WAITING FOR THE KICK

JAMES TARR

BOOKS

Vinci Books

vinci-books.com

Published by Vinci Books Ltd in 2025

1

Copyright © James Tarr 2019

The author has asserted their moral right to be identified as the author of this work in accordance with the Copyright, Designs and Patents Act 1988. This work is a work of fiction. Names, characters, places and incidents are the product of the author's imagination or are used fictitiously. Any resemblance to actual persons, living or dead, places and incidents is entirely coincidental.

All rights reserved. No part of this publication may be copied, reproduced, distributed, stored in any retrieval system, or transmitted in any form or by any means, including photocopying, recording, or other electronic or mechanical methods, nor used as a source for any form of machine learning including AI datasets, without the prior written permission of the publisher.

The publisher and the author have made every effort to obtain permissions for any third party material used in this book and to comply with copyright law. Any queries in this respect should be brought to the attention of the publisher and any omissions will be corrected in future editions.

A CIP catalogue record for this book is available from the British Library.

Paperback ISBN: 9781036707132

Printed and bound in Great Britain by Clays Ltd, Elcograf S.p.A.

By James Tarr

James Tarr Conspiracy Thrillers

Failure Drill

Splashback

Splits and Transitions

Whorl

Waiting for the Kick

Ghosts and Madmen

The Subsection

ANDAMENTO

As industrial parks went it was rather small and forgettable. Situated in the Northern Neck area of Virginia, it was roughly 75 miles from Washington D.C., although there was no quick way between the two. There was only one entrance with a small sign "WESTMORELAND INDUS-TRIAL PARK".

The access road was barely wide enough for two tractor trailers to pass. An outfit which manufactured small trailers was on the immediate left, a packaging company on the right. Two more buildings housing bland enterprises on either side, then the short street terminated in a low rolling gate and a guardhouse.

The guard didn't step out of the booth as Colman rolled up and held his unmarked ID badge in front of the scanner. When the slow-moving gate was finally out of the way he drove his vehicle toward the only building visible.

From the outside it appeared to be a good-sized warehouse, newer steel construction with siding on the exterior, with a lot of windows, most of which were tinted. The parking lot was nearly full. On the far side of the nondescript building nothing was immediately visible other than a thick belt of trees.

There was a large sign out front of the building, THE O'HARE GROUP, which gave no indication of the type of business conducted inside. The only clue that the building might be a bit unusual for an industrial park was the small sign on the front door leading to the lobby, PERSONAL FIREARMS AND LIVE AMMO ARE NOT PERMITTED ON THE PREMISES.

Colman got out of his car, stretched, and then headed for the plain side door. In the distance he could faintly hear squealing tires from the precision driving course, and gunfire from the pistol ranges, none of which were visible from the road. He swiped his ID for entry. Inside, the building was no warehouse but rather a warren of hallways filled with classrooms, offices, a cafeteria, and private rooms slightly better than the dorm rooms found in most colleges. As he passed a classroom he glanced through the narrow window in the door and caught a brief glimpse of about twenty backs facing a PowerPoint presentation. All he caught on the slide was the heading—Bureau of Diplomatic Security: Courier Protocols.

Colman headed toward the center of the building. He found the short corridor he was looking for, ending at an unmarked door. He swiped his ID to enter, and found himself in a small vestibule before another door. His cell phone went into the plastic box hanging on the wall, then he punched his code into the access panel beside the door. When the green light appeared he opened the door and stepped in. His boss was already seated at the table.

Colman looked around and waited for the door to close before he spoke. "I haven't been in a SCIF in a while." He pronounced it 'skiff'. The room could have been a small windowless meeting room in any office building anywhere, with only a few clues it was something more: the panels on the wall which looked like acoustic tiles on steroids. The phone on the table with several interesting buttons. Then, of course, were the security measures to get in. The interesting thing about Sensitive Compartmented Information Facilities wasn't the actual rooms themselves, but rather what was discussed in them. And that the intelligence information discussed inside was shielded from any sort of outside monitoring, electronic or otherwise.

Colman sat at the rectangular table. His direct supervisor looked around and stated, "I thought it prudent." Very few people even inside the building knew who the man was, but as the Deputy Director of Operations for the Defense Intelligence Agency's Defense Clandestine Service (try getting all that on a business card) Winston Elliott was one of the few people in the U.S. intelligence community who actually had the power to order people killed...among other things. He smiled. "We have a new Sheriff in town. And for all the Boy Scout 'America First' rhetoric about extreme vetting and enhanced interrogation, I'm not sure our new President actually understands how nasty the business of national security can sometimes be. So we are trying to clean up any messes, or potential messes, we still have on the books before they look at the books and we are told in no uncertain terms to cease and desist certain types of operations. Does the name David Anderson ring a bell?"

It took Colman half a second, but then he nodded. "Oh yeah." The one that got away.

"He came to our attention because of a certain unique characteristic. Two, actually. Fingerprints."

"I remember. That matched other people. And he burned them off, so I was recalled from the field."

"After clearing up a few loose ends, if memory serves me right. Things got a bit complicated. The media was involved." Elliott raised an eyebrow.

"Outside my assignment," Colman reminded him. "Anderson apparently had a run-in with a high-ranking criminal figure prior to his coming to our attention, and the FBI had the working theory that this mobster hired my team to take him out. Revenge. It had absolutely nothing to do with us and was a perfect cover when things went sideways, so we just backed away and let it run." His eyebrows pushed together, forming a vertical line above his nose. "It's been a while, so the exact details are a bit vague."

"You haven't kept tabs on the story? On Anderson?"

"I was given an assignment. Once it was completed, I moved on."

"Just like that? No personal investment? No plans to revisit him some night? He killed your team. We've lost Ground Branch teams before, just never on U.S. soil." The Deputy Director kept his gaze steady.

Colman didn't respond, and his expression was unreadable. Eventually his supervisor went on. "Anyway, it's been two years. And the human body is an amazing thing."

Colman frowned. "You're worried he…grew them back? If I remember correctly he all but barbequed his fingers. That's why he was no longer deemed a security threat." He'd declined to correct his supervisor—Ground Branch was CIA, not DIA, but Elliott had started his career in Langley.

"Stranger things have been known to happen. Last medical report we could find is over a year old. He's still got all of his fingers, and apparently they're working properly, more or less, but one thing the doctor doesn't mention is whether or not he's got any fingerprints left in and among the skin grafts and scarring. Not medically pertinent, I suppose." Elliott set a flash drive on the table in front of Colman. "We want you to track him down. Not sure how long it'll take."

"It only took me a few days last time, and he was on the run."

"I reviewed the reports." Elliott gestured at the flash drive. "Copies in there to refresh your memory. I'm not so sure you found him. Maybe he let himself be found. After all, what happened when your team showed up? Did we ever conclusively determine exactly what did happen? How six highly trained operators ended up dead?"

Colman pursed his lips. "I obtained copies of the police reports. Officially Anderson only gave one statement after he recovered from his wounds, that he was sitting at home minding his own business when some guys showed up and started shooting at him, then at the deputy who pulled up. He provided no details, and no motive. At least on the record. But I'm not sure I believe what's in those reports. Or rather, what's not in them."

His supervisor drummed his fingers on the table. "You think he said more than that?"

"There is no way the local cops would have let him be if all he'd said was what was in that incident report. If they knew more, learned enough to know they couldn't put it into any report…" He shrugged. "That is the most plausible scenario for me. It's Tohono County, John Osterman's domain. He's no stranger to…controversial incidents, shall we say. Smart, by all accounts. And very politically savvy. I think he's the one who contacted the media."

"Ah, yes. You had a run-in with the Sheriff if I remember correctly. Trying to secure Anderson afterward."

"Don't remind me."

"Well, here's a second chance for you. Anderson dropped off the radar over a year ago, actually months before that last follow-up medical examination. No record of him for a while before he showed up at his doctor's office, and nothing since. Tax return says he's living in Michigan, but the address is a mailbox at a UPS store. He sold the two properties he owned, but if he bought another house somewhere it wasn't in his name. No utilities or driver licenses or arrests or car registrations after selling the one he owned in Michigan. Well, the one that's not still in the police evidence garage full of bullet holes. His Social Security Number hasn't been entered into the system since that last doctor's visit. If he's ever Googled himself we weren't able to spot it. He has no online presence, nothing in social media. He hasn't obliged us by sending his DNA to one of those ancestry websites to find out about his genetic makeup."

"We're into those databases?"

"We're into everything, are you kidding me? Siri and Alexa do so much of our work I'm surprised they're not covered by government health insurance. The only thing we know for sure is that shortly before selling his house he bought a few guns in Michigan. Then nothing."

"David Anderson is a pretty common name."

"Yes, but the computer can cross check data points, as you well know. Height, age range, all of that in addition to online points of contact. Known interests. No hits at all. He's abandoned his email, Facebook account, everything. No trace of him."

"I sense a 'but'. Is that why I'm here, now?"

The Deputy Director nodded at the flash drive. "The

computer flagged something. What little we have is on that flash drive, everything retrieved through PINWALE, STELLARWIND, PRISM, and whatever else they've got spinning up there. Possible matches off social media and assorted websites from facial recognition software. Both cherrypicked and bulk data. Sorted, but not analyzed or of course acted upon. Plus, the flagged item." He pointed at the flash drive. "That is only computer data, with no human intelligence. No one has started pulling any of those threads, making phone calls, talking to people, reading whatever the algorithms snaked out of the internet and flagged. Put human eyeballs and a brain looking at the data. Which is where you come in. And be aware, this wasn't exactly a priority item, so you won't have the luxury of following a fresh lead. That possible hit on him is close to two months old already. You'll have your work cut out for you."

"And when I find him you want me to find out if his fingerprints have grown back? It was only two fingers, if I remember correctly."

"Yes."

"What if I can't determine whether or not that specific problem is once again a problem?"

"If you can't say for sure it isn't, then you need to act accordingly. This is not something we can leave to chance. It shouldn't have been punted this long."

"Understood." Colman paused. "You understand, we're in the intelligence business, and we still don't know exactly what happened the last time we sent a team after him. But I was told to cease and desist, so I followed orders. That's always bothered me. It was my team. I sent them. And I don't like unanswered questions."

"Yes, I don't blame you. I've read the incident reports from Tohono County as well. I don't know what the hell happened, how the team could have screwed up so badly. I know the kid didn't win a six-on-one gunfight, which is what the report seems to suggest. Which tells me that the whole report is bullshit." Elliott ran a hand through his thinning hair. "Bombs and fires and getting into a gunfight with a deputy? One of Shotgun John's deputies to boot, the man can't stay off Fox News. Did your men ever hear the term *clandestine*? Jesus. Thank God we used deniable assets and cutouts. I hate to speculate, but I imagine he went to the Sheriff, told him a convincing story, and it was Osterman's men who put down your team. Maybe used the kid as bait, set an ambush. I really don't see any other way those men, with all their combat experience, could have ended up dead." He sighed. "You said you backed away, didn't maintain an interest. Are you aware just how much media attention that got? They were talking about that clusterfuck on Billy Parr's show, even though nobody knew anything."

"Why would Billy Parr be talking about that?" Colman got a dismissive wave in response.

"He was doing a show on gun control and one of his guests who's against it mentioned Anderson. How him having guns and knowing how to use them saved his life. Forget about that. Yours weren't the first men to go after him, just the first pros. That FBI Agent got himself recorded hiring dirty cops to go after him." Elliott sighed. "If I would have known how big that was going to blow up I would have cancelled your mission. Or at least postponed it. Talk about fertile ground for the conspiracy theorists, they were ranting about the mafia and the FBI everywhere, including Parr's show. The mafia angle was a clever bit of misdirection, whoever thought of it. I wish I could take the credit. But that media attention is why we backed off of him, not just his possible lack of prints. Which is how he managed to disappear. This time I want it just to be you. I think you're perfectly capable of handling something like this by yourself, don't you? Without making headlines? Discreetly?"

"Of course."

"I'm under the impression he never actually saw you, is that correct?"

"The only time we were face to face he was in a medically-induced coma. And even that was over two years ago. Osterman might recognize me, but I don't plan on running into him." Colman smiled, then frowned. "Could Anderson be in Arizona? Instead of Michigan?"

"The data the computer flagged seems to indicate he is. Or was." The Deputy Director nodded at the flash drive. "He sold the property he owned in Arizona, we know that for sure, but everything else is just AI guesswork. He could be dead, or out of country. But we have to plan for worst case scenario."

"Arizona's still hot after that terrorist attack last month. If he's down there…"

"We were just using the word discreet. I trust you know what it means. And that wasn't terrorists, it was cartel."

"We're making that distinction now?"

The Deputy Director snorted. Then he leaned forward and tapped the flash drive. "There's no doubt he'll have some scarring and damage based on the medical records I've read. It'll be up to you to determine if whatever prints he has left are enough to cause this country any trouble." He leaned back and smiled. "I don't know if or even when word may come down from on high telling me to shut down certain types of operations. But if I was ordered to tell my people cease and desist, I would of course not be able to contact those teams or individuals who were in the field and operating under emcon until their missions were complete. No matter how long their missions might take. Are we clear?"

Emcon. Radio silence. "Yes sir. Perfectly." Colman thought. "Since I'm going to be out in the cold and in the dark for the duration, I'm thinking I ought to requisition a few items. Since I'm here."

"Whatever you need."

PART I
TERMINAL

Chapter One

Dave was still, after all this time, on east coast hours. Waking up ridiculously early. Or maybe it was just that he didn't want to sleep, didn't want to close his eyes, because… well, for a lot of reasons.

As he blinked in the dimness he realized there was a bit of pale light seeping through the narrow horizontal blinds, but to his experienced eyes it wasn't anything more than starlight. Still a way to go before dawn. He listened carefully, wondering if anything other than his internal clock had been the reason for climbing out of the uneasy sea of sleep. There wasn't much to hear. The faint ticking of a clock. The low hum of the refrigerator from the kitchen. So faint it was barely perceptible the sound of a single vehicle moving at speed. Between the thin dry air and bare hills all around forming a bit of an echo chamber there was no way to tell exactly how far away the car was or even in what direction.

He lay on his back, staring upward. The ceiling and walls appeared light gray. Soon they'd brighten to their true white hue when dawn arrived. The walls were almost completely bare; the only photos and pictures he'd hung in the place weren't for looking at.

The air in the bedroom was a little chilly, just the way he liked it. It made it easier to sleep. Well, less difficult, at least. As they were every morning, his fingers were cold and stiff whether he slept with them under the comforter or not.

With a grunt he pushed the comforter aside and sat up. The cold air raised goosebumps on his legs, and the rough carpet was cool on the soles of his feet. The clock on the small bedside dresser table gave off a muted blue glow and he glanced at it. Four-thirty, on the dot. So he'd gotten less than six hours sleep, but that was all he seemed to need lately, no matter how tired he was when he dropped off. Some nights he couldn't do better than three or four hours before he was wide awake and staring at nothing. Beyond the glow of the clock the packed wood bookshelves lining the dark bedroom were a featureless brown-black wall.

He sat on the side of the bed and opened and closed his hands for a minute or so, squeezing his fists, then massaged each of his fingers in turn from base to tip. They didn't hurt any more, didn't ache, the skin didn't feel tight as it had for so long. They were just cold. Always.

Sighing, he bent over and grabbed his sweatpants off the floor, locating them mostly by feel as they were dark blue cotton on brown carpet. He stood and stepped into them, then knotted the cord at his waist. He found a t-shirt with his toes and pulled that on as well. Finally, he picked up the Glock 19 from the bedside table and headed into the kitchen.

The surprisingly spacious kitchen was in a back corner of the house and brighter than the bedroom. It was the brightest room in the place. He supposed that was due to the two windows at ninety degrees to each other, their blinds raised, and the white cabinets and appliances reflecting whatever light there was. The window on the left gave him a view of the neighboring residence. He'd never been inside but was pretty sure they had a mirrored layout of his, so the curtained window facing him from twelve or so feet away should open onto their kitchen. The window on his right gave him a view of his back yard, such as it was. Dirt and gravel and a few small juniper and Manzanita shrubs, planted by the previous owner. Beyond it was more of the same, dirt and gravel and juniper and Manzanita, landscape design by Mother Nature. While that window was halfway open, it was latched so nobody could just slide it up the rest of the way and make silent entry, they'd have to break something.

The night air coming through the window was chill and dry, but then it always was. It was a rare morning he didn't wake up with a dry nose and mouth, snot hard as pebbles, the arid air sucking the moisture from him all night as he breathed. Three hundred days a year of sunshine, that was plastered all over the city's website, presumably to attract retirees and tourists. But you'd better apply Chapstick like it was a new form of religion or your lips would crack and peel and bleed—*that* should be on the city's website.

He set the Glock down on the kitchen counter next to the sink. Squinting his eyes against the expected bright light he opened the refrigerator door and retrieved a bottle of water. Drank it standing at the counter, the cold water making his teeth ache, and ate a protein bar. While he chewed he bent his face close to the window and peered upward. He was looking east and a little northeast. The city to the west put out a glow, but still the light pollution here was nothing like what he'd grown up with. In small part because there was no moisture in the air to catch the light. He marveled at all the stars. Maybe it was the dry air, but the sky was always bright with stars as if someone had thrown a thousand glittering diamonds across black velvet. Bright stars didn't translate into much light on the ground, though, and the moon was already down below the horizon. At night, with no moon, it was *dark*.

In the Midwest, after a fresh snowfall and with a full moon the dark of night disappeared. You could shut off your headlights and drive home at 2 a.m. without a worry. While the pale landscaping gravel which was seemingly everywhere in this neighborhood (including his back yard) did reflect some light, it was nothing like a white blanket of snow covering everything.

After a quick detour to the bathroom he swapped his sweat pants for shorts, pulled a sweatshirt on over his t-shirt, laced on his running shoes, then sat on the carpet in the middle of his front room and stretched. The palm-sized bruise on his right thigh no longer hurt, and its edges had blurred as it shifted colors from purple to greenish yellow. The bruise on his left arm just below his shoulder still didn't look bad, just a slight swelling and a small purple-red mark, but it still hurt almost too much to touch. By the time he was done stretching he was a little warmer, and his hands were no longer stiff and cold.

Fanny packs were out of fashion for just about everyone but distance runners and fat middle-aged couples wandering through Disney World. He was not the latter, and his was on a table in the front room. Walking with a weighty fanny pack poised above your groin was one thing, jogging was another. The first time he'd gone running with the fanny pack he'd worn it in front, as it didn't feel secure bouncing behind his back. But he'd discovered that there was just no way to wear it in front without suffering RTI—Repeated Testicular Impact. The endorphins coursing through his system while running had dulled most of the pain, and when they'd worn off he'd been sore for days. Who even knew you could bruise your pubic bone? So he was forced to wear the fanny pack on his fanny—not that he'd ever used that term in his life when referring to any part of his body. Still, 'fanny pack' sounded more polite than 'butt bag'.

He peered out the front window, but there was nothing to see. Only a few porch lights. Mrs. Leslie across the street was still asleep, her place dark. Probably sleeping curled up with her creepy hairless cat. He looked left and right. Dark cars parked in driveways in carports, nothing parked on the street—but that was as it should be, nobody parked on the street. Nothing moving. He locked the front door behind him, stuck the key in the front pocket of the pack alongside his phone, then twisted the little pack around until it was over the small of his back. He hopped down the three porch steps to the concrete walk and checked his watch.

The walks and low wheelchair-friendly curbs all through the neighborhood were made of concrete, but the street itself was asphalt. And, since it had been poured barely five years before and saw almost no traffic, the asphalt remained black and smooth as an oil slick. In the dim starlight jogging on the asphalt was like swimming through the blackness of space. It didn't reflect any light at all but rather soaked it up. He couldn't actually see the asphalt at night, and it was a little disconcerting. He had to be careful not to look down while running or it would mess with his balance and depth perception. It was as if he was staring into nothing. What was that phrase, be careful because when you stare into the abyss, it stares into you?

Something like that. Probably wasn't written about fresh asphalt, but whatever.

The street had been poured before any of the homes had gone in, which meant everything in the neighborhood was fresh and bright and new. Most of the houses had light-colored exteriors, white or pink or peach or the ever-present light tan/orange "adobe"—it was the Southwest, after all. And light colors helped with the heat when the bright sun of summer was overhead.

He guessed it was below fifty degrees as he set a good pace down Hydrangea Place and then turned left on Poinsettia Boulevard, which ran through the middle of the development. That was one term the builders used for the place: "development". "Planned neighborhood" was another. They might even use the expression "modular residence" to describe the homes. If pressed they might get technical and refer to Glassford Meadows as a manufactured housing community. They would never ever be caught dead uttering the words "trailer park" even though that's how he thought of it. And, it seemed, how most of the residents thought of it. Perhaps they weren't being fair—the homes here were homes, they were never trailers or intended to be moved once they were assembled. It just so happened that they were built in sections at a factory and then assembled on site. Which made them surprisingly affordable. The fact that they resembled double-wide trailers was a result of their manufacturing.

He'd spent a lot of time in various grades of trailer parks and "manufactured housing communities", including, ironically, the one Eminem had grown up in. While maybe one day several decades hence Glassford Meadows might fall into disrepair, right now it was bright and shiny new. Instead of beer-drinking lotto-playing types with low-paying blue-collar jobs and more than a passing familiarity with the process required to obtain a restraining order at the local courthouse, the residents here were mostly all retired Midwesterners trying to be smart with their money.

Unlike the true trailer park a few miles down the road, Glassford Meadows didn't have a 55+ age restriction. Still, he was one of the youngest residents in the neighborhood, and one of the newest. As for the place he lived in... Roger MacDonald, sixty-three years of age, eight years retired from TRW, had bought the double-wide trailer—er, manufactured home—from the builder as the neighborhood went in. MacDonald had been happy to get away from Ohio winters, and was near enough to his daughter and grandkids in Phoenix that he could visit easily without being too close. Four years and change later he dropped dead of a heart attack in his front room. Perhaps because MacDonald's body hadn't been found for a week the realtor found it a bit difficult to sell the residence. The carpet had been swapped out for wood laminate and every flat surface in the place had been scrubbed down, but still some days there was a faint smell...and if someone died in a house, real estate laws required disclosure of that fact, so every prospective buyer soon learned the exact origin of that odor. The realtor dropped the price just to move the place, as it was a low-ticket item to begin with compared to some of the houses in the nearby suburbs.

The very next day Dave drove through the neighborhood and saw the For Sale sign. At the end of a cul-de-sac, no neighbor on one side and nothing but desert behind it? He'd thought it had been the perfect place to plant his feet, and wasn't bothered with it being the site of Roger MacDonald's passing. When offered cash they were willing to drop the price even further. And the rest, as they say, is history.

The strip down the middle of Poinsettia Boulevard was barely six feet wide and filled with rocks, without a blade of grass visible. It hardly merited the term boulevard in his opinion. One thing that always amazed him, running past the generally neat and well-maintained residences, was how so few of the yards sported anything green. Coming from the Midwest, a yard was supposed to be grass. Maybe with a few weeds or bushes, but yards were green. Period. But as he ran along the flat curving ribbon of the street there was little grass to be seen anywhere. Many of the yards sported landscaping and vegetative decoration, but in the high desert that consisted of cacti and succulents and maybe a yucca or two. Plus lots and lots of decorative gravel and the odd gallon-jug-sized picturesque rock.

A few homes, their residents probably transplants from the Midwest as well, sported small table-size squares of grass, as lovingly tended as pets, mementos of the residents' pre-desert lives. They had to be watered every day by hand, and as twenty square feet of grass was more a tiny gesture of defiance to the arid environment than an actual *lawn*, almost nobody owned a lawn mower. The green squares were usually cut by hand via electric weed trimmers bought at the nearby big box home improvement store.

At the end of the boulevard, right at the entrance to the neighborhood, was the wooden sign for Glassford Meadows. Just a simple rectangular forest green sign with a cream border and gold lettering. There was one small streetlight illuminating the intersection, and past the small circle of gold-tinged light was inky blackness. The only decision he had to make was which direction: left or right on Old Fain Road?

Glassford Meadows had been built in the middle of what had been nothing but grazing land for cattle. And still, for the most part, was. Cows in the Midwest ate grass; cattle in Arizona ate whatever they could, and what little there was usually had to be supplemented with feed. There were tufts of wild grass everywhere, but it always seemed to be brown—he wondered how and when it grew. The few weeks a year in the late summer when Arizona got a few inches of rain? There was also a lot of low scrub, including small bushes, only some of which were junipers. Whatever the bushes were, the cattle ate them, as well as the tough dry grass. If it had more organic content than lava rock he'd seen a cow gnawing on it.

Most of the land around the subdivision was empty, and Old Fain Road, all six-plus miles of it, was still gravel. Of course, it was supposed to have been paved by now, but whatever deal the builder had struck with the county to get that done had apparently fallen through. As had the plans for other manufactured housing communities around Glassford Meadows, which a lot of the retired residents (more than a few from Michigan) smilingly called GM.

If he felt in the mood for cross-country running (and trespassing) he could just go straight and keep heading west. If he was willing to hop a few fences and climb a small line of hills, maybe scare some cattle and rabbits, dodge a rattlesnake or three, in two miles or so he'd run into the county fairgrounds. If he turned left, south-southwest, Old Fain Road ran into just plain Fain Road spitting distance from State Route 69, right at Grapevine Industrial Park. As industrial parks went it was a bit small, with four short streets home to the usual types of businesses—a recycling center, a construction equipment rental facility, and a FedEx warehouse among others. Between GM and Grapevine was a whole lot of nothing. Well, dirt, hills, juniper bushes, dozens of rabbits and even more tiny skittering lizards, but no buildings or people. High desert, in other words.

If he turned right there was more nothing, that is until the cement plant on the left. There Old Fain dead-ended at State Route 89A. Other than the plant, mostly off the road out of sight, the only thing to see at that intersection was the Mingus West subdivision. If there was a universal list somewhere of unfortunate names, he was pretty sure Mingus was near the top of it.

Old Fain Road was level—okay, not level, nothing in that hilly part of Arizona was level, but it had an even surface, so it provided a fine running track. No huge potholes or rocks big enough to turn an ankle. He impulsively went left and headed south, trying to find the familiar rhythm. His breath moved in and out, and his gait smoothed as he settled into his regular pace. The only sound the crunching of his shoes on the gravel and his breathing. No iPod, no earbuds—little traffic is not the same thing as no traffic, and he wanted to hear any cars coming before he got run over jogging in the dark. He kept to the right, near the edge of the road, just in case. And, as it often did when he ran, his mind began to wander.

He'd been almost completely out of shape when he'd started running again, and adding to that challenge was the elevation here. Officially Prescott Valley was 5,300 feet above sea level, just a tic over a mile. The gentle slopes of the road didn't add up to more than fifty feet or so of elevation change, although compared to the table-top flat Midwest fifty-foot hills were mountains.

Maybe five miles west of GM, on the other side of the city, was Glassford Hill, a local landmark and extinct volcano named after Colonel William A. Glassford. After seeing the Glassford name around town a few times he'd looked the guy up, and learned Glassford had been sent to the area in the late 1800s to keep his eye on the Apaches, among other things. The summit of Glassford Hill was over 6,000 feet, and there was a trail leading to the top, but he'd never been.

He was only a little chilly, and just for the first few minutes. The dry air sucked the sweat off of him almost as fast as it came out of his skin, but after a couple of miles his armpits were a little damp. He was also in the groove, moving at a speed he was happy with. He wouldn't win any awards or break any speed records, but the more regularly he ran the faster his natural pace became. Five days a week was his usual schedule, although sometimes he did six if he couldn't sleep. Every once in a while he'd head out for a second run in a day. When in doubt, work out.

There was a cattle guard across the road a hundred yards or so before the industrial park. Between the cattle guard and the bright fences of the industrial park was a small house, little more than a shack. Its large yard was enclosed by a rusty fence that had seen better days. Inside the fence were llamas, although he didn't know if the owner was raising them for fur or meat or something else. He had no idea what you did with llamas, all he knew was that they looked weird. Their proportions were all wrong, like crayon drawings of horses done by little kids. Except they had sheep-ish fur, or hair, or whatever it was.

He crossed the road before the metal grating—he was always afraid that trying to run over a cattle guard he'd turn an ankle, which is exactly why cattle wouldn't walk over them—and started back toward his house along the opposite shoulder.

He was sweating freely as he passed the Glassford

Meadows sign, and as usual he sprinted the last two hundred yards to his place. The sky was still dark, although there was a tiny bit of glow to the east. He checked his watch as he passed the walk leading up to his porch, then walked the length of the street twice to cool down.

There were lights on inside several of the nearby homes but he didn't see any movement. Surprisingly few people in the neighborhood actually worked, they were mostly retired, but he'd discovered the stereotype was true—the elderly tended to wake up early. A big percentage of the retired residents would be up by seven a.m.

He set the fanny pack down with a thunk on the table just inside the front door and headed for the kitchen. He drank another bottle of water so cold it threatened brain freeze while eating half a protein bar. He wasn't hungry, but he found he needed a little something in his stomach when he was doing anaerobic exercise. As there was no chance of a car sneaking up on him inside the house he went to his laptop and clicked his way to his iTunes workout playlist, making sure the small speaker was plugged in. Then he pulled off the sweatshirt and threw it in the hamper.

The floor in the main room was wood laminate, but it was the expensive stuff, and looked and felt like hardwood. He rolled up the Persian (fake Persian, Pakistani, Pennsyltucky, who knew, he'd found it at a garage sale) rug and knocked off thirty push-ups as Eminem angrily cleaned out his closet. Well, Eminem did everything angrily, that's why he was great to work out to.

He took exactly thirty seconds to catch his breath, watching the second hand on the wall clock, then hooked his toes under the front of his couch and did fifty crunches. Thirty seconds rest, then thirty burpees, finishing just as Linkin Park hammered from the speaker, which had a surprising bass range. Although he made sure it wasn't too loud—his windows were open, and sound carried remarkably far in the dry air.

Burpees kicked his ass, especially after running, so he took a full minute to catch his breath then did ten pull-ups on the bar he'd put across the doorway to one of the spare bedrooms. Thanks to his long arms he had to bend his legs at the knees, and still his knees almost hit the floor. He then repeated the series—thirty pushups, fifty crunches, thirty burpees, ten pull-ups, with the same resting intervals. By the fourth series the sweat was dripping off his nose as he did the pushups. Even though RHCP's *Breaking the Girl* had the exact right beat to motivate him he was gasping like a landed fish as he got on the pull-up bar for the last set. He was quivering for the last three pull-ups, afraid his sweaty hands would slip off the bar (it had happened before, and his knees had been sore for days), but he made it.

He staggered to the laptop as The Kills' *Future Starts Slow* boomed out and turned the volume down. Then he just stood there trying to catch his breath as the music played. He knew it wasn't as fierce a workout as actual weightlifting but overall he thought he had a good full body workout routine. He didn't do the same thing every day because he didn't want to get bored or burned out. *Future Starts Slow* ended and Ted Nugent's epic *Stranglehold* began. The burning brought him out of his reverie and he pulled off his shirt to wipe the sweat out of his eyes, then shut off the music. Then he grabbed another bottle of water out of the refrigerator but just sipped at it for a few minutes before heading into the shower.

Once a week he spoiled himself and had breakfast at the Wagon Wheel Café in downtown Prescott—pronounced *Preskitt*, otherwise everyone knew you weren't a local. The narrow café right off the sidewalk was across from Courthouse Square in the old downtown. The walls were covered with all sorts of interesting cowboy and Old West memorabilia, but he went for the food. The Wagon Wheel had the best bacon he'd ever tasted, and everything else was damn good too.

By the time he was ready to head out to breakfast it was just after seven and the sun was up, although still low in the sky. Early enough traffic wouldn't be too bad, and the drive would maybe take ten minutes if he hit most of the lights green. To cut the morning chill he'd put on a long sleeve canvas shirt unbuttoned in front over a t-shirt and jeans. He glanced out the front window, then headed out to his vehicle parked in the carport. Carports in Arizona were simple things, usually just an aluminum roof to provide shade, as the intense desert sun could turn a car into an oven in just a few minutes.

The Jeep Wrangler started right up. Obeying the 15 mph speed limit he drove through Glassford Meadows, then sped up as he headed south on Old Fain. About a mile up there was a vehicle on the side of the road, and he thought he recognized it. He pulled up next to the Toyota SUV and rolled down his passenger window.

The girl behind the wheel didn't notice him at first, she was trying to start her car. When she saw the Jeep idling next to her vehicle she jumped a little in her seat. She stared angrily at him but didn't roll down her window. They stared at each other, and after a few seconds he figured out the power windows were dead in her SUV, and she couldn't open her door without hitting his vehicle. He put the Jeep in reverse and pulled in behind her, then got out, looking around.

When he walked up to her door she didn't seem any less

upset or happy to see him, and didn't open the door. "I don't know a lot about cars, but if you pop the hood I can take a look," he volunteered, talking through the closed window. "If you're getting nothing when you turn the key, and the window's not coming down it's probably electrical. Maybe you've got some loose wiring." The Toyota was only a few years old, so it wasn't a wear issue. Some electrical Tab A must have popped out of Slot B. Up close she was just as pretty as he'd thought, with dark blonde hair pulled into a ponytail.

"That's okay," she said, her voice muffled and flat through the window. He couldn't tell if she looked more angry or sad, but she seemed pretty upset.

"You need me to call a tow truck?"

She stared at him through the window glass. "I've got a phone," she said firmly.

He paused, trying to read the situation. "I'm your next-door neighbor," he said, trying a smile on her.

"I know who you are," she said flatly, her voice inside the car slightly muffled.

He stood there for a few seconds, then shook his head. A hint of a smile ticked the corner of his mouth. "I was trying to avoid that whole creepy stalker vibe, but apparently I wasn't successful." He looked around. There was nothing to see but bushes and hillocks and dirt below clear blue sky. Brown, brown everywhere, but at least there wasn't snow. "Okay, fair enough. I don't want to leave you out here all alone, though, so I'm going to go back to my Jeep and sit inside it until the tow truck comes. I'll stay in there and won't come out."

He walked back to his Jeep and then, after thinking about it for a few seconds, backed up thirty feet or so, that way he wasn't right behind her vehicle. Less threatening that way. He turned on the radio and surfed around the dial, but there weren't a whole lot of options. As he was fiddling with the radio he saw her get out of her vehicle and walk his way. She stopped beside his door, purse in hand. She looked angry, but she also seemed about to cry. In fact, was that a tear in the corner of her eye?

When he rolled down his window she admitted, "My damn phone's dead." Her voice was thick. She looked away, then back at him. "Listen, I...I need to go pick up a prescription. For my mother. It's pretty important. Can you...?"

"Sure," he said. She seemed surprised when he opened the door and stepped out. She was shorter than he expected, maybe five-three or so. He towered over her, and took a step back so as not to seem threatening. He looked around, then gestured at the empty driver's seat. She gave him a confused look.

He raised his hands, palms out, and took two more steps backward. "Do whatever you need to do. Bring it back whenever you're done." He stuck his hands in the front pockets of his jeans.

Her eyebrows pushed together. "No, I...you'd let me take your car?" The disbelief in her voice was huge.

He shrugged. "It's just a car." And from the simple way he said it she could tell he meant it. "I can walk back easy. And I know where you live," he added, with a smile. He took a couple more steps up the road, ready to start walking. The mile back wouldn't take him long at all.

She stared at him. He had wide shoulders and was so lean he looked taller than he actually was. His beard was thick, but trimmed short enough that she could see the scar running along the left side of his jaw. She hadn't noticed that before. "I don't…how…can you just give me a ride? I don't want to take your car," she told him.

The idea that he'd just let her take his car seemed an alien concept to her. "Sure. Not a problem." He waited until she walked around the front of the Jeep before climbing behind the wheel. "Where to?" he asked as she opened the door.

"Walmart. They've got a pharmacy." She looked around the inside of the Wrangler. It was probably fifteen years old, but the interior was spotless. No garbage. No nothing, actually.

"You remember to lock your car?" he asked her. She hit the remote as he drove around her car, and its taillights flashed. Hmm. So it had some juice, but none was getting to the starter. The Jeep cycled through the gears as he headed down Old Fain, the gravel knocking against the undercarriage, the knobby tires humming.

"Do you have a charger? I took mine out of my car and never put it back."

He glanced at the phone in her hand. "Not for an Apple. You can use my phone if you want to call for a tow or whatever." He gestured at it sitting in a cupholder. It was a basic flip-phone with no data capability. She frowned at it.

"I don't know the number. I guess it can wait 'til I get back." She sighed and threw her phone back in her purse.

Once they hit pavement the Walmart wasn't much more than ten minutes away. He was content to just pilot the Jeep, and the fact that he wasn't talking to fill the silence surprised her. Most guys weren't like that. She noticed him unconsciously flexing his fingers from time to time. They were covered with scars and looked as if they'd been chewed on by some sort of rabid animal.

"Isn't there a CVS right at the corner of 69 and…

maybe Windsong? Have to drive right past it to get to the Walmart, and it's a lot closer." He was still learning the local roads but knew the CVS was on the north side of the road heading toward Prescott.

She shook her head. "Prescriptions I need to get are a lot cheaper at the Walmart."

He shrugged. "Okay." Then didn't say anything else.

"I'm Lori," she said finally, when they were three traffic lights away from the Walmart.

"Jack," he told her. "Jack Burton." She turned her head and gave him a funny look, but didn't say anything. And that was the extent of their conversation until he pulled up in front of the Walmart.

"I don't know how long this'll take," she admitted. She seemed embarrassed to have asked for the ride.

"I'll be right here," he assured her as he scanned the parking lot. "Don't worry about it."

She glanced at him, then got out of the Jeep and walked inside. She'd thrown on a baggy plaid shirt over a tank top and yoga pants, and wasn't wearing makeup. She probably thought she looked a mess. He snorted a little thinking about that. Just because he wasn't interested didn't mean he was blind. He kept an eye on the clock, and she was back out twelve minutes later. She looked…well, not happy, but less stressed out. And no longer on the edge of tears.

"I really appreciate this," she told him, climbing back into the Jeep.

"It's not a big deal."

They rode in silence for five minutes, which she found rather odd. Guys never just sat there, not in her experience, and here he was doing it again. Guys talked, either out of nervousness or ego or to fill the silence. Not him. And it wasn't because he was shy, that was obvious.

They were bouncing back on Old Fain Road when he asked her, "Is it cancer?"

She squinted at him. He shrugged, and looked back at the road. Then he said, "We live spitting distance apart. You can probably hear when I flush my toilet. I've seen you with your mom a lot. She's got good days, but I can tell it's something bad. That usually means cancer."

She stared down at the bag in her hand holding the prescriptions. After a while she answered. "Yeah. Brain cancer. Inoperable." She sighed. "They gave her six months when she was diagnosed."

"How long's it been?"

"Seventeen, almost eighteen months." She smiled at the small victory.

"Do not go gentle into that good night," he said quietly, nodding. He drove past her dead car, still sitting on the side of the road. "How old is she?"

"Fifty-five. She's…well, I don't know how long she's got. Not any more." He could hear the pain in her voice and shook his head.

"That sucks. That a nurse I see coming over couple times a week?"

"Yeah. I'm trying to do everything myself, but sometimes I can't. Some days she can hardly walk. And I'm not going to put her in fucking hospice," she said with sudden fury. "I came back home to be with her."

He turned into Glassford Meadows and they rode in silence for a few turns. He pulled up in front of her mother's house, which was pale blue with white trim. Right next door to his house. She and her mother had been there since he'd moved in, but other than a passing nod or wave he'd never interacted with either of them. He didn't talk to people much any more, but he realized belatedly that was no reason to be rude. He'd become aware of their situation months ago, not long after moving in, and never offered to help. Kind of a dick move, the more he thought about it.

"Thanks a lot, I really appreciate it," Lori told him, opening her door.

"You need a ride back to your car, or to the repair shop, just let me know," he told her. "Borrow the Jeep if you need to. Or, you know, if you need help with your mom, I'm right next door." He pressed his lips together and looked out the windshield. "People are heavy."

Standing in the open door she looked at him appraisingly. She opened her mouth and closed it. "Thanks," she said finally, then closed the door. She strode quickly toward the front door of her home.

He watched her until she was inside, and sat in the Jeep for a few seconds, thinking. Then, after a quick look around, he put the Jeep back in gear and headed out. He still hadn't had breakfast, and was starving.

Chapter Two

Sheriff John Osterman pushed through the front doors of the station at 6:35 a.m, which meant he was uncharacteristically, almost unforgivably, late. But he'd been unable to find his darn phone. There was no way he was going to wake his wife up to ask if she knew where it might be or to help look for it; after forty years of marriage he'd long ago learned that as much as he adored his beloved she was useless until the sun was up and she had three cups of strong black coffee in her. He'd finally found the phone on his workbench in the garage, having no recollection of ever having placed it there. Sure, he'd be turning 70 in a few months, but just because lapses in memory for someone his age weren't uncommon didn't mean he had to be happy about it.

"Morning, gentlemen," he called out. He preferred to come in the front door as opposed to the employee entrance in back. He wanted to see the station the way the public did.

The two deputies behind the security glass smiled and

nodded at him. "Mornin', Sheriff," the younger one said reflexively.

"Morning sir." The older deputy had been with the department for over a dozen years. He glanced at the clock on the wall and did a doubletake. "Sir, you're almost five minutes late," he said with mock alarm. His voice rose. "And you have no coffee. Did the zombie apocalypse start?" He pretended to peer out the glass of the front doors. The younger deputy behind the desk snorted.

"I would tell you to mind your insubordinate tongue, but tardy is tardy," the Sheriff admitted. Truth was he made his own schedule, and could show up for work at nine a.m. if he wished, in a polo shirt and khakis, but Sheriff John Osterman had never been easy on anyone, including himself. He'd been showing up for work at six-thirty a.m. in full uniform since first being duly elected Tohono County Sheriff twenty-six years before. That the search for his phone had taken so much time he'd been unable to stop for coffee on the way in to work was especially painful. The stationhouse coffee was suitable only for cleaning brake drums. He'd still drink it without a hint of complaint, but it truly was wretched awful stuff.

He was buzzed through the door and made his way toward his office. Morning road shift didn't start until seven-thirty, so most of the men had yet to start rolling in and suiting up. The station was quiet, most of the offices still dark.

Osterman unlocked his office door and flipped the light switch. He squinted as the fluorescents came on. Or maybe the stacks of paper on his desk were what made his eyes twitch. There were two prep radios in charging cradles on the table behind the desk, one on with the volume down low. He rounded the corner of the desk and stared down at the paperwork, then at his computer. He hated it even more than the paper, because its capacity for irritating him was infinite. There were probably a hundred emails stacked up in his Inbox since he'd left work the day before.

"Trying to glare it into submission again?"

Osterman looked up to see his right-hand man on the far side of the desk, smirking. Sam Wheaton had creased and tanned skin and the moustache of a cowboy poet. Much more important at the moment, however, were his hands, each of which held a coffee cup with a plastic lid.

"I swear you have some psychic powers," Osterman said, thankfully taking the proffered cup.

"Getting tough to find a place that makes good coffee which doesn't seem obsessed with spouting off about lefty politics or using customer money to support whackadoo causes," Wheaton observed, taking a sip of his coffee. "This is from the new place in the Crossroads center that has all the snowflakes melting just 'cause of its name. Thought we should try it out."

"Owned by vets, right?" Osterman sipped at his black coffee. It was good and strong, and he nodded appreciatively.

"Owned and operated. The Aloha Snackbar." Wheaton snorted. "Fella poured us these lost a foot in Afghanistan."

"You paid full price?" Osterman asked. It wasn't a question.

Wheaton nodded. "And left a tip."

"Good man." He took a few more sips of the coffee and surveyed the work sitting on his desk. "It's demoralizing, is what it is. You know what it isn't? Policework."

"So retire then already. You've been Sheriff of this county so long people have forgotten they're allowed to vote for someone else."

"I'd retire if I thought someone could get elected to replace me who wasn't an imbecile or a disgrace. Thomasen in that last election, he nearly beat me with that smile, and you know what he was up to. Hell, six months after the election the FBI was knocking on his door for interstate fraud."

The phone on Osterman's desk rang and they both looked at it. Bit early for the phone to start. The Sheriff hit the button for the speaker. "Osterman."

"Sheriff! Oh, good, you're in. Wasn't sure you'd be there. This is Rhonda in dispatch. I've got Deputy Webster on the phone for you. He's out on the road right now, on a call."

"His radio broken?" Osterman had a prep radio on his belt and it had been relatively quiet on the way in, just a few units calling in traffic stops.

"No sir, but he said he had something out there that probably shouldn't go out over the radio." The two men glanced at each other. Osterman's expression hardened.

"Put him through." When the phone clicked, he identified himself, somehow knowing it was bad news.

"Sheriff, this is Paul Webster. I've got a situation out here."

Osterman thought he remembered which face went with the name, although it was tougher every year. The young deputy sounded out of breath. "Tell me what you've got."

"It came over as a noise complaint on South Pleasant. I actually got it...shit, almost an hour ago. Shouting, maybe fireworks, that's how the call went out. Higgins and I were busy cleaning up an accident on 89A so we didn't roll out on the call until the tow trucks cleared the scene. Since he was right there he rolled up with me to the address, we thought we'd check it off the list before coming off shift."

"What did you find that you didn't want going out over the radio?"

"Bodies, sir. Latin males. Two of 'em, all hacked up, one still tied to a chair. Blood everywhere inside the house and on the back porch. We cleared the house then backed out without touching anything. From the amount the blood has dried I'd guess it all happened late last night, maybe early this morning." The deputy paused. "When the call went out." He sounded guilty.

"It's okay son, we can't be everywhere at once. Unfortunately, most of what we do is just clean up. Even if you'd gone straight there after getting the call I'm sure it would have been all over. Hacked up, you say?" At that Sam looked like he'd eaten something sour.

"Yes sir. It's ugly. If I had to guess, I'd guess cartels. Or someone just went totally nuts, but this seems more deliberate than crazy."

"Dammit. Pardon my French, son. Okay, I will be there forthwith. What's the address?" When he had it he hung up with the deputy and picked up the phone to call Dispatch. "Rhonda? Send four cars over to assist the units on Pleasant, and a Sergeant to manage the scene. Don't put out any details over the air, but we've got a couple of bodies in bad shape, maybe tortured."

She sighed. "Oh, Lord."

"As soon as day shift checks in swap the men out so we're not racking up the overtime. I'll have Wheaton arrange the crime scene unit and a detective." He pointed at Sam, who nodded and headed out the door. "I'll be heading out to the scene. I'll have a prep, but if you need to talk details about this one call my cell."

"You got it, Sheriff."

The neighborhood wasn't a bad one, he didn't need to see it or the house to know that; the map of the county and associated crime rates was hardwired into his head. It could be a home invasion gone bad, maybe a lover's quarrel gone nuclear, but Latin males tied down and cut on did sound a lot like cartel business. He wouldn't be surprised if a check on the house showed it was a rental. Which meant the investigation would probably go nowhere. But still, they had to try.

Osterman parked at the curb several houses away from the crime scene. It was early, and nobody was using either their lights or sirens, but still there were already a few neighborhood residents on their porches. He knew he'd be recognized, which meant they had fifteen, maybe twenty minutes before a news van showed up.

The Sergeant on-scene met him in front of the neighboring house. "Joel," Osterman said with a nod. "It as bad as I was led to believe?"

"I just peered in through a window, but it looks like something out of one of those torture-porn movies that somehow pass for entertainment."

Osterman sighed. "Well, until the evidence techs get here make sure no one goes inside. You've got somebody behind the house? I don't trust the news people not to try and sneak in that way."

"In the back yard. There's a fence of sorts, half chain link, half wood, that'll slow 'em down."

"Where's the first deputies that were on-scene? Webster and, um…"

"Higgins. Higgins is talking to the neighbor who called in the noise complaint." The Sergeant nodded at the next-door neighbor's house. The deputy was talking to a pale man in his sixties just inside the front door. "All I've heard so far is that the place is a rental. That's Webster right there." He looked at the young uniformed deputy standing on the sidewalk in front of the house.

Osterman nodded and strode up to the man who'd found the bodies. He'd been with the department five years or so, if Osterman's memory served. "Deputy, walk with me."

The house had a raised front porch. Osterman studied the cement sidewalk leading up to it before walking on it, as he didn't want to destroy evidence. Kicking a shell casing or stepping in blood was decidedly unprofessional. Not that he hadn't done both, one time or another. The sun was just up over the horizon, which meant the street was all streaks of light and long shadows. By comparison the sheltered porch was dim. Osterman paused at the base of the stairs and pulled out his flashlight. He ran the bright light over the stairs and the roofed wood porch. "You said there was blood on the porch?"

"Back porch, sir. And on the inside of the back door, which was a bit open."

Osterman nodded and took the stairs carefully. There was a small window at the top of the antique front door. Leaded glass, looked like, too high to see through. He bent down and peered inside the front window, playing his light inside.

"You can't see much from here," Webster said.

"I can see enough." Osterman sighed. Such as a hand, not connected to its owner. The coffee soured in his stomach. He took the steps down slowly, then shone his flashlight on the yard in front of the house. It was hard-packed dirt with a few weeds, nothing that would provide a usable shoe impression.

He walked around the side of the house into the bright

morning sun, boots crunching. He shielded his eyes as he looked down, but he couldn't see any footprints in the narrow strip of yard between the houses or anything else that might count for physical evidence. Around the corner into the backyard he stepped into the shadow of the house to the rear of the property and his face suddenly felt cool. He nodded to the deputy standing in the back corner of the yard about thirty feet away and looked up at the rear of the house.

Another raised wood porch, four steps up off the ground. "There's a little blood on the railing there," Webster told him, pointing. "And on the porch right in front of the door. Some on the inside of the door."

Osterman turned and called out to the deputy at the rear of the yard. "Any blood on the fence back there?"

"Not that I've seen, Sheriff."

"You thinking someone ran out of the house? Should we get a canine unit?" Deputy Webster looked at the nearby houses.

"Hmm." Osterman stood and tapped his flashlight against his palm, then stuck it back in the holster on his uniform belt. Webster stood nearby, waiting for a decision.

The neighborhood was gradually waking up. In the distance Osterman could hear car doors slamming, engines starting, the unmistakable sound of a mother lecturing a child. Much closer, somewhere nearby, he heard a small sound. Sounds. Probably an animal. The sun was just showing its face, so the soft little noises were most likely a possum or some other nocturnal creature.

Osterman cocked his head and got very still. He stood that way for a good minute. Then he pulled the flashlight from his belt, turned around, and squatted on his heels. He directed the bright beam underneath the porch, his other hand resting lightly on his gun.

The young woman underneath the porch was bloody and wide-eyed. He doubted she even realized she'd been whimpering. She was shivering, perhaps from the cold as much as shock. Underneath the dirt and blood she appeared to be naked.

Osterman shut off the flashlight. "*Policia*," he said softly. "*No te preocupes. Estas segura.*" Over his shoulder he said, "Mr. Webster, I'm going to need a blanket."

It was nearly one o'clock when his detectives got back from the hospital where they'd interviewed the woman who they'd determined was, in fact, a victim. He met them in his office, where he was slowly working his way through the paperwork and emails that made up so much of his job.

Because the vic was female and knew little if any English he'd made Maria Flores the lead in the case. She'd been a detective for close to eight years and knew her stuff. Her partner, Norm Hill, had four years as a detective, and they made a great team because they were complete opposites in every way. Osterman figured he had every base covered between the two of them.

"First, what's her medical condition?" Osterman asked. Considering he was the person who'd coaxed her out from underneath the porch and wrapped the blanket around her shivering bloodstained body, he was sincerely concerned for her welfare.

"Medically? Medically she's not too bad at all," Flores said, nearly growling. She was dark-skinned and short and affectionately nicknamed The Pitbull by her coworkers. "Borderline hypothermia and minor lacerations. Bruises and swelling to the face from a few punches. The gunshot wound is across her lower left back, one long gouge. Nasty and bloody, took a lot of stitches to close, probably hurts like hell, but it was never life-threatening. Emotionally? Psychologically? That's a whole other story."

"She's still in shock, but she's a fighter," Hill told him. "That's why she's still alive." The man was pale as milk, nearly six and a half feet tall, sporting a barrel chest and stubble for hair. Flores looked like a midget next to him, but truth be told she was the more dangerous one. A guy the size of Hill had tried to throw her around when she was in uniform, grab her gun, and she'd bitten a big chunk out of his arm before shooting him in the leg. Hence the Pitbull moniker. It made a funny story now, but for most of a year afterward she'd had to go in and get her blood tested to make sure she hadn't picked up anything nasty from the junkie perp.

Osterman looked at Flores, and she pulled out her notebook. "Reina Isabella Martín, age twenty-four. Originally from Guadalajara, she came into the States about two years ago. Not a U.S. citizen."

"Reina. What's that mean in English, princess?"

"Queen. She works afternoon shift at a diner just off 17 on the north side of Phoenix. Was coming off work day before yesterday—"

"Thirty-six hours before you found her," Hill told Osterman.

"...and she got grabbed by two guys," Flores went on. "Juan Miller and Enrique Peña, according to their IDs, which are Arizona Driver Licenses that are the best fakes I've ever seen. Didn't know they were fakes until I tried to run them and the numbers came back to other people. Even got the, whaddayacallit, seal that only shows up under UV light. Anyway, they punched her in the face, threw her in the trunk. Near as she can tell they drove straight to the house on Pleasant. Got there when it was dark. Dragged her inside." The detective's face grew even darker. "They raped her off and on for the next twenty-four hours or so while drinking beer, making phone calls, and watching TV. For some of the time she says she was tied to the bed, but then I guess they figured she'd been tamed and cut her loose. When she wasn't being raped they locked her in a bedroom."

"Any particular reason they grabbed her?" Osterman asked. "Any prior contact with either of these guys? Any gang or cartel activity at this place she worked? She involved with a gang? I'm just wondering why her."

"We're not aware of any connection," Flores said. "She said she had no idea who these guys were, never remembered seeing them before. That maybe, maybe, they'd been customers at the diner."

"She's smoking hot," Hill said. "Hard to tell under the bruises and blood, but the girl is world-class pretty. Maybe she was just a target of opportunity for a couple of shitheads."

"And from what I've gathered, the two men who abducted her are the ones who ended up in pieces on the floor?"

"Yes."

"At least that scale's been evened out a bit," Osterman said with a sigh. "So who did the cutting?"

"Three males arrived at the house very late last night. Maybe early this morning. Two big guys, potentially bodyguards for the third man, a fancy-looking guy in a suit. That's how she described him, 'fancy'. *Sofisticado*. She was in the bedroom at this time, but could see most of what was happening through a crack between the door and the frame. It's an old house, and I went back there to check out her story. The bedroom where she says she was kept, the bed in there is a DNA minefield. There's blood on rope fragments, a little blood on the sheets...and you can smell the semen." She shook her head. "As for the door, there's at least half an inch gap, and with the door closed I could see the chairs."

"Where these two men were tied. Where they were tortured."

"Yes. Apparently after talking for a short time, the three newcomers all pulled guns and tied the two rapists to chairs they pulled in from another room. Then they proceeded to torture them. Some hitting, but mostly cutting."

"Neighbors didn't hear screaming?"

"Gagged with blankets. She said fancy suit was in charge, and he was asking the guys who were tied up questions, but she couldn't actually hear the questions. She thought the torturing went on for a couple of hours, and looking at the bodies I believe it. At some point she couldn't watch any more, but she could still hear it. Until she couldn't take listening, either. She forced the bedroom door open, surprised the hell out of them, they never checked the house, never knew she was there, and made a run for the back door. One of them shot at her and gave her that nasty wound in the back. It was her blood all over the door and the back porch. She apparently had enough of a head start that they thought she jumped the fence when all she did was hide under the porch."

"Girl's damn lucky to be alive," Hill said soberly.

"They searched the neighboring yards for a minute or two, then took off." Flores checked her notes. "She heard them talking. One of them said, 'I know I hit the bitch, she's probably bleeding out in a gutter somewhere'. And they saw the blood. The other one said something like, 'You better hope so'. Her English is okay, but I did the interview in Spanish. She says that they were all speaking Spanish."

"When do you think she'll be ready to sit down and look at pictures? Or meet with a sketch artist?"

Hill rubbed his face. "Maybe a day or two, but I don't know if it'll do much good. The two deceased, they're Mexican nationals, and seems a good bet that the three guys including Mr. Fancy Pants are as well. I'd be surprised if they're not already back over the border."

Flores raised a finger. "She said they were Mexican, from their accents. She never saw their car, and we don't have any photos, but I did put in a call to ICE and the Border Patrol. To keep an eye out for three Mexican males travelling back over the border. One possibly in a suit, and one with a badly cut left ear."

"Cut ear?"

Flores ran a finger across her own ear. "Not fresh. It's an old scar, a bad one, on one of Mr. Fancy's thugs. It's a long shot, but maybe we'll get lucky. Anyway, I made the call, didn't think you'd mind."

"No, that's a good idea." Osterman made a face. "Mexican nationals, recreational rape, torture, murder...cartel business, or something else?"

"If I was a betting man I'd say cartels, but what the hell are they doing way up here?" Hill said. "We're four hours from the border and not on the way to anywhere. Not directly."

"We're between Phoenix and Vegas," Flores pointed out. Hill shook his head, then shrugged.

Osterman thought for a bit. "Turn the dead men's effects inside out. Have we located their car yet?"

Hill nodded his big head. "Rental out of Sky Harbor,

parked on the street. It's been towed back here, but I don't know if the evidence techs have been through it yet. We're checking with the airlines to see if these guys flew in, and from where. Waiting for a call back."

"And the landlord of the house?"

"He's out of Flagstaff. Uses an internet company to rent it out a week at a time, hires a maid service to clean it out between customers, hasn't been to the house in months. He's been cooperative, we're running down the name and the credit card of the company that rented it for this week." He turned to his partner. "You could say Flagstaff's between Vegas and Phoenix too. And it's bigger." She didn't answer.

"Company rented the house?" Osterman asked.

"Yeah. Lot of loose ends on this one that might lead somewhere."

"You need more bodies, you let me know. I want to know why they were here, and what the hell this was all about. If this is cartel business, I will not have them moving into this county. They are a cancer. You don't coddle cancer, you kill it with poison or you cut it out." He looked between the two of them. "Is that it?"

"For right now."

Osterman nodded. "Keep me updated."

"Yes sir."

He was sitting at his desk ten minutes later when a knock at his open door made him look up. Sam Wheaton was standing there, eyebrows raised.

"Yes?"

"Don't you have someplace to be before too long?"

"Not that I recall."

"No interview?"

Osterman frowned, then checked the clock. "Darn it,

that totally slipped my mind with this double homicide. Sally's off sick today, otherwise she'd have been all over me." Sally Harrison was his secretary. "Good thing you're paying attention."

A little over two and a half hours later Osterman was sitting in a chair in the Fox network affiliate in Phoenix. They'd dusted a little makeup on his face, not that he'd ever be pretty, but apparently parts of his face were a bit shiny. He had an earpiece in so he could hear the anchor in New York, but had nothing to look at other than the lens of a camera. He knew there'd be about a second or second and a half delay in the audio from New York, and possibly people standing behind the camera he was talking into, but he'd done enough of these over the years to not be distracted.

"We're going to be going to you in about thirty seconds," the floor producer told him. "Eight-and-a-half-minute segment, if I didn't tell you that already." Osterman nodded but didn't say anything. The audio feed got switched on in his earbud. He heard music as the network came off a commercial break, then the anchor's voice in his ear.

"In this next segment we'll be talking immigration. The new administration has taken a tough stance on it, and it's been in the news for months. Here to talk about it are two of our regular guests, Doctor Neil Lightman from the Southern Poverty Law Center, and Sheriff John Osterman in Arizona. Gentlemen, good to see you."

Osterman waited for Lightman's greeting, then added, "Good to be here, Mindy."

"Dr. Lightman, let's start with you. The SPLC is one of

the plaintiffs on the most recent immigration lawsuit filed against the administration, specifically naming the Department of Justice and ICE. You claim the new immigration restrictions are illegal and unconstitutional, something that the administration flatly denies. What can you tell us about it?"

Osterman sat still as Lightman, who was both a professor and lawyer and spoke as if he got paid extra for big words, detailed the SPLC's position. Osterman did not have a law degree but knew gobbledygook when he heard it. He waited patiently until the anchor cut off the longwinded lefty.

"Sheriff Osterman, you've been sitting there quietly waiting your turn, thank you. Being in Arizona, your department often has to deal with people of dubious immigration status. What do you think about this new lawsuit against the administration? You've been very vocal in your support of this administration's tougher stance on this subject."

Osterman smiled. "Mindy, first, thanks for having me on again. And I want to commend Mr. Lightman and the Southern Poverty Law Center for discovering that this country does, in fact, have a Constitution which protects the rights of its citizens against the power of government. For years they've seemed unaware of that fact. But I must admit I'm seriously confused. I thought I was here to talk about the heavy toll illegal immigrants have had on my county and America."

"It's *Doctor* Lightman," he heard in his ear, but ignored the man and continued.

"Instead Mr. Lightman keeps using this inaccurate and misleading term *undocumented worker*. First, a huge percentage of illegal aliens in this country aren't, in fact, working hard to earn a living but are, instead, on government assistance. Especially in states such as California which give out taxpayer money to anyone who asks, apparently." He'd always been a hardliner on immigration, and things were only getting worse. The double cartel-style homicide and the bloody young woman whom he'd wrapped in a towel that morning didn't leave him conflicted about his views. In fact, he was feeling a bit combative.

"That is completely untrue!" Lightman spluttered in outrage. "Migrant workers are the backbone of agriculture in this country. Hundreds of thousands, perhaps millions of undocumented workers come to this country and work hard to support their families—"

Osterman cut him off. "How would you know? If they're undocumented, how would you know how many there are, where they're working, or anything about them?"

Lightman huffed. "Because luckily there are places in this country that treat them like human beings, not an existential threat to humanity. Sanctuary cities and states, where undocumented immigrants can register."

"Exactly!" Osterman interjected. "Register for what, exactly? Governments don't give out jobs anymore, all they do is give out money. The days of the WPA are long over. So if these illegal aliens are registering with the state, it is to get benefits. 'Assistance'. Money, in other words. Money produced by law-abiding hard-working Americans…and being given to foreign criminals. Thank you for making my point."

Mindy Tonaka was an experienced host who knew good TV when it was happening, and she just sat back, shut up, and let it happen.

"Criminals?" Lightman nearly shrieked in his ear. "Surely you're not suggesting that these undocumented workers who just want to make a new and better life for their family are criminals."

"That's exactly what I'm saying," Osterman said calmly. "All of them. They are illegal aliens. Note the term 'illegal'. Their very presence in this country is evidence that they have broken the law. Federal immigration law. Which makes every illegal alien, by definition, a criminal. Every. Single. One."

The outrage and indignation nearly had Lightman apoplectic. "So we should, what, lock them all up? Put them in jail? Put them in camps like the Japanese in World War II?"

"I'm not in charge of federal immigration law," Osterman said calmly, with a smile. "But I will point out that those Japanese citizens, as poorly treated as they were by a Democrat President, were still American citizens, and had many rights under the law. Illegal aliens are not American citizens and are not entitled to the protection of the Constitution."

"That's fascism!" Lightman shouted. "I always suspected you were a fascist, and I'm glad it's finally come out."

"The U.S. Constitution only applies to Americans," Osterman said slowly, as if he was explaining a difficult math problem to a child. "I never went to law school but I know they cover that on Day One of Constitutional Law. So you being a lawyer and a professor have to know that. Yet you're advocating for the rights of criminal foreigners against the people of the United States. Which begs the question…why do you hate America?" And he sat back with a polite look of confusion on his face for the viewers as Lightman exploded in outrage. Even in law enforcement a Minor in Theater could be very useful.

Osterman was halfway back to Prescott in his department vehicle, a fully-marked Ford Explorer, when his phone rang. He knew there was some way to make the vehicle itself answer his phone so the caller echoed around the car but he didn't want that. When he wanted to talk on his phone he'd talk on his phone, not talk to his car. You drove a car, you talked into a phone. He put the phone up to his ear.

"Osterman."

"Sheriff, it's Flores. Where are you?"

"Coming back from Phoenix. Maybe an hour out. What's going on?"

"What's the phrase about hard work producing luck? Border patrol picked up our suspects, trying to cross back at Nogales."

"There are a lot of quotes, but my favorite is Jefferson's. 'I am a great believer in luck, and I find the harder I work the more I have of it.'" Osterman smiled, then frowned. "They the right guys? Did the victim already make the ID?"

"Not yet. But I've got a feeling. Three guys, one with a split left ear, the third, in the backseat, in a suit. All Mexican nationals."

"Who are they?"

"I've got names but haven't had a chance to run them yet. I just got the word from Border Patrol fifteen minutes ago."

"Make sure BP knows these guys are suspects in a double homicide and they might have blood or other evidence on them or in the car. They need to make sure everything and everyone is locked down tight until we can take custody. If these are the guys, I want them."

"Three guys, cut ear, suit? It's gotta be them. They're already asking for a lawyer, which is interesting, since they haven't even technically been arrested yet."

"Worrisome is the word I would use, but let's work this right, nail them down tight. Assuming it is them, good job. That was some damn fine police work. Closed the case in eight hours."

"Thank you, sir."

"Don't thank me yet. I've got the bad feeling that there's a whole lot more going on here, and two murders are just the tip of it. You make a plan yet to pick them up?"

"Hill and I are going to head down there tomorrow morning, take custody, bring them back up."

Osterman thought for a few moments. "Take a prisoner transport van. And a uniformed deputy. No, two."

"Sir, I don't really think that's—"

"It's not a request," he said firmly. "You're not picking up drunk drivers or men who were arrested on bench warrants for overdue child support. These gentlemen hacked up a couple of their fellow human beings. Into pieces. Treat them as if when they get the chance they'll do the same to you. And if they are cartel, they will have lots of friends with just as little humanity. Two deputies, and they're cuffed at all times. Am I clear?"

"Yes sir."

Chapter Three

They hit a bump and the new guy almost fell out of his lawn chair. Aaron, sitting in the captain's chair rescued from some RV in the distant past, laughed. The captain's chair was bolted to the floor. And had cupholders.

"These roads suck. It's worse than driving around Iraq." The new guy nearly had to yell to be heard over the road noise and creaks of the truck body and the roar of the diesel engine.

"Yeah, they do, but these trucks magnify every bump. It's because they don't have shocks, only springs." They both looked around the box of the battered armored car in which they were riding. The walls in a previous epoch had been painted white but now were mostly bare steel with rivets showing. The floor sported several overlapping carpet remnants, but they were tattered and dirty. Where there were gaps in the carpet the steel floor underneath was scraped and rusty. This particular truck smelled dusty and rusty, which was a distinct improvement over some of the trucks in the fleet. The back of the armored car was empty but for the two of them and the two chairs. And their rifles.

"What's your name? Timmy?"

The new guy shot Aaron a dirty look. "Tim. Tim Lee." He looked to be in his late twenties, with short black hair and a muscular build. In the bright white uniform shirt and creased black pants he looked as much like a cop or ex-military as anyone in the company. By comparison Aaron's uniform shirt looked gray and ancient.

"You ever been on a Fed run before?" Aaron patted his shirt pocket and found the pack of Marlboros, but stopped there. He was trying to cut down on the cigs, so he wasn't smoking inside the truck any more. The fact that it meant less people pissed at him for the secondhand smoke was irrelevant.

"No," the new guy said with a shake of his head.

"How long you been with the company?" Aaron asked him. "Month?"

"Nearly two."

Aaron nodded. "Well, it's because you bounced around in Asscrackistan that I requested you for this run. It's an easy gig if nothing happens, great way to spend half the day. But if something bad happens, it's going to be really, really bad. Like CNN headline bad. But the company finally got their shit together after all these years and listened to me and put some actual guards on the trucks, which is why we are sitting back here living the dream. Before this run they didn't have anyone just standing by and keeping an eye out during the offload, they were all just slingin' cash. That we should have rifles was a no-brainer, but you'd have thought I was asking for underage hookers."

"You requested me?"

"Yeah. Coupla tours, right? Marine Corps? I figure you

knew how to work a rifle, not like most of the humps work here. No offense Tony," Aaron called out to the driver on the other side of the ventilated partition. "You know I'm not talking about you." He looked at the new guy. "Tony's a former jarhead too."

"Yeah?" Tim looked at the driver through the metal grille. He had to be at least in his fifties if not older, with solid gray hair and beard. "How long were you in?"

"Eight years active. Then I got out and put in twenty-five with Ford before retiring. Sat at home with the wife for two years until I was ready to kill her, then started doing this. More for the scenery than the money."

"You see any action?"

Tony glanced back over his shoulder into the dim interior of the truck. "In the Corps? What there was, back in the day. I was in late seventies and early eighties. 3rd ANGLICO. Spent some time ducking snipers in Lebanon. Went to Grenada, but there were about a hundred of us for every bad guy there, it was like a parking lot after a rock concert. Seen more excitement doing this, tell you the truth."

"Really?"

Tony shrugged. "Some asshole takes a potshot at you while you're walking down the street in Beirut with twenty of your closest friends, all gunned up and wearing armor, that's one thing. Everybody empties a magazine into the window where he was half a block down, and then if it's allowed under the ROE and somebody's got a '79 or a '203 you send a grenade or two in his direction. If you get him, actually find a body, you have no idea if any of the holes in him came from you. It was a team effort, high fives all around. This job, if somebody comes at you it's a lot more up close and personal."

"Tell him your burger story," Aaron prompted.

Tony glanced over his shoulder again. "You want to hear it?" he asked the kid.

"Sure."

Tony shrugged. "Okay, well, I make a regular pickup at White Castle on Warren Ave. I walk out the back, bag of cash in one hand and eating a burger with the other. The truck is right there, and a guy steps out from behind the back of the truck with a shotgun, like twelve feet away. My driver, he's got his face buried in the Free Press as usual."

"Oh shit. So what happened?"

"Guy points the shotgun at me and pulls the trigger. Shotgun goes *click*."

The Marine Corps veteran sat and thought about that for a second. His face went pale. "Oh, man. Shit. Jesus." He got chills.

"Yeah. So I threw the burger at him, pulled my piece, and shot him in the face. Then I pulled my driver out of the cab and beat the shit out of him."

Aaron laughed. "When the cops showed up they thought the dead guy had done it. Tony's my fucking hero. And let me tell you, that made all the drivers get their shit together and pay attention like they're supposed to, at least for six months or so."

"Cops also checked out the shotgun," Tony said. "It went boom when they pulled the trigger."

"Damn."

"Whole thing was caught on security cam, so the entire investigation took about ten minutes. About as close to a walk-off home run as you'll ever get killing somebody. Dead guy had a record, of course."

Aaron looked at the new guy. "So what're you, Chinese, Japanese, Viet Cong?"

"Lee's Chinese." He'd gotten no end of razzing in the Corps, so Aaron's attempt to get a rise out of him fell on deaf ears.

"Okay, good, an expert. So tell me, why is 'Oriental' an insult?"

"What?"

"Used to be we called Asians Orientals. But now 'Oriental' is an insult or something stupid like that. Do you know why? 'Cause I sure don't."

"No."

"Well shit. It's like changing Peking to Beijing and... whatever the hell it used to be to Mumbai." He thought for a second. "Bombay. Wasn't Mumbai Bombay? It's Bombay Gin." He glanced around the truck but just got dumb looks. "We getting close?" he asked Tony with a sigh.

"About five minutes."

"You manage to lose Stuey yet?"

Tony laughed and glanced in his side mirror. The second truck was still behind them.

Aaron nodded, then looked at Lee. "Okay, you've never done a Fed run, so let me tell you about it. I'm not sure what gate we're going to end up at, so I'm not sure what the exact layout's going to be. The fenceline, it could be a couple hundred yards away or it could be half a mile away. Which is why we have rifles. But if anybody comes from that direction on foot they've got a lot of open ground to cover, I'm not worried about that. No, the thing to keep your eye on is the building and any vehicles. Any vehicles, I don't care how they're marked, anybody approaching on foot, that's who you eyeball. It's supposed to be a secured area, so there shouldn't be too many people just wandering around."

"Got it."

"The two trucks will back up side by side, more or less. I'll go left, you go right, we need to be on the outside of the trucks. Between the two of us we'll have three-sixty degree coverage. Plus everybody else should have their eyes open, and they're all carrying guns, but we're the early warning system, you got me?"

"Yeah."

Aaron eyed him. "So what's your job on this run?"

"Get out, go to the right, protect the cash."

Aaron shook his head violently. "No, screw that, the cash is insured. I don't care what company policy says. Your job is to protect the people. Me, Tony, the morons with Stuey in the other truck. If things go crazy insane and it gets like *Die Hard* out there, you pull everybody back with you into the truck and close the doors, let the assholes take the cash. I can't see that happening, we've got too many people with guns, we'd need to get hit by a small army, but it's fucking Detroit. A word to the wise, you got me?"

"Yeah."

"And afterward you get back in here, that way nobody's confused about who's in what truck. Makes the head count simple. You wearing a plate?" Aaron rapped his knuckles against the steel armor plate covering his heart. It was in the chest pocket of the soft body armor he wore religiously. Soft body armor worked great against handgun bullets, but you wanted a plate if any of the bad guys had rifles.

Lee had spent a great deal of time wearing armor plates when in the Corps. The thick SAPI plates issued to soldiers could take multiple hits from armor-piercing rifle bullets, but they were heavy and expensive and Detroit wasn't Fallujah. He shook his head. "Just soft body armor. But it's rated to stop anything handgun."

"And that might be all you ever need. But it might not. It got pockets for plates?"

"Yeah."

"I'm not sayin', I'm just sayin'," Aaron said pointedly. He sat back and eyed the new guy again. "So, Chinese. That means you know karate, right?" The corner of his mouth fought a smile.

"Karate's Japanese."

Aaron waved a hand indifferently. "Whatever, tomato, potato." Lee snorted and shook his head. He'd gotten it ten times worse from the guys he'd served with.

"Gate," Tony called out, downshifting.

The two trucks rolled up to a manned guardhouse in front of a tall chain-link fence topped with razor wire. The gate was electric and on rollers. The uniformed agent took Tony's driver license through the gun port and then walked to the second truck and did the same with Stuey, then jotted down the license plates. He went back into the gate house and after two minutes of glancing at a computer terminal, making notes on a clipboard, and talking into a radio, he handed their IDs back and the gate rolled open.

"He tell you where to go?" Aaron asked. The guard had said something to Tony through the small gunport, but it was lost in engine noise.

"Yeah. It's not too far. And they got here early, so we are good to go right now." Tony put the truck into gear and it slowly accelerated through the gate.

The trucks rolled across the concrete for half a mile before hooking a left around the end of the building. The ground crew saw them coming and waved them in around the back of the plane, positioning them at the end of the mobile conveyor belt used for unloading baggage.

"Hold the fuck up," Aaron said. He called to Tony,

"Have Stuey and his guys take a look around before they just jump out of the truck like popcorn. Check out the side window," he told Lee. Aaron moved to the back window and pressed his nose against the armored glass, looking left and right. A handful of baggage handlers waited beside the conveyor belt, as well as a middle-aged white guy in a suit, holding a clipboard. That'd be the courier. The jet towered over the two trucks. The ground crew had yet to pilot the jet bridge out to the aircraft, so it was still buttoned up, a metal cigar-shaped island on the concrete.

Tony grabbed the handset. "Stuey, you guys see anything?" There was a few seconds pause, then Stuey's voice came back over the radio. His response was unintelligible. "I think that was a 'No'," Tony said.

"Right. You got anything hinky?" Aaron asked the new guy.

"No."

"Okay then, let's do this." Aaron pulled out the pack of Marlboros, stuck one in the corner of his mouth and lit it, then grabbed his rifle and popped the door. "You're right, I'm left," he reminded the former Marine as he jumped down.

The airport tarmac was windy, but then it usually was. Between all the open space and the jet engines still winding down there always seemed to be a lot of gusts. Aaron walked around to the left side of his truck and up toward the cab where he could keep an eye on the airport terminal building and the other vehicle. Past the airplane was a whole lot of concrete, then grass, then more concrete. The fence line was way out there, half a mile or more. Or maybe it just seemed that distant because of all the open space.

Tony walked up to the courier and they compared

paperwork as two guys jumped down out of the back of the other armored car and stood nearby. Every Absolute Armored employee was uniformed and wearing a pistol. The courier nodded to the baggage handlers, and one of them climbed onto the angled conveyor belt and popped open the door to the baggage compartment. He adjusted his knee pads and crawled inside. Another man turned on the conveyor belt. Ten seconds later the first bundle was tossed onto the belt and made its way slowly downward. The courier took out a sharpie and made a mark on the clear plastic of the bundle, and repeated it for each and every bundle that appeared. Above them faces were pressed against the windows of the passenger jet, watching the unexpected event.

As they reached the end of the conveyor belt the armored car employees grabbed the plastic-wrapped bundles and began tossing them into Stuey's truck. Each one weighed about thirty pounds. Aaron had to force his eyes away from the men working to scan the surrounding area. The threat would most likely come from the terminal so he eyeballed it, and any nearby vehicles. He sucked at the cigarette and kept his hands on his AR-15, muzzle down, safety on.

When the first truck was full—or as full as was possible while still leaving room for the men to climb back inside—they began tossing bundles into the second truck. After ten minutes the last bundle was placed on the conveyor belt and initialed and numbered by the courier as it went by. He watched it tossed into the armored truck and then exchanged paperwork with Tony.

Aaron was staring off into the distance when he heard Tony say, "All done, let's go!" He took a long slow look around, checking for anything dangerous or just out of place, and when he didn't see anything he moved toward the back of the truck and climbed up.

The bundles of cash took up so much room the loaders had collapsed the folding chair and placed it atop a stack of bundles. The new guy was sitting on an identical stack, looking around himself in minor disbelief. Aaron climbed in, slammed the door shut, and waited until he could see Stuey's guys were all inside before he called out, "Okay, let's roll."

"Jesus, I didn't think there'd be…how much cash is this?" Lee was wide-eyed.

Aaron looked at the bundles. Each one was two packets of bills wide and tall, so what was that, five by twelve inches? And the packets were stacked about eighteen inches tall before being shrinkwrapped in heavy duty plastic. The plastic was clear, for easy identification of the bills inside. No mixed bundles, each contained the same denomination of bills. About half the bundles were showing $20 bills, a quarter of them were $100s, and the rest were $5s and $10s and $50s. All brand new bills straight from the Federal Reserve.

"I don't know. Sixteen million? Thirty-two? Sixty-four? It's some multiple of sixteen, I can't remember," Aaron said.

"Sixty-four," Tony called from up front.

"And they just ship it in the belly of a passenger jet with one unarmed courier?" Lee said in disbelief. He'd never thought about it before, but it made sense that the Federal Reserve would have its own planes. The Government never seemed to shy away from spending money on everything else.

"Armed guards load it in after all the passengers are

buttoned up, and we or whoever unloads it in a secure area, with the passengers still all locked up. And even if they weren't locked up but standing around on the ground watching us, they've all been through TSA screening, metal detectors and whatever they call those naked body scanners. In-between there and here it's thirty thousand feet in the air. No need for an armed courier." He saw the younger man looking around the truck. Looking at the stack of cash he was sitting on. Aaron had to admit it was a surreal sight.

"This isn't the shipment you want to rob anyway," Aaron told him knowingly.

"What? Why not?"

Aaron waved a hand. "This is all brand-new cash. Straight from the mint. They've got a record of every single one of these serial numbers. You steal it and try to spend one of those bills the Secret Service'll jump on you faster'n Oprah on a donut."

"Yeah." Lee didn't sound convinced, looking around at the stacks of cash filling the truck. Aaron understood—the idea of that much money was unnerving to most people. Being able to see—and touch—tens of millions of dollars of cash was fantastical. Something very few people ever got to do. Aaron had been doing the job long enough that it wasn't money to him anymore, it was just work. Each cash brick was just thirty pounds of pain in the ass. Besides, he ever decided to retire on the job, steal a truckload and disappear, it would be used bills he'd take. Untraceable.

"Don't zone out just yet, we're not safe now. Well, you're never safe in this job, even if you've got no cash in the truck nobody knows that, you're just a big dollar sign driving around. But until we get downtown and drop this stuff off keep an eye out the windows." On the way back they were behind the other truck, and its square back end filled the windshield.

"Right." Something occurred to Lee. "Hey, if something had happened. Or ever does happen. Do we have first aid kits in the truck? IFAKs, blow out kits, tourniquets, QuikClot, whatever? In any of the trucks."

Aaron stared at him for a few seconds before shaking his head and swearing. "Shit. No, no we don't."

"Those two new trucks do, but they're just about useless, Band-Aids and aspirin and shit like that," Tony said from the front. "No tourniquets or gauze pads or anything you'd need for a gunshot wound."

"I gotta talk to Joe about that. We should probably all have basic first aid training, too, but they'll never pay for that shit. I knew bringing you along was a good idea. Even if nothing happened." Aaron looked at Lee pointedly. "And if you do your job right, and your driver is paying attention, probably nothing will happen. You'll see it coming and shut it down before it does happen. Or just leave so nothing happens. People get robbed in this business it's usually 'cause they got their head up their asses, like Tony's driver. This is Detroit, we don't have DeNiro and Pacino looking to take down trucks after two months of detailed planning, we've got D'Shonquiel and José and tweaker Eminem wannabees making shit up as they go. Which means that because so many people in this company also have their head up their asses a lot of them have been robbed. Or at least gotten into gunfights."

Tony laughed in the cab. "You remember Cornell's robbery?" He glanced back over his shoulder at Aaron.

Aaron snorted and looked at Lee. "Coupla guys try to rob him on a stop, or so the story goes. Cornell pulls out his Beretta 92 and blows through the entire mag and then two more. Forty-five rounds, and all he hit was parked cars, a parking meter, a telephone pole, and an apartment building. Good thing the company's got insurance, that would have cost them ten grand in body work and windows instead of whatever their deductible is."

Lee glanced at Aaron's pistol. It was a stainless Colt Delta Elite 10mm, which was a bit flashy and pimptastic. Especially with the cocked hammer. It didn't strike him as a serious working gun, it looked more for show. But then again it was Detroit, sometimes it paid to make an impression. And then there was the shop talk he'd heard, although gossip was a more accurate term. "I hear you have a fast draw. You the resident gunfighter?" He was wondering what kind of story he'd get. The bigger the tale, the more it would tell him about Aaron.

Aaron leaned back in the captain's chair. "Yeah, I've got a fast draw. I've had to point my gun at more assholes than I can count, but I've never had to pull the trigger."

"Your old partner, on the other hand…" Tony said. Aaron made a sound and shook his head.

"What, he not pay attention out on the job?" Lee asked.

"He was fucking awesome out on the road," Aaron said defensively. He threw an angry glance at Tony for even suggesting otherwise. "All of his gunfights were on personal time."

Lee laughed, thinking it was a joke. Then he saw Aaron's expression. "Wait. What?"

"Local mob boss thought Davey killed his kid in a hit-and-run," Tony volunteered when Aaron didn't say anything. "Hired a bunch of dirty cops to take him out. No-shit SWAT team guys. When Davey killed them he hired a bunch of retired Special Forces fuckers, and Davey took them out too. Now he's in witness protection somewhere."

"Bullshit," Lee said, trying not to laugh at the ridiculous story. Aaron gave him such a flat stare that it killed any impulse he had to laugh. Lee frowned. "Do they even have mob in Detroit?"

"Not as much as they used to," Tony said. "FBI's been putting everybody in jail. Especially after that clusterfuck."

Aaron, a bit irritated, stared out the back window as Tony navigated I-94 toward downtown Detroit. At freeway speeds the engine was a constant loud roar and he was getting a headache. He thought about lighting up inside the truck just to piss the new guy off, but he knew Tony had some lung issue—asthma, emphysema, something like that. So he just sat and stewed.

It was five minutes later when Lee said, "Hey, is this what you were talking about?" He held up his smartphone. Aaron leaned over to look at it. The story was from the Detroit News. Aaron didn't have to read it, he recognized the headline.

"Yeah."

"What was this, two years ago?" Lee squinted at the date. "I was still in Iraq. This guy, David Anderson, he was your partner?"

"Yeah."

"He really did get into a gunfight with a SWAT team? Holy shit." Lee skimmed the story.

Aaron scowled. "Four cops who were on a SWAT team. Detroit PD, dirty cops. Out on bail after being arrested by the FBI. For robbing strip clubs. Fuckin' Detroit, I swear to God, there should be circus music playing on loudspeakers when you cross over Eight Mile."

"He killed them?"

"He killed three of them, an Oakland County deputy killed the other one when they started shooting at him too."

Aaron didn't want to talk about it, but he wanted the facts right if they did.

"Damn. What about that other thing, the Special Forces guys? I don't see that in this story."

"It happened later, in Arizona. Don't know how much of it made the Detroit papers. Fox News covered it."

"Sorry, but that still sounds like bullshit." He'd met too many guys who talked about how much combat they'd seen, how many guys they'd killed, and it all turned out to be lies.

"I was there, I saw the fucking bodies. Don't you fucking tell me it didn't happen," Aaron spat, now angry, jabbing his finger. "I was there with a DPD detective. Local deputy got shot too, one of Shotgun John's guys, heard of him? He's the one who called Fox News. Seven fucking bodies, two of 'em burned to a crisp. I had to pull Dave out of the fire or he'd have died too. Sat by his side in the hospital for a fucking week while he was in a fucking induced coma because he got shot three times in addition to getting cooked like a turkey so don't you fucking tell me it didn't happen." He pulled out a Marlboro and lit it with his Zippo, the flame bright and tall inside the truck. The end of the cigarette flared as he sucked at it.

Lee blinked in surprise at the angry explosion. "Okay, sorry." He bent down to his phone and started typing in search terms, trying to find a story on the incident in Arizona. "And this was all because some mob guy thought your partner killed his daughter?"

"Mob boss," Tony corrected him from the cab. "His adult son died in a hit-and-run. After he killed Dave's parents drunk driving. Guy figured it was a revenge thing."

"That's the story," Aaron said, his voice flat. The smoke curled around his head.

"He do it?"

"Cops tried for years to pin it on him. But they never found shit," Aaron growled around the bobbing cigarette.

"Aaron, can you put that out? You're killing me up here," Tony pleaded. "Kid didn't know. I'd call bullshit on the story too if I didn't know better."

Aaron grumbled, then stubbed the cigarette out on the carpet. The truck's engine roared and then faded as Tony downshifted and followed the other truck up the off-ramp. "Two minutes. Five if we hit every light," Tony called out.

"Eyes up, put the phone away," Aaron said. "We're not there yet. When we are, we're going to be unloading in a completely secure area. Basically we're driving into a vault. Which means no rifles, we'll be throwing bricks with everyone else. Then it's back to base and see if they've got anything else for us. If not it's a short day."

The company was light on afternoon work, but there was one short run available. Aaron jumped on it as the messenger (seniority had its privileges) and got Eddie Rogers as a driver. Eddie had been with the company for close to ten years and was a good driver who paid attention, and he got Aaron's sense of humor, so they made a good team. He had a round head, round arms, round thighs, round belly... it wasn't that Eddie was fat so much as he looked to be under extreme pressure.

"So how short is this 'short' run?" Eddie asked as he waited behind the wheel of the idling truck for the steel door to roll up.

Aaron scanned the paperwork in back. "Eight...no, nine stops, most of them in Dearborn, gas stations and party stores. Two to three hours tops, maybe half that if we don't have to wait anywhere. You in a hurry to get home or do you need hours?"

Eddie shrugged. "I've already got forty hours this week, but I still don't want to go home at noon, I got bills. Still, sooner I get home, the sooner I see my boys. Unless you need the hours?"

Aaron shook his head. "A black man that actually wants to spend time with his kids? Who am I to get in the way of that?"

Eddie turned around and looked at Aaron, but he was smiling. "That's mighty white of you."

Forty-five minutes later Aaron jumped out of the truck and headed into the imaginatively named Greenfield Party Store…on Greenfield Road in Dearborn, not too far from the Ford Headquarters. As with most of the party stores in Detroit it was as much a small grocery store as it was a place to grab alcohol and cigarettes and lottery tickets. It was a lot easier for the local residents, especially the senior citizens, to walk a block or two to the "GPS" than it was to try and arrange transport to the nearest true grocery store, a Kroger over a mile away for most of them.

Aaron eyed the two people lined up at the counter and tapped on the security door with his clipboard. The counter ran along the entire front of the store and featured security glass two inches thick. The glass ran up to the ceiling and enclosed the cash registers.

Ronnie, the owner, popped the door and stepped back into the crowded area behind the counter. "Give me two minutes," he said to Aaron in lightly accented English. They kept all the likely-to-be-stolen items on the counter behind the glass or under the counter, items such as cigarettes, alcohol, scratch-off lottery tickets, and pre-paid cell phones.

Ronnie's real name was Rahmani, and his brother working the register was Armani or something like that but everybody called him Art. Art was chubby and hairy and had such a weird personality he came off as borderline retarded to Aaron...except he effortlessly memorized the price of every item in the store and apparently had an accounting degree.

"I just got to get the cash out of the safe and bag it up," Ronnie said, bending down in front of the ancient steel floor safe. "It's already counted."

"I'm in no rush," Aaron told him. He watched Art punch out daily lotto tickets for the two people on the other side of the glass. They looked as if they could barely afford clothes and there they were dropping twenty bucks on low payout lotto tickets. And probably did it every damn day. Aaron shook his head as they shuffled out of the store, in no hurry to get on with their lives.

As Ronnie was stuffing what looked to be five grand or so into a security envelope Art turned to look at Aaron and gave him a big smile. "How you doin' boss? You need cigarettes? Marlboro red, right? Box, right?" His accent was a lot thicker than his brother's.

Aaron hadn't been to this store in a couple of weeks, and hadn't bought smokes there in maybe two months, yet Art remembered. Aaron was impressed. He remembered something Dave had said to him one day when Aaron had been bitching about immigrants with accents so thick they were hard to understand—"His English is a hell of a lot better than your Arabic." As much as he hated to admit it, his old partner had a point. Aaron told Art, "Yeah, might as well get me a box while I'm here." He paused, then pointed at one of the plastic clamshells hanging on a display on the counter. "And one of those too."

"You got it boss!" Art said enthusiastically as Aaron pulled out some cash.

As Ronnie sealed the security envelope Aaron noticed the small silver crucifix around his neck. Aaron was pretty sure that meant he was Chaldean, and Chaldeans were Christian Arabs...although he wasn't sure about the exact details. Like the difference between Sunni Muslims and....whoever the hell the other guys were. Something like *Sheeit*, but he knew that wasn't right. All he knew was that if the barbarians were at the gates they'd want to kill Ronnie and all of his kin as much as they would Aaron. Chances of that were low, though. That was the one good thing about the area—even though Dearborn had one of the highest populations of Arabs outside the Middle East, the Detroit area was so economically depressed there weren't a whole lot of juicy targets if you were a suicide bomber. You'd get a lot more attention blowing yourself up in Chicago or New York.

On the way out the door Aaron passed a black woman not much more than five feet tall who seemed nearly as wide. He actually had to turn sideways to fit past her in the vestibule and still it was tight. And she was the one glaring at him, as if it was his fault. He looked past her and saw Eddie watching from the truck, a big smile on his face.

"Damn, you see her?" Eddie said when he got back in. "That's a whole lotta groceries right there."

"I thought you bruthas liked 'em big," Aaron said as he triple-checked the amount Ronnie'd written on the tamper-evident security envelope with what he'd written on his clipboard, then stuffed the cash envelope into the canvas bag he used for small items.

"I like curves, woman's supposed to have some curves, but she's only got one curve and it goes all the way 'round. Bitch be built like the Death Star. You still with Arlene?"

"Yeah, why?"

"Nothin'. Just, she built like a coat hanger. Skinny girls…there's just nothing to squeeze."

"Then you're grabbing 'em in the wrong spot."

Eddie snorted. "Where next?"

"Head back to Michigan Avenue," Aaron told him. "We're doing a big circle today, and it's time to start heading back. When you hit it take a left."

"Got it."

As Eddie put the big truck into gear Aaron pulled out his pocket knife and cut open the plastic packaging on the pre-paid phone he'd just bought. It came with twenty free minutes of talk time, and the battery was partially charged, so he set about powering it up and getting it working. He'd gone through the process enough times that it only took him a couple of minutes.

Aaron called the number from memory and got a computer reciting the number and telling him to leave a message at the beep. He sighed as the beep sounded in his ear. "Dude, just checking in. Haven't talked to you in… Jesus, I don't know how many months. Give me a call back, let me know you're still alive." He read off the number of the new phone in his hand. "It's a prepaid drug dealer cell phone, and I'll pull the battery when I'm done with the call, check it once a day, all that spy shit, but maybe we can arrange a time when I can actually talk to you. Playing phone tag is bullshit. Anyway…just worried about you. Hit me back." He closed the phone and stared at it for a minute, lips working as he silently talked to himself. With a shake of his head and a frown he pulled off the back, removed the battery, and stuck it into his pocket.

From the cab Eddie said, "You talk to him, you tell him I said hi. Brother's been through it, that's for sure. Witness protection, man, dudes gunning for you, I don't even want to think about it."

Aaron just stared out the window at the passing cars, frowning.

Chapter Four

"You were late. I was wondering if I was being stood up."

Pietro Bufonte turned slowly to look at West Bloomfield Detective Billy Dixon, who was smiling as he got into the car. Bufonte didn't think the man was funny, but then he didn't find much anything funny these days. The smile faded from Dixon's face.

"You sure this is wise? Meeting face to face? I don't have to tell you how much attention you're getting." Dixon shut the door and looked around.

Bufonte sat for a minute without saying anything. Dixon did his best to hide his nervousness. He'd shown up in a car that couldn't be traced to him, and was wearing a hat to shield his face from random security cameras, but if the feds had found out about this meeting, or Bufonte was being tailed, none of that mattered.

"And why is that?" Bufonte said finally.

Dixon blinked. "Well, the FBI—"

Bufonte cut him off. "The FBI is a pack of jackals snapping at me, waiting for me to make one final mistake so they can take me down. Gut me. I am sure all of my businesses—those they haven't shut down—are under surveillance. I know my house is. I have to assume both my home and my vehicles are bugged. I'm forced to cower in the back seat of this foreign shitbox just to get out of my own house undetected." They were sitting in the back of a Toyota Camry that had seen better days. It belonged to the girlfriend of one of Bufonte's few remaining loyal men. The man was standing a dozen feet away, out of earshot, smoking. Outside the windows in all directions was a sea of cars, and every minute or so they could hear the roar of a plane taking off. "And do you know why? David Anderson."

Dixon sucked some air in through his nostrils before he spoke. "Yes. Although you weren't exactly unknown to the federal government before that whole incident," he felt obliged to point out.

Bufonte's face darkened and he looked at Dixon. "Business is one thing, but it seems clear that the Detroit office of the FBI has taken it as their personal mission to not just put me in jail but destroy everything I have," Bufonte said tiredly. "Because I corrupted one of their own, bribed an FBI agent to hire some dirty cops to kill David Anderson. Because I believe he killed my son, in revenge for Paulie killing his parents in that accident."

"They'll never come out and admit that it's personal for them, but yes, that's what is going on."

"Except I never bribed an FBI agent. Never tried to kill David Anderson. I assumed that fact would eventually become clear. But it's been over two years and it has not. My lawyers just shake their heads at me and tell me it's almost impossible to prove a negative…while charging me hundreds of dollars an hour. I asked you to look into it.

Find out everything you could. We're meeting because you signaled that you had something."

Dixon squirmed a little in the seat. "I've got...well, I think I've got all there is to get. I don't know if you'll be satisfied—"

"Forget whatever personal arrangement we have, it is your job to find out who killed my son. Five years. Over five years ago he was killed, run over like a dog in the street, and no arrests. It's been your investigation from the start."

"I told you two years ago, right before Anderson got involved in...whatever the hell he got involved in, that near as I can tell, Anderson started dating his girlfriend when she was working as a stripper at the club Big Paulie managed. That can't be a coincidence, especially since he had to have seen the guy, and never mentioned to his girlfriend that hey, that's the drunk driver who killed my parents."

"So he was stalking my son?"

"Doing surveillance is my best guess. Gathering intelligence. And within six months Paulie gets run over by a car. Twice. Will I ever be able to prove Anderson did it? I don't think so. God knows I've tried, but there's just no evidence. But I know he did it. He had to." Dixon huffed. "And I told you that, two years ago."

"And what was I supposed to do with that information? It had barely come into my possession when the local TV stations are all over my front lawn, asking me about bribing FBI agents, hiring SWAT officers to take out Anderson. The FBI camped out in my offices for months, harassed and detained me and my men, put microphones in all of my businesses. Subpoenas, never-ending harassment. My legal bills are twenty-five thousand dollars a month. I didn't try to kill him, I didn't send those men, but the only cop who believes me, who will ever believe me, is in my employ." He looked at Dixon pointedly. "So I have pretended to forget all about the boy, for almost two years. But two years is long enough. Which is why I asked you to look into it. Into him. And for all their certainty that I tried to have him killed for killing Paulie, none of them are looking at him as a murderer. Investigating him. Because if I want to kill him, he must be the murderer of my son. But do I get any justice? Does Paulie?"

Bufonte was just blowing off steam. He knew the situation as well as anyone, but Dixon felt he needed to remind him. "They've said—and they've had to say it publicly because of all the attention this case has garnered, that they have no evidence tying him to the death of your son."

"'They' being the FBI."

Dixon nodded. "And they are only repeating what they heard from my chief, as it's been our investigation, not a federal matter. Although the case is still open. Anderson had motive, everyone admits that, but no one has been able to in any way prove he had anything to do with Paulie's death. I've found more than anyone else, and what I've got wouldn't stand up in a trial. It's not even enough to arrest him. It's a thin connection, nothing else. It's convinced me, and I think you, but actual evidence tying him? There's nothing."

Bufonte scowled at nothing for several minutes before speaking. "Any luck finding out exactly who was trying to kill him? Because I know it goddamn well wasn't me!" he said with some force. He took a breath, then said more calmly, "And where he is? I presume that's why you contacted me."

"Because I actually have a legitimate reason to be investigating Anderson I haven't had to be subtle. Luckily," Dixon added. "He's the only person of interest I have in the only unsolved homicide we've got on the books. But…the more I look into this, the stranger it gets. Four Detroit cops, SWAT officers out on bail for armed robbery, arrested by the FBI, attempt to kill him. That goes wrong in an epic way. Anderson skips town, and a few weeks later ends up in a hospital in Arizona, burned, blown up, and shot three times. There were seven bodies at his cabin out there, most of whom were identified as decorated Special Forces veterans. The next day Arizona Sheriff John Osterman comes forward with an audio recording that seems to be of a local Detroit FBI Agent asking one of those Detroit cops to take out Anderson, in return for which he'll make evidence disappear. Actually he was the Assistant Special Agent in Charge of the Detroit FBI office. Peter Hartman."

"And the extra-special FBI Agent was working for me. To arrange Anderson's death."

"That's the working theory."

"This I know."

Dixon nodded. "The Assistant Special Agent in Charge of the Detroit office Peter Hartman was suspended pending an investigation of the recording. He was found dead the next day, an apparent suicide. His boss, the Special Agent in Charge of the Detroit office of the FBI, Mitchell Boehmer, died of a heart attack two weeks after Anderson was attacked in Arizona. Very young age, completely unexpected. Home alone, at the time. So I did some more digging into the FBI. The Director of the FBI Lab in Virginia died in a hit-and-run car accident the day before one of the bodies at Anderson's Arizona cabin was identified as Michael 'Mickey' Mitchell, one of his employees who had gone missing weeks before. Mitchell's ID never made the news. And I still haven't figured out his role in all this. FBI won't tell me shit about him, officially or off the record.

But it sure looks as if the FBI was trying to have Anderson killed...and either the FBI is having a bad run of luck, or somebody very good or very connected or very both is trying to quietly clean up loose ends over there."

"What about the other dead men in Arizona? They weren't FBI, they were all former military."

"All former Special Forces, at least the bodies they could identify. There was one inside the cabin they couldn't ID, shot in the face with a shotgun before getting burned down to the bone. None of them were officially currently employed by anyone, which tells me they were probably working for the government off the books. But why they were after Anderson...well, the official FBI position, or suspicion, is that you're responsible for that. Revenge for your son's death. You bribed Hartman, and he hired dirty cops. When they didn't work out, he, I don't know, called Dial-A-Mercenary or something."

"Do you know why the FBI wants Anderson dead? This I find very curious."

"No. That still is a mystery. I can't even guess as to what it might be, but apparently it went all the way up the chain to the FBI Lab in Virginia. To be honest, it's like a freaking spy movie, all these accidental deaths. But how Anderson is involved I have no idea."

"But then they stopped trying to kill him."

"Even if they still wanted him dead, for whatever reason, after all the press that shootout in Arizona got, after the shootout here, after the media shitstorm from that recording Osterman had, which was brought to him by a Detroit detective who'd gone out there trying to track down Anderson, they didn't dare. Even though he would have been an easy target; he was in recovery, and physical therapy, for six months or more. But then he disappeared."

"Is he still alive? Do you know where he is?"

Dixon shook his head. "Last address I had for him is a year old. I can do whatever I want to track him down without trying to hide it, he's part of a homicide investigation, but he's totally off the grid. He might be dead, they—whoever 'they' are—might have finally gotten him, but I'm thinking he's just in hiding somewhere. He either knows why the FBI was trying to kill him and is still scared out of his mind, or he has no clue and thinks you were the one trying to kill him. Either way, he's in hiding, I'd bet on it. But no, I don't know for sure."

"I want his location," Bufonte growled.

Dixon nodded. "I know you do. And I'm still working it. If he's still alive, and I think he is, he'll turn up eventually."

"I want his location, and soon. I'll pay you half a million dollars for it."

Dixon blinked. His mouth opened and closed a few times. "I—well, I know you want him. Trust me, I've been doing everything I can to track him down for you. I want to talk to him myself, find out just what the hell is going on. This is a once-in-a-lifetime kind of case."

"Do more. Do whatever it takes. But don't take too long."

Dixon blinked and regarded the older man with some concern. "I'm convinced Anderson killed Paulie, but I told you that two years ago. The FBI is still all over you and your people. I understand, Paulie has waited for justice long enough. But this rush seems...unwise. Is there something I should know?" He gave a little laugh. "Are you dying?"

Bufonte sighed and looked out the window. "Aren't we all?' he said flatly.

Dixon studied the man. Bufonte had always been thick, but his body seemed to have sagged around him. And there were a lot more gray hairs on his big block of a head. The constant and aggressive FBI investigation of him and his business ventures was now two years old, and it had to be taking its toll on the man himself. But was that it? Or was there more? Dixon sat there, and finally Bufonte turned and looked at him. "My lung cancer's back. My remission is in remission. Even if I beat it again I know it will eventually kill me. Five years from now. Two. Sooner, rather than later. I start chemo next month if they can't cut it out. So, half a million. Plus whatever expenses you incur. I can't take it with me, but knowing the ratfucker who killed my Paulie went first will make it...not so terrible."

Chapter Five

State Route 69 was the main drag in Prescott Valley. It struck off northwest from Interstate 17 halfway between Phoenix and Flagstaff before curving west and heading into Prescott itself. In many ways it reminded him of a river—in the old days, everyone lived along rivers, because they were the highways of the era.

Everything was so damn new along Route 69 that it made him wonder just what the hell had lined the road twenty years earlier. Then again, Prescott Valley billed itself as "the fastest growing community in Arizona". Considering how the population had tripled since the '70s there probably hadn't been much of anything lining SR69 twenty years ago. Now there were strip malls and new buildings everywhere, chain stores including Lowe's, Costco, Bed Bath & Beyond, and Trader Joe's all just in a half mile stretch, supported by the ever-increasing number of Phoenix residents who came north to escape the heat. Although most of the very new stores were closer to the Prescott city limit, his destination was a few miles before that.

He stopped at the light, turned the Wrangler onto Yavapai drive, then hooked a quick left into the strip mall parking lot. He took the speed bump at a sedate ten miles per hour, then pulled up behind a beige Toyota Camry at the stop sign and waited for the driver to make the turn. And waited.

He sighed. The percentage of post-retirement-age drivers in Arizona had to be higher than a lot of places based on what he'd seen, and navigating parking lots during the middle of the day was always an exercise in patience. It didn't help that his destination was three doors down from the Safeway, and all the senior citizens seemed to do their shopping in the middle of the day.

The thing was, he knew even without being able to see the driver that most likely the apparently comatose pilot of the vehicle in front of him was old. It was the vehicle.

It wasn't that old people drove Camrys, although they did. It was the type of vehicle, combined with the color. If it was a boring sedan, foreign or domestic, in some shade of tan or gold, the chances that the owner was at least in their fifties if not older he placed at 75% or higher. It was simply an observation based on years of experience. And he wasn't the only one, in the classic *Fletch* Chevy Chase referred to the bland car driven by that weasely accountant guy (or whoever he was, Dave couldn't exactly remember, it had been a while since he'd seen the movie) as a "tan Oldsmobuick". Boring people drove boring cars. It was one of those undeniable facts of life not written down anywhere.

He stared out the windshield at the Camry. Sure, the left turn signal was on, but that didn't mean anything. It could have been blinking for days. He checked his mirrors and was just about to drive around the Camry when the driver apparently woke up and powered through the turn at near walking speed. Dave followed in his Wrangler, passed the Camry on the left when the car stopped at the curb between businesses for no apparent reason and no signal—yep, old lady, seventy years old if she was a day, big knobby knuckles all over the steering wheel behind which she was sitting close enough to kiss—and found a parking spot somewhat close to his destination. He looked around before he got out, then looked around again.

The Personal Defense Institute of Prescott—"P-Dip" to all the students—was sandwiched between a hair salon and a pet store. Physically the exterior of the place was as unimpressive as the rest of the strip mall, but online it had gotten a lot of good reviews. For once the internet hadn't failed him, the reviews had been accurate.

In a previous life the space had housed a pool supply store. Occasionally he caught a whiff of chlorine. The owner, Mackie, did everything he could to keep the place from smelling like dirty socks, but with all the mats and punching bags soaking up sweat every day it was a constant battle. Ironically the nicest-smelling space in the place was the locker room, as it had a tile floor and could be mopped with bleach.

He nodded to a few of the other students as he walked toward the locker room. About half the time he wore a karate uniform, a *gi*, but the rest of the time he was in regular street clothes. That was one of the things he liked about the place; while he did teach straight karate classes, half of them to kids, for his true self-defense classes Mackie wasn't a narrow-minded dogmatic worshipper of one discipline. He was interested in teaching people how to defend themselves using what worked, and so he stole techniques from every martial art and fighting style he'd ever learned or been exposed to—judo, karate, wrestling, jiu-jitsu, boxing, and a bit of aikido. He tailored the techniques he taught so they could be performed by average people. The end result was closer to MMA fighting than anything else. Considering he was trying to teach people how to defend themselves in the real world, Mackie had no problems if people wanted to practice while wearing their actual clothes—minus jewelry, of course. Jewelry got hooked on clothes far too easily.

When Dave came out of the locker room in his *gi* he set his small backpack against the wall, doublechecking the top was unzipped for easy access. He then moved to where the other students were and began stretching with them on the mats. Including him there were ten in this small late-morning class which met for ninety minutes three times a week, but usually at least one or two students couldn't make it. He'd initially chosen this class because it was the only beginner class with an opening. Most of the other students worked afternoon shift based on their comments.

Mackie was over by the heavy bags with Tina, a pudgy thirty-something secretary who was new to P-Dip. She'd had a bad scare and wanted to learn how to defend herself, but had a bad habit of curling her fingers around her thumb when making a fist. If she ever punched a heavy bag—or a person—that way with any force she'd break her thumb.

"What kind of class were you in?" Mackie asked the woman. "Box aerobics?"

"Kickbox cardio."

Mackie made a face. "Well, those kinds of classes are great exercise, but they don't teach you jack about how to actually hit or kick anything. You're just throwing your hands and feet out there to get the heart rate up."

James 'Mackie' MacKenzie was a former U.S. Army

Ranger who'd managed to get himself shot, hit by shrapnel, and set on fire (just a little bit) early on in the Iraq war. He'd been an avid martial artist before medically retiring from the service and got even more interested in "real world" hand-to-hand techniques after recovering from his wounds. He'd competed in some state-level MMA tournaments with some success until, as he put it, "I got tired of waking up three days later still too sore to walk."

"Zombie, you remember what we're going to be doing today?" Stephen asked Dave as he stretched. Stephen—not Steve, he'd be the first to correct you—was effeminate, biracial, and had the build of a supermodel. Even though Prescott was trendy and artsy, there were assholes everywhere. Stephen had had a scare as well, but it was more of the "I'm going to beat your ass, faggot," type than Tina's "No doesn't mean no" near-rape.

"Maybe heavy bag techniques, I can't remember for sure." Everyone in the class called him Zombie, even Mackie. He couldn't even remember why, now.

"No more ground fighting, please, my butt is still sore from practicing falls," Melissa groused.

"Mackie says most fights that last more than one or two hits end up on the ground," Stephen told her. He'd never punched anyone, and had never been punched, although he'd been shoved a few times. The class for him was more about building up his self-confidence to actually stick up for himself than actually learning how to beat on people.

"I've started a low carb diet, hopefully it'll give me more energy, I'm always exhausted after class," Renee said. She worked afternoon shift as a cashier at Walmart. "Zombie, you never even get sweaty in class, it pisses me off."

He shrugged. "I work out pretty hard in the mornings.

This is more learning technique and practicing it than it is exercise."

"Maybe for you," Melissa said. She was a shift supervisor at a small injection-molding place just north of town. Walking her dog was the only other exercise she got.

"You go to a gym?" Stephen asked him.

He shook his head. "Work out at home. Pushups, sit-ups, pull-ups, basic stuff like that. I guess you'd call it bodyweight CrossFit. Plus I run."

"How far do you run?" Stephen wondered. He was skinny, but he hated cardio. Zombie had a great body, and apparently he worked hard for it, but he wasn't Stephen's type at all. Too intense. And he never smiled.

"Six miles or so. Usually five days a week."

"Five days a week? Jesus. No wonder you're so skinny," Renee said enviously. She wanted to lose weight, but she hated running. Running six miles a day sounded like torture…and her boobs would give her black eyes. Not that Zombie, the only good-looking straight guy in the class, had apparently ever noticed she had them. He barely even spoke, this was the most words out of his mouth during a class in months.

"D'you already work out today, before coming here?" Stephen asked him.

"Yeah, I always work out before coming here. That way, on the days I take off, I don't do anything. I take the whole day for rest."

Stephen's eyes widened. "You do this shit after running six miles? Damn, dude, that's hardcore. I gotta give you props."

"Okay, now you just have to practice that until it comes naturally, so you don't have to remember it when you're tired or scared, it just comes naturally," Mackie told Tina as they walked back from the gently swinging bags. He was in a well-worn judo *gi*, which was made of a thicker material than the average karate *gi*. It made him look even stockier than he was. Mackie looked at the assembled students down on the mats, stretching. "Everybody here? Anybody not here, raise your hand. Today we're going to be working on all sorts of knee strikes. You knee someone hard enough, in the right spot—and no, ladies, I'm not talking about the balls, get your minds out of the gutter—" that got smiles and a few laughs, "a knee in the right spot will end the fight. Or at least let you get out of there. Even if you're dainty, your knee is a near-solid piece of bone and muscle twice as big and heavy as your fist, powered by some of the most powerful muscles in the human body. You don't need to be a barrel-chested steely-eyed bearded SWAT-team Jesus to seriously hurt somebody with your knee. And the great thing is knees never run out of ammo as long as you've got the will to use it. Finish stretching, and then we'll get to work. I'll demo one technique, we'll practice it on the heavy bags, then the next one, then the next, and then we'll pair off and do a little bit of street dancing."

Mackie always called it street dancing instead of sparring. He looked at his students and pointed. "Zombie, get up here again, let me demo a few things, we'll get this show on the road."

He was underneath the Wrangler changing his oil when he heard a car pull up in front of his house. He scooted quickly out from underneath the vehicle and sat up. His canvas work shirt was unbuttoned, and he pulled it open as his eyes registered a dark sedan. The sunlight was bright to his eyes after being underneath the Jeep, and so he couldn't see who was in the vehicle. Then he saw the vehicle was a black Mercury Marauder, the commercial version of the Ford Crown Vic police cruiser, and this one had custom red piping along the sides. He relaxed as he recognized the car, and a second later John Osterman stepped out. The Sheriff was in plain clothes but he still wore them as stiffly as if they were a uniform. He hitched his belt up before closing the car door. Osterman was about to head toward the front door when he saw Dave sitting on the concrete behind the Jeep.

"I catch you at a bad time?" Osterman asked, walking up the driveway.

Showing him his grimy hands, Dave shook his head. "Just changing the oil."

"You a gear head? Didn't strike me as one."

"No. But I've been learning how to do everything I can with this thing. Helps stretch the money out." He stood up, favoring his right leg. His thigh was still sore from the nerve plexus knee strikes Mackie had dealt him. He was several inches taller than the Sheriff.

Osterman nodded. "Always cheaper to do it yourself." Osterman's eyes dropped to the work shirt. There was only a slight bulge, but his experienced eyes could spot the pistol underneath. Not that his carrying a gun was exactly a surprise, quite the opposite. Osterman's eyes moved over to the boy's dirty hands. "How are your booger hooks?"

The young man blinked, then burst out in surprised laughter, and it lasted for quite a while. "That is about the last thing I expected to hear come out of your mouth," Dave said when he could finally catch a breath. The hands in question were lifted, the grimy fingers opened and closed a few times. "Still working."

"I'm glad," Osterman said warmly. He looked the young man in the face. "How about you? How are *you*?"

He got a shrug in response. "Getting by. Still alive."

Osterman huffed breath out through his nose, not pleased at all with the responses. He squinted at the young man, then looked around. Bright sunny morning, nice new houses, but nothing moving. A lot of that had to do with the fact that the median age of the residents was well past retirement age. "Not exactly a glowing endorsement for your state of mind. You can't hide out here forever, *Jack*."

Osterman felt a chill as he watched the young man look off into the distance and say vaguely, "I don't think it'll be forever."

Osterman licked his lips. "I worry about you. What you've been through…"

The young man smiled and looked at him. "Don't you have kids of your own to express your disappointment with?"

"The Lord did not bless my wife and me with children. So I take care of this county as if it were my own. As well everyone in it who needs help." Osterman gave him a pointed look. "Some more than others."

"I'm fine. Really," Dave said with a smile that was almost convincing. "I appreciate you stopping by from time to time to check on me. And everything else you've done."

Osterman looked down at his shoes, shaking his head a little. Then he took a deep breath and nodded. "Well, you get tired of waiting, and want to start your life back up again, that job offer still stands. But don't wait too long, I won't be Sheriff forever."

They both glanced over as an SUV pulled into the driveway next door. Lori was visible behind the wheel. She looked at the two of them talking as she got out of her vehicle, squinting in the bright sunlight. She was carrying several plastic bags from Safeway.

"You've been Sheriff since Wyatt Earp was swinging a gun around these parts. I bet you've got a few more years in you." In the late 1870s, Wyatt and Virgil Earp as well as Doc Holliday were patrons of The Palace, still standing and serving drinks and food on Whiskey Row in downtown Prescott. It was perhaps the town's oldest tourist destination.

The Sheriff waited until the pretty blonde was inside her residence before answering. "A few. But none of us are here forever, and it's up to us to make the best use of our time while we're here." He held out a hand, not caring that a handshake would mean grease and oil all over him. When the young man took his hand, Osterman clenched it tight and looked him in the eye. "You remember that."

"Yes sir."

Osterman nodded sharply, then released his hand. "I will be back to check on you."

"Is that a promise or a threat?" But Dave said it with a smile.

Osterman was walking back to his car when he heard someone shout "Sheriff!" He looked around, and across the street was a woman about his age on her porch. She had a pruny hairless cat under one arm and was waving the other. "I love you!" she called out. "I've voted for you every time!"

He smiled and waved back. "Thank you," he said warmly. He then turned back to Dave. "So much for civilian clothes and my personal car," he said quietly. The Mercury Marauder had actually been seized ten years before by the Sheriff's Department. It had belonged to someone who'd ultimately been convicted of drug distribution. Personally the red stripe down the side was a little fancy for Osterman, but apart from that he'd liked the looks of vehicle, and had bought it off the county at auction for pennies on the dollar and been driving it ever since. But he had to admit, not only did it resemble a police cruiser, the spoiler on the back and the red stripes down the sides made it immediately identifiable as his car.

"It's hell being famous."

With a roll of his eyes and another wave to the neighbor on her porch, Osterman got into his car and drove away.

"Isn't he the greatest?" Mrs. Leslie called out as he knelt down to crawl back under the Jeep. Dave just waved back, not wanting to have another conversation.

An hour later he was finishing lunch, scrambled eggs with chunks of cheddar cheese and salami. He stuck the dishes into the dishwasher, then stood in the kitchen for a while, massaging his fingers.

They were warm at the moment but his fingers were cold, very cold, in the morning. Every morning. He was worried that meant there was a problem with his circulation, but the doctors repeatedly assured him that everything was just fine. Well, they never used words like "fine" or "normal", they preferred writing long complicated sentences in his file full of medicalese, maybe to justify how much they'd taken out in student loans for their degrees. "Nominal" was a word he heard a lot, as well as "acceptable", usually in terms of range of motion. Most importantly, they'd stopped using the term "impairment". More than once he'd stolen a peek at his file when the doctor was out of the room, but deciphering the medical abbreviations was beyond him.

His hands had been through a lot, and looked it—truth be told they were far from normal, they'd never be normal again, but they worked. That was what was important, and it had taken a lot of work to get them there. *Use it or lose it* was the philosophy he'd adopted during recovery and physical therapy, and it seemed to have worked. There was nothing—medically or functionally—wrong with them. At least not now. Despite half a dozen medical professionals telling him that would never be the case. There were a few numb spots where the nerves hadn't grown back, but they were small. And after a year of constant minor pain, none for months.

From the front bedroom he could see all the way across the house. If he stood in one spot he was looking across the big front room past the front door. If he moved a step to the right he could see down the main hallway which ran the length of the place. He hung actual targets from time to time, but usually he just made do with the photos he'd hung on the far walls. They were of varying sizes, and at varying heights, none higher than a person's head. He opened the horizontal blinds in the front window to let in as much light as possible, then went to his laptop and opened iTunes.

His dirty covering shirt had gone into the hamper, revealing the Glock 19 on his belt. He unloaded it, triple-checked to make sure it was empty, then reholstered it, grabbed the shot timer, and moved to the spare bedroom. He always left the timer alone when warming up or refining technique, but used it when working on his speed. He'd set a par time, move at the beep, and see if he was done by the second beep. Then he'd make the par time shorter and shorter while making sure his technique was solid instead of sloppy, his sight picture steady.

Letting his hands hang loose at his sides he focused on the eight-by-ten photo on the far wall that was always his initial target. Without trying to go fast—that would come later—he scooped up the Glock with his right hand, and as he pressed it forward his left hand came up and joined the other on the pistol. He pushed it out and as the sights came up and on target his finger found the trigger and pressed. The Glock went click.

Good sight picture, good clean trigger press, although he did see the front sight wiggle just a little bit. Little sloppy on the grip, apparently. He cycled the slide just enough to recock the striker and holstered the pistol. Then did it again. And again.

After ten minutes of drawing to the one photo—a blonde in a daisy field, the photo that had come in the frame—he began using the timer, gradually increasing his speed, and began drawing to other photos hung on the walls. He'd paced it off, and they were all between seven and ten yards away as he stood inside the bedroom, his back close to the wall. Then he began engaging more than one photo at a time, tapping the trigger once for each target, then twice. The secret was to move your eyes to the next target and have your gun follow it. He'd long ago learned that when swinging from target to target he had to try and stop the front sight at the leading edge of the target. Inertia carried the muzzle to the center of the target, especially when he was pushing himself to go as fast as possible.

After twenty minutes of engaging multiple targets he practiced reloading the pistol. He'd draw to a target, pull the trigger once or twice, then hit the mag release. The magazine in the gun would fall to the floor as he grabbed a new one off his belt, and he'd stuff it in the gun.

The first time he'd picked up a gun after charbroiling his hands everything had felt wrong. The familiar curves of the Glock felt foreign. His fingers felt like they belonged to someone else, and were stiff and clumsy. After a year of daily practice the things on the ends of his hands finally felt as if they belonged to him, although they still felt stretched and tight. He doubted they'd ever feel normal, but at least they worked.

After his reload drills he worked at shooting on the move, drawing the pistol as he moved forward on bent knees, moving the pistol from photo to photo while pulling the trigger, trying to walk and shoot as fast as possible without making the muzzle bounce crazily. It was a constant, frustrating battle, but that was why shooting on the move was the hardest practical shooting skill to master.

It was hard not to get burned out doing the same thing every day for hours, no matter your motivation, so he tried to change up his dryfire routine the same as he did his workout routine. After half an hour practicing shooting on the move he grabbed another canvas work shirt, put it on, and practiced drawing from concealment. He planned to do that for twenty minutes or so, then practice drawing the Glock from the fanny pack. He didn't practice that enough, and it was a more involved procedure than just grabbing it out of a holster on his belt.

He'd been practicing drawing his pistol from underneath his covering garment for fifteen minutes, the par time set at .9 second, when someone knocked on his front door. Frowning, he picked up the loaded magazine from the table, quietly chambered a round, and kept the Glock along his leg as he walked to the door. He peered out the front window, and his eyebrows went up.

"Uh, just a second," he called out. He holstered the Glock and made sure it was out of sight under his shirt as he headed toward his bedroom. The Beastie Boys were pretty loud and he turned the volume way down on his laptop. He pulled the timer off his belt and set it on the table.

Even with the blinds all the way open the sun was

painfully bright in his eyes as he opened the door. His next-door neighbor was standing there, a bemused look on her face. She was wearing an expensive-looking light blue sweatshirt over pink yoga pants.

"Hey," he said. "What's up? Music too loud? Your car okay?"

"Yeah, it's fine." She cocked her head to the side. "Okay, so who the hell are you?"

He blinked. "What?"

"I guess who doesn't matter so much as what, what are you? But I know you're not fucking Jack Burton."

His mouth opened and closed twice. "I'm...excuse me?"

She pushed past him into his house as she said, "Like I've never seen *Big Trouble in Little China*?" She looked around, taking the place in. "This for sure ain't the Pork-Chop Express, and you're not Kurt Russell." She then peered at him. "So are you undercover, or are you in witness protection or something?"

"Uh..."

"I live next door. So does my mom. So I figure we've got a right to know. You don't want to tell me, you can't tell me, fine, but just don't lie to me." One of the photos on the wall caught her attention and she peered at it, then looked at the others. They all still had prices listed in the corner of the pictures. They weren't even real photos, they'd come with the frames. All of them. Interesting. She wondered if the furniture was even his.

He frowned, then closed the front door. She stared up at him, a few feet away, unafraid. He took the time to choose his words carefully. "Why do you think I'm...that?"

She rolled her eyes. "I saw who you were talking to before, I'm not blind." She turned and marched across the room and into the front bedroom. He followed her. She stood right where he'd been just a minute earlier, practicing his draw, and pointed at the window. The horizontal blinds were open, and outside, ten feet away or less, was an identical window. She pointed at it.

"That's my bedroom," she told him. "If your blinds are open, like they are most of the time, I can see you in here doing your draw and pretend shooting even during the day, although you're mostly a silhouette then. At night I can see everything you're doing. Practicing your draw and reloading and all sorts of gun stuff. And what the hell is that goddamn beeping?"

He opened his mouth, then closed it. Of course she could hear the shot timer going off. Even with the music on. Their house was so close, she could probably hear it even if all the windows on both homes were shut. He was an idiot.

"Never mind," she said, cutting him off before he could answer. "First time I ever saw you doing that I was freaked out, wondering if you were a terrorist or going to go on a school shooting rampage. Especially since you'd do it every day for what seemed like hours. No, for what was hours. But you don't have that nutjob vibe. You kept doing it without ever popping off psycho, plus you're always working out in here, don't think I can't hear that. And I've known bad guys, a few ex-cons. You seem more like the Iraq veterans I've met than a criminal. Then I saw you talking with the Sheriff early one morning. He was in regular clothes, and an unmarked car, but I recognized him. Then and today. There's no way he's going out on nine-one-one calls, and you guys seemed to know each other. So I figured you were an undercover cop, most likely. And I know you're carrying a gun right now, I was just watching you practicing your draw again." She nodded at his untucked shirt. "So what's your story?"

He stared out his window at hers. So close. He hadn't realized just how close the two houses were. Hadn't realized that room was her bedroom. He slept on the opposite side of the house in the big bedroom, but it only made sense that in her mirror-image house, her mom was in the master bedroom. He felt very weird knowing that she'd been watching him practice his draw. For months, apparently. "How long ago was this?"

"That I figured it out? Five, six months ago."

He frowned and turned to look at her. "And you never said anything?"

She made a face at him. "What, like you're talkative? You said ten words in that car ride to Walmart, and that's the first time we've talked. How long have you lived here, a year? But I saw the Sheriff over here again today and figured I ought to know. In case it's dangerous. You working to infiltrate white supremacists or meth cookers or something?"

He wasn't sure how to react to her. He wandered out of the bedroom and sat down on the couch in the front room. She followed him out. "No, it's…" He wasn't sure what to say. He hadn't been expecting to have this conversation with anyone. A denial seemed stupid. And she wouldn't believe him if he did try to deny it, that much seemed obvious. She was pretty and blonde, but she wasn't dumb. Where's a good stereotype when you need it? "It's closer to witness protection than it is undercover work," he said after about a minute. "But I'm not going to give you any details."

"Okay, fine," she said. She nodded to herself and wondered if that was why he'd grown the beard. He didn't seem a beard kind of guy, and he kept it short, as if he didn't really like it. "Are my mom and I in any danger?"

He shook his head. "No."

She sat on the arm of a chair. "So what's your name? And don't fucking tell me Jack Burton."

He smiled. "That's the name on my driver's license."

"Who picked that, you? It's better than Indiana Jones, I guess, but still."

"Most people never get the reference, and even then it's a pretty unremarkable name. You don't strike me as a big movie geek, though."

"My mom and I watch a lot of TV together. We've got Netflix and Hulu and Amazon. Well, I got her all those, she still had a VCR. Blinking twelve o'clock. She's a big fan of eighties movies and sci-fi. I never watched much TV or saw many movies before coming to live with her, so it's all new to me. She enjoys me watching her favorite stuff with her. It's like I'm…sharing in her memories. Of when she was younger." She sighed, thinking about her mother, then looked at him. "I know you don't know me, but I can keep my mouth shut. You don't have to worry about me."

"I'm not worried."

She waited, but when it appeared he wasn't going to say anything else she gave a little nod and stood up. "I better get back to mom."

He stood up too, and followed her to the front door. "I was serious, you need help with your mom, just let me know."

She turned around, a bit surprised to see him right there behind her. She had to look almost straight up. She guessed he was maybe six foot two, which wasn't that tall unless you were five-three. With any other guy his offer would have been a lame come-on, a way to get into her pants using her mother. With him, though…she was getting no sexual vibe off of him, whatsoever. He wasn't pinging her gaydar either, he just wasn't there. Not sexually. Not that he was asleep at the wheel, he was intense as hell. Always looking around, staring at everything. If he was in witness protection, that explained a hell of a lot. Maybe even his lack of interest in her, although she did dress like a slob most of the time now, and had put on a little weight.

"Don't offer if you don't mean it. She doesn't have a sprained ankle. She's in a diaper just in case, some days she's furious at everything, or forgets who I am…" She swallowed loudly. "It can get ugly."

"I can handle ugly," he said, opening the door for her.

She stepped through it, then turned and looked at him. The weight in his voice was palpable. He wasn't bragging; he knew he could handle ugly because he had handled it. That much was crystal clear to her. Yet he was so tightly wrapped, he was a cable vibrating under tension.

"Okay. Maybe I'll take you up on that. Later." But she stood there on his porch, her head slightly cocked to the side, looking at him. There was so much about him that intrigued her. Everything about him was so…unexpected.

He sighed. "My name's definitely not Dave," he told her. "It's Jack," he said firmly.

A little smile twitched her mouth, and she nodded. Then she turned and hopped down the steps. As she cut across his front yard Dave looked past her. The street was quiet and empty. Mrs. Leslie was the only moving thing he saw, watering the flowers along the side of her house. Her pink horror of a cat stalked along behind.

Dave shut the front door and just stood there at the unexpected turn of events. Then he looked around and cocked his head. The room seemed somehow much emptier than it had before she'd barged into his house. It also smelled like girl.

PART II
ESCHAR

eschar (/ˈɛskɑːr/; Greek: eskhara) a slough or piece of dead tissue that is cast off from the surface of the skin, particularly after a burn injury

Chapter Six

Flores, with Hill right behind her, knocked on the Sheriff's open door and stuck her head in. The Sheriff was behind his desk, but she wasn't expecting to see two other men present.

"Sir?"

"Hill with you? Good. Come on in and give me the update on your case. Detectives, have you met Assistant U.S. Attorney Scotty Grimes? And this other fellow with the poor taste in clothes is Doug Harlin, the Special Agent in Charge of the DEA's Phoenix Division. I guess I've known him for about fifteen years." The men stood up as Hill and Flores stepped into the Sheriff's office. The Sheriff's office wasn't big, and with four of them in front of the desk it was a little crowded.

"Scott, please," Grimes said, throwing an exasperated look at the Sheriff. He was slender and in his thirties. He had dark hair and was wearing a gray suit that looked expensive.

Harlin was about fifty and thick. He had a shaved head

and was wearing a Hawaiian shirt over blue jeans. His mouth curled up in amusement. The four of them shook hands all around and the two detectives eyed the unexpected visitors.

"I apologize for my casual look, I actually just came straight from the airport," Harlin said.

"Hawaii?" Osterman said, eyebrows raised. It was obvious he didn't care for the shirt.

"Disney. With the wife and kids."

Osterman nodded. "Then you get a pass. This time."

"Sir?" Flores said again. She was the lead on the case, and they were meeting the Sheriff to give him an update on it, but talking about an ongoing investigation in front of visitors, much less one who was an attorney, was generally frowned upon.

"Mr. Grimes and SAC Harlin in particular, and Uncle Sam in general, apparently have an interest in the three men we have in custody. We'll get to that in a moment, but get us up to speed on the investigation. Actually, first, how is our survivor?"

"As well as can be expected," Flores told the Sheriff.

"Maybe better," Hill added. "What happened to her was horrible, but at least the guys who did it to her won't be doing anything to anyone ever again, and she knows it. So she's got some sense of closure."

Flores shook her head. "She's been talking to a counselor. From the hospital. Which I'm glad to see." She glanced at her partner. "And you called it right, she is a survivor. She's tough. Which is good, since she's our only witness." She looked at Harlin. "Special Agent in Charge? Does that mean you're the head guy at the Phoenix Division?"

"That'd be me."

Hill flipped open his notebook while Flores eyed the DEA supervisor. "The three men picked up at the border are Angelo Rodriguez, Roberto Muñiz, and Hector Salamanca. Currently sitting in our jail. They have secured the services of Richard Condelle, Esquire, noted local attorney and defender of scumbags."

The Sheriff frowned. "Hector Salamanca? Why is that name so familiar?"

"It's a character on *Breaking Bad*," Hill told him, glancing at the DEA agent. "I had that same reaction, and Googled it. The OG who had the stroke, in a wheelchair. Now he's on the prequel, *Better Call Saul*."

Osterman had gone through Marine Corps boot camp in 1968 with a recruit named Robert Mitchum who was in no way related to the actor, but still. "Is it a fake ID?"

"That's the name on his ID. But it was Mexican ID, so take that for what it's worth."

"It's his real name," Harlin said. "Or at least he's been using it for years, since he was first arrested at age twelve or thirteen in Mexico City. But every time I see it I have that pause. Reminds me of one of the first guys I arrested, told me his name was Roger Rabbit." The two detectives looked at the DEA SAC, then each other.

"Which one was in the suit? The one in charge?" Osterman asked.

"Muñiz," Flores told him. "Our witness had no problems picking his photo out of a six-pack, but couldn't ID the other guys, the muscle. But we may have caught a break. There were droplets of blood on Muñiz's sleeve when he was picked up by ICE, on the cuff. They were small, so there might not be enough for a DNA match to the vics, but I'm hopeful. Be another week or two before we get the results back from the lab, if we're lucky."

"Maybe I can light a fire under their butts," Osterman said.

"They've finished processing all the evidence collected at the scene. The dead men's fingerprints are all over the house, not to mention their blood in the front room and semen in the bedroom, but our three suspects, if they touched anything they didn't leave a print. Oh, but we had a partial shoeprint at the scene, in blood, and it sure looks like it came from Salamanca's shoe. Bobby in the lab won't commit, though, says there's not enough to say for sure one way or the other."

"You test the shoe?"

Hill nodded. "Yeah, but didn't get anything. Probably washed it off, knowing they'd stepped in blood. We collected all their clothing, but the only thing we got that might be gold are those blood drops on Muñiz's sleeve."

"And they asked for a lawyer and got Condelle?"

Flores snorted. "I checked the camera footage at the jail. Muñiz knew his phone number by heart. All he's done is ask for a lawyer, the other two haven't said word one. They might as well be mute." She paused. "Those two, Salamanca and Rodriguez, they're stone-cold killers. You can see it. I'm not surprised to hear at least one of them has a record." She glanced at Grimes. "We've requested records from Mexican authorities, but so far haven't gotten much but a runaround. You here to help with that?" she asked the Assistant U.S. Attorney.

"Not specifically, but I can look into it," Grimes told her. "I know people who know people."

"Okay, what about the background investigation?" Osterman said, frowning. "The two dead men, their rental car out of Sky Harbor, the company that rented the house where this happened?"

Hill flipped through his notebook. "Okay, well, we collected fingerprints and DNA from the two dead guys. We've also run their names, just in case they were using their real names, only on fake IDs, but Juan Miller and Enrique Peña appear to be aliases. Trying to track down where they got the fake drivers licenses, but nothing yet. We've reached out to ICE and Homeland and Customs and everybody else to see if they've got a record of these guys coming into the country or travelling out of the States on those fake names, but so far nothing. And no pings on the prints or DNA yet, on either side of the border." He looked at the Assistant U.S. Attorney. "Any help there?"

Grimes smiled. "The only thing I can provide beyond what you're already doing is if you get us some photos of their faces, we can circulate those with the DEA guys," he nodded at Harlin, "our Host Nation Counterparts in Mexico, see if either of them gets recognized."

Flores nodded. "We can get you those."

"They rented the car out of the airport, but they didn't fly in. At least, not under their own names," Hill said, reading his notes. "I've had someone out there reviewing security camera footage at Customs, but he didn't spot them the day of the rental, or the day before." He looked up. "Which is weird, right?"

"Maybe they rented it at the airport because it's a big facility and they wanted to blend in with the crowd," Osterman said. "It's offsite, so they wouldn't need to even go near TSA. Security camera footage of them renting the car?"

"Murphy is the one tracking all that down for us," Flores told him. "You said if we needed some help we could poach other detectives, so Murph is helping with some of it. Juan Miller used a credit card to rent the car, so Murph is running that down, and the company that rented the house on Pleasant."

Osterman nodded approvingly. Dick Murphy usually worked white collar and financial crimes, so having him track down credit card and business info was a smart move.

"What was the name of the company that rented the house?" Grimes asked.

Flores checked her notes. "Telefond, R.A.," she read off. "Which is a subsidiary of Capítal Holdings, a Mexican corporation. Which is owned by another company, apparently. Murph said it's like peeling an onion, all of them appear to be shell corporations." She flipped back and forth through her notes, and then looked at her partner. "And that appears to be it, you're up to date on where we are."

She looked at the Sheriff, who looked at his two visitors and held his hand out, giving the men the floor.

Harlin went first. "Muñiz is why I'm here. The other two are low level muscle. Sure, they're killers, but they're just soldiers, there are a hundred more where they come from. Muñiz, on the other hand, is a high-ranking member of the *La Fuerza* cartel. How high up we're not exactly sure, but he's way up there. Inner circle, maybe the number two or three in the organization."

"*La Fuerza*? Never heard of it."

Harlin nodded. "It's smaller, and newer. Popped up a few years ago in central Mexico and has been making moves. Lately they've been in a turf war with *Los Zetas*."

Flores frowned. "I admit we don't get much cartel stuff up here, but aren't *Los Zetas* the biggest cartel in Mexico?"

"Yes, and *La Fuerza* has decided to go to war with them. So you can imagine it's been a bit bloody and brutal even for the cartels. Luckily for us almost all of that has been happening south of the border, but maybe that's changed.

This is the first I've heard of Telefond, but I think Capital Holdings is a shell company owned by the Zetas." He looked at the AUSA.

Grimes nodded. "It is."

"Shit." Flores made a sour face, then her eyes darted toward the Sheriff. "Sorry, sir."

Osterman smiled grimly. "No, while I don't approve of the language I completely understand the sentiment."

Grimes had a wry smile on his face, amused by a cop discussing rape and torture who had a problem with swearing. But Osterman was a known entity, consistent as death and taxes, known as a strong Christian who didn't condone swearing and yet he'd killed more than a few men in the line of duty. Most of them with a shotgun, hence his moniker Shotgun John. He'd been Tohono County Sheriff since before Grimes entered high school.

Osterman rubbed his chin. "So the Zetas rented the house, and the new gang in town shows up and after exchanging pleasantries tortures the Zeta soldiers to death? I'm not quite as current on my cartels as maybe I should be, but weren't the Zetas formed when a bunch of Mexican Special Forces soldiers joined up with a faction from another cartel?"

"Pretty much," Harlin confirmed. "They trained up all of their cartel soldiers on weapons handling and tactics, which is how they got to be number one."

"And Muñiz's cartel is going up against them?" Hill asked.

Grimes nodded. "And so far holding its own. If we can ID the two dead guys it will doubly confirm it, but it looks like this war might be spreading to our side of the border. Spreading in general. *Los Zetas* and *La Fuerza* usually operate in central Mexico. In this area on both sides of the border the Juarez Cartel controls things. So maybe *La Fuerza* is pushing against them as well. If so, that's news to us. Bad news. Anyway, Muñiz would be a big fish even if his cartel wasn't at war with *Los Zetas*. They're dropping bodies on a daily basis over there, and it's only getting worse. As it is...let's just say the Department of State and the DEA want to get their hands on him, and they are only the two most interested federal agencies of a whole long list."

"Tell 'em to stand in line," Flores growled, flicking her dark eyes at the DEA representative. "He's ours."

Osterman put his hands up calmingly, smiling at his detective. He looked at Harlin, then the Assistant U.S. Attorney. "Do you have specific charges you want to bring against Mr. Muñiz, or is he, as they say, just a person of interest?"

"No charges, at least in the States, but he's wanted in connection with a few murders and tortures in Mexico," Grimes told them. "And the State Department always wants to play nice with our allies, especially one with whom we share a border."

"High ranking cartel guy?" Hill said dubiously. "Even if anyone down there has the balls to arrest him, wouldn't he just buy his way out of jail, or kill judges and cops until the only people left were too scared to go after him? Isn't that how it works?"

"Sometimes," Grimes admitted. "Cartels don't seem to have any qualms about targeting law enforcement in Mexico. And corruption is a widespread problem. But that doesn't mean we don't give them a chance at the guy."

"We work with locals and the *federales* and the Mexican military all the time," Harlin told them. "As many problems as they have, they are the front line against the cartels.

Handing this guy over to them would really smooth over the bumps that have popped up with this new administration."

Both his detectives opened their mouths to protest but Osterman held up his hands to cut them off. "I think we can all agree that Mr. Muñiz appears to be a serious bad guy, and a lot of serious good guys want to have their turn at him. And they will. However, we now have him in custody. We have an eyewitness who puts him and his two friends at the scene of a double homicide." He looked pointedly at Harlin and Grimes. "You can talk to him all you want in our jail, while he's awaiting trial, but until he has been convicted or found innocent in a court of law for those crimes, he is not leaving our custody."

The DEA Agent looked amused and unsurprised. Grimes smiled thinly. "I think the State Department might argue that—"

Osterman put a finger up to cut the man off. "Scotty, please. Let's forget for a moment that there are many esteemed legal scholars who say that a county sheriff is the highest-ranking law enforcement official in his county, local, state or *federal*, due to being directly elected by the citizens of that county. Let's forget for a moment the successful track record this department has suing the Justice Department over immigration enforcement, civil rights violations, any number of issues. And need I point out that almost all of those mostly successful lawsuits were against the previous administration's Justice Department, which was helmed by some of the most anti-American Godless people to ever hold public office? Or that I happen to be personal friends with both the current Attorney General and the new President of these United States, or that the President has stated several times publicly that I am a 'great American'? No, I won't even mention any of that," Osterman said with a twinkle in his eye. "Instead, let me just put it simply, in grade school terms—we've got him, and you can't have him until we're done with him."

Both Hill and Flores fought back smiles. Even his enemies admitted Osterman was a fierce opponent, a true believer, unwavering in his convictions.

"Possession is nine-tenths of the law?" Grimes said with a frown. "Finders keepers?" The DEA Special Agent was fighting back laughter.

"Something like that," Osterman said with a quick grin, leaning back in his chair. "Lot of turnover in your office lately, I hear. You've moved up."

"Always happens with a new administration. Lot of people were asked to resign. Those who didn't were fired."

"That's because most of them were left of Ché Guevara," Osterman observed. "Which was just peachy with the previous administration, our former President had no problems traipsing down to Cuba and having his photo taken in front of murals of communist terrorists. You seem a bit more centered. Have shown yourself to be a moral servant of the law. I'm guessing you might have actually read the Constitution a time or two, and not just so you could find the loopholes."

"And if I returned with a federal writ compelling you to turn him over to the Justice Department?"

Osterman glanced at Harlin, who wasn't saying a word. "Even if I was a slave in chains the federal government couldn't compel me to do anything I didn't want to do," Osterman said with a wide smile. "We can have our lawyers duke it out in court, wasting taxpayer money, if you want. But you know me, I love a fight, and our department's lawyers make me look like a wilting daisy. You can talk to him—or try to talk to him, he doesn't seem especially chatty

—inside our walls all you want. His lawyer, Condelle, is just a peach, I'm sure he'll give your request to talk to his client the utmost respect. You, the DEA," he gestured at Special Agent Harlin, "and anybody else, federal, state, or Mexican. But until Mr. Muñiz has had his fair day in court and answered to the people of Arizona for *this* crime, the only way you are wresting him from our custody is if you mount an armed assault on our jail. And I wouldn't recommend that. I really wouldn't."

"Glad to see you haven't mellowed in your old age, John," Harlin said, shaking his head but unable to hide a smile.

"You bring a tear to my eye, sir," Hill said, deadpan.

The Assistant U.S. Attorney glanced at the two detectives then back at Osterman, rolling his eyes. As he dug in his pocket he sighed. Well, it had been worth a try, but things had gone pretty much how he'd expected. "With whom do I arrange visits from my people to talk to Muñiz and his two goons?" He pulled out a twenty-dollar bill and handed it to the DEA Agent.

"Me," Flores told him. "And it all gets recorded, by us, or it doesn't happen."

"Of course."

Osterman hadn't missed the money changing hands. "You lose a bet?" he asked the attorney.

"We had a wager about you giving up Muñiz."

"And you bet I would?"

"No, I'm not that dumb. I just thought your refusal would stay along legal lines." The attorney glanced at the DEA Special Agent. "Harlin was sure you'd say the only way we'd get him is if we came in shooting. Which is ridiculous, or so I thought. Silly me."

"You can try to talk to him, but you'll be wasting your

time, though," Hill told him. "Condelle won't let him say one word. One syllable."

Grimes shrugged. "You never know till you try."

"That's the spirit," Osterman said warmly.

"And the witness? She's safe?" Harlin asked.

"We have her in protective custody," Osterman told him. "I won't tell you where."

"And I don't want to know. Honestly. Just make sure the men guarding her know how serious this is." He paused. "Does she? Is she aware the man she identified is in a cartel?"

"She's been told," Flores said to him. "And she's scared shitless. But she's willing to testify anyway. I think she believes that if she doesn't testify, since she's an illegal we'd deport her. And then she'd be back in Mexico, where they can get to her more easily and would kill her just in case. She believes she's between a rock and a hard place, and I don't know that she's wrong. We're certainly not going to argue otherwise."

Grimes nodded. "Still, that takes guts." He looked at Osterman. "You maybe want some help from the U.S. Marshalls? They do witness protection all the time."

"I appreciate the offer, but I'd rather keep this in-house."

Harlin glanced between the detectives and the Sheriff. "I'm sure your people have done an excellent job debriefing the witness, but if we had a few follow-up questions for her?"

"Absolutely," Osterman told him. He nodded at Flores and Hill. "Contact my people, and they'll make sure she's available to answer your questions. Here. Everything recorded, of course."

"Of course."

Osterman stood up and offered his hand. "Gentlemen, until next time?"

"I can hardly wait," Grimes said, taking his hand for a quick shake.

"Come on down to the office some time, haven't seen you there in a while," Harlin told him. "I'll take you out to lunch. I promise to wear long pants."

Osterman smiled. "It's a date."

The three of them watched Grimes and Harlin leave, and Osterman sat back down. "Is that all, sir?" Hill asked.

Osterman held up a finger, and picked up his phone. He punched in the number for the control room of his jail.

"Benedetto."

"Benny, who's the officer in charge of the jail today?"

Benedetto had been with the department for eighteen years and recognized the Sheriff's voice immediately. "That'd be me, sir." Every deputy with the department had to cycle through the jail. Most of the deputies didn't like it, they would much rather be working the road, but Osterman thought it was important so they could see real criminals firsthand, and how they behaved.

"You have three prisoners there," Osterman said into the phone while eyeing his two detectives. "Angelo Rodriguez, Roberto Muñiz, and Hector Salamanca. Suspects in that double homicide on Pleasant."

"Yes sir?"

"I want you to put a note in the computer, but I also want you to, in person, tell whoever is in charge of lockup on night shift. Heck, and everyone else there, too. I want the word spread far and wide. Under no circumstances are you to release any of those men, to anyone. I am especially concerned about federal government employees showing up with impressive-looking paperwork. I don't care if the documents are signed by the Governor—heck, I don't care if the Governor himself shows up to take custody of those men, they are not to be released. And if anyone does show up to try and take them, I want to be notified. Immediately, day or night. Is that understood?"

"Yes sir." Benedetto paused, then asked, "Are we suing the feds again, sir?"

Osterman smiled. "Not yet. And hopefully that won't be necessary in this case. But these three men have cartel ties. I don't need to tell you what that means. Are they segregated?"

"Yes sir. We don't get so many murder suspects we have to double them up in the cells."

"And hopefully that won't change. Thank you." Osterman hung up the phone and looked at his detectives.

"You think he'd try that, go behind your back?" Hill asked.

Osterman shrugged. "You plan for your enemy's capabilities, not probabilities. And on that note, make sure one of you goes to the front desk here, make sure they're up to speed as well. Put it into the system, but also tape up a big memo next to their monitors." Osterman was a firm believer in actual hardcopy notes. "This thing could be even bigger than we think it is, so I'd prefer a daily briefing. Four o'clock tomorrow, if that works for you."

"Yes sir."

Osterman pointed at Hill's waistline. "I understand we are in a secure facility, but at least until our investigations are concluded and these gentlemen are no longer in our custody, I want you wearing your sidearm at all times when on duty."

"Yes sir," Hill said, chagrinned. His Glock was in his

desk drawer. Sitting in his desk chair with it on was uncomfortable.

"You really think they'd try something here?" Flores asked.

"Cartels have military hardware at their disposal and have shown they are happy to use it. And well trained in its use. And they've got big numbers. They've shown no qualms torturing and beheading people, even women. Hung corpses from overpasses. They've battled the Mexican military to a draw in running gun battles and bombed police stations. I doubt they would try that here even though the previous administration was happy to sell them all the guns they wanted." The BATFE's 'Fast & Furious' gunwalking operation was a sore point with the Sheriff since one of the first victims of that debacle had been a Border Patrol agent killed in Arizona. "I would guess they'd try bribery or blackmail, or go after the witness in the courthouse during the trial long before they stormed a secure facility like this full of armed police trying to rescue their man. But I don't know that, and neither do you." He pointed at Hill's beltline. "Gun."

"Yes sir."

Osterman watched his detectives depart, then grunted and pulled out his cell phone. Luckily his wife had shown him to increase the size of the lettering on the screen or he'd need to pull out reading glasses every time he wanted to use the darn thing. He found the deputy's phone number under recent calls and punched it.

"Kling."

"Deputy, how are things?"

"Fine, sir. No problems."

"Is our witness keeping her head down?"

"Yes sir. She's still recovering from her wounds anyway,

but she's quiet. She watches TV and reads mostly when we're here."

"Aren't you there all the time? You're still in the pink safehouse, correct?" The house had been seized by the county the year before and was still in limbo. The previous owner had painted the exterior a pale peachy pink.

"Yes sir. But every other day she's visiting the counselor in the hospital."

Osterman frowned. "You can't get the counselor to come out there?"

"No sir. I asked, but she says she's too busy, the travel time would take too much out of her day. And I...I really think it's doing the witness some good. She had a rough time of it."

"It's not over. I just had a visit from the head of the Phoenix Division of the DEA and an Assistant U.S. Attorney who confirmed all of my worst fears about the people that young lady will be testifying against."

"Cartel?" Kling said quietly, so he wasn't overheard.

"Very much so. Who's with you there today, Dino Saunders?"

"Yes sir. We've been doing twelve-hour shifts, two men per shift, as you instructed."

"Hmm." Two men wouldn't be nearly enough if the cartel found out where she was, but that information was very tightly held even within the department. And he couldn't burn all the department's manpower budget on guarding one witness. It would be months until the trial. "Long guns?"

"Yes sir, department M4s, and pistols. And we're in plain clothes and unmarked vehicles, so there's no flashing cop sign out front for anyone driving by."

"Still, the neighbors will know who you are," Osterman observed. "I might start moving you around a bit."

"Whatever you think is best, sir. You actually think the cartels would try to make a run at cops all the way up here?"

"The last time I tried to play the odds on what an enemy might do the Viet Cong showed me just what a mistake that was, and I still have the scars. But they taught me a valuable lesson. Assume the worst and plan accordingly. Those who are ready for trouble rarely have any. I think Teddy Roosevelt said that."

"Didn't he go out looking for trouble?" Kling asked. "Picking fights around the world?"

"In the military vernacular that would make him a Subject Matter Expert," Osterman said with a smile. "Stay safe."

Chapter Seven

Mackie stood in front of the class, clad in his usual worn judo *gi*. "Melissa was asking about krav maga. Krav maga is the cool new martial art. Krav maga is the James Bond of martial arts right now. But the philosophy behind krav maga is the same one I use—take what works, leave the rest. The Israelis looked at all the techniques that actually worked on real bad guys in real world situations. It's a mix of judo, aikido, boxing, and wrestling—sound familiar? 'Krav maga' just means contact combat. An IDF guy I know—that's Israeli Defense Forces—described krav maga as beating the shit out of somebody while two guys beat the shit out of you, because a lot of time they're working in crowds to take down bad guys, and bad guys often bring their buddies along. It ain't pretty, but it works."

He smiled. "Now look, none of this is rocket science. Sticking your thumb in someone's eye has worked since we've had eyes. And thumbs, I guess. And you don't need to practice that to refine your technique. Which is a good thing, because it's kinda hard to practice. Same with throat punches, and kicking somebody in the side of the knee." He held up a finger. "However, while we won't be doing any eye-gouging or knee-breaking today, I'm going to show you when you'd want to use them, and how to set up to do those techniques. Show you how hard you'd need to punch a throat, or what kick you'd want to use to take out someone's knee. But first we're going to practice those punches and kicks we have learned, because practice makes perfect. Line up on the bags." He clapped his hands.

After class Mackie came up to him just to make sure he was okay. Dave was blinking his right eye a lot, and it was still tearing up. There was a red line across the side of his head to the corner of his eye.

"Zombie, let me see your eye again," Mackie said, leaning in. He reached up and checked Dave's cheek and eyelid, then studied the eyeball. "Look around the room, so I can see it. Okay, no scratch on your eye. I guess she just poked it good through your eyelid."

"I'm really sorry," Melissa said again. She looked at her nails. "They're not even that long." She hadn't even been trying an eye gouge, or even going for his head. She'd just kind of panicked when they were sparring, and lashed out as she was falling.

Mackie smiled encouragingly at her. "And that's why nails are great in a real fight. You stick your thumb in a guy's eye who's trying to rape you, really dig it in there, he'll start thinking about all the bad decisions in his life that got him to that point. Accidents happen, but be careful. My insurance is already high enough, if one of my students loses an eye…" Melissa made a face as she grabbed her stuff and headed into the locker room.

"Came out of nowhere, didn't even have time to flinch," Dave said. He was disappointed in himself. And the socket around his other eye was bruised badly from where he'd been sparring with Mackie right at the end of the class when everyone else was cooling down. He'd taken a real beating today. With everyone watching.

Mackie looked at his student. He'd been coming to classes three days a week for most of a year, but they'd barely exchanged fifty words in that time. "Why'd you start taking this class?" Mackie asked.

Dave shrugged. "I know my way around guns." He stopped, considered, then went on. "But I realized one day that I'd never been punched. Never punched anyone. Didn't know anything about hand-to-hand." He reached his fingers up to the scratch on his face. The red line was stinging, and the other side of his face was throbbing. "Apparently I still don't, after all this time."

Mackie smiled. "Well, you said you wanted to go all out." He looked around to make sure everybody else was in the locker rooms or out of earshot. "With someone who wasn't a hausfrau." He bent and started folding up and stacking the mats.

Dave could feel the throbbing around his eye socket. "What was that, your elbow?"

"Yeah, when you came in to my body I got you with the elbow." Mackie demonstrated it, and fought back a wince of his own. Full contact sparring with minimal pads could leave some serious bruises, and Zombie knew how to hit.

Dave shook his head. "Been coming here almost a year, I was hoping I'd do better than that."

"You're a lot better than you were when you showed up. Then you didn't know anything."

"How long does it take to get really good? Like you?"

His teacher shook his head. "Lot more than a year. Years and years. I've been involved in martial arts for twenty years."

Dave made a face. He didn't have that kind of time.

"Hey, don't sweat it. Look, you're still working at mastering the basics, but you've got a good start. You're big and have a long reach, and you've got great reflexes. You know how to hit. And you're in stupid good shape, which makes you seem better than you actually are, you don't get winded. You're an average fighter…but man, you can take a beating like nobody's business."

Dave frowned. "I'm not sure what you mean."

Mackie stopped putting away the mats and turned to look at him. "Why do you think I started calling you Zombie?"

Was it Mackie who'd started that? He honestly couldn't remember. "I don't know, because I came in tired a couple of times and stumbled around? I don't remember the first time you did it."

"No, it's because you take the hit and keep on coming. Zombies only go down if you head shoot them. They just shrug off shots to the body."

Dave frowned. "What are you talking about? It hurts like hell when I get hit. Especially when *you* hit me. The girls here punch like girls. You know how to hit."

"Yeah, but you don't let it stop you. You don't even let it slow you down. I can tell it hurts, but you don't care, you just keep coming. Most people are afraid of the pain, try to avoid it. You're not and you don't." His eyes were drawn to the scar along Zombie's jawline that the short beard didn't quite hide. "Why do you think none of the other students ever want to spar with you? You haven't noticed that it's you and me almost every time I have you guys pair off?"

"I just thought that was because…I don't know…we had an odd number of people."

"No, it's because when we're doing full contact sparring, even if they hit you perfect they almost can't tell because you suck up that pain as if it's…I don't know, like you think you deserve it. Like you expect it. I hit you harder than I meant to with my elbow and all you did was blink—then hit me. Anyone else in this class, if I hit them that hard they'd be on the mat crying. One on one I could kick your ass in a real fight, but I know I'd have to break a couple of joints or beat you unconscious to get you to stop coming after me. You eat up the pain like candy." He paused. "Look, I may be stepping out of bounds, here, teacher to student, but… have you ever talked to the counselors at the VA?"

Dave frowned. "The VA?" There was a big VA hospital on the north side of Prescott.

Mackie nodded. "Yeah. They've got some good guys there. A lot of them have been through it themselves, and even those that haven't, they deal with this stuff every day. They know what you're going through."

Dave was shaking his head. "I'm not sure what you think I…"

Mackie held up his hands, then pointed at Dave's. "Hey, I know gunshot wounds and burns when I see them, I've got them myself. I'm not going to jump into psychology mumbo jumbo but I can see you're working through some stuff. I've lost people too. You don't want to call it PTSD, or survivor guilt, fine, but I know a lot of world-class tough guys, and none of them adjusted to civilian life without a few twitches and hiccups, know what I mean?" He paused, considered, then dived all the way in. "I mean, you usually end up sparring with me because I'd rather it be me if today's the day. I'm afraid you'd hurt one of them."

"What does that mean? The day for what?"

"The day you lose it. You hide it well, you're very tightly wrapped, but you're one of the angriest people I've ever met."

"Me?" Dave blinked in surprise. "I'm not angry." Why would Mackie think he was angry?

Mackie straightened up and debated saying something more, but just shook his head and went back to folding mats.

He'd done a full workout before getting his ass beat in class, so Dave felt he'd earned a few carbs, and he'd been sticking to the budget he'd made, he still had plenty of money. The new coffee place he'd heard about apparently offered some killer sandwiches and was less than three minutes from P-Dip. After changing he drove straight there.

The Prescott Valley Crossroads was a newer—hell, what wasn't new around there?—open shopping mall near the border with Prescott. There was a Cracker Barrel out front and a Home Depot anchoring the big building in back, with a lot of chain restaurants and assorted businesses in-between, both attached and free-standing. He'd heard somewhere that the place had 58,000 parking spaces and he believed it, the sprawling mall was huge.

Aloha Snackbar was right next to a Chipotle Mexican Grill and they'd obviously spent a lot of money on the interior. It was as upscale as any Starbucks he'd ever been in, only with understated military and patriotic memorabilia on the bare brick walls.

There were half a dozen customers at the small tables and two guys behind the counter when Dave walked in. The air inside was thick with the aroma of coffee. Good coffee. The business was relatively long and narrow, with the tables set in front of the windows which ran down the side of the building. One door in front, and one at the far end of the place which was marked Emergency Exit and probably locked from the outside. He set his tablet down on an unoccupied table and moved to the counter.

"What can I get you?" According to their nametags Matt was the redhead who moved with a slight limp, and Mike had scar tissue running up his left arm out of sight under his sleeve and reappearing again above his collar on the side of his neck. They looked to be in their early thirties.

The board on the wall behind them listed a lot of coffees and Dave frowned at it.

"If you want just a pure black God Bless America caffeine rush to the heart I'd recommend the BlackJack," Mike told him. "We get it from the Black Rifle Coffee Company. If you're into flavored coffees I'd recommend the Highlander Grogg. It's out of South Dakota, sort of a butterscotch caramel, but it doesn't taste artificial at all. Personally I prefer a mix of the two."

"I'll take a large BlackJack." Dave pulled a bottle of water out of the refrigerated case. "This too, and a chicken Caesar wrap." He pointed.

After he'd paid, Dave sat at the table facing the front door. The tall windows were along the wall to his right, and a brick column at his right elbow. It looked and felt like real brick as opposed to decorative facing. Hung on the column a few feet above his head was an antiqued copy of the Declaration of Independence. He glanced out the window, which was tinted against the Arizona sun, glanced at the front door, then punched in the code to unlock the tablet. He sipped at his coffee as he tried to find the wi-fi.

"Hey, do you guys have public wi-fi? I thought you did,

but all I can find is Aloha REMF, and it's password protected."

Matt reached over the counter and tapped a plastic jug. "A five-dollar donation will get you the password for the wi-fi, which is good for the whole month."

Dave got out of his seat. "Donation? To what charity?"

"Changes every month. This month it's Disabled American Veterans. Last month it was the ASPCA."

Dave found a five in his pocket and stuffed it through the slot in the top of the plastic tub. The redhead nodded at him in thanks, noticing the scars on Dave's hands but not saying anything. "Password is bacon," he said as Dave went back to his seat.

"No, that was last month. Today is the first of the month," Mike corrected him. He looked at Dave. "Password is America."

"You guys the owners?" Dave asked them, sitting back down.

"Yeah. Thought we were done getting up at oh-dark-thirty when we got out of the military, then we get the great idea to open up a coffee place. When do people most want coffee? Early in the morning." Mike peered at Dave, saw him touch the screen of his tablet a few times. "You in? Good. That means you capitalized America, the way it's supposed to be."

"'Bacon' should have been capitalized too," Matt said.

His partner shook his head. "It's not a proper noun," he said.

"It is to anyone who eats it." He jabbed a finger at a wood plaque hanging nearby, on which was etched a quote —*A society should be wholly judged by its attitudes on bacon and dogs.*

Dave snorted and sipped at his coffee as he checked the websites of the Detroit area papers and TV and radio stations, WJR, WXYZ, WWJ, DetNews, Freep…even the Macomb Daily and the Oakland Press. He wasn't looking for anything in particular…but it was what you didn't know that could get you killed.

He'd bought the tablet used at a local pawn shop, and never used it in any way that could get traced back to him personally. He never signed in to any personal account with it, no email, no Netflix, and never used it to pay his bills. Never never *ever* did a Google search of his real name or the one on his current driver's license or the names of anyone he knew before coming to Arizona. It was sterile, in other words, and he meant to keep it that way.

Forty-five minutes later he'd checked all the usual websites without finding anything of concern or interest. His coffee cup was empty, he'd finished the water, and the only thing left of the Caesar wrap were a few bits of Parmesan cheese on the plate. It had been a damn good sandwich. He picked the cheese crumbs up with his thumb as he dug a phone out of his pocket, along with its battery.

After first double-checking to make sure he'd grabbed the right one, the burner phone, he installed the battery, powered it up, and punched in a number. While he listened to it ring he eyed a sign on the wall near the front door, made to look as if it was from the old west—GUNS ARE WELCOME ON PREMISES. PLEASE KEEP ALL WEAPONS HOLSTERED UNLESS NEED ARISES. IN SUCH CASE, JUDICIOUS MARKSMANSHIP IS APPRECIATED. That got a smile out of him. It wasn't the first time he'd seen such a sign in a local business, and was one of the reasons he loved Arizona.

He got a generic recording asking him to leave a message. "Hey, it's me. I got your messages. Yes, the number is still good. And I'm still alive. I'm just…." He sighed, and shook his head. "I'm not being a dick. Well, I'm not trying to be a dick, I'm trying to keep you safe." He looked at the palm of his free hand, and flexed it. It creased in odd places and looked like a partially fried piece of Spam. The shiny scars reflected the lights in the coffee shop. "Don't worry about me, okay?" He opened his mouth to say something else, but couldn't think of anything. After a pause he shut the phone, pulled the battery out, and stuck it back in his pocket.

"Hey, thanks man, you didn't need to do that," Matt said to him as Dave brought up his dirty dishes. "You interested in a little dessert? The brownies we've got are killer. We don't make them, a lady does, she supplies a lot of the local businesses. Aunt A's Sweet Treats. Makes 'em fresh every day."

"No, thanks, I'm good." Dave had lost whatever appetite he'd had left. Leaving the message for Aaron had gotten him thinking about the past, and the future, and that never put him in a good mood. He scanned the parking lot automatically before exiting the coffee shop, reflexively, the way he checked his mirrors for a tail whenever he drove anywhere. And his eyes continually swept the area as he walked. There was a woman sitting in Chevy Malibu near his Jeep, and a guy just getting out of a Ram pickup the next aisle over, but nothing that pinged his radar. His mind stayed on other things.

As he drove back to his house he knew he was in a bad mood, and from past experience knew the dark thoughts would drag him down unless he distracted himself. That was why he worked out all the time—you couldn't worry or obsess when it was all you could do to breathe. Same with practicing his draw—with the proper focus everything else was pushed away. He hadn't practiced his draw at all yet today. Maybe two hours of that, with the music on real loud, would keep him from thinking too much. Then bingeing some more Netflix. He couldn't do daytime TV. He'd tried, but every show on the major networks during the day seemed designed to lower the IQ of the viewers. Or the morale. Daytime network TV was a parade of, by, and for human debris. Talk about depressing. Netflix kept him sane when he was too burnt to work out or practice his draw but not so tired he could sleep. Not that he ever slept much. He was halfway through the five seasons of *Person Of Interest*, and was hooked. It had started out as a modern-day version of that old TV show The Equalizer and was turning into something truly epic.

As he drove down his street he noticed a second car in the driveway next door. He recognized it as belonging to the nurse helping Lori with her mother. As he climbed out of the Wrangler he heard someone calling a name. After a second, he realized the name belonged to him.

"Jackie. Jackie!" He looked across the street and saw Mrs. Leslie waving at him. "Can you help me move a few of my planters?"

"Sure." He trudged across the street. His neighbor always had a few planter boxes and big flower pots on her porch and along the side of her house, usually positioned, he'd noticed, where they could get some shade from the relentless Arizona sun. He recognized carnations. Or maybe they were daisies. He didn't know flowers.

As he drew close he saw that she'd just finished watering all the pots and planters. The soil inside was dark, the water leaking through the drain holes in the bases. No wonder she didn't want to lift them.

"What's going where?" he asked.

She smiled at him. Rose Leslie was in her seventies and

was originally from Ohio or Indiana...somewhere in the Midwest, he couldn't remember exactly. She and her husband had retired at the same time at 55, then her husband had gotten bored, discovered Viagra, and started working his way through the neighborhood ladies. So she'd gotten a divorce, moved out West, and never been happier...or at least that was the story she was sticking to. She was skinny and kept a cane handy, but he'd never seen her use it. She stood next to the front porch and pointed at the planters along the side of her house.

"These poor things are getting baked here," she told him. "Can you slide them up toward the front of the house, closer to the porch? They'll be in shade longer there."

"Sure." The planters were plastic things colored to resemble clay, shallow troughs two feet long filled with soil. Dry they'd probably only weigh five pounds apiece, but the water she'd just added tripled that. Dave grabbed them one at a time and relocated them according to her pointing bony finger, trying not to trip over her hairless cat, which he'd learned was a Sphynx. Such a distinguished, sophisticated, classy title for such an ugly animal. It didn't look like a cat, it looked like an alien. Hell, it looked like an aborted alien fetus. Its only redeeming quality was the name she'd chosen for it.

"Mr. Bigglesworth! Get out of there or you're going to get kicked!" Mrs. Leslie scolded the cat. It looked up at her with that royal expression of disdain reserved for use by cats and French supermodels, then went back to sniffing at Dave's shoes as he moved back and forth.

When he was done playing musical planter boxes she thanked him and he headed back across the street. Halfway there he saw Lori standing in her driveway. He debated, but there was no way to pretend he hadn't seen her, the houses were too close together.

"Hey," he said, stopping on his concrete walk in front of his porch. Then he frowned. She looked lost, and it wasn't until he took two steps toward her that she even reacted.

"What?" She was in a baggy t-shirt and yoga pants, her hair pulled back into a ponytail.

"You okay?"

She looked at him, bit her lip, and gave a long shuddering sigh. "Yeah. No. Mom's having a bad day. Bad couple of days. Vicki's over, the nurse, and she told me to take a break, but…" She gave a little sad laugh and gestured at the cars. "I'm parked in." She glanced back at her house. It was obvious she didn't want to go back in. And felt guilty about it.

He smiled at her and stuck a thumb over his shoulder. "You want to borrow my car? I keep offering…"

She smiled back at him. "No, I…" her voice faded away and she looked past him at nothing. He recognized the look. He saw it quite frequently in the mirror.

Dave frowned. "You want to come in? Talk, not talk, watch some TV, read a book, whatever?" He really didn't want to talk, wasn't in the mood for company, but he still had a soul. He knew just how horrible it must be for her, living and dealing with a parent slowly dying. It was probably worse than he could imagine.

Lori looked around, but he wasn't sure if she was seeing the street and houses around them. She looked at the nurse's car blocking hers in, then back at her house. "Yeah, I guess," she said finally.

"All right, now he's really starting to piss me off," Aaron said, closing the burner flip phone with some force.

"Who?" Arlene asked.

"Who do you think? Who else do you think I'd be calling on this piece of shit?" He waved the phone around. On the couch Peanut perked her head up, wondering if Aaron was about to throw something. They hadn't played catch in a few days. The thing in his hand didn't smell like a toy, but you never knew. She studied him intently in case he threw it, and also on the odd chance any steak fell out of his pockets.

"What's he doing? Is he okay?"

"I don't know," Aaron said as he pulled the battery out of the phone. "That's the fucking point. I haven't talked to him in close to six months. We're just leaving messages back and forth." He glanced at his girlfriend, looking for a sympathetic ear.

She frowned. "He is in hiding, you know. Maybe he's just trying to keep you safe. I mean, you're using a fucking burner phone. And pulling the battery out of it like *Mission Impossible*. For a reason. He almost died. You showed up five minutes earlier, you might've died. Five minutes later he would've for sure, right?"

"Yeah, but no, that's bullshit. He's not doing it to keep me safe." He frowned, thinking.

"You sure about that?" Arlene looked at him. "You worried about him?"

Aaron didn't say anything for a while, then shrugged. She took that as a yes, and it was about as close as he was going to get to talking about his feelings. "Well, what are you going to do about it? If he's not answering when you call…"

"I could go down there."

"You know where he is? I mean, I know you know about where he is."

"Yeah. He told me when he landed where he's at now." Dave had also told him the fake name he was living under. It had taken all of Aaron's self-control not to Google Dave's alias.

Arlene frowned. She pulled two bottles of beer out of the refrigerator, twisted the caps off, and handed him one. "I don't know if you should go all the way down there without checking with him first. Maybe he's got other stuff going on."

"I'm not showing up with a wedding proposal, I just want to make sure he's fucking okay." He fumed. "I don't think he's got anything else going on. I think he's just sitting down there. That's what I'm worried about."

"Jesus." Dave saw the drop of sweat trembling on the end of his nose and carefully rolled to the side. It fell onto the wet sheets instead of into her eyes.

"Yeah," Lori gasped. There was a puddle of sweat in her navel.

"I guess I had to get that out of my system. It's been a while." He glanced over at the clock, had to blink a few times to get it in focus. Three hours? No wonder they were both covered in sweat. He looked over at her. She looked great naked, and even better naked and sweaty. Not that he had anything left to give her at the moment.

"It's been a while for me too. Couple years." She said it as if she couldn't believe it had been that long. She looked around to find the clock, tried to remember when she'd come over. Wow. Yep, she was going to be sore tomorrow. Hell, she was sore already, but it had been worth it.

"Yeah? Same here, couple years." He had his reasons for being antisocial, but her default position in his male brain was 'pretty blonde', and pretty blonde girls shouldn't have any trouble getting laid. So it took him a few seconds to compute why she'd had a two-year dry spell. Ah. "Guess moving back in with your mom cuts into your dating life." Living next door to her, and spending a lot of time at home left him subliminally aware of her activity level even though he wasn't paying any particular attention. She spent more time indoors than he did, and half the time when she left her house for any length of time it was with her mother. He tried to remember if he'd ever seen a guy over there. No one under the age of fifty, at least.

She glanced over at him. "I've lived next door to you for what, nine months?"

"Closer to a year."

"And you never did much more than wave."

"Yeah, I'm sorry about that. I should have offered my help. I can't even imagine what you're going through."

A line appeared between her eyebrows as she frowned. "No, I'm not...that's okay, you don't have to apologize for that. She's *my* mother, you don't have any responsibility for that." She sat up on one elbow. "How old *are* you?"

He frowned back at her. "Twenty-eight. Why?"

"Because you act a lot older than you look."

"How old do I look?"

"Twenty-eight."

He pursed his lips together and didn't say anything for a while. "It's not the years, honey, it's the mileage," he finally said, with a little smile. Then he snuck a look at her. She was grinning too. "What are you smiling at?"

"You think if I got a *Big Trouble in Little China* reference I wouldn't recognize a quote from *Raiders of the Lost Ark*? No,

I'm not talking about helping with my mom, I'm talking about you. Nine months living next door and you didn't even introduce yourself. I more than half figured you were gay."

He blinked, then laughed. "No, not gay."

She saw him looking at her tits and smiled. "Well no shit."

"How old are you?" he asked.

"Don't you know you're never supposed to ask a woman that?" She scowled at him, then laughed to show she wasn't serious. "Thirty. Why, how old do I look?"

"Forty-eight."

"Asshole." She hit him with a pillow as he laughed. She studied his face, then ran her eyes down and back up his body. She'd seen the scar along his jaw before, but the gunshot wounds—and that's what they had to be, she'd never seen one before but what else made holes in people but bullets?—one in his arm and one in his leg, those were new to her. Healed, and scarred over, so not new to him. She couldn't say she was surprised. He seemed the kind of guy who'd have bullet wounds, and they looked like they'd been less painful than the burns on his hands. Guess he really did have a lot of miles under the tires. Still, she didn't ask about any of it. Not her business, not after one afternoon sex marathon that was as much stress release, for the both of them apparently, as it was sex.

Still, it had also been sex. Great sex. She eyed him some more. Six foot two, wide shoulders, big hands, big feet…and every appendage in proportion, which had been her experience, with very few exceptions. And three *hours*, with just two short breaks to rehydrate. Not a bad way to end a two-year dry spell.

She glanced at his eight pack abs, then moved her eyes

further down. He was good-looking all over and had the skills to match. If they weren't both already exhausted she'd jump right back on him, sore or not. Some bikes were meant to be ridden.

He was still smiling, but it almost looked a little sad. "I just wasn't...looking for anyone. Anything."

She squinted at him. It occurred to her that they'd been neighbors for a year, and they'd been looking past each other the whole time. At least until that day her car had broken down. She looked around the room. Every wall was lined with bookcases, and they were all packed with books. Paperbacks, hardcovers, dictionaries, even an old encyclopedia set. "You rob a library or something?" she asked.

"Something like that." He smiled at her, and kept looking. If she was just going to lie there naked, he wasn't going to be shy about staring at her. "You have the softest skin I've ever felt," he said. "Maybe it's been so long I've forgotten." Maybe it was his hands. He glanced at them. Burned on the inside, bruised and callused on the outside from the heavy bags at P-Dip. Everything was soft compared to his hands.

"Laser hair removal," she told him. "Worth every penny. No shaving, no stubble, and no one will ever be able to say I'm not a real blonde."

He snorted, then stared up at the ceiling for a few minutes, quiet. "What time is your mom expecting you back?" he finally asked.

She stared at him in surprise, then ultimately laughed. Hard. "Wow. Seriously?"

"What?"

"I've kicked more than a few guys out when I was done with them, but I've never had it done to me." It was funny. She couldn't decide if she should be angry.

"No, that's not what I meant. I, uh..."

She laughed at him again. "Don't worry about it. I'm just giving you shit. I do need to get back, though." She glanced at the clock to double-check, her eyes sliding over the pistol on the bedside table. Guns didn't scare her. Bad guys were another matter, whether or not they had guns. Jack/Dave/whatever he wanted to call himself might be serious and intense, but he wasn't a bad guy. She'd been pretty sure of that before, and after fucking him she was positive. More often than not a guy's true self came out in the bedroom. He was hiding a lot of anger and maybe sadness, but he kept it buried so deep it only came out in hints—a glance, an inflection in his voice, and the incessant clenching of his hands. But it wasn't anger at women, not like some guys she'd known. "Is that a Glock?"

"Yeah. Glock 19. Pretty stock except for the Trijicon sights and a three-and-a-half pound connector. Why?"

She shrugged. "Just curious. What's that orange thing?"

"Orange? Oh, the front sight. Orange so you can see it easier when you're in a hurry. The Glock factory sights suck." He'd liked the Hornady Critical Duty +P ammo even before the FBI chose it as their new duty load, and it filled every one of his pistol magazines. It was designed to work well even if you had to shoot through auto glass or car doors.

Lori nodded but didn't have a clue about Glock anything. But from the amount of time he spent practicing his draw and doing the other stuff with his gun she had a good idea that he knew what he was talking about. Which made sense, considering his undercover cop/protected witness/whoever/whatever-the-hell-he-was situation. With bullet wounds. Before him her only experience with guns was seeing a few drunk assholes waving them around.

She glanced at the clock again. She knew she was

putting it off, but the thought of heading back to her mother sucked the energy out of her. "Vicki is supposed to leave in ten minutes. She's probably wondering where the hell I went, if she's seen my car is still out there." With a grunt she stood up and began collecting her clothes. As she moved she could feel that she wasn't just sore, she was swollen too. And exhausted, even though he'd done most of the work. She was out of shape. Her hips felt like they'd been popped out of their sockets. Or maybe it was just that he did too much damn cardio. Three hours straight, with barely a rest. After two years of nothing. Well, nothing but her own hands. And a few toys.

Dave sat on the edge of the bed and watched her dress. As he'd suspected, she hadn't been wearing anything under the yoga pants.

"You're going to want to wash those sheets," she told him, fastening her bra. The whole room smelled of sex.

He glanced over his shoulder. "Yeah." He realized he should show her out, and found a pair of shorts to put on so he didn't flash Mrs. Leslie when he opened the front door.

Lori pulled the shirt on over her head, and he followed her toward the front of the house. She stopped in the front room, and turned to him as he unlocked the door. Several things ran through her head, but what she said to him was, "Don't be a stranger." Then she kissed him, opened the front door, and went out.

Chapter Eight

Ramos looked up and down the river as far as he could using the binoculars, taking his time, but saw nothing moving save a few circling birds of prey, and the river itself.

The banks on either side of the river were green, but the green didn't reach far from the moving water, not this time of year, probably not ever. The hills on the far side of the river were as brown as the hills behind him. Topographically the hills were nearly identical, geographically they were less than a mile apart. Politically, though, they were worlds apart.

Ramos lowered the binoculars and nodded to the coyote standing at the base of the hill. The man nodded back, then bent to speak one last time to the five men standing before him. Then the men turned and began walking away—directly northeast, toward the river.

El Rio Bravo del Norte was a little faster and deeper here than in a lot of spots, but that was exactly the point. It wasn't the easiest spot to cross so hopefully the law enforcement presence on the other side would be busy elsewhere. If he wanted easy there were a lot of other places to cross. There was that new tunnel outside Ciudad de Juarez. But…tunnels were a big project, only dug by bad people looking for big rewards smuggling drugs or other high value items north. Which meant there was a higher chance the Americans had them under surveillance to see who or what came across. Anyone who snuck across the border using a tunnel was not just some peasant hoping for a menial job or to suck on the American government's teat. No, the peasants went across on foot, in the open.

The five men reached the edge of the green border on this side of the river. They were all dressed as the men they were, day laborers, denim jeans, cotton shirts, and boots. Ramos was wearing the same thing himself.

The men reached the edge of the water and with only a second's hesitation waded out into the fast-moving water. He would hope they didn't hesitate, he'd paid them quite a bit of money for doing something they'd all already done at least once. Normally they'd have to pay the coyote.

When the water got deep enough the men had to swim, and he watched the current take them downriver quite a distance until they reached shallow water again.

"Water's fast," Ramos commented in Spanish. His accent marked him as a local.

"I told you," the coyote told him, trudging back up the small hill. "But if you know how to swim it doesn't take long to cross."

A minute later the men were all standing on dry land again. On that side the river was not known as El Rio Bravo del Norte but rather the Rio Grande. He raised the binoculars. He could see them talking briefly, then the men separated and began walking quickly, each heading roughly northeast but angling away from the others. Shotgun pattern, as he'd explained to them.

"The American border patrol has drones, helicopters, patrols, maybe even satellites, I don't know, but they don't often come out here because there is nothing," the coyote said, waving his hand at the far side of the river. "No houses, no paved roads within twenty kilometers of the river. One ranch, maybe fifteen kilometers east-northeast from here. The river here is faster and deeper than in some places. Too fast and deep for women and children. Good place to cross, good place."

The man wasn't telling Ramos anything he didn't already know. All of those reasons were why he'd chosen to cross here. But the coyote was nervous around him, knowing who he worked for, and would rather talk to fill the silence.

"Do you truthfully think they will build a wall, or a fence, all along the border, as the American President says?" the coyote asked him. The man frowned and studied the land before them.

Ramos shrugged. "Politicians lie. It is what they do." That answer seemed to make the man happy, but what Ramos said next didn't. "But this one, he is new to politics. He has no history as a politician. But he has a very long history of building things."

The coyote growled low in his throat. This tough talk about immigration was already cutting into his business. Actual construction of a "wall", even if it ended up being just a fence, would do so even more. Fences could be climbed, walls could be breached, but just knowing they were there would discourage a lot of people looking to come north.

Ramos used the binoculars to check on the progress of

the men on the other side, then glanced at the watch he'd chosen for this job. It was a cheap watch, but durable, as were the jeans and plaid shirt and Nikes he was wearing. He'd bought them all at a secondhand store and had nothing in his pockets but a hundred dollars in American money, a folding knife, and a small compass.

"You said wait ten minutes?"

"It is a guess, but yes," the man said.

After ten minutes all but one of the men on the American side was out of sight, and he was just a faint moving smudge on a distant hillside. Ramos had seen no spotter aircraft, no vehicles or ATVs or dust trails which could be the result of speeding Border Patrol vehicles. If they did somehow become aware of men crossing the border at this point, they would first go after those five men. They were the distraction, the decoys, and none of the men was so stupid as to not realize that. Which is why they'd been paid for the crossing. That, however, was all they knew. Ramos handed the binoculars back to the guide. "If you see a vehicle and I'm still within earshot, whistle and wave," he told the coyote again.

"*Si, Señor*," the man said nervously, bobbing his head like a bird.

Ramos finished the water bottle at his feet, then strode down the slope to the river. The grass on the banks was thick and brushed against his jeans as he headed toward the water. The river was noisy, and he looked back for the coyote just in case the man was whistling and he couldn't hear it, but the man was standing there unperturbed, the binoculars to his eyes.

The water was colder than he was expecting, and faster. He knew how to swim...but it had been years, and he panicked a little when he kicked off the bottom and felt himself being swept downstream. He began working his arms, stroking hard, and in just a short while he was touching the bottom on the far side.

Wet clothes and shoes were an annoyance, but a temporary one. He walked up to the top of the nearest ridge and looked around. He didn't see anything moving on the American side. Behind him the coyote was still there on the small hill, not waving or gesturing at all. Ramos pulled the compass out of his pocket, took a rough bearing, marked a spot on a distant ridge, and began jogging.

The dirt road was roughly three kilometers from the river. And probably used more by the Border Patrol than anyone else, if he had to guess. There was no sign of human life anywhere between the river and the road, unless barbed wire fences counted.

By the time he reached the road his shirt was totally dry, his jeans nearly so. His socks, however, were still wet. He stopped on the shoulder of the road, panting lightly, and looked left and right. Nothing in sight. He'd checked his compass heading several times, so he knew he was roughly in the right spot. He turned left and began walking northwest on the dirt road. He hadn't been running as much as he should lately, but still a three-kilometer jog, even one cross country, was nothing.

Five minutes later he saw the plume of dust in the distance. He stopped and waited. If it was the Border Patrol there was nothing to be done, and he couldn't run far enough or fast enough. He had no ID, and had committed no crime other than the illegal crossing. They would perhaps take his photo and fingerprints, run whatever name he gave them, and check to see if he had a record. He did not, not in America—and none of the men he'd chosen did. That was his main criteria for picking them, that and fluency in English. That was why he'd been chosen as well. The worst that would happen to any of them is that they'd be held for a short period of time before being sent back.

The vehicle under the tail of dust was gradually revealed to be a small green station wagon, far from new. It slowed down as it neared him, and the dust plume passed it by, then the driver did a U-turn. Ramos walked up to the passenger door and bent down to peer inside the open window.

"Sir," Gabaldon said to him with a nod.

"Gabby." Ramos got into the car and Gabaldon started driving back the way he'd come. "Were you able to get the IDs?" he asked as he put on the seatbelt. Their previous document forger in the area had recently been arrested by the FBI, and the new one had not yet proved himself.

"In there." Gabby pointed at the glove compartment. Ramos opened it and pulled out the cards and papers inside. "They are not perfect, to my eye, but very good. They should get us clear if we get pulled over by *La Migra*."

The ID card and paperwork would do. The only issue was the name on them. "Ruben Hernandez?" Ramos said, looking at his new identification.

"Yes? Is there a problem?"

"Do I look like a Ruben to you? Do I look like I should be pinching the bottoms of chubby young boys and watching *telenovelas*?"

His young lieutenant glanced at him, saw the look on his commander's face, and snorted. Apparently Ramos was in a good mood after successfully crossing the border. "No sir. But…what about Ruben Blades?"

Ramos waved his hand dismissively. "One exception." He peered out the windshield at the dirt road disappearing into the distance. "How long of a drive?"

"At least two hours to the safe house in El Paso, probably closer to three. And there is a good chance we will be stopped by *La Migra* before we get there."

"How far is it from El Paso to Phoenix?"

"Over six hours. The safe house there is set up as well."

"And how many have made it?" Ramos asked.

"Eight, before I left to pick you up. How many do we…?"

"At least a dozen. But it is still early, and some might have been delayed for reasons other than being stopped by the Border Patrol." He clapped his lieutenant on the shoulder. The young man looked worried. "Do not fret. The men are resourceful, and we have plenty of time. That is why we are crossing so early, so everything is in place when it is time to act."

Osterman looked up at the knock on his door jamb. Maria Flores was there with a curious expression on her face. "Sir? Do you have a few minutes?"

"Absolutely."

"Can you walk with me to the interrogation room? I've got something to show you."

Osterman stood up. "I see the witness in here earlier?"

"Yes, and that's what I wanted to talk to you about." They walked down the hallway side by side. She and her partner had been giving the Sheriff updates on the case several times a week, although lately there hadn't been much to report. "Muñiz and his thugs have been refusing to talk to anyone," Flores said. "As you know. Or rather their lawyer Condelle has been refusing on their behalf. But everyone has tried. DEA, Department of Justice, FBI. Offering deals if they'll talk." She caught Osterman's sharp look and she held up a hand. "It's all smoke and mirrors, don't worry. They know they have no legal position to offer any deals until we're done with the suspects, but they've been throwing everything out there, just to see if they can get Muñiz or his goons to blink. *Nada*. Both the DEA and the Department of Justice have also talked to our witness. Interviews done here. We gave both organizations access to full copies of the witness' statement, and it is a full and complete statement, but they still felt it their duty to ask all the same questions I did about what she saw and heard."

Osterman grunted. It was nothing that he hadn't expected. They reached the hallway where the two interrogation rooms were and Flores led Osterman into the observation room, where all the recording equipment was situated. Her partner, Norm Hill, was leaning against the wall, making the room feel even smaller.

"Sheriff," he said with a nod. He had the same look on his face as Flores, both curious and confused.

Flores told the Sheriff, "She hasn't remembered anything new, and nothing in her story has changed."

"Who wanted to interview her today?" Osterman asked his detective.

Flores smiled. "That's the interesting thing. Special Agent Joe Clark, DHS."

"Department of Homeland Security? Federal or state?" Arizona had their own state-run Department of Homeland Security. When your state shares a border with a foreign country, sometimes a little initiative is called for.

"Federal."

"He with ICE? Or Border Patrol?"

"He contacted me from the Phoenix office over on North Central Ave. And I called him back there through their switchboard. He only ever identified himself as being with DHS. And I verified his credentials."

"Hmm." The Department of Homeland Security was an umbrella organization formed after 9-11, designed to ensure cooperation of several existing federal law enforcement agencies. While DHS had their own credentialed agents, most of the badge carriers working under the aegis of DHS were employed by other federal agencies, usually ICE or Customs and Border Protection.

"He's who just left," Flores told him.

"He only talked with her about ten minutes," Norm Hill said. "Most of it was rehashing her statement, seeing if she remembered anything else. Nothing special there, although you might have to take Flores' word for it." He nodded at his partner, then cued up the video of the interview on the computer.

Osterman saw DHS Special Agent Joe Clark was slender and blonde, dressed in a bland gray suit with a dark blue tie. He looked about thirty-five and very Ivy League, as if he'd spent a lot of time in his youth playing lacrosse. Clark was sitting across the table from their witness, whom Osterman was happy to see looked in excellent health. Reina Isabella Martín had proven quite resilient, and the physical signs of her abuse had all but faded from her skin. Clark was smiling, and the witness seemed relaxed. Flores was just visible at the edge of the frame, leaning against a wall. Hill clicked Play, and Osterman blinked as the video ran. After about a minute the Sheriff stepped forward and paused it.

"Okay, wow," Osterman said, scratching his head. His Spanish was decent and still he'd barely been able to follow the conversation.

"Yeah," Norm Hill said drily.

Flores said, "He's not just fluent as a native, he's speaking with an accent. A *Chilango* or *Defeño* accent, which you hear around Mexico City. Most of the Spanish we hear is variations of *Norteño*, the northern dialect."

"Impressive," Osterman observed. "And...interesting."

"Considering he looks as whitebread as me?" Hill said. "Yep."

Flores glanced at her partner, then back at the Sheriff. "Isn't it though. Hit Play again, and watch this next part, it's why you're here. You should be able to follow it."

Osterman used the mouse to click Play. Clark was overly friendly and grateful. "I very much appreciate your taking the time to talk to me," Clark said to the witness in smooth Spanish. "Maybe one more question. Or two. Do you ever remember hearing the name Diego Garcia while you were in that house?"

Reina shook her head. "No. I told you, everything I remember is in the statement I gave to the police."

Clark smiled reassuringly. "I understand, but sometimes hearing a word or a name makes something pop into your memory that you didn't remember before. How about the word 'tentpole'?" He used the English word, as well as the Spanish translation, *poste de la tienda*.

"'Tentpole'" she said in accented English, frowning. "No, never."

Flores stepped forward and shut off the video. "And that's the end of the interview. He thanks her, and us, and heads out. After smiling some more at me and refusing to elaborate just what the hell was with his last few questions."

"So what do you make of that?" Hill asked the Sheriff. "Diego Garcia? Isn't that one of our military bases in the Caribbean?"

"Indian Ocean," Osterman corrected him. "But it just as well could be a name, I suppose."

"And 'tentpole'?" Flores asked.

Osterman shook his head. "Don't have a clue. But if I was going to pick a random word that might come up in the conversation between cartel thugs as they're torturing some fellows, tentpole wouldn't be it." His eyebrows thrust together.

"I know that look," Maria Flores told Osterman. "What are you thinking sir?"

Osterman chewed his lip for a bit more, then finally shrugged. "We'll probably never know. But I wouldn't be surprised if Special Agent Joe Clark spelled DHS with three different letters, possibly CIA. And 'tentpole' sure sounds like a codeword to me."

"You thinking one of the guys in the house, maybe one of the dead guys, was undercover? Or, what do the spooks call them, an 'asset'? Maybe an informant?"

The Sheriff shook his head. "As I said, we'll probably never know. But…go check on their bodies. Re-examine their personal effects. And see if anyone interesting or unexpected has signed in down there to examine their corpses."

The detectives exchanged a look. "Yes sir."

Preliminary examinations were cursory things. Usually.

In Michigan, a defendant who is charged with a felony or high court misdemeanor has a right to a preliminary examination. The hearing is held in front of a District Court judge to determine if there is probable cause to believe that a crime occurred, and that the defendant committed the crime. It didn't establish guilt or innocence, but rather whether or not the probable cause was sufficient to warrant a trial.

The defendant and the prosecution both have the right to waive the preliminary exam. The defense often took the opportunity to ask the judge that the charges be thrown out for lack of evidence, but that almost never happened. Still, it didn't hurt to ask…

The preliminary exam for the huge retail fraud case Detective Billy Dixon was a part of was two days away, and he was reviewing all of his paperwork in case he was called to testify in front of the judge.

Retail fraud—Michigan's term for shoplifting. This wasn't teenagers stealing condoms, though, this case was huge. So far twenty people had been arrested in this shoplifting ring, and the amount of stolen merchandise in the warehouse in Highland Park was staggering. Its initial estimated value was over a million dollars. Detectives from five Detroit suburbs were involved. Dixon, on behalf of West Bloomfield, had one of the smaller pieces of the evidentiary pie. As a result he doubted he'd even be called to the stand in the preliminary exam. He honestly would have been surprised if any of the detectives were called to testify, but better to be prepared than to embarrass yourself.

"You working your white whale?"

Dixon looked up to see his chief standing in front of his desk. Steve DeKerk had started out in uniform, then spent fifteen years as a detective before making Chief. The West Bloomfield Chief of Police was pudgy and pale, his skin even whiter against the dark blue of his suit. He had thick arms and puffy hands that were surprisingly hairy.

Dixon leaned back from his computer screen and rubbed his eyes. "No, but I was planning on talking to you about that."

"Yeah, I heard you pulled in a witness last week." The fact that Paolo Bufonte was the son of a well-known Detroit mobster was only a small factor in the case. No matter who he was, his case was still an unsolved homicide, in a city that didn't have any unsolved homicides. Hell, they had years with no homicides of any sort.

"David Anderson's girlfriend at the time of Bufonte's murder. Brought her in to get a recorded statement." Dixon dug around on his desk until he found a hardcopy of the transcript and handed it to his chief.

"You've talked to her before, right?" The Chief said as he skimmed the statement.

"Yes, but knowing which questions to ask…"

Dixon watched his chief's eyes moving back and forth. He flipped through one page, then another.

"Hmm. Okay. So when he met her, Anderson's girlfriend was working as a stripper at the club that Bufonte was managing. Not exactly a smoking gun."

No, but it is, or rather she is, an actual direct connection between the deceased and Anderson."

"Aren't Anderson's dead parents that?" the Chief said, playing devil's advocate. The blood drawn after the accident showed Paolo "Big Paulie" Bufonte had a blood alcohol level nearly three times the legal limit. However, he hadn't been arrested for drunk driving but rather being belligerent to the responding officers. It was only at the hospital, where he was being treated for a minor cut, that a nurse smelled the alcohol on him and took some blood. The lack of consent by Bufonte and lack of a warrant by the police department had enabled Bufonte's lawyer to get the blood test results quashed. The lawyer had called expert witness after expert witness to the stand to discuss the slippery roads and traffic patterns and do whatever they could to muddy the waters, with the end result Bufonte pleading guilty to reckless driving and having his license suspended for six months. After killing two people while driving drunk.

Dixon made a face. "I mean after Bufonte got off on his bullshit technicalities. This is the first time we have anything linking Anderson to him directly, after his parents' deaths."

His chief shrugged. "Could be a coincidence," he said, still playing devil's advocate.

"You know what they say about coincidences."

"Yeah, they take a lot of planning. You know, from the transcript," his Chief looked up from the document, "...it sounds as if you might have had some of this information already."

Dixon nodded, not denying it. "Yeah. And I was trying to work it, but I got nowhere. So I got a recorded statement from her. I'm hoping that's enough to do some more digging. Get a few warrants."

"For what?"

"Her phone records, for one thing. From the time she met Anderson until right now. She says she hasn't seen him or talked to him in over a year, but I don't know if I buy that. She claims she doesn't know anything, but I don't know if I buy that either. Who knows what she might have written in a text last month, last year, three years ago."

"You ran his cell phone already, correct?"

"Back when this all started. But not hers. Maybe he had another cell phone we didn't know about, a burner—transcripts of her texts would tell us that. Remember, he lawyered up immediately, and never would sit down for an interview with us. He only had one friend that I could find, and he told me to fuck off. I think Anderson told the girlfriend not to talk to us either, because she wouldn't come in. The only reason I got this information out of her now is because she thought I was working that big gunfight he was involved in, not his parents' murder. I want her phone records, and I'd like to take another run at his old partner at the armored car company."

The Chief rubbed his chin. "You've still got nothing on him but knowing a stripper who worked for the deceased." He cocked his head. "And motive. A big damn motive, Paulie killed his parents and got away with it."

"I know. But...I think he did it. Pietro Bufonte thinks he did it, look how many times he's tried to kill the kid." Dixon paused. "Allegedly."

"Allegedly. Right." The Chief rolled his eyes.

"Heck, even the FBI is acting like they think he killed Big Paulie, but they don't seem to care, all they're after is the big man himself. And maybe Paulie deserved to get run over twice, if not for Anderson's parents then something else we don't know about, and hit-and-runs are not specifically FBI jurisdiction. But still."

"Do we know where Anderson is now? Didn't you say he's in the wind?"

"Right. I'm hoping pulling these records might turn over the rock he's hiding under."

The Chief handed Dixon back the transcript and pulled at his belt absently. "Well, I'd hate to retire with an unsolved homicide still on the books. I think you've got enough for a warrant on the girlfriend's phone records going back to when they met, but that's up to the judge. And if you want to take another run at the partner I don't see an issue. But I don't see that you've got a whole lot to work with. It'll be a big fishing expedition." He paused. "The partner been cooperative when you've talked to him?"

Dixon snorted. "Fuck no. But maybe I can yank his chain hard enough to shake something loose."

Chapter Nine

He found himself on his feet next to the bed, gun in hand, before he was even fully awake. He didn't question why or doubt his body's reaction. He just waited, fingers tight around the Glock.

Dave stood there silently, tense, listening to every sound, every creak of the trailer, every wisp of wind past the windows. He didn't move, didn't do more than cock his head for the first five minutes. He never shifted his feet, even tried to breathe shallowly so there was absolutely no sound coming from him. Had he heard a noise? Was his jumping out of bed a reaction from a nightmare? He couldn't remember if he'd been dreaming. Best to assume something, some strange sound, had woken him up.

The bedroom was dark and cool. The yard outside was lit up with starlight and a sliver of moon, but nothing was moving. He heard the howl of an animal far away, and the faint clicking of insects. The cold air moved in vague currents around his legs, and he felt goosebumps rise, but he muscled back a shiver through force of will.

After what he guessed was ten minutes, standing there silently without moving a muscle, the Glock down along his thigh, Dave relaxed. The idea was to outwait any potential intruders, but after ten minutes of no sound or movement from him, if there had been anyone already in the trailer they would have made some kind of sound, however slight. Still, he proceeded to clear the rest of the trailer slow and quietly, Glock up in two hands, tritium inserts in the sights glowing bright green in the darkness.

All alone.

Back in the bedroom he glanced at the clock and saw it was 2:43. Way too early to be up, but there was no way he'd be able to get back to sleep. So, as he'd done every other time he'd woken up in the middle of the night—and it happened at least once a week, although he didn't always find himself standing there gun already in hand—he put on his running clothes, stretched, and went for a run.

He loved running at night—the stars, the quiet, the feeling that you were the only person awake for miles around. The stars were beautiful. He didn't see a single car. He did his normal six miles, and it felt like nothing.

Back at the trailer it still wasn't even 4 a.m., so he wasn't about to pull out the shot timer and get it beeping as he practiced his draw. Instead, he sat down in front of his laptop and pulled up Netflix. No headphones or earbuds—you couldn't hear shit with those on, somebody could be sneaking up behind you with a running chainsaw and you'd be none the wiser. Even though the speaker on the laptop wasn't the greatest, it would have to do. He turned the volume down low, so it didn't carry outside of his bedroom.

While he still hadn't finished *Person of Interest*, and it was getting intense, he wasn't in the mood for intense, so he pulled up *Supernatural* and watched a few episodes as he munched on energy bars and drank a couple glasses of water.

By the time dawn rolled around he was burned out on watching videos and antsy, as if he hadn't already gotten a run in. He stared at his laptop for a few seconds, sighed, then went to his Bookmarks.

One, maybe two days a week Dave's chest workout was just thirty pushups. But they were the hardest thirty pushups he'd ever done in a simple but brutally tough chest workout called the "Bring Sally Up Pushup Challenge".

He'd stumbled across it by accident. He'd gone Googling, trying to discover the name of the song played during the opening credits of the otherwise utterly forgettable *Gone in 60 Seconds* remake with Nicholas Cage and a young Angelina Jolie in bizarre blonde dreadlocks. The song had a great beat, with the same lyrics repeated over and over—"Bring Sally up, bring Sally down".

Turns out the song was called *Flower*, by Moby, but Googling "Bring Sally Up" led him to several YouTube videos touting the Bring Sally Up Pushup Challenge. And it was simple—get into pushup position, and follow the directions in the song. Bring Sally up—push out to full extension. Bring Sally down—lower yourself until your chest was a few inches off the ground. Then hold it, until it was time to push up again. It was hovering just a few inches off the ground that was the killer, and you never got to pause at the top with your arms locked—"bring Sally up" was always immediately followed by "bring Sally down".

He'd counted once, and obeying the lyrics like the commands of a drill sergeant only resulted in doing thirty pushups, but they were spread out over three and a half minutes, and holding yourself two inches off the ground inbetween them was a special kind of torture. He'd been working out steadily for months before he'd been able to make it all the way through the song. He could do it now, but he still was sweating and sometimes shaking by the end of the song.

He eyed the YouTube webpage. After procrastinating for a minute he took a couple of deep breaths, then hit Play and got down on the floor. By the time the fifteen second lead-in had finished he was in position, and went to work to the beat of the music. After the song was over—he remembered liking the song a lot more before he started torturing himself to it—he did a hundred crunches, then put on his plate carrier and did ten chin-ups and fifty squats. The cordura nylon vest by itself weighed less than two pounds, but the ballistic steel plates inserted front and back, rated to stop high-velocity rifle bullets, added about twenty pounds. He alternated between chin-ups and squats until he'd done four sets of each, then pulled the body armor off over his head and took a shower. There were salt stains on the nylon from him sweating, but he wasn't sure if he could (or should) put the vest in the washing machine.

Small purchases added up, so he tried to watch every dime spent, no matter how trivial. So even though there was a gas station close by he tried to limit his snack purchases there to the times when he stopped to fill the Jeep's gas tank. The Jeep wasn't quite on Empty, and he had no plans to go anywhere (P-Dip was tomorrow)...but he had a real hunger for some junk food. And he was still feeling restless. So he bent his rule.

Bouncing down Old Fain Road he had a rabbit dart across the road right in front of him, so quick he didn't even have time to touch the brake. He'd been seeing a lot more rabbits lately. Not just the "regular" rabbits, as he thought of them, but jackrabbits as well.

What he thought of as regular rabbits the locals called cottontails. He'd seen as many or more jackrabbits, and they sure as hell weren't something he'd ever seen in Michigan. First off, they were huge, much bigger than the cottontails. And they were just plain weird, with their long ears and oddly shaped bodies. They looked more like small kangaroos or mutant dogs than bunnies. They seemed to be everywhere.

At first he'd thought it was just the time of year, but he'd heard someone at the Maverik gas station talking about it as well a few weeks earlier. A local guy, likely a farmer from his clothes, Dave had seen him at the station a few times before. As a lot of the locals did he wore a pistol openly on his hip, in his case a dusty Smith & Wesson auto in a monogrammed leather holster. He also had skin that resembled old leather, brown and lined.

"Is it the weather?" Dave had asked him.

The man, in a work shirt and a sweat-stained and battered ball cap, shook his head. "No, winter wasn't anything special. It's the predators, coyotes and javelinas. If the rabbit populations are up, predator population must be down. Everything goes in cycles. Two, three years, you won't see a damn rabbit all season."

Dave nodded knowingly. When he got back to his house he looked up "javelina" online, although it took him a few attempts to spell it right since the j was pronounced as an h. Arizona had small wild pigs roaming the countryside? Who knew?

The Maverik was at the corner of State Route 69 where Fain Road dead-ended into the entrance to the Prescott Country Club. There were condos all around the golf course, in tight rows down the curving streets and all of them nearly identical. Like they'd been planted and grown from seeds.

Dave parked at the pump and went inside to pay with cash. He had a debit/credit card in Jack's name, tied to a checking account, but only used it for emergencies. Just inside the front door he had to step aside for two girls, presumably sisters. The older one was maybe eight and had a roller skate on one foot and a flip-flop on the other. With every step she did a shuffle-roll-hop as she held her little sister's hand. Dave smiled as he watched them head out the door, wondering just what the story was there. He stared after them for a while. The fact that he'd never know the why or how she'd ended up in just one roller skate, that when she was older she'd probably forget the incident entirely and it would get lost to time, made it both beautiful and sad. What the hell was that line at the end of *Blade Runner*? "All these memories will be lost in time, like tears in the rain." Something like that.

He bought a Diet Coke, a Snickers, and a Tabasco Slim Jim and handed the clerk a twenty. "Put what's left on pump four," he told her.

The clerk was very pale and a little pudgy, with black lipstick and a nose ring. She looked down at the Tabasco Slim Jim, then glanced up at him. "So you're getting gas for your car…and yourself?"

Dave snorted. "Nice."

Pulling down his street he saw the nurse was back at Lori's house. Used to be the nurse only came by once or twice a week, but the past few weeks she seemed to be there more often than not. He knew what that meant.

Dave had taken off his work shirt to reveal the Glock and was just about to turn on his iTunes playlist for the start of his daily practice session when he heard the knock. He doublechecked through the spy hole in the door before opening it even though he knew it was probably Lori.

"Hey," he said. She was in a tank top and shorts and looked frazzled.

"Hey," she said, and walked past him into the house, not even glancing at the gun on his hip. By the time he got the door closed and locked she had the tank top off and was heading into the bedroom without a look back. Dave shook his head and followed after her.

"Your mom have insurance?" he asked her not quite an hour later, as they lay side by side taking a break. "A visiting nurse can't be cheap."

"She's not a full RN, she's a home health care aide or something like that. CNA, Certified Nursing Assistant? But yeah, you're right, she's not cheap." Lori brushed her sweaty hair out of her face. "Luckily my mom's insurance covers her. Covers just about everything. I've got a lot of money saved up from when I was working, but we'd be just about through it by now if I'd had to pay for her medical care."

Dave opened his mouth, then closed it. He wasn't sure if asking more about her mother was the appropriate thing to do...after all, he was pretty sure she was coming over to his place to forget about all those troubles.

She waited for him to say something else, but when he didn't she wasn't surprised. "You know, you're going to give me a complex," she told him. "I'm initiating every time. Sure you're not gay, and just doing this out of pity?" It had been almost a month since that first time, and he had yet to even knock on her door or call her on the phone. After she'd made a point of giving him her phone number. Every time, it had been her knocking on his door.

He looked over and saw her smiling. "Yeah, I'm totally gay." He eyed her naked body, just because he could. He sighed and gave a little shake of his head. "I figured you were sick and tired of guys coming on to you anyway, so I deliberately kept my distance. Maybe more than I might have, otherwise."

She frowned. "What do you mean?"

He looked at her. "I'm a twenty-eight-year-old single heterosexual male with high speed internet access. What do you think the chances are that I wouldn't recognize you?"

She seemed stunned by his answer. Her mouth opened and closed a few times, and he could almost see the thoughts racing through her head. Finally she said, "I honestly don't know. I don't go online and search for me. When'd you know?"

"The first time I saw you I thought you looked vaguely familiar. About the third time it finally clicked."

She sat up. "And you never said anything? Most guys would've been hanging around, trying to accidentally run into me. Maybe following me. Telling all their friends about the porn star who lives next door. I can't get you to even fucking call or walk ten feet and knock on the Goddamn door."

He gave a little shrug. "I guess I'm not most guys."

Yeah, no shit, she thought, but didn't say it out loud. So he knew. She'd been wondering when to tell him. If she should tell him. It wasn't as if they were even dating, not really, but she knew he'd want to know. Well, a normal guy would want to know.

"I will admit to some performance anxiety, though, that first time," he said.

Her eyebrows crawled up her forehead. "When you went for three hours?" She'd been sore for days afterward… but it had been a good sore. Every time she got a twinge afterward it made her think of him, and the sex, and forget about her mom's troubles. At least for a little while. That was why she kept coming back. Plus, the sex was great, and it had been way too long. And he wasn't an asshole; hidden deep down behind the scars and silence was a nice guy.

"I didn't want to disappoint. I know how stressed out you are about your mom. And I figured you…" he tried to figure out how to word it, "…had high standards," he finished. She'd been on the "A-List" of porn actresses for most of her career. Honestly, he was surprised it had taken him so long to recognize her. Maybe it was because she'd been so out of context. And wearing normal clothes. Wearing clothes, period.

She shook her head. He'd known…and said nothing. Given no indication he'd known. Treated her normally. How many guys would do the same? Shit, she didn't know any. "Wow. You are something different."

"You quit to take care of your mom? I know you're not still working, you barely leave the house. You make me look sociable."

"Yeah. I told you that first time it had been two years for me, and I wasn't lying." Lori frowned as she remembered. "She called me and told me. At first I thought she was joking. Cruel joke, but we hadn't been close for a long time. When I got off the phone I cried for an hour. Next day I put my condo up for sale and drove down to be with her. And haven't left. Had my stuff shipped down and put in a storage locker. It's been horrible, but…it's also been the best time we've ever spent together. We even went to Disney together earlier this year, before she got too sick. Expensive as hell…and worth every penny. When I was in high school we fought every day until I moved out, and I barely talked to her. Now we talk all the time, about all sorts of things. We're both older now, and wiser, I guess. At least I am. And fucking cancer…it makes all the little stuff seem unimportant."

"The little stuff is unimportant, and most everything is little stuff," he told her.

She eyed his gunshot wounds. She supposed getting shot tended to reorient your lifeview as much as a parent getting cancer did. She'd already known he was good at keeping his mouth shut, so it shouldn't surprise her that he'd known who she was and just didn't say anything. "Yeah, I guess you're right." She rubbed a thumb over the bullet scar on his leg, then eyed the one on his arm. "What's the other guy look like?"

His face grew dark. "They're all dead," he said brusquely. "You want something to drink? I've got water and Diet Coke in the fridge." He was off the bed quickly.

Okay, touchy subject, probably should have guessed that, she thought. Still, 'they're *all* dead'? He didn't say it as if he was bragging, he still sounded pissed about it. As if he was upset they could only die once. "Yeah, a Diet."

She watched him walk away and come back. He looked just as good naked as anybody she'd ever worked with, and he didn't have psychological issues. Well, other than burying a lot of anger, but it wasn't anger at women. He wasn't a misogynist like so many guys who were in porn, didn't have the fragile ego of a model, didn't do drugs. Maybe she'd just spent too much time in porn, or in California, and had forgotten what a normal guy was like. Although…was he normal? Alias, bullet wounds, anger issues? Probably not. But compared to some of the guys she'd dated…

"What time do you have to get back?" he asked her, getting back on the bed. "You want to watch Netflix or something?"

"Seriously? That's all we're going to talk about the porn thing?"

"You want me to ask you questions? I can ask questions, if you want."

She looked at him. In many ways he was just a blank wall. It wasn't just anger, it was sadness too she saw. "No, it's just...like you're hiding in a cave. Wow."

"I've got questions, I just figured it was none of my business."

As he said it she realized she felt the same way about him. She didn't know exactly who he was, only that he was involved with—or used to be involved with—some serious things. What did she really know about him? He was using a fake name, worked out a lot, carried a gun, had a lot of scars, and was friends with the Sheriff. Except for the last part that would make him a bad guy to be avoided. He wasn't a bad guy, she'd spent enough time with him to know that, but just exactly who and what he was...was still pretty damn vague. And she realized she didn't care about the details. She liked him. She liked him even more now, knowing that he knew about her background and didn't care.

"I've never been with anyone who did porn before," Dave elaborated, "but I dated a stripper for years, so I'm not exactly coming into this all wide-eyed and innocent. I know I'm stress release for you as much as anything else, and I'm guessing you've had enough of guys asking you stupid personal shit."

"Not lately. Nobody's recognized me in months. At least that they've come up to me and said something." When was the last time? Maybe that guy at Disney, who was with his kids and wife. He didn't say anything to her, but he did a comical doubletake and nearly walked into a Mickey garbage can. "In L.A. it was every day, and I had a lot of stalkers. I am fat now, I guess I look different. And I dress like a slob. Not that I wore latex and four-inch heels much off-camera, but I haven't dressed up in forever." She still had all the outfits and underwear. Somewhere. Probably in one of those boxes in the storage unit, with a lot of her more exotic toys. She doubted much of it would fit, she hadn't worked out in a year.

"You're not fat, Christ. You've just got more curves now than when you were working. From your muscle tone back then I'm guessing you did aerobics or whatever a lot. But it looks good on you. Your boobs are a lot bigger. I think. In person's different than watching a movie."

She looked at him. "Yeah? How much of my stuff have you watched?"

He shook his head, smiling, and pointed toward her house. "I'm surprised you couldn't hear it, you can hear everything else I'm doing in here apparently. You can probably hear when I flush the toilet."

She smiled. Since all the cards were being put on the table... "I'm surprised you couldn't hear me over there a lot of the times you were practicing your draw."

He frowned in confusion. "Hear you doing what? Flushing the toilet?"

She moved her hand between her legs and rubbed a little with her fingertips. It took him a second, then Dave's eyes went wide. "What? While watching me practice my draw?"

"Damn straight. It's hot." Handsome badass working a gun? Hell yeah, she got wet watching him once she figured out he wasn't crazy or dangerous, and it was only a small step from that to taking care of business while he put on a show.

He blinked rapidly. "How long have you been doing that?" His voice crept up an octave. Her in her bedroom watching him practice his draw was one thing, but he was having a hard time wrapping his head around *that*.

Lori smiled. "Six, eight months."

"Jesus." He thought about it for a while, then laughed. "I guess we're even then." He took a drink of the soda. "I'm going to have to close those damn blinds if I ever want to get a good practice in now. Otherwise I'll be thinking of you over there, doing that, and forget to unload my gun and shoot a hole in the wall. Or myself."

She smiled, and took another sip from the can. "You up for round two? Now that it's all out in the open we can relax and have some fun."

"Weren't we already?" He saw the look on her face, and he jabbed a finger at her. "See, dammit, that's what I was talking about when I mentioned performance anxiety." He was only half joking, and her giggling didn't help.

"I just mean you've been great so far, especially considering how long the dry spell was for the both of us. But I've been on my best behavior, trying to act like the girl next door. But I'm not and you know it. And now I know you know." She gave him a pointed look. "I'm in the mood for something that isn't so vanilla. Unless you have an objection?"

She considered what they'd done so far vanilla? Holy shit. He raised his hands in surrender. "You're the professional."

"Very funny."

Chapter Ten

The knock on the front door came just as Aaron sat down on the couch with dinner. Peanut jumped up, barking. Aaron looked at Arlene, but she just shrugged.

Cursing, he put his plate down on the side table and stomped to the door, Peanut bouncing along in his wake, tail wagging fiercely. He peeked through the window, cursed again, and opened the door.

"Mr. Abruzzo? Detective Billy Dixon." Dixon eyeballed him. Still the same porn 'stache, still the same big gun on his hip. It had been two years since he'd talked to the guy, and it was as if no time had passed at all.

"I know who you are. I remember you."

Dixon smiled. "I've got a few questions. Hope I can come inside and talk to you, just take a few minutes of your time."

"Did I win the lottery?"

"What?"

"If you're here to escort me to Lansing to pick up a big

pile of cash, fine, but if you're here to ask me more questions about Davey I ain't sayin' shit."

"You mean Dave Anderson?"

"Yeah I mean Dave Anderson. He's why you're here, isn't it? What the hell else do I have to do with West Bloomfield? You puttin' in a trailer park there, lookin' for people to move?"

Dixon smiled. "Have you spoken to Mr. Anderson recently?"

Aaron opened his mouth to respond, then shut it and stared at the detective for a few moments. "How many years has it been? What, like five fucking years, and you're still trying to pin that thing on him."

"It's an unsolved homicide Mr. Abruzzo." He raised his voice, letting it carry. "A murder. A man was brutally killed. Run over repeatedly. You sure you want to discuss this with me out here?"

"What do I care, my neighbors already hate me. Yeah it was a murder. Of a fucking fat douchebag. Who ran over Dave's parents, and got off cuz of some bullshit loophole, but he was in the fucking mob, too. Maybe you should look at those guys instead of trying to pin it on Dave. Five years. If you had any evidence Dave'd be in jail, right? But he's not, because you don't have shit. Fuckin' leave him alone already."

"Are you in contact with Anderson?"

Aaron scowled at the detective. "Five years and you still haven't solved it? Maybe detective isn't the right job for you in law enforcement. Maybe you should look into becoming a conservation officer, it seems more your speed."

Dixon blinked. "Excuse me?"

"Possum cop," Aaron said helpfully. "Grouper trouper. Tree police?"

Dixon fought back his temper. "Do you know Anderson's girlfriend? Former girlfriend, apparently, since she hasn't talked to him in over a year. Gina?"

"Yeah?"

"I just had a very interesting conversation with her."

"Yeah, I bet. She's got great tits, and they're right at eye level for you."

Dixon ignored the short joke. "Did you know that she was working at the same club as Paolo Bufonte when she met Anderson?"

"What?"

"She was an exotic dancer—still is—and the club where she was working, when she met Dave Anderson, Bufonte was the club manager."

Aaron didn't say anything for a second. "Yeah, and?"

"Don't you think that's suspicious?"

Aaron made a face. "There are only so many strip clubs in Detroit, and God knows how many of them are run by the mob."

Dixon shrugged. "Well, that was only one of the very interesting things she told us in her statement. I was just curious as to whether or not you were aware of it, seeing as you were working with Anderson when he was dating her, correct? He ever talk about how they met?"

Aaron stood there for a second. Finally he looked back at the detective. "Thanks for coming by, but I'm pretty sure this is the part where I tell you to fuck off and leave my friend alone." His face split in a wide fake smile, and he slammed the door.

"That guy's just a dick," Arlene said as Aaron retrieved his now lukewarm dinner. She'd heard the whole conversation.

Aaron sat back down on the couch with the plate on his lap. Jeopardy was just coming on. "Five fucking years," he said to her, shaking his head. Were they ever going to let it go?

She sat down next to him. "So she was working there when Dave met her. So what? Could she know anything?" She nodded toward the door. "He said she said a bunch of things. What would Dave have told her? Would he have told her anything?"

"No," Aaron said, staring at the TV but not seeing it. "I don't think so." He sat and thought. "Shit, I don't know."

Arlene didn't say anything, just watched her boyfriend as he sat there. After a minute he cursed and pulled out his phone. Not one of the burner phones. She couldn't see who he was calling, only that it was a stored number.

"Yeah," Aaron said into the phone. "You got time to meet, maybe tomorrow? It's about our mutual friend." He listened for a while. "See you there."

Ramos got out of the dusty green station wagon. He shrugged his shoulders, trying to loosen them. He still carried some muscle, leftover from his younger years when he was with *El Policía Federal*, what everybody on both sides of the border called the *federales*, but it had been far too long since he'd had a regular workout schedule. "Which house is it?" he asked Gabby in English. They only spoke in English now, it helped them watch their words and drew slightly less attention than speaking Spanish. Slightly. Hearing Spanish spoken in Arizona, anywhere in the state, was as unusual as snow in Alaska.

Gabaldon nodded at the tan house in front of them and

the two men walked to the curb. The house was one story, and small, with no garage. There was a short driveway and a carport in-between the house and its neighbor, a nearly identical small house clad in pastel green siding.

Ramos looked around. There was plenty of parking on the street. The house was half a block down from a major street with constant traffic, and a hundred yards in the other direction was the back end of a hotel. Many more parking spots there.

He blinked, and tried to widen his perspective. He saw the houses, the cars passing on the street, the occasional pedestrian. He had no doubt that there was little to no crime in the area, none of the horrors that were so common south of the border. His much younger self would have been sad that his countrymen knew so little of that peace and security and innocence. His current self just saw the tactical advantage of the situation; their soft life made the Americans weak and unprepared. Easy targets.

"Let's go inside, and show me on a map where we are."

Gabaldon nodded, and Ramos followed him. The early morning air was cool, but already the Arizona sun was hot. The house was well maintained but devoid of furniture. They would have to buy some—chairs, couches, beds—whatever they needed to seem normal in case the landlord came by. Nelson and Ronaldo were inside, and they nodded to him.

Gabaldon spread a map of the city out on the kitchen counter and the four men clustered around it. He had bought the map at a nearby gas station and had spent hours driving around the area the day before, learning the roads. "Here is where we are," he said, pressing a square fingertip against the map. "On Alarcon." He moved his finger to the south. "The Sheriff's Department is less than three blocks away, on Gurley."

"Less than three blocks?"

"It is a big county, but this is the only real city in it, and it is more a small town," Gabby assured him. "We are on the west side of the city, near the old downtown, which is where the tourists go. About two minutes from Prescott Valley, which is about the same size, but newer. Malls and neighborhoods there. Between the two cities they have over a third of the population of the county. This road right here —" his finger moved to E. Sheldon, the busy street half a block away, "it gives us quick access east or west."

"And the other house?"

Gabaldon's finger moved north. "About half a mile on the other side of the police station."

Ramos stared at the map for a while, and the other men waited silently for their commander. Finally Ramos said, "Three blocks is closer than I would like, but I suppose this is not Juarez. And the renting of the houses?"

"Each for six months. Which we can extend."

"I doubt that will be necessary, but good. We will need to get some furniture. Used. You can handle that?"

"Of course."

Ramos went to the front windows and peered out. "All the men made it here from Phoenix?"

"Yes."

So they had fourteen men, including him. All but one had made it over the border without incident. Hopefully that was a sign. The fifteenth would join them when and if he could. Currently he was in the custody of the U.S. Border Patrol, and they might hold him for a while before sending him back. There was no guarantee he'd make it across the border without getting picked up again. "How many vehicles do we have?"

"Three. Although the truck, I do not think it will last long. There is a used car business half a kilometer from here if we need to buy another."

"The tan one?" They'd stayed at the Phoenix safe house for a few days before heading north to Prescott. He'd seen a truck there.

"Yes. I think it threw a rod. Not something Manuel can fix here." Two of the men in the group, Manuel and the small man everyone called Moro, had at one time in their lives worked as auto mechanics. However, they only had access to simple tools, and a thrown rod was not something that could be fixed with a crescent wrench and screwdriver.

"See if you can get it repaired locally for a reasonable amount. It resembles a work or utility truck, which could be useful. And with fourteen of us already here, I am guessing we will need at least one more auto." He turned back to the men. "Half the men here, half at the other house?"

"That's what we were thinking. Diego and David have been staying here. They are currently out buying groceries. Also Raul has been *aqui*, but he and Francisco are out picking up more *armas*. Unless you had another idea?"

"No, that should be good. English, Gabby," he gently reminded the man. "And I will say it again, no one does anything that attracts the attention of the neighbors. No music, no shouting, and as little coming and going as possible. I do not want our numbers obvious."

"Yes sir. I've told the men already, and will tell them again. Ummm...drinking?"

Ramos smiled. "I think if you lived next door to a bunch of Mexicans and they weren't drinking beer, that would be suspicious, no?" The men laughed. "But *cerveza*, beer, no tequila, no hard liquor, and no one is to get drunk, ever. Any drugs and I will send you back home, and failing on an important mission like this...well, we all know what that means." He wasn't worried about any of that, all the men had been picked specifically not just for their skills but for their experience, but it never hurt to remind them where things stood. "We are here to do a job, *comprenden*?" He stopped himself, smiled, and repeated it in English. "Understand?"

"Yes sir."

Ramos looked at one of them. "Ronaldo. What weapons do we have so far?"

Ronaldo was the biggest in the group by far, six-foot-five and blocky with muscle from years of weightlifting. He counted them out on his fingers. "Four handguns. One AR-15 rifle. Five AK-47s. Enough magazines for all the guns we have, and some ammo. Raul and Francisco should be returning with more rifles, but I am not sure how many."

"The guns, they work?"

"They are mostly new. Do you want to look at them?"

Ramos shook his head. "No, I trust you, this is why you are here. But make sure they are not lying around in case the landlord stops by."

"Yes, of course. I will be taking them out and shooting them, making sure they function and hit where they are aimed."

"Where can you do that?"

The man smiled. "There are many local shooting ranges."

Ramos frowned. "Is that wise?"

His man smiled even wider. "I have already been, to look around. They do not even ask for ID, all they care about is the money to use the range. And if we do not get all of the ammunition we need with this last purchase of rifles, I can buy it at the range."

"No identification needed?"

Ronaldo shook his head. "Not for ammunition, not in Arizona. And they do not check the serial numbers on the guns."

Ramos frowned, then nodded. "As you say. Do not take risks."

"If I was Arab I think they would be on the phone to the FBI before I left. However, a Mexican with a gun is no worry here. Everyone has guns. An open gun on the hip is legal, and you do not even need a permit to carry it. I have been seeing them all over town. They all love to think they are cowboys."

Ramos nodded again, then looked at their main technician. Nelson, because of his skills, was the most important to the mission. The mission couldn't start—at least as it had been planned in Michoacan—until he made it across the border, with his electronic toys, no matter how long or how many attempts that took. There'd even been some talk of having him cross legally, with a visa, but Ramos had been against that. There wasn't just this mission to think about, all these men were valuable employees, and the fewer records of their travels the better. Leo with his computer skills was their backup man, but it was Nelson who, more than anyone else, could ensure the success of this mission. And, as an added bonus, he could speak English without trace of an accent. "Have you begun your work?"

"Along with food, Diego and David are buying a few cleaning supplies. A little here, a little there, so as to not attract attention. I gave them a list. Yesterday one of the men went to several hardware stores and bought chemicals, some fertilizer and a bit of wire. Gasoline we can get at any time. No matter what I decide to make, the stove in this kitchen will suffice for a heat source. Construction will take a few hours, if I take my time."

"Please," Ramos said, and the men laughed.

Nelson smiled and went on. "I will be using a cell phone trigger, and Gabaldon bought several phones at a gas station. But it will be very safe, have no worries."

"I trust your skills, that is why you are here. We have a simple plan, but we need several things before this can happen," Ramos told all of them, but looked pointedly at Nelson. "Location information on the target being the first. Current information, it would not surprise me if they move her."

Nelson told him, "Leo has been working on his laptop, trying to break into the police computer system. Even if he succeeds there is no guarantee the information we need will be there."

Ramos knew of the friendly rivalry there. "You are betting on your phone idea?" Ramos said. Nelson nodded. "How are you going to find him, get close enough to him to clone his phone?"

"As you said, this isn't Juarez. From what I've read he shouldn't be too hard to find, he's on TV and doing interviews all the time. He's a Hollywood Sheriff. I don't even think he has a bodyguard."

"Well, that will make things easier down the road. But we have no way of knowing if this will work, or if it does that it will get us the information we need. It could take days or months...and the longer it takes, the greater chance of something going wrong, of our being discovered. So this is your priority. The diversions are a good idea, and we have been instructed to send a very strong message, but there is no reason for diversions if we can't find the target of the mission. Everything at the proper time. Ask for any help you need."

"What if she is at the jail?" Gabaldon asked. "What if they are keeping her safe there, or inside the police station? Our source was able to tell us that she is with the county sheriffs instead of the American federal agents, but that is all."

"We have no one in this police force taking bribes who can tell us where she is?" Ronaldo asked.

Ramos shook his head. "No. In Phoenix or Tucson this would be much easier, yes? But here? No, we have no one. If she is at the jail, we will have to wait months, until the trial. But I don't think she's there. Nobody sleeps at the police station, and they would not put her in the jail with the criminals."

"She is an illegal," Ronaldo pointed out.

"They don't care about that," Gabaldon told him.

Ramos looked at the men. "By the time Nelson gets this cloned phone he is dreaming of, everyone should know where the police station is, the jail, the courthouse where the trial will be held, access points and escape routes. We all need to learn the area. We are not tourists, and we are not on vacation. I will be going over to the other house tomorrow, and tell those men the same thing." He grabbed the map, then looked at Gabby. "Let me study this for a while, then we can drive around. I need to see this city for myself."

The National Coney Island restaurant was on Van Dyke Avenue directly across from the General Motors Tech Center, which occupied more than a square mile in the center of Warren, Michigan. Over twenty thousand people worked at the facility which was situated just four miles from the Detroit city limits. In true capitalistic fashion the east side of Van Dyke opposite the Tech Center was lined with restaurants, and those restaurants were usually packed at lunch time by the white-collar workers employed at the giant GM facility.

John Phault sipped at his cup of coffee and watched the dozen or so waitresses in their logo'd t-shirts, black slacks, and utilitarian polyester aprons whir through the busy lunchtime crowd like bees, stopping to pollinate tables with food and drink before disappearing once more into the hive behind the counter.

He guessed half the customers were from the GM Tech Center; the rest came from the nearby Warren City Hall and the various banks and other businesses lining Van Dyke. In his polo shirt and khakis he was dressed like half the men in the place, which was intentional.

"You need that topped off, hon?" His waitress was stout and dark-haired and looked like she'd been waiting tables since Nixon was in office. Probably could do the job in her sleep.

"Not quite yet," Phault told her. He had the right proportions of half-and-half and Splenda in his ceramic coffee mug, and a top-off would just ruin it.

She nodded and was off, a busy bee with other tables to pollinate. Across the aisle a skinny young waitress with obviously a lot less experience was taking the orders of four guys in a booth. From their badges clipped to belts he saw they were from the Tech Center.

"This place is hopping," Aaron observed, sliding into the vinyl booth across from Phault. The seats were red vinyl, the booths barely big enough for two people on each side. There was a lot of neon on display inside the restaurant, giving it a slightly retro feel.

"I'm surprised you're not out slinging cash, middle of the day like this," Phault said to him. He hadn't seen Abruzzo in at least a year and a half, maybe more, and the guy looked just the same. Wearing a black button-down work shirt untucked to cover the big gun not-so-concealed at his waist.

"I'm surprised you're not out sneaking and peeking," Aaron responded.

"I am," Phault responded, taking another sip of his coffee.

Aaron's eyebrows went up. "Really. You're working right now?" At Phault's tiny nod Aaron looked around the restaurant. "Who's the douche?" He flipped over the ceramic coffee cup in front of him.

"One of the waitresses," Phault told him. "Got a lawsuit going against her former employer, alleging knee and ankle injuries that restrict her ability to work."

"Coffee?" Phault's waitress was back, and eyeing Aaron's now-upright cup.

"You got it. And two Coneys."

"With everything?" she asked, filling his cup. Everything on a Michigan-style Coney dog meant chili, onions, and yellow mustard.

"Yeah."

"Coming right up." And she was gone just as quickly.

"Her?" Aaron asked, tilting his head in the direction of their departed waitress.

"No. Younger one, working some nearby booths."

Aaron nodded, then eyeballed the PI. Phault had a backpack on the seat next to him in the booth, but it was closed. Aaron half-stood inside the booth and looked over the far table edge. The P.I. wasn't wearing a gun on his waist, but considering the stories he'd heard about him from Dave…

Aaron nodded at the backpack. "That thing heavy?"

Phault hid a smile. "Very."

"Whaddaya carrying?" Aaron asked, curious.

"I used to carry a 1911," Phault told him, looking pointedly at Aaron's waist where his holstered 1911 sat. "But I ran out of ammo in a gunfight once so for a while now I've been carrying a SIG 226. Single action only."

Aaron's Colt Delta Elite was fed by a nine-round magazine, with one more round in the chamber. And he carried a spare magazine on his hip. Nineteen rounds was probably fifteen more than he'd ever need in a gunfight…and this friend of Dave's ran out of ammo? Didn't sound like the guy, Dave had said Phault had been in a few dustups, put more than a couple guys in the ground. Supposedly knew how to shoot.

"Having problems finding your front sight that day?" Aaron inquired, honestly curious.

"Nope."

He could see Phault wasn't about to volunteer any more information and shrugged. "Okay. Nine millimeter, right? Fifteen round mags?"

"Standard. But they make flush eighteen-rounders." Phault had enough gun and ammo in the discreet tactical pack—quickly accessible through a zipper—to kill half the people in the diner, if necessary. There was a panel of body armor in the pack that would stop every incoming pistol and shotgun round. And he had a rifle in his SUV, with four loaded thirty-round magazines. He never wanted to die for lack of shooting back, and after having once run out of ammo in a gunfight he never wanted that to happen again.

Aaron noticed Phault had his phone sitting on its edge,

leaning against the napkin dispenser on the table. "Filming with that?" he asked quietly, eyeing the phone.

"And my watch," Phault admitted. The rechargeable camera in the watch could record for two hours on the micro SD card at 1080p. "And I've got a video camera set up in the car in the parking lot. Don't get much through the glare on the windows, but I get some." He looked at Aaron. "The longer I sit here the better, but I know you're not here to give me cover."

"You heard from Dave?" Aaron asked him quietly.

Phault shook his head. Dave had been working for him, doing surveillance, when four disgraced Detroit S.W.A.T. cops out on bail had tried to kill him. Then he'd taken off for Arizona, and gotten into another gunfight, one that had almost killed him. "Haven't talked to him in maybe a year and a half. Haven't seen him since he was in the hospital." Phault had flown down to visit Dave in the Arizona hospital. He still remembered how horrible the kid's hands had looked with the burns. "Why?"

"I had that detective from West Bloomfield banging on my door, making noise. Saying he'd been talking to people. Building a case against Dave for that old hit-and-run."

John Phault sighed and took a sip of coffee. He stared off into the middle distance for a while. "He's trying to shake the tree, see what falls loose," he finally told Aaron. "He called me," he admitted.

"Yeah? What'd you say?"

Phault bit back a sharp word and looked at the man in front of him. The man that he knew was Dave Anderson's friend, who'd ridden around with him in an armored car on the days he wasn't doing surveillances. He knew Dave trusted this man with his life. Had trusted him with his life. That Aaron had been the one who'd pulled him from the burning wreck of his house, out in the Arizona desert. He'd been at Dave's bedside in Arizona when Phault had flown down to visit.

Phault didn't directly answer the question. "You know," he said, "the first time they sent a guy to kill him, Dave was doing a surveillance for me. With me. I spotted the guy, called him out to a DPD unit. Thought he was another P.I. on a surveillance. Guy killed those two cops, shot half a dozen other officers before he was put down. Didn't even know it was connected to Dave until months later." Phault looked out the windows to the bright parking lot. "Then Bufonte sent two carloads of dirty S.W.A.T. cops after him. Then those other guys in Arizona, whoever the fuck they were. Private contractors, whatever." It sounded insane to his ears even now, even though he knew it was true. He eyed Abruzzo. Phault was pretty sure he hadn't gotten the full story of what had happened in Arizona, and after he'd checked out of the hospital down there Dave had just disappeared. "So maybe I saved his life calling out that minivan. I definitely got those cops killed."

"You didn't kill them," Aaron said to Phault's frowning face.

"I sent them right over to the guy who did."

"That was their job. Sucks that they bought it, but that's the job. And you killed the guy who did it, you chased him down, right?"

Phault didn't say anything for a while. Finally, he finished the coffee in his cup and said, "My point is, Dave and I have history. He was doing CPR on those cops, blood up to his elbows, while I chased that asshole down and put two in his chest." He looked Aaron straight in the eye. "I don't know if he ran over Paul Bufonte. Big Paulie. And I don't care. I owe him. So I very politely told the detective to pound sand." He watched Abruzzo nodding in satisfaction. "But just because I think he was fishing doesn't mean he didn't get an interesting nibble from someone else. Somewhere else." He paused a second. "You talk to Dave at all?"

"Not in a long time," Aaron said honestly. He chewed on his lip until his food arrived.

Chapter Eleven

Dave studied Lori as she returned from his kitchen with two bottles of water. He still appreciated that she had no issues walking around naked. Neither did Gina, his former girlfriend. Actually, thinking about her, Gina with her big implants and toned body looked more like a porn star than Lori ever had. But when it came to performance he'd discovered there was a definite difference between an amateur and a professional. He said, "No tattoos, no piercings, no implants. Aren't you violating some sort of porn actress ordinance?"

She snorted as she sat down on the bed. She handed him one of the bottles. "I didn't get into porn because I was crazy or hated myself or needed money for drugs, I got into porn because I was horny and loved to have sex. The idea that I could make money having sex with hot guys seemed like a dream job. Plus, by the time I was in high school I'd discovered I had a...what's Liam Neeson's line in *Taken*? 'A unique skill set'. Something like that."

"High school?"

"Well, I discovered I could drink milk and shoot it out my nose in grade school. By accident the first time, in the cafeteria, then I did it all the time to gross the other girls out. I discovered I had absolutely no gag reflex in middle school. Combine those two skills with a certain moral flexibility and you can make a lot of money doing porn. A hell of a lot of money."

"Yeah, that definitely is your trademark move. Was." He paused and blinked. "'Certain moral flexibility'? Did you just quote *Grosse Pointe Blank*?"

She laughed in delight. "Wow, you recognized that? Yeah, I watched that recently with my mother. I love that movie. I'm surprised you got it."

"I've been watching a lot of movies too." He frowned and remembered what she'd said. "You discovered you had no gag reflex in middle school?" Jesus.

"On a cucumber. Or maybe it was a banana. But I know you're not one of those people who think girls only get interested in sex the day they turn eighteen. Or boys. I was with a bunch of other girls and we were screwing around at somebody's house on a sleepover or something. The girl whose house it was laughed at how surprised I was I got the whole thing down my throat. It was weird that first time, I remember. One of the girls got really angry at me when she saw what I could do. Like she'd lost a competition or something, and she stopped being my friend right that second. It was *sooo* educational once I figured out what happened, and why. So many women just hate you, stab-your-eyes-out-and-set-you-on-fire hate you, when you do porn. Not because they're religious but because you're a threat to them. And not because you're prettier than them, most girls in porn aren't beautiful, they're just average to look at. It's because other women know that you'll do stuff they won't. Stuff that guys like and want, and these women know guys like and want it. Heck, most porn is just fantasies depicting what guys want in the bedroom, there's no mystery there. But somehow it's all porn's fault for giving guys unrealistic expectations. You want to know what a guy wants in the bedroom, it ain't rocket science, watch porn.

"Honestly, guys are too afraid to ask for what they want most times, and women pretend ignorance, or just won't do it, or stop doing it once they've got the ring on their finger, so the guy is either unhappy or goes somewhere else for the sex he needs. I'm telling you, I learned so much about psychology and people while in the porn industry. It's not so much the porn as it is people's reaction to it. Tells you so much about them and their issues. Anyway, one of the other girls there that night—back to the cucumber—thought it was really hot how I could shove something down my throat like it was nothing. She was actually the first girl I was ever with, that was over a year before I ever had sex with a guy."

"So the bi stuff wasn't just for the camera?"

"I never did anything on camera that I didn't do on my own first. And liked. Trust me, you don't want it to be on camera the first time you're trying something new, on-camera sex is usually not like regular sex. Those girls who hate what they're doing never last long in the business. That's true about any job. You can't have a lot of limits and be successful in porn these days." She paused, and squinted. "You remember that movie with Melanie Griffith where she plays the porn actress?"

Dave blinked at the unexpected question. "Um, maybe. A murder mystery or something, right? Directed by Brian DePalma I think. From the eighties?"

"I don't know who directed it, I just remember one scene where she's being considered for a job by a guy posing as a director and she's listing all the stuff she won't do in porn. That's a good example of how porn has changed, tastes have changed since the eighties. She'd never get a job in porn today. You have to do all that stuff now if you want to keep working. And the girls who keep working are the ones who don't just do it but like it."

"Would you ever go back to it?"

"What, porn?"

"Yeah."

"No," she said without hesitation. "For a lot of reasons. I liked it, mostly, while I was doing it, and the money was great, but I wouldn't want to start doing it again, you know? And I didn't plan it that way, but it sure looks like I got out at just the right time."

"Yeah, why's that?" He knew every few years there was an AIDS scare in the porn industry.

"Money."

"What money?"

"There's just so much free porn on the internet, more every day, that fewer and fewer people are willing to pay money for it. So a lot of the studios are cutting back, paying less, or just plain closing their doors, such as Kink-dot-com in San Francisco. The only girls still making good money in the industry are the ones going into business for themselves, running their own websites, generating their own content."

He laid there next to her for a long time, not saying anything, a small vertical line between his eyebrows.

Finally she said, "I hate to do that girl thing, but what are you thinking about?" She wondered if he'd gotten upset at the thought of her doing porn. He didn't seem the type, but she'd deliberately tried not to talk about porn with him. Not because she was ashamed of her past but because of how guys usually reacted.

He smiled. "Economics, actually. Porn went from being an illegal or gray-market commodity to being everywhere after the internet came along. You could get whatever you wanted right in your own home without having to go down to the video store and be weirded out by the creep in the trenchcoat. But then everyone downloads the pay content and posts it for free, in combo with seemingly everyone with a smartphone posting homemade porn online with the push of a button. I'm wondering if in a generation there won't be any professionally made porn at all, because nobody will be able to make any money at it. Because of how much is out there already, for free, and all the new free amateur filmed-on-a-phone stuff."

She turned her head slightly to look at him. So many things he said and did were completely unexpected. Most of the guys in the industry were either brainless idiots or assholes, just like the women. Heck, he was the first guy she'd talked to at length, about anything, since quitting porn. The guys she'd met outside of the industry, when they found out what she'd done, most couldn't get past the porn. A few became obsessed with it. Not him. He was sitting there next to her when she was naked, thinking about the *economics* of porn. Maybe he was an alien disguised as a human. That would explain a lot.

"It won't disappear entirely," she told him, "but I think you're right, the pro stuff will struggle. But you get a good enough looking girl, or guy, maybe somebody with a unique body or skill, let's say, like Hot Kinky Jo or Bailey Jay," she'd worked with both of them, "there's always somebody willing to pay to watch. Somebody will always pay, remember that."

"Unique skill…like you?"

She shrugged and smiled. "I guess. Also, to many girls

these days, porn is just a gateway to escorting. Even if the acting jobs don't pay much, the videos get them noticed, gets their faces out there for guys to see. And try to hook up with. Apparently escorting is where the real money's at these days, I hear you can get a grand or two an hour if you're a big name in porn."

"You ever do it?"

"Escorting? No, but I will admit that there's not much difference between escorting and porn. Actually, there's only one real difference. You know what that is?"

"No, what?"

"Who pays."

He thought about that for a bit. "Hunh." He put his water bottle down on the bedside table and stood up off the bed. "I have to head to the bathroom. If you're hungry, you're welcome to whatever you find in the kitchen."

"Okay." She watched him walk away, then shivered. Just lying there the air in the bedroom was a bit cool. She found his t-shirt on the floor and put it on.

She really felt it when she bent over. "I'm going to be sore tomorrow," she said loud enough for him to hear. "I haven't had my legs behind my head in forever."

He wasn't sure what to say to that. "Um…sorry?"

She laughed. "It was my idea. And no, you're not." She heard him chuckle.

On her his shirt hung down nearly to her knees. She was looking over all the books in the bookcases when she heard the knock on the door.

She padded over to the door and looked through the peephole. She didn't recognize the guy but between the borderline mullet and the porn moustache and the cigarette dangling from his lips he just had to be an undercover cop checking in on Dave. Lori pulled open the door and smiled at him. "Yeah?"

The guy's eyebrows drew together until there was a vertical line up his forehead, and his mouth pulled down into a frown behind the cigarette. He looked at her, then backed up half a step and doublechecked the address on the front of the house. He took the cigarette out of his mouth. "Um, is Dave here?" He continued staring at her, eyeballing the t-shirt and the bare legs below it. "I mean Jack. Shit." His eyes went back up to her face.

When the guy backed up she'd seen the shiny pistol on his hip. Yep, one of Dave's friends or coworkers or something, had to be. She laughed. "Yeah. Jack!"

From deep in the house she heard, "Was that the door?" Dave stuck just his head around a corner as he was still naked. His eyes went wide when he saw she had the door open, and when he saw who was on his porch.

"You asshole!" Aaron yelled at him. He jabbed the cigarette at Dave. "You motherfucker. I don't know if you're dead or goddamned alive, can't get you to make one fucking phone call. For weeks. Shit's going on, and I come all the way down here, don't know if I'm gonna find you dead in a ditch or what the fuck, and here you are playing fucking house." He looked at Lori. "No offense." He looked back at Dave. "Are you fucking naked? Are you shitting me? You know, I had visions of you while driving up here, shot in the head, Colombian necktie, poisoned, whatever, wondering what the fuck I'd find. You rocking out with your cock out was not on the list."

"Jesus, come on inside before the neighbors call the cops," Dave said.

Aaron angrily flicked the cigarette toward the street and stepped in past Lori.

"What's going on? What happened?" Dave asked him.

"Go get your damn clothes on first," Aaron growled at him. "Just 'cause I saved your life doesn't mean I want to see you naked."

"Okay. Um," he hesitated, then pointed. "Aaron, Lori. Lori, Aaron."

"Yeah, we've fucking already met," Aaron spat, waving a hand. He looked at her and paused a few seconds. "Big fan," he said finally, then glanced back at Dave. "Asshole," he said again.

When Dave had his clothes on and came out Aaron was still fuming in the front room, Lori standing right next to him. She looked happy or something, which was weird.

"Are you even fucking carrying a gun?" Aaron asked, peering at Dave's loose work shirt.

"Yeah, I'm carrying a gun," Dave said defensively, pulling the work shirt out far enough to show the Glock 19 on his hip. His eyes darted from Aaron to Lori and back. "Okay, you, um, maybe want to go out and get a coffee? Sounds like we've got a lot to talk about." He wanted to get Aaron away from Lori considering he didn't know what they needed to talk about. And Aaron seemed in a mood.

"Yeah, whatever." Aaron wanted another Marlboro but knew that Dave probably didn't want him smoking in the house.

"I'll get dressed," Lori said quickly, and headed for the bedroom.

"Um," Dave said to her, about to protest.

"Oh, hell no," she said, holding up a finger as she strode past him, never slowing down. "I'm coming too." She pulled the shirt over her head and headed into the bedroom for her clothes. Dave stared after her, then looked back at Aaron, who'd gotten a split-second view of her naked butt.

"Asshole," Aaron said definitively one final time. He huffed. "I'll be outside smoking."

The ride to Aloha Snackbar passed in uncomfortable silence, but Aaron's mood improved slightly as soon as he walked through the front door and smelled the coffee. There were a few tables occupied, and two guys and a girl behind the counter.

When it was Aaron's turn a limping redhead took his order. "I'm looking for something flavored, with a lot of cream and sugar," Aaron said to him, still frowning. He glanced back at Dave and Lori taking their seats at a small table.

"We've got a caramel macchiato, a vanilla cream, and some Highlander Grogg flavored coffee, those are the three I'd most recommend," Matt told him. He eyed the big stainless 1911 on the guy's hip, then saw the red triangle on the pistol's grips. "That a 10 millimeter? You expecting the zombie apocalypse? Or are you a pimp?"

"I'm from Detroit," Aaron said by way of explanation.

"So...both?"

That got a smile out of Aaron, but it didn't last long. When he got his coffee he sat down at the table and frowned at Dave. Dave was skinny. Really skinny. The short beard didn't do much to hide the angles on his face. Aaron's frown got deeper, and he turned it on Lori. "Okay, you let her tag along. How much does she know?"

"Not a damn thing, why do you think I wanted to come?" Lori said brightly, sipping at her espresso. She didn't know much about Dave, but she knew human nature. Aaron was angry and yelling because he was scared and worried, not because he was actually angry. Guys always had trouble expressing their emotions. It seemed clear the two of them were close. Interesting.

Aaron growled deep in his throat and shook his head. Dave stared at her but didn't say anything. Lori thought it was weird that Dave and Aaron were sitting next to each other until she realized they were both seated facing the door.

"Okay, you remember that West Bloomfield dick? He was back, banging on my door this week. He said he's been talking to Gina."

Dave frowned. "It's not the first time."

"Yeah, well, apparently they finally figured out she was working at the club Big Paulie managed when you guys started dating."

"Yeah, and?"

"Well, it's a connection. One they didn't have before. He said she was telling them all sorts of other stuff too. What does she know? What can she tell them?"

Dave shook his head. "Nothing. He's fishing. He was just trying to rattle you, get you to give up something. They—" he stopped and looked at Aaron. He remembered the car parked on the street in front of his house. "You get a rental at the airport? Was that what you parked in front of my house?"

"Yes, but no. I got a rental at the airport, but it was a Chevy, fucking Government Motors. Loaded with GPS or tracking devices or whatever in that OnStar Big Brother bullshit they got going on. So I drove to a local car dealership and arranged a test drive. Just moved to Arizona, don't you know, and need a new car. Still a fucking Chevy, but not tied to me in any database." They'd Xeroxed his Michigan driver's license and proof of insurance. "That's what I drove to your place, the airport rental is at the dealership. With my phone inside it, so they can't track it to you."

"Yeah, but they could track you to Arizona. To Prescott."

"Maybe if you'd answer your fucking phone—" Aaron began, his voice rising.

Angry both at Aaron and himself, Dave took the first sip of his coffee. He made a weird face, and sniffed at the cup. Then he put the cup down and smelled his hands. His eyes darted toward Lori and back. "I need to hit the john, wash up," he said.

"Yeah," Aaron said, unsurprised. He looked at the girl as Dave got up and headed toward the back of the business. Even from across the table she still smelled like sex. And coconut.

She smiled at him and sipped at her drink. "Sooooo, how do you know Dave? Er, Jack. Shit." She'd made the same mistake he did.

"We used to work together. How do you know him?"

"Neighbors. I live next door."

"Seriously? For how long?"

"Two years."

Aaron blinked. So she'd been living there for a year before Dave moved in. Was she the reason he'd picked that house? "How long have you two been a thing?"

"A month or two. Although I'm not sure what we are. He's not exactly chatty. He was living there six months before he even said hello."

Aaron frowned. It had taken him all of three seconds to recognize her. "What are you doing in Arizona? You, uh, working?" Prescott, Arizona didn't seem a likely location for a porn production company.

Lori smiled. "No, I'm out here to take care of my mom. She's got cancer."

Aaron studied her. "My mom passed from cancer last

year. Fought it for almost five years. What kind does she have?"

"Brain tumor. Inoperable."

Aaron sighed, and some of the tension left him. "That sucks." He stared down at his coffee, thinking of everything he'd gone through with his mother. "Enjoy your time with her, as much as you can."

"I'm doing my best. She's lived three times as long as they said she would." Lori eyed him. "Is Gina the stripper he used to date?"

"He told you about her? Yeah. Smokin' hot, but not a lot going on upstairs." He eyed her and pursed his lips. "Lori? Lot better than Jizzabelle. Who came up with that?"

"I did," she said, chagrinned. "Junior year of high school when I started to think about porn as a career. After a few years I thought about changing it, but then it was too late because I had name recognition. I didn't want to be one of those girls that worked under half a dozen different names. By the time they found one they liked they were burnt out. Still better than that nickname the asshole reviewer at Hustler gave me."

Aaron shook his head. He didn't know it.

"PorkSnorkle," she admitted.

Aaron snorted...and then cocked his head and nodded. It worked as a nickname—funny, unique, memorable, and accurate. She rolled her eyes at him. "You and, shit, almost did it again, Jack, work together in Detroit?"

"Yeah."

"Doing what?"

"Armored car, but he had a lot of other stuff going on."

Hmm. Interesting. "So what exactly is going on with D—Jack? You seem pretty worried." She gave him a big smile.

Aaron opened his mouth, then realized at some point she'd set her not-so-small tits on the table in a not-so-subtle effort to shut his brain off while his mouth was running, and he'd been staring at them while doing just that. He appreciated the effort, but shook his head to clear it. "He wants you to know, it's up to him to tell you." He glanced up as Dave came back to the table. "Speak of the fucking devil."

"What'd I do now?"

"You didn't answer your phone, that's for sure."

"Okay, for fuck's sake, I get it. I'm sorry. I should have called you back. But I'm not on vacation down here."

Aaron shook his head. "It's been two years. If anything was going to happen, it would have happened."

Dave's face darkened. "You don't know that. And your ass isn't on the line if you're wrong."

"So, what? Is this forever then?" Aaron waved a hand around. "You going to hide until, what, all your money runs out? You even get a job yet?"

"I don't want to talk about it."

"Yeah, no shit."

"I thought you were working for the Sheriff," Lori said, looking at Dave.

Aaron looked at her, then Dave. "Sheriff?"

"Osterman. He's come by a few times. He's worried about me too."

Aaron took a sip of his coffee. "Well that makes two of us who still care whether or not you live or die. Seriously, I pulled you out of a fucking fire. You probably don't remember, because you were fucking shot eighteen times. Maybe I should have left you there to burn, is that it?"

"No, I…"

"If you wanted to die, why'd you fuckin' fight in the first place?"

Dave was getting angrier and angrier, which meant his voice was getting softer and softer. "I don't want to die. Not then and not now. But what I want's got nothing to do with it."

"Bullshit. You went into a hole when your parents died and you haven't come out of it. Hell, you just keep digging deeper, scared to even look up."

"You a shrink now?"

"No, I'm your fucking friend. Maybe the only one you've got."

The two of them glared at each other for several minutes, until the polite "Excuse me," broke the tension. All three of them looked up to see the redhead co-owner of the place standing at their table. He was looking at Lori. "I hate to bother you, but…are you who I think you are?"

Dave and Aaron looked at each other while Lori smiled up at him brightly. "I don't know, who do you think I am?"

"Um, uh." Matt struggled with how to respond. If he just flat out asked if she was a porn star, and she wasn't… well, that conversation would not end pleasantly. A paying customer never to return to the store. He went with the most innocuous description he could come up with. "An actress? You do this trick with your nose…" he said tentatively.

She laughed. "That'd be me," she said.

"The PorkSnorkle herself," Aaron agreed, fighting a grin. Dave glanced at him in confusion.

Matt turned around and jabbed a finger at Mike behind the counter. "I told you," he said. He looked back at Lori. "I didn't mean to interrupt, but if it was you, I just wanted to say thanks." He gestured at his business partner behind the counter. "We both spent some serious time in the Suck, and," he paused, trying to figure out how to phrase it, "your movies helped lower the stress level. You were real popular."

"The Suck?" Lori repeated, thinking he was somehow talking about porn.

"Iraq and Afghanistan."

"Oh. Ah." Yeah, she was real popular with military guys. All porn was, and always had been. There was no mystery about what guys liked, especially young guys full of testosterone. "Well, I'm glad you made it back."

"Most of me. You visiting the area?"

"I live out here. I'm retired now. Most of you?"

"I lost a foot over there. Well, I didn't lose it, I know right where it is." He glanced at the two guys with her. "Look, I'm one of the owners, me and that jarhead behind the counter. You come back in here, any time, you drink free."

"You don't have to do that."

"It's the least I can do." He smiled. "The world needs more girls like you. Hey…can I get a selfie with you? A lot of the guys I served with, we're friends on Facebook, and they'll shit when they see it's you."

"Sure."

Dave and Aaron waited while the co-owner pulled out his phone and Lori smiled through several photos. Then he shook her hand and waved at them and then went back to work. Aaron looked at Dave and said drily, "This is keeping a low profile?"

"We've never gone out together before," Lori told him defensively. "He didn't know. It happens, but not nearly as much as it used to, and I'm so used to it I don't even think about it. It's my fault I guess." She looked at Dave with concern. "You're in hiding or whatever, it was dumb of me to—"

"Forget about it," Dave said. "Not your fault."

Aaron checked his watch. "I better get that car back to the dealer before they report it stolen."

Dave sighed. "Yeah."

They rode back to the house in silence. Dave pulled into his driveway and got out. He looked at the new car parked on the street, then at Aaron. "You coming back after you drop that off?" Lori got out and stood behind him.

Aaron stared at the car for a while before answering. "No. I just wanted to make sure you were still alive. And I already might've fucked things up enough just coming out here."

Dave thought about the car swap, and the fact that Aaron hadn't brought his phone anywhere near his house. "It's probably okay. I'm sorry I haven't called. I'm still…I'll try and keep in touch. Maybe set up a time to actually talk, instead of trading voicemails?"

"That'd be good." The two of them shook hands, then hugged briefly. Aaron looked at Lori. "It was nice meeting you," he said to her, walking backward toward the car. He smirked. "You look almost as good with your clothes on."

"Thanks," she said, but was smiling.

Aaron pointed at Dave, then at Lori. "Teach her not to open your fucking door unless she knows who the fuck's knocking, or PorkSnorkle's not going to be the worst nickname she's got." Aaron got into the car, gave a wave, and then drove off. Dave and Lori stood in the front yard and looked at each other.

"So he's shy," she said.

Dave laughed. "Yeah. Um, PorkSnorkle?"

"Don't ask, jeez." Vicki's car was still in her driveway, and Lori checked her watch. The nurse would be leaving any minute. "Have you ever met my mom?" she asked him.

"Waved a couple of times," he told her. "Maybe said hi."

She nodded and tilted her head toward her house. "Come on. Come meet my mom."

Aaron was still in a mood as he parked the test drive vehicle in front of the dealer's showroom. Apparently he'd been gone a little too long, as the salesman popped out of the door before he'd even had a chance to lock up the vehicle.

"Great, glad you're back!" the salesman said, looking relieved. He was wearing a white shirt and black slacks, with a red and gold striped tie. "So what'd you think?"

Aaron tossed him the keys and the man caught them awkwardly. "Are you kidding me?" Aaron said in disgust. "What kind of window-licking retards would buy such an overcomplicated overpriced nanny-state turd of a vehicle? The seat pokes you in the ass if you change lanes without signaling. Parking assist for, what, lazy or one-eyed owners? Lights flash if someone's in your blind spot. Auto start/stop so it shuts off if I stop rolling even for a second, which officially makes it neutered, but I knew it didn't have any balls the first time I touched the gas pedal. And it beeps a reminder at you when you shut off the car to make sure to check the back seat. Should've named it the Chevy Maxi-Pad, because the only thing that belongs inside it are pussies."

The salesman stared at Aaron, blinking erratically, his mouth open.

Chapter Twelve

Walking into Lori's house Dave had an immediate and visceral flash-back to visiting his grandfather in a nursing home. He'd been ten years old or so, there with his parents for Father's Day or something like that. It was the smell that brought him back, a mixture of antiseptic and medicinal chemicals and, faintly, urine. That nursing home had been the saddest place Dave had ever been. Ever seen. To his young eyes it seemed as if all the old people had given up and were just sitting around, waiting to die. Some of them going through the motions of life, others just sitting there staring at nothing. His grandfather had been cheerful enough, even though he'd been wheelchair-bound, but still the despair of the place had haunted Dave for weeks. And Lori's house felt and looked and smelled exactly the same to him. Death's waiting room. Jesus, no wonder she needed to get out from time to time.

They met the nurse or whatever she was in the front room, packing her bag. She was a thick middle-aged black woman with her hair pulled back in a bun. Her skin looked flawless. "Vicki, this is Jack, he lives next door."

Vicki smiled at Dave, but he didn't miss her eyes going up and down appraisingly as she held a hand out to him. "Nice to meet you." She looked at Lori. "She's in the kitchen, watching the little TV. She's had a good day."

"Good, I wanted her to meet Jack. Are you back tomorrow?"

Vicki shook her head. "Day after tomorrow." She hoisted her bag. "Ten a.m."

Lori nodded. "Okay, thanks." She opened the door for Vicki and then closed it behind her. She took a deep breath, then called out, "Mom, I'm back. And I brought a visitor."

Dave followed her down the short hallway to the kitchen. Her mother was sitting at a small oval table, watching a video on a tablet. Up close she looked much more frail than she had the few times he'd waved to her. Or maybe her health was just failing that rapidly. He had no idea how brain cancer affected the rest of a person's body, but it had to be wearing on her emotionally. Both her and Lori. Her hair was blonde fading to white, and her face was narrow. Her skin was grayish-white and hung in wrinkles from her neck. But she had a big smile on her face as she looked up from the tablet.

"You do? Who is it?" she said brightly.

"This is Jack, he lives next door." She gestured at him.

"The young man you're always talking about?" Her watery blue eyes danced about.

Lori made a face. "I'm not always talking about him," she said, glancing from her mother to Dave.

Dave grinned, feeling a little self-conscious. "Nice to meet you, Ms…is it Hoskins?"

She held out a hand, smiling. "Grace, please. And she is always talking about you, the handsome police officer next door." She shook his hand, hers feeling light and delicate in his palm. Her other hand was trembling. Dave glanced at Lori and back at her mother.

"I guess you're never too old to have your parents try to embarrass you," Lori said, the corner of her mouth curling up.

Grace let go of Dave's hand and made a raspberry sound. With her parchment-like lips it was the driest raspberry he'd ever heard. "Me embarrass you? Please." Then she stopped and peered at Lori, then swiveled her gaze back to Dave. "You have told him, haven't you, about what you used to do? I assume you two aren't spending all that time over there playing euchre, so it's something he should know."

Lori blew out a long breath. "Yes, Mom, he knows."

"We've all got a past," Dave told her.

Grace stopped at that, and nodded. "That we do." She shot her eyes sideways at her daughter. "Some more colorful than others."

"Mom," Lori began, but then she saw her mother was deliberately having fun with her. She was having a good day. "Did you eat?"

"Yes, Vicki made me some soup, although I needed some help with the spoon. But I asked for soup, so I can't complain."

Lori nodded at the tablet in front of her mother. "Are we interrupting something? What were you watching?"

"Just some YouTube videos." She paused. "You know, speaking of it, I guess I'd like to play euchre. But we'd need a fourth."

"You want me to ask Mrs. Leslie?"

Grace shook her head at her daughter. "She'd insist on bringing over that horrid cat. Looks like a plucked chicken." Dave snorted. She glanced at him and said defensively, "It's true."

"I know the rules for three-handed euchre," Dave volunteered. "I learned them from a friend. I don't know if they're official or not, but it works. If you're up for trying to learn a few new rules." He looked back and forth between the two of them. He had no idea if Grace was really up for playing a card game, much less an unfamiliar one. Lori waited for her mother to answer.

"That sounds nice," Grace told him.

They had a great time. They played euchre for almost an hour and a half, and while Lori's mother had occasional lapses of concentration, when she was focused she was all there, and a ferocious card player.

"If I was twenty years older I probably would have gotten into bridge," Grace admitted at one point. "My parents were in a bridge group, played every Friday night, every week at a different person's house. But it always seemed so intimidating. The local paper used to print nationally syndicated bridge strategies, written by Omar Sharif. They looked like math formulas."

Dave blinked. "Omar Sharif? The actor?"

She nodded. "Oh yes. He was a famous bridge player. Or maybe it was contract bridge. I honestly don't know the difference. Bridge seems a combination of math and chess. It always appeared too complicated to be much fun."

"I feel that way about craps," Lori said. "I guess if you know how to play the odds are pretty good, but I'd rather play blackjack. It's a lot simpler, and the odds are just as good." She looked at Dave.

"I've never been much of a gambler," he admitted.

Grace's eyes danced between the two of them, and she was smiling as she opened her mouth. Lori jabbed a finger at her. "Don't even," she said, but with only mock seriousness.

Grace smiled, but then got serious and looked at Dave. "Have you ever seen her movies?"

"Mom, what are you—?"

"Shh." She waved a hand at her daughter.

Dave blinked, wondering if this was some sort of trick question. "Yes," he said, after only a brief pause.

"Did you know what she did before you started dating?"

Dating? What they were doing, did it count as dating? He wasn't sure about that, but said, "Yes."

"When did you know?"

"I'd been here about a month before I recognized her."

She made a face and leaned back, then glanced at her daughter. "He did play hard to get." She smiled at Dave. "She's been staring out her window at you for months."

"Mom, God." Lori's neck turned red.

After a fiercely fought game that Lori narrowly won, Dave noticed that her mother's hands were getting a little shaky. He glanced at Lori as she was gathering up the cards and raised his eyebrows. She saw the look.

"Mom? You want to take a break? Maybe watch a movie?"

"Yeah, I'm tired. Can you help me to the couch?"

Dave stood to the side as Lori helped her mother out of the chair. "Anything in particular you want to watch?"

Grace turned her head to look up at Dave. "You're tall."

"I'm standing on a box."

He said it so seriously that she glanced down at his feet, then blew a raspberry and shook her head. "Oh, you. He's quick, this one," she said to her daughter.

"He's something," Lori said with a smile.

"You know what I haven't seen in a while? *Romancing the Stone*."

"Is that a movie?" Lori asked.

"Yes, a great one. With Michael Douglas and Kathleen Turner. See if we have it on our Netflix thing. Have you ever seen it?" she asked Dave.

"No." Although he'd heard of it. Dave followed them out to the front room. Lori got her mother situated on the couch in front of the big screen TV and then pulled a big remote out from between the cushions. The movie wasn't on Netflix, but it was available on Amazon and they settled in to watch it, Lori seated between her mother and Dave.

It had been so long since he'd enjoyed a normal family activity, like sitting around a kitchen table playing cards or relaxing on a couch and watching a movie together, that Dave had forgotten the feeling. The movie was great, a romantic comedy with a lot of ridiculous action. Sitting on a couch watching it with a girl and her mother gave him flashbacks to high school, back to a time when he had a family, when he'd had girlfriends.

Lori was warm against his arm, her thigh pressing along his, as she and her mother laughed at the funny parts. Lori held her mother's quivering hand a few times to still it and he pretended not to notice.

Dave felt disconnected, a voyeur to this scene of familial love and tenderness. It was as if he was watching the scene in a movie rather than being a part of it. Maybe that was because he wasn't a part of it, wasn't really there; he was just visiting.

Two-thirds of the way through the movie Dave looked over and saw a tear running from Grace's eye. It wasn't just one tear, it was a steady stream, a glistening line down her cheek, but her mother didn't seem to be crying, she was enjoying the movie. He nudged Lori gently, and nodded at her mother, a bit worried.

Lori reached across Dave and grabbed a Kleenex out of a box. "Your eye's leaking again," she said matter-of-factly, dabbing at her mother's face, then went back to watching the movie. As the credits rolled Dave looked over and saw that at some point Lori's mother had fallen asleep.

He looked at the movie winding down, at Grace, then at Lori. Lori was holding her mother's hand. "I suppose I better get her into bed," Lori said.

"Do you want me to help?"

She glanced at him and shook her head.

Dave pursed his lips together, then asked quietly, "Do you want me to go?"

"No, you stay here. Well, maybe help me get her up. Mom, come on, time for bed."

She was gone ten minutes, then came back and dropped onto the couch next to him like a puppet whose strings had been cut. She seemed exhausted. Dave hadn't been blind to how extra cheerful she'd been ever since they'd entered the house, and knew that didn't come cheap.

She brushed the hair back from her forehead, then looked at him. "Okay, so what's your deal?" she asked.

"What do you mean?"

"I didn't get involved with you because I was shopping for a husband. I wasn't looking for anything other than to forget for a few hours. At least that first time. But compared to you I'm a clingy guilt-ridden Catholic schoolgirl. I can see there's a good guy inside you, somewhere, but the outside, you've got this dead shell or something. What the hell is up with you?"

Dave didn't answer for a long time. He wasn't sure if he should answer at all. Finally he sighed. "I'm a lot like your mom," he said. He shrugged. "My days are numbered."

She frowned. "What the hell are you talking about? You're the healthiest person I know. You work out for hours every day. It pisses me off, actually."

He gave a little smile. "I don't have cancer." He debated, even then, telling her, then did. "It's just that...at some point...some guys are going to show up and kill me. They've already tried a couple times. And I hope I survive another attempt or two. But eventually they're going to get me. Actually, I'm surprised it hasn't already happened."

She turned to face him on the couch. "What? Who? Who wants you dead?"

"The who doesn't matter, and I'd really rather not say. I think it's safer for you."

"The fuck it doesn't matter. And how could me not knowing be safer? You're sitting here on my couch, my mother in the next room, you live right next door, it fucking matters who might or might not be coming to try to kill you."

Dave sighed. Then, for some reason that he couldn't quite explain, he told her. Told her everything while staring unseeing at his scarred hands. Told her how he used to have fingerprints that matched two other people. Had been blissfully unaware of that fact until the lab tech at the FBI was so delighted at his discovery he thought it should be shared with the world. Cue the sinister music as the government tried to cover up everything and eliminate the evidence, which included Dave. Mickey, the now former FBI lab tech, barely survived an attempt on his life before finding Dave and explaining to him why people were trying to kill him.

Telling him how he'd screwed up Dave's life, not to mention destroyed his job prospects with the FBI. Dave explained to Lori how a team of dirty SWAT cops and then private contractors had been sent after him, but almost nobody knew the truth about why, not even the guys sent out to kill him.

It seemed almost too fantastical to be true, but she'd seen his scars, remembered the comments his friend Aaron had made, which at the time hadn't made much sense to her. "So why do the cops think it all happened?"

"My parents were killed by a drunk driver. Just so happens the guy who killed them was the son of the biggest mob guy in Detroit. Detroit still has the mob, who knew? Anyway, he got off with a slap on the hand due to a bullshit technicality. Then got killed in a hit and run not long after. Everyone thinks I killed him, and that all these attempts on my life were paid for by Pietro Bufonte, the mob guy. Revenge for his son."

She stared at him, eyes huge. "Are you shitting me?"

He shrugged. "It was the simplest explanation, and I never said different."

"No, not that. You had the FBI and the Detroit mob trying to kill you? Seriously? You're not fucking with me?"

"It's not paranoia if people actually are trying to kill you. But it was only the FBI. Actually a small group inside it. The mob just got the blame for it."

She waved a hand violently. "Whatever. You're serious?"

"I met Osterman when I was in the hospital down here. After private contractors, a bunch of retired Special Forces dudes, made a run at me at my grandfather's cabin at the north end of the county. Aaron came down with a Detroit Police detective who'd thought he'd figured it all out. But they were a little late. By the time they showed up I'd been shot a few times and hit with a little bit of shrapnel. From my own bomb. And burned. Aaron wasn't joking when he said he pulled me out of a fire."

Parents dead in a car wreck, and then the FBI tries to kill him? Well that explains a lot, she thought. Her head was spinning. "Did you kill him?"

"Who?"

"The guy who killed your parents."

"Doesn't matter. Everybody thinks I did."

"The hell it doesn't matter. If you did kill him, then maybe I guess you feel like you deserve everybody coming after you. If you didn't kill him, and everybody thinks you did, well, that's horrible. I can't even imagine that. And you don't have to tell me, I don't want to know, but don't tell me it doesn't matter." She paused. "That's what Aaron was talking about? A cop still asking questions about that hit and run? Because you're, what, the main suspect?"

"Yeah."

"Does the Sheriff know? Does Osterman know?"

"About what?"

"I don't know, you tell me. He knows something, I can see that the way you two look at each other when he's over."

Dave sighed. "He knows everything. Including the fingerprint stuff."

"Well, what is he doing about it?"

Dave shook his head. "He doesn't think they're coming. He thinks it's over, if it hasn't happened by now. That I'm safe. Hell, I don't have fingerprints anymore." He looked down at his hands and flexed his gnarled fingers.

"Right. No? Why not? Isn't he the expert? He's the Sheriff."

Dave shook his head again, sharply. "I can't think like that. I'm assuming the worst. And planning for it. If I'm wrong nothing happens. If I just start wandering around like everything's fine and he's wrong, and they come for me…" He looked past her, staring at nothing. His mouth was pinched together, and some color came into his face. "Well, I'm not doing that," he finished. "I'm not going down without a fight. And I've got a pretty good track record against these guys."

"What happened to that lab tech?"

"He died in the fire that burned down my house. Maybe in the gunfight that started the fire, I don't know." He huffed. Because Mickey had been honorable, honest, and true, it had ruined Dave's life. Mickey could have just shut up, figured Dave's matching prints were an anomaly, and now Dave would be an FBI Special Agent and Mickey would still be working at the FBI Lab at Quantico. It was hard to stay pissed at Mickey for what he'd done, though. It was Mickey's own honorable convictions that had gotten the idealistic lab tech killed. Actually, it was Dave's fingerprints that had gotten Mickey killed. That and Dave failing to protect him during the attack on his grandfather's cabin. And Dave knew it. He couldn't forget it.

Lori sat and stared at him for a long time. "That is such bullshit," she said with sudden force. "You want to tell yourself you're fighting, that this brave front is all about going out in a blaze of glory, but it's not. You're sleepwalking through life, waiting to die. You're a zombie." The use of the word shocked him. She'd never been to P-Dip, never heard their nickname for him, and yet there the word was again.

"Is that why you didn't care, don't care that I've done porn? Am I one last fling for the condemned man? Is that why you didn't seem to give a shit about birth control even after you knew I worked in porn? Never asked about HIV or anything? 'Cause you figure you'll be dead before anything you catch from the porn star will do you any serious damage? I've got an IUD and was tested for everything six months after I quit in case you were wondering. Which you weren't. Oh my God." Everything was so clear now. She jabbed a finger at him.

"You need to come out of your cave. You're not dead. You're not even dying. And don't fucking tell me different. I know. I KNOW. I go through that with someone who is fighting every second of every day for more life. Tonight was awesome, she was almost her old self, but don't think that's how it usually is. My mother has brain cancer and half the time doesn't even know who I am and has to wear a diaper and she's more engaged with the world than you are. It's like you're watching a timer on your life wind down. You might as well be in hospice. Stop it. You're alive." Then she punched him in the arm. "Fucking act like it." She punched him again, hard, and stomped off into the kitchen, fighting back tears. Dave stared after her, stunned.

She never came back, and he never went after her. After five minutes he let himself out and went back to his house.

Lori heard him go. She was sitting on her bed, not quite crying. After a few minutes she wiped at her eyes angrily, then paused. She thought for a second, then grabbed the tablet. She Googled "Dave David SWAT team Detroit gunfight hit-and-run mob mafia Osterman FBI murder Bufonte", although she wasn't quite sure how to spell the name. She figured the more details she could enter into the search, the quicker she'd be able to find out whether or not the fantastic story he'd told her was true. Sure, he seemed like a nice guy, and not crazy, and something sure was going on with him or the Sheriff wouldn't be involved, but his story was just so out there she didn't know whether or not to believe it.

Reading the newspaper articles and watching the videos that turned up in the search kept her up past 2 a.m.

"Holy shit," she said. All of it was true. No wonder he was so messed up. And so paranoid. It didn't excuse his behavior, but it sure explained it.

Chapter Thirteen

"You're a horrible person and I hope you die!"

Osterman smiled at the wild-eyed woman. "Good morning," he said cheerfully, noting her saggy t-shirt and what looked like pajama bottoms over flip-flops. Excellent attire for puttering around the house, but not exactly what he would consider appropriate clothing in which to appear in public. He responded to her, but he didn't stop moving down the sidewalk. The woman was standing next to a rattle-trap minivan and glaring daggers at him as he passed by, but she seemed startled by his cheerful response. The Sheriff didn't turn his head to keep an eye on her but Sam Wheaton did, walking next to him, until they were a good distance away.

"You see her kid she was putting into that car seat? Beefaroni-stained Ninja Turtles t-shirt over sweatpants and Kool-Aid lips. We'll be arresting him in fifteen years for stupid petty crimes, you can bet on that. Sure we can't require licenses to get pregnant? Just for a few years?" Wheaton asked conversationally, his voice low.

Osterman chuckled. Sam Wheaton knew his views on rights as well as anyone, and just because someone was hateful and stupid didn't mean they should lose their rights. As much as he understood the impulse.

Wheaton looked in the direction they were headed, then across the street. "Why do you insist on walking?"

They were walking down East Gurley to the Wagon Wheel Café. And 'down' wasn't just a meaningless descriptor, from the Sheriff's Department offices it was a continuous downhill walk to the narrow restaurant, although the slope wasn't steep.

"I am not wasting taxpayers' dollars on gasoline to travel a tenth of a mile," Osterman scolded him, as he had a dozen times over the years. "I am not so old and feeble as that." He hiked up his uniform belt, which provided a comforting, constant creak as they strode down the sidewalk. He eyed Sam Wheaton, who didn't have an ounce of fat on his body. Both of them were in full uniform, including Kevlar vests. "Neither are you."

"Morning Sheriff!"

"Morning," he called back, cheerfully, to the man entering the realty office.

"It's closer to half a mile, but who am I to argue," Wheaton said with theatrical shrug of his shoulders. "And you are so loved by everybody, not a thing to worry about."

Osterman looked pointedly as his Number Two and gestured around them. "I work for them. So do you, for that matter. Whether they voted for me or not. And as you well know, I'm not afraid to put myself out there." Osterman waved back at a woman on the far side of Gurley. Wheaton frowned behind his moustache but didn't say anything.

The Wagon Wheel Café was right across the street from Prescott's Courthouse Plaza, which consisted of a small courthouse sitting in the middle of a block surrounded by a lot of lawn and a number of old trees. The interior of the Café seemed dark after the bright late-morning sun on the sidewalk and it took a few seconds for their eyes to adjust.

"Mornin', Sheriff." Marla was such a stereotype of a diner waitress that she seemed more an actress playing a part. Her thick curvy body, drawn on black eyebrows, and big mane of blonde hair hardened with half a can of hair spray perfectly matched the painfully kitschy Wild West-themed uniforms the Wagon Wheel employees wore. "All the booths are full. Want to wait?"

Osterman smiled at her. "A table's just fine. How's Robbie?" Her son was a heavy equipment operator, but he was a heavy equipment operator with the United States Marine Corps, stationed in Okinawa, so Osterman always asked after him.

Marla blew a lock of blonde hair out of her eyes as she reflexively grabbed a couple of menus for them. Her breath barely made the hair twitch. "Getting serious with a local girl, which I don't think will be anything but trouble, but you can't tell kids anything. Especially ones that think they're in love. C'mon."

She waved over her shoulder and they followed her toward the back of the narrow restaurant. Half the people in the restaurant waved or called out a hello to the Sheriff and he nodded and smiled as he wound his way through the tables. He shook a few hands, per the usual. She set the laminated menus down on one of the thick wood tables and looked at the men. "Coffee?"

"Do you even need to ask?" Wheaton said to her with a small grin.

She snorted and whisked off as the men sat down and turned the thick porcelain coffee cups on the table right-side-up. She was back two minutes later with an insulated carafe of coffee. After she set it down she whipped out her pad. "Whatcha havin'?" She put the eye on Osterman. "Lillian still on you about your cholesterol?"

The Sheriff smiled. "My wife does surely love me, but if the good Lord didn't want me eating bacon he wouldn't have given me a mouth. Four strips, if you please, and three eggs, scrambled, with a bit of cheddar."

"You got it." It hadn't slipped her notice that the two men were sitting elbow to elbow, facing the door. "And you, hon?"

Wheaton looked up from the narrow menu. "The fruit plate. And a Belgian waffle. Lots of butter please."

"Coming right up." And she was gone.

Osterman's eyebrows crowded together on his forehead at Wheaton's order, and as he watched the man pollute his coffee with cream and some sort of artificial sweetener. "Sure there's not estrogen in there?" he asked, nodding at the yellow packets. "You're eating like a teenage girl."

"We can't all be as manly as you," Wheaton said through his droopy cowboy moustache.

The restaurant was about two-thirds full, which was a bit unusual for the hour. Eleven a.m. was late for breakfast and a bit early for lunch, as most of the Prescott residents didn't start their day as early as the Sheriff.

"Sheriff, do you know how long they're going to take with that sinkhole up on Cortez?"

Osterman turned in his seat and saw the voice belonged to John Chapper, who leased out close to a dozen buildings within a half mile radius of the Wagon Wheel. He was sitting with three other locals in a booth.

"Chappie, didn't see you there, good morning! Well, technically, that's not my department, unless that sinkhole gets a little rough with its spouse or starts driving under the influence, but I hear tell everything should be back to new or thereabouts by the end of the week."

Chapper didn't appreciate the Sheriff's attempt at humor, but then he never did. He huffed, then said, "What about that double murder? That your department?"

"Now you know I can't talk about that, ongoing investigation and all."

One of the other men in the booth spoke up. Osterman recognized him, but the man's name escaped him. "But they caught the guys, right? We don't have to worry about some psycho who's watched too many horror movies wandering around town."

"Arrests have been made," Osterman assured him. "And it appears to have been an isolated incident that's over." That got one of Wheaton's eyebrows to twitch, but he didn't say anything, just took another sip of his coffee.

"That was cartel business," Chapper said sourly. "Cartel business is never over." But he let the matter lie. At some point when the Sheriff was digging into his bacon Chapper's group left the restaurant, which was far less busy than when the Sheriff had arrived.

When Marla came over with a busboy to collect the tip and clean the table, Wheaton asked her, "So is Chapper one of those rich cheapskates who don't tip or is he a big tipper to show just how important he is?"

Marla turned around and put a hand on her hip. "Now what kind of waitress would I be, Sam Wheaton, if I divulged information like that to just anyone who asked? She gestured behind her, where the busboy was finishing cleaning the booth. "The table's like a confessional, what happens between a waitress and her customers is confidential."

Wheaton was smiling. "Good to know."

Marla smiled. "Unless you're a lousy tipper. Then I'll tell everyone." Osterman snorted as she sped off, smelling of bacon and hair spray. Two minutes later she was seating a construction worker—had to be with the hard hat and reflective vest, probably working on the sinkhole repair—at the cleaned booth. The man had a thick hardcover book in one hand, but he set it on the table unopened and pulled out a smart phone as he sat down. Osterman nodded at the man and went back to eating.

"So what's the word on that thing?" Wheaton asked him around a mouthful of waffle. "Anything new?" He knew the Sheriff was still getting daily updates on the double homicide but Wheaton wasn't sitting in on them.

Osterman kept his voice low. "Not of note. Murphy is doing a good job running everything down, but the trails don't lead anywhere. House rented by a shell of a shell of a shell corporation, and that's the strongest evidence we've got that it's cartel business. Any credit cards involved go to newly established accounts that aren't linked to anything or anyone. The guys in custody haven't said two words to us, and nothing to anybody else. Other than a presumed turf war between the Zetas and the other one, I forget it's name—"

"*La Fuerza*, I think."

"Sounds right. Well, we don't know the details of why it happened. It seems a good guess that the feds know more about the what and why than they're willing to let on, but that's par for the course. There's something going on behind the scenes, that's for sure, an operation in progress or an informant, but I'd be surprised if there wasn't. The torture probably means the suspects were trying to get information out of those two now-dead men, but maybe not."

"Do we care? There wasn't enough blood on Muñiz' cuff for a DNA match, but the witness ID'd his photo. And picked the other guy's mangled ear out of a six-pack line-up of mangled ears, that was a genius idea by Flores. She's been just flat-out fabulous as a detective. Boy howdy, whoever hired her really has amazing judgement." He tried on an innocent look, which the Sheriff ignored. Wheaton made the final decision on all the hiring for the department. "Eyewitness and two rock-solid line-up picks? That's better than a confession. Well, just as good. Even if the other two who were with him never talk, Muñiz is going away forever."

"We still have this pesky thing called a trial that needs to happen before we can declare anybody guilty," Osterman reminded him. Juries were never a sure thing. He took a sip of coffee. "And I'd feel a lot better knowing why it happened. So I'd know whether or not it was likely to happen again. And I would have preferred our local paper not making it known to all and sundry that we had a witness."

Wheaton grunted. "Cartel's only one that counts, and they already knew. First thing those assholes in custody did when they met with their lawyer was tell him about her, and considering he's owned by the cartel I'm sure it knew about her ten minutes after he left the station. And presumably they've been looking for her ever since."

The Sheriff's cell phone rang and he fished it out of his trouser pocket. He looked at the number and saw it was a local extension. "Osterman," he said politely. Sam Wheaton watched boredom settle into the Sheriff's features, and he heard someone's faint voice going on and on and on.

Finally the Sheriff interrupted. "Stan. Stanley. Stan! I appreciate you thinking of me, but this is a Board of Adjustment matter. I don't have anything to do with zoning variances. I'm a county employee, remember. Not city. They didn't? Why don't you call Maureen, she's the City Clerk. Hmm. Have you talked to a lawyer? Well, then, I suggest showing up for a City Council meeting and giving them your two cents when they've got to sit there and listen to you. Second and fourth Tuesday of every month if I remember correctly, but the time escapes me. I'm sure they've got it posted somewhere. Yessir. Sorry I couldn't be of more help. Yes, you too." Osterman sighed as he ended the call.

"Do I even want to ask?" Wheaton said.

"Apparently half the people in the county think I'm the Mayor and every other high office-holder in this county," the Sheriff observed, and not for the first time. His second-in-command snorted.

Ten minutes later they were done and left a big tip for Marla before heading out the door. From his seat inside the booth Nelson watched them go, then looked around. No one in the diner was close or even in a position to see, so he opened the hardcover book, revealing the cavity that had been cut out of the pages. The rectangular cutout was just big enough for the electronic device he'd stuffed inside, a top-of-the-line Lamprey that made the hulking (in comparison) Harris KingFish seem like an Atari 800 computer. It and the supporting electronics and software had cost the cartel close to a quarter million dollars, and they'd bought it solely at his recommendation. He was supposed to be the expert. If they only knew.

He studied the readout on the Lamprey against the screen on his phone. Then he smiled, and relaxed. The Sheriff's phone had been successfully connected to, and as soon as Nelson got back to the safe house and entered a few commands he'd be able to listen in on all of the man's phone calls (while recording them) and the lawman would be none the wiser.

On their reconnaissance drives around town Nelson had seen all of the road construction going on, and thought the reflective vest and hardhat would be a good way to hide in plain sight. If he had to follow the Sheriff day after day, he'd have to change his appearance somewhat, and all anyone looking at him would see in this outfit was the vest and hardhat. But that was no longer necessary—his idea had worked on the very first try.

Nelson let the cover of the book drop and signaled to the waitress.

"Getcha somethin' else, hon?" Marla asked the construction worker.

Nelson hoisted his coffee cup. "A refill?" he asked without a trace of accent, unable to hide a smile of triumph. He had work to do, but even Ramos wouldn't begrudge him a cup of coffee in celebration of success. Maybe two. It had been a long road to get here.

"Comin' right up."

PART III
CONTROLLED BREAK

Chapter Fourteen

Dave paused the video on his laptop when he realized he had no idea what was going on in the Netflix movie. He wasn't sure when he'd zoned out, but it had been so long ago he didn't recognize the location on screen or the actor in the scene.

He was exhausted, physically, but that wasn't the problem. He couldn't stop thinking, that was the problem.

His brain wouldn't shut off, and it kept running in circles. It was why he'd been working out like a maniac all week. And the week before. He'd done his six miles this morning, flat-out sprinting the last mile. Then he'd done a full-body workout indoors, pushups, squats, pull-ups, crunches, lunges, more pull-ups, burpees, pull-ups again, and finally push-ups until his arms gave way and he found himself on the floor in a puddle of sweat, fighting back tears and not sure why.

He'd barely been able to lift his arms to eat a protein bar...and two hours later he'd been so antsy he'd gone for another run. Done four more miles at a near sprint, for a total of ten for the day. Then he'd practiced his draw and reloads and movement and target transitions and use of cover for almost four hours, until his shoulder was aching and he was getting a sore spot on his palm through the existing callus, precursor to a blister. But still he couldn't relax, couldn't focus, couldn't even sleep. It was why he found himself sitting in front of his laptop at 1:41 a.m., eyes blind to what was on-screen, mind racing.

Dave frowned at the still image on the screen of his laptop, the anonymous actor frozen in mid-sentence, his mouth open awkwardly. The image seemed to dissolve, the pixels growing as Dave stared at it, until the pattern vanished and they were a random mix of colored squares.

He blinked, shook his head twice, got up and paced around the place. At one point he glanced through the open door of the spare bedroom at the window, now covered with closed blinds. Just a few feet beyond that was Lori's bedroom. They hadn't spoken in over two weeks, since she'd yelled at and hit him. Staring at the window he made a sound in his throat and returned to his laptop. He closed out Netflix, opened a browser, and began typing. He wasn't sure if it was a good idea, in fact he thought it might be a very bad idea, but he needed to do something, and it was all he could think to do.

He stared at the search results, clicked a few links, and looked at the schedule. Second Sunday of the month. Well, they had a full schedule all month long, but that seemed the next likely event.

The date and time were at the lower right corner of his computer screen, but he couldn't remember what day of the week it was. He pulled up the laptop's calendar and checked the date. As he sat there it was very early Friday morning. The Second Sunday of the month was two days away.

Dave heaved a big sigh. "Well, hell," he muttered.

His destination was east of Phoenix. Google Maps told him it would be just over a two-hour drive, and he was hoping to get there half an hour before the start time of eight a.m. He barely slept at all, again, and found himself starting up the Jeep before five a.m. When the sun came up the baseball cap on his head would keep the sun out of his eyes, but he liked how it shielded his face for more than just that one reason. He stopped at the Maverik to top off the tank and grab a cup of coffee, then hit the road.

There were already ten cars in the sandy lot when Dave pulled in over an hour early, and he sat in the Jeep biting his lip. Was this a horrible idea? Or was it something that he had to do? Maybe it was both.

"Shit," he said, and got out.

Dave walked over to the small building. There was a sliding window, and a middle-aged man was sitting inside. Dave took a deep breath, then said, "Here for the match."

"That'll be twenty bucks. You need to fill out this waiver too." The man handed Dave a clipboard. "USPSA number?"

"Um, it's pending. I just joined."

"Gotcha. Good to see you. Is this your first match? You need a new shooter orientation?"

"No, I...I've been a member before, but my membership lapsed. I've shot matches."

"Cool. What division you shooting today?" Competitors were separated by the types of firearms they used for a more level playing field.

"Uh...Limited." That way he could load his magazines

up fully, the way they always were anyway. "Nine millimeter, so Minor power factor."

Colonel John Dean "Jeff" Cooper was the iconic figurehead who popularized the idea of holding handguns with two hands for faster and more accurate shooting. In the 1970s he started the American Pistol Institute—Gunsite—located in Paulden Arizona, about half an hour north of Prescott, where he developed and taught the "Modern Technique of the Pistol" which was now used by just about everybody on the planet even if they'd never heard of Cooper or gave him credit. He was also one of the founding members of IPSC, the International Practical Shooting Confederation, whose American arm USPSA (United States Practical Shooting Association) was the largest action pistol sports proponent in the world.

If Gunsite was the Mecca of practical shooting, then the Rio Salado Sportsman's Club in Mesa, Arizona, was its largest church. Located in the Usery Mountain Shooting Range, it was the home of at least three practical pistol clubs—Rio Salado, Hosemasters, and Red Mountain. Checking the calendar, Dave had seen there were three or four action pistol matches there a week. Most ranges around the country would be lucky to hold one match a month.

He'd been living in the area for two years, but he'd never been to Rio Salado before. Never even looked them up online, not until two days earlier, but he'd heard of it. Everyone who'd ever shot USPSA had heard of Rio Salado.

He hadn't typed anything having to do with competition shooting into an online search bar since he'd been shot. He'd been an avid competitor for years, and credited the skills he'd learned in competition—and practicing them religiously—with saving his life on several occasions. But he'd severed all ties with his previous life to keep himself safe. He still practiced with a gun every day, practiced more than he ever had when he was actually competing, but he hadn't fired a live round in two months. Gun shops and indoor ranges always had security cameras, and facial recognition software was in regular use by the exact people who'd come after him before. Matches required registration.

However, he couldn't get what Lori had said out of his mind. He'd been thinking about it since she'd said it. Couldn't stop thinking about it. He wasn't sure if he was there to prove her wrong...or because he knew she was right, if only a little bit.

Dave looked around at the lot filling up with cars and returned a few friendly nods from competitors. Then he went back to his Jeep, got inside, and without making it obvious unloaded the Glock on his hip. You could see a gun on every competitor's hip at USPSA matches, but they were all unloaded. Only the guy on the line had a loaded weapon, and then only after he'd been given the command to "Make Ready".

He could see twenty people from the driver's seat of the Jeep, and nearly half of them were already sporting handguns on their belts. It was probably the safest place he'd been in years, but still he was uneasy. He made sure to keep one magazine fully loaded with hollowpoints in the mag pouch at the small of his back, and one in the cargo pocket of his shorts, just in case. Then he put his empty pistol back in its holster and got out of the vehicle.

There were seven courses of fire or "stages" and he went out to look at them. Each one was on a separate range bay with a U-shaped sandy berm, although the ultimate backstop was a mountain maybe half a mile distant, dotted with saguaro cacti. The shortest stage required a minimum twelve shots to complete—five regulation cardboard silhouettes which needed two shots apiece and two falling vaguely-human-shaped steel "Pepper Poppers". The longest stage was a thirty-two-round field course that involved a lot of running and shooting around walls. 153 rounds total for the match, if you didn't miss or have to fire any extra shots.

Dave had a total of six 15-round magazines for his Glock 19, a holster, two magazine pouches, and he'd brought his second identical Glock just in case the first one broke in the middle of the match. It was his daily carry gun, and daily carry gear, nothing meant specifically for competition. While he'd been practicing a lot, he had no illusions about winning his division, and wasn't even going to try. He was here…he wasn't sure why he was here. To prove to himself that he wasn't hiding, wasn't scared? Wasn't acting like a dead man walking?

It had been two years. Whether that was long enough to be hiding, or far too soon to risk something as potentially stupid as this, he didn't know. He just knew that he needed to do something. He'd realized Lori was, at least in one way, correct—what he'd been doing for the last two years was, in fact, nothing.

The morning was a little chilly, and he took the opportunity to head to the Safe Area—where handling your unloaded firearm was permitted—and practiced his draw for ten minutes with his unloaded Glock. His fingers felt cold as icicles in the early morning air, and he massaged them a few times before he started. By the time he was done his fingers felt as if they belonged to him, although they were still quite cool to the touch.

Nearly ninety competitors showed up for the match. He was squadded with ten other guys and one woman, whom he learned in short order was married to a guy on another squad. Apparently they couldn't shoot together without arguing. His squad started on the short twelve-round speed shoot. All the targets could be engaged from one spot if you didn't mind a huge lean, but from the left side of the barricade three-quarters of one of the Poppers was hidden behind a wall. Dave suspected most of the competitors would hit the silhouettes from the left side of the barricade and take a short step to see—and hit—the two Poppers from the right side of the barricade, where they were clearly visible. Easier shooting, but the movement added time. Unlike just about every other shooting sport, competitors in USPSA didn't have to shoot the targets in a certain order. Figuring out the best plan of attack was part of the sport. He put in his earplugs and donned safety glasses and waited.

He watched two of his squadmates shoot the stage before it was his turn. Both of them shot all the paper targets from the left side of the barricade, then moved to the right side to engage the steel, just because the lean to hit the steel Poppers from the left side of the barricade was huge, and when doing so only a fraction of the one Popper was visible. It was a tough shot. One shooter ran the stage in just under seven seconds, the second one shot it in just over six seconds. He guessed they were maybe B-class shooters, which would put them in the middle of the pack.

When Dave was up he stepped into the rectangular shooting box and loaded his Glock at the Range Officer's command. He knew he'd been practicing an insane amount, hours every day, but he hadn't fired a live round in forever so he wasn't going to try to go fast. His goal was just to be smooth and have good hits. The carboard silhouettes were between seven and ten yards away, close enough that not only would he aim for their center "A" zones but he should be able to fire rather quickly. As for the Poppers…

that visible portion of the one half-obscured Popper wasn't much wider than his front sight when viewed from the left side of the barricade, but that still should be an easy shot, provided he didn't jerk the trigger. And wasn't the point of this whole exercise to challenge himself? Get out of his comfort zone?

The RO held the shot timer up behind Dave's head and used the codified commands. "Are you ready? Stand by." Behind the RO was the scorekeeper. The RO watched Dave, and the gun, and the scorekeeper watched the targets. The RO held the electronic shot timer, which beeped to signal the shooter and could "hear" the gunshots.

When he was competing regularly and trying his hardest to win matches Dave was always stressed standing in the shooting box. Palms sweaty, heart racing. Sure, he'd been in a gunfight once before, when he was younger, but he assumed that was an outlier, an isolated incident, and so let "match nerves" bother him, if just a little. Now, after surviving several no-shit gunfights, not to mention getting shot in the face and almost burning to death, Dave felt calm as he stood there. He had a loaded gun on his hip, and no one was likely to try and kill him, at least for the next few hours. He could relax, and just play the game.

At the beep he snagged the Glock in a solid draw and punched it forward in a two-handed grip, the sights already on the center of the leftmost silhouette even as he pressed the trigger. The recoil of live ammo felt strange in his hands, yet familiar. He worked the gun from left to right, tracking the front sight as it moved up and down in recoil, two shots each per cardboard target, the transitions between targets just as fast as the splits between shots. Then he went up on one leg in a lean and took one quick aimed shot at each Pepper Popper.

He knew they were good hits on the steel targets even before he heard the pings, and he saw the smudges on the paint, but because of the angle the targets were a bit slow to fall. Dave kept his eyes on the Poppers until it was clear they were on the way down, then ran his eyes back over the silhouettes. He saw all his hits were in the A zones and nodded.

"If you are finished, unload and show clear," the RO told him. "If clear, hammer down and holster." Dave pulled the nearly empty magazine out of the Glock, ejected the live cartridge from the chamber and caught it, pulled the trigger on the empty gun while it was pointed downrange to verify it was clear, then holstered his pistol.

As Dave stepped out of the shooting box, thinking back on the run and distractedly rubbing his right hand, the RO looked at the time displayed on the shot timer and then showed it to the scorekeeper, his eyebrows sliding far up his forehead. The scorekeeper looked at the screen. **3.56** Just as fast as it had seemed. Surreptitiously he pointed at Dave with a wondering look on his face. *You know who the hell he is?* was the obvious question on his face.

The RO just shrugged and shook his head. Then he called out to the waiting squad members, "Range is clear! Target pasters please. And don't forget to reset the steel. Who's the next shooter?"

Dave moved back from the firing line still thinking about his draw. He hadn't been completely happy with how his front sight had appeared in the notch of the rear as his arms had reached full extension. He'd been smooth and quick and all of his shots had gone where he'd intended, so he was satisfied. Mostly satisfied.

The squad had more than enough people to help paste the targets in-between shooters, so he went back over to the

Safe Area and practiced his draw for another five minutes until he was satisfied with where his front sight was popping up. Then he rejoined his squad.

Dave thought about leaving right after the match, but curiosity got the better of him. After putting his range bag in the back of the Jeep he wandered back toward the "stat shack", wondering just how he'd done. All the scores had been entered on Nooks, and several people had mentioned how it usually only took the staff ten or fifteen minutes from the end of the match to get the results done.

"You had a damn good match," Dave heard. He looked up, and it was one of the guys from his squad.

"Thanks," he mumbled. He gave a half smile, then wandered a few feet away without making eye contact, not wanting to get into a conversation with anyone. He'd barely traded six words with anyone on his squad all day. He glanced around and saw that there were still a lot of people hanging around for the results. They clustered in groups under the covered shooting areas at the rear of the bays or between the vehicles in the parking lot after loading their range bags into their car trunks or truck beds.

He hadn't had a miss for the match. In fact, he hadn't missed a piece of steel or had to fire an extra shot at a paper target. After that first stage, where he'd felt a little sloppy and choppy firing live ammo after months of doing almost nothing but dryfiring, he'd pushed himself a little. Not to the raggedy edge, but just to point where the smoothness started to disappear. He still wasn't sure why he'd decided to shoot the match, but he was glad he'd done it. He'd had a good time, gotten in some good practice, and nothing bad had happened.

Dave walked back over to his Jeep and grabbed a piece of gum out of the center console. The nearby rifle range was very busy, and from time to time he could hear a machine gun cut loose on full auto. Eventually he wandered back toward the gathered crowd. He hadn't been rude or antisocial, but from his body language it seemed clear to the rest of the shooters in the squad that he wasn't interested in socializing, and apart from meaningless niceties he hadn't spoken to anyone all day. So he was shocked when someone just a few feet away blurted, "Dave? Dave Anderson? Gunfighter? Jesus, man, holy shit, that is you! Fuck!"

Dave froze, then his left hand went behind his back to grasp the magazine loaded with hollowpoints as his right settled on the Glock still in its holster. But as he turned he realized he recognized the voice, and recognized the face of the man staring at him with complete surprise.

After a two-beat pause Dave let go of his pistol and, forcing a casual tone, said, "Hey Frank." Frank Falmouth, one of the regulars at his old club, standing there with his hands on his hips looking at Dave, smiling wide. Jesus, what were the chances? Running into somebody he knew, halfway across the country, especially FoulMouth Frank. Shit. Actually, considering how many people from the Midwest retired to Arizona, maybe he should have expected something like this...

"Jesus, dude, it's awesome to see you. Fuck. You just fucking disappeared after doing your John Wick impression. Almost didn't recognize you with that beard. You move down here too?" Frank stared at Dave. Between the beard and being so skinny, anywhere else he probably wouldn't have recognized him, but at a match his brain had clicked when he'd seen him in profile.

Dave didn't answer for a second, then shook his head.

"No, just in the area." He kept his voice low, hoping that Frank would follow suit, but Frank kept right on talking as if he was trying to be heard over loud music.

"That's fucking awesome," Frank said. "I'm glad I ran into you. You been shooting a lot?" He didn't wait for Dave to answer. "I haven't been shooting a lot of matches, since I retired down here it's been all rifles. Not a lot of four- and six-hundred-yard ranges in Michigan, but here all the rifle ranges go out forever. You ever do any long range rifle shooting?"

Dave shook his head again. "No, just 3-gun. That bench rest kind of stuff, I never really liked it. Slowly squeezing the trigger, that controlled break, waiting for the kick, it's not my style. I always get impatient and tired of sitting there and jerk it because I want the gun to go off. But you do that benchresting and you throw the crosshairs all over the place. At least I do."

Frank laughed. "So do I, but I'm trying to train myself to stop. You shoot the match today? How'd you do?" His eyes dropped down to the compact Glock at Dave's waist. "You shoot that?"

"All right, combined results," he heard someone calling out. Dave turned and saw one of the overweight guys in the stats shack thumb-tacking several sheets of paper on the corkboard on the side of the building. "They'll be divided by division when we post them to USPSA tonight."

The two dozen shooters in the immediate area clustered around the sheets, and everyone else began moving in that direction. Dave was twenty feet away when he heard someone exclaim loudly, in a British accent that seemed totally out of place in Arizona, "Who the fuck is Jack Burton?"

Dave looked over and saw a balding middle-aged guy

with glasses and a bit of a gut staring at the posted scores, looking more perplexed than anything else. Feeling a bit anxious, Dave squeezed between two shooters, getting close enough to the printouts to read the results. There, fourth down from the top, was the name "Jack Burton".

Fourth place was a better finish than he was expecting, and Dave ran his eyes over to the right. He immediately saw that he'd shot 94.13% of the overall match winner, which wasn't bad at all. Then he saw that the guy just above him had been competing in Open Division, where the shooters used tricked-out custom space guns that looked like something out of a sci-fi movie. His Glock could hardly be compared to those race guns. Dave had signed up for Limited Division, where custom guns were allowed, but no electronic red dot sights or ported muzzle brakes.

His eyes moved up one place. The guy who'd placed Second overall had also been shooting an Open gun. Hmm. Dave looked at the first place finisher. He didn't recognize the guy's name, but he was also shooting in Open Division.

"No, seriously, who the fuck is Jack Burton? An unclassed shooter? What bullshit is that? Any of you guys heard of him?" Dave turned around to see the apparently British guy close behind him, looking around.

"What's up, Angus?" somebody asked him. "You're tuning up for the World Shoot, right?"

Staring at the bespectacled, tanned Brit Dave frowned, then turned and looked back at the results. There, in fifth place, was Angus Hobdell, who had shot 94.09% of the first-place shooter. Dave had never seen him before, but he recognized the name—Angus Hobdell was a professional shooter, sponsored by CZ, who'd been going around the world and winning championships for twenty years. He ran the CZ Custom shop outside of Phoenix. It was then that

Dave finally realized that not only had he won Limited Division, he'd also beaten a professional shooter, albeit by a fraction of a percent. Dave looked at Hobdell again, glanced at the scores once more, then started to slide through the crowd toward the parking lot. He was so surprised that he didn't know how he felt.

Frank stepped over to the printout. His eyes went up and down, looking for Dave's name. "Where are you? I don't see you."

Dave stopped and shrugged. He grudgingly admitted, "I'm Jack Burton."

"What?" Frank laughed. "Well shit, you won Limited."

Frank looked at Dave, then at Hobdell. Dave followed the gaze, and saw the pro shooter looking at him.

"That's what I get for not pushing hard at a local match," Hobdell said ruefully. He looked at Dave. "Good show." His eyes dropped down, and he frowned a bit. He nodded at Dave's waist. "You shoot that today? Is that a fucking Glock 19?"

Dave looked at the Glock 19 on his hip. "Yeah."

"Dude, you kicked Angus' ass shooting a Glock 19?" Frank said. "Holy shit."

"Four hundredths of a percent isn't exactly an ass-kicking," Hobdell contested. He glanced back at the posted scores. "'Unclassed' my arse."

"It's just a local match," Dave said reflexively, looking from the pro shooter to Frank.

Frank wouldn't be shut down. "A local match at Rio Salado. And you beat Angus Hobdell shooting a Glock 19. At fucking Rio Salado. That's like winning the Daytona 500 driving a stock Corvette. Fuck."

"What ammo did you use?" Hobdell asked him. He and most serious competitive shooters hand-loaded their ammo to make it as soft-shooting as possible. Less recoil meant faster follow-up shots.

"Winchester white box," Dave told him. Hobdell made a face. The Winchester bulk ammo was inexpensive but recoiled quite a bit more than the handloaded stuff he was shooting.

"You been practicing?" Frank asked him.

Dave felt like he was stuck in a spotlight that he didn't know how to shake. "Some. Two, three hours, maybe more."

"Couple hours a week?"

Dave shrugged, wanting to disengage from the conversation and just fade away. "A day," he admitted.

"Two to three hours a day?" Frank repeated.

"For how long?" Hobdell asked him with real curiosity, peering at Dave from behind his glasses.

"Most of a year," Dave admitted. Hobdell nodded after a beat. That would do it.

"I didn't know you were British," Frank said to Hobdell.

"I'm American," came the immediate reply.

Frank frowned. "You've got an accent."

"The problem," Hobdell said slowly, "is you're listening in American, but I'm talking in English."

That confused Frank for a second, but he shrugged it off. He'd never let being confused stop him before, and he was practically bouncing on his feet looking at Dave. "No wonder you're kicking ass. Man, it's great seeing you. I haven't heard about you since Taran bitchslapped Billy Parr. Which was fucking awesome." He frowned and leaned a little closer, staring. "The fuck happened to your hands?"

Dave looked at his hands almost reflexively then blinked twice as what Frank had said registered. The confusion evident was on his face. "What are you talking about?"

Dave had been casual friends with a pro shooter, Taran Butler, who was gaining some notoriety as a technical advisor to a lot of Hollywood actors, but hadn't spoken to him since he'd assumed his new name. "Billy Parr?"

Frank looked stunned. "What, you don't know about that? Taran talking about you to Billy Parr on HBO?" He studied Dave's shocked face. "How have you not heard about that? Where have you been? Dude, you're a fucking legend."

"That was you?" one of the nearby competitors said to Dave, peering at him curiously. They were generating a bit of a crowd, the nobody who'd beaten Angus, and now talk of Taran Butler and his celebrated appearance on Billy Parr's HBO program FacePalm.

Dave felt as if he was a small animal caught in the headlights of an oncoming car, and was trying to figure out how to disappear without causing even more of a scene. But he and Frank and Hobdell had become surrounded by curious competitors.

"I heard about that on the Enos forums. Just like most legends, it was probably bullshit," somebody else said. "FBI and mafia and a gunfight with a SWAT team." He made a rude noise. Frank turned on him immediately, jabbing his finger.

"Fuck you!" Frank nearly shouted, seeming to take the comment as a personal insult. "I was fucking there when it happened. It was four against one and he got three, and scared the fourth so bad he ran into a cop car. It was fucking incredible, skidding cars and flying glass and brass in the air. And are you calling Shotgun John Osterman a liar? Those asshole crooked SWAT cops couldn't shoot worth shit, so the mob guy hired a buncha private contractors, sent them into Tohono county after Gunfighter here.

And look who's still fucking standing." He stuck a finger at Dave. "Osterman had a big news conference about it all over Fox News coupla years ago."

"I remember that," Dave heard. Everyone was now listening to the conversation.

"That was real? I read about that on Arfcom and thought it was just a story," someone else said.

"Was it true two of those contractors were former Delta Force?" a skinny guy asked Dave, pushing close.

"I don't know," Dave said, looking left and right for an opening.

"That was you? You the same guy?" Hobdell asked Dave. The transplanted Brit had been living in Arizona for years and had heard a lot of crazy stories and met a lot of interesting people. Iraq and Afghanistan combat veterans were easy to find in the shooting sports; people who'd been in multiple gunfights inside the borders of the U.S…not so much.

The professional shooting circuit was not large, and Hobdell counted Taran Butler as a friend. He'd heard the truth about Dave straight from Taran himself. Just about everyone active in the small world of practical shooting knew the story. It wasn't every day one of your fellow competitors made national news. The shootout with the SWAT team had been witnessed by half a dozen local competitors and had assumed legendary status, but the actual details of the gunfight that had happened under Sheriff 'Shotgun John' Osterman's watch were closely guarded. Still, Hobdell knew a lot of local deputies, and they'd described the scene to him, a bomb crater and burned-out cabin and most of a dozen people dead in the desert. And this was the kid, the sole survivor? Hobdell's eyes dipped down to the Glock and back up to Dave's face.

So he hadn't been beaten by nobody. Far from it, actually. Still didn't make him happy about it though.

"Hey, Angus," somebody from the back of the pack said. "You go to the Scottsdale Gun Shoppe much? They've got some of your guns for sale there, whole CZ Custom case. Place is fabulous. Got a separate range for VIP Members, got a rectal scanner and everything."

Hobdell was a serious competitor, and had expected to win, which meant he wasn't in the best of moods, even if he'd lost fairly. "Is it mounted on the floor?" he asked. "Do you stand on a ladder to use it?"

The other shooter looked confused. "No."

"Retinal," Hobdell snapped. "It's a retinal scanner." And he stomped off toward his car, vowing to put in more practice time on Monday.

Frank scratched his neck and peered at Dave. "You hungry? You want to catch a bite to eat?"

Dave flashed a tight smile at him, feeling like his head was about to explode. "Sorry, I've got to go. Good seeing you again." He pushed through the crowd and fought the urge to run to the Jeep. When he climbed behind the wheel he found his hands were shaking, and sweat was freely running down his sides under his shirt. He grabbed the steering wheel and clamped down until his knuckles were white to stop his shakes. When he looked up he saw at least a dozen pairs of eyes across the parking lot staring at him. Dave cursed under his breath and drove away as fast as he could. He was several miles away before he realized his Glock was still empty. He pulled onto the shoulder of the road and loaded his pistol, then just sat there. He closed his eyes and shook his head. His head went back and forth faster and faster, then his shoulders started going up and down and he found himself laughing out loud. He laughed for quite some time until tears built up in the corners of his eyes.

That had either gone exactly right or perfectly, horribly, comically wrong. He didn't know which. Couldn't know which, until something happened. But wasn't that how he'd been living anyway, doing nothing but waiting for something that might never happen?

"Shit," he said finally. He laughed again, sighed, wiped his eyes, then put the Jeep into gear and pulled out into traffic.

Dave found the episode of HBO's FacePalm with Billy Parr —or most of it—uploaded onto YouTube by some user named PasghettiJelly. It had been aired almost eighteen months before. Hands both cold and sweaty, Dave stared at the thumbnail of the video on his computer screen for five minutes, then finally clicked Play.

Parr started off with a nearly ten-minute monologue about current events, which now were not so current, and then he introduced his guests. There was a skinny bearded professor from UC Berkeley who'd gained some notoriety organizing protests against the new President, a comedienne who was slightly past her prime, Irish actor Aiden Gillen most well-known for portraying Petyr "Littlefinger" Baelish on Game of Thrones, and Taran Butler, who was introduced as a professional shooter and technical advisor for movies. Butler's hair, as usual, looked fabulous. The episode had been filmed in front of a live audience.

Parr and his guests sat around a table and talked about the news of the day for a few minutes, then the topic of Hollywood came up. Parr asked Butler about training actors in Hollywood, and they played the famous clip of Keanu

Reeves shooting live ammo—"Keanu Shredding With Taran Butler", currently just shy of ten million views—that Butler had uploaded to YouTube during his training of the actor for John Wick 2. Unlike most actors, Keanu Reeves could actually run a gun in real life. It was here that the professor jumped in.

"Don't you think that perpetuating the use of guns in movies is exactly the wrong thing to be doing in today's society?"

Dave shook his head at the question and watched as his friend Taran Butler blinked in confusion, then said, "What?"

"With all of the gun violence against African Americans and inner-city youth by the police, not to mention all the mass shootings we've had in the past few years—I mean, come on, it's an epidemic. Don't all these movies that you're working on just glorify guns and violence? You should be ashamed of yourself."

Taran looked startled, and Dave could tell the direction of the questions surprised him. "Excuse me?"

Parr jumped in. "There's always been that argument that violent movies and video games encourage violence in people, or at least numbs them to it."

"Video games these days are frighteningly violent and bloody," the comedienne agreed, nodding.

"These automatic rifles and pistols that everyone seems to be using in movies, any crazy person can buy them, and they've got no place in a civilized society," the professor went on, leaning forward.

"Gun control has always been a very important conversation in our country," Parr seemed to agree. "Especially when it comes to military-style guns." He turned to Butler.

"The kind of guns you train actors to use. And, if I'm not mistaken, you also sell."

The professor jumped in almost before Parr had stopped speaking, leaning across the table toward Butler. "Wouldn't you agree, that these automatic rapid-fire guns should only be for the military and police?" He looked at Aiden Gillen. "Aiden? Back me up here."

Aiden Gillen smiled wryly. "I'm from the UK. Gun control is pretty total over there." He gestured at Butler. "I've only ever seen guns, and shot them, while making movies. I wouldn't know even how to comment on this. It seems a uniquely American problem." There was scattered clapping from the audience.

Butler looked as if he'd eaten something sour as he looked at Parr. "I thought I was here to talk about training actors," he told the host. "Hollywood shenanigans." Then he turned toward the professor. "I'm not even sure what an 'automatic rapid-fire gun' is."

The man waved a hand. "Whatever the technical term is. In a civilized society, only the police and military should have access to those kinds of things. Not to mention the combat training that you seem to be doing. Not just actors, but regular people. If you're a civilian, all it seems good for is learning how to mow down children at a school."

"Hold on now, I don't think—" Parr started to say.

"Excuse me? Combat training?" Butler said, equal parts confused and irritated.

"That shooting stuff you do, those competition matches, where people are training to kill each other."

"It's a sport," Butler said, now visibly angry. "Action pistol shooting sports have been around, really, since the 1950s. It's fun, the whole family can participate, and their safety record is amazing. Nobody is training to kill anybody."

"It's simulated combat, though, isn't it?" the professor insisted. "Human silhouette targets and everything? Aren't you just practicing killing people? Anyone who would want to participate in these kinds of activities seems like a borderline sociopath to me."

Butler still looked non-plussed. "I came on here to talk about training actors for Hollywood, for movies and TV," he said. "Keanu shredding, and helping the Punisher up his game. Making sure actors playing soldiers and cops actually look and move like the heroes they're portraying onscreen. Now we're talking gun control? I feel like Tom Selleck on the Rosie O'Donnell show. What's the phrase, 'ambush journalism'?" He glared at Parr, then back at the professor. "You ever heard of self-defense? Or the Second Amendment? Or 'innocent until proven guilty'?" Butler asked him. His ears were actually red. "Action shooting sports are not just a lot of fun, they teach you proper gun handling skills that could be very useful in a defensive situation."

The professor scoffed. "The Second Amendment was not written about AK-47s. As for those combat shooting schools for civilians, let's be realistic, when would a person ever need to know how to shoot like that? Only the military and police should have that training. Your entire so-called 'sport' is nothing but training psychos to kill. It should be called Future School Shooters of America." There was laughter and clapping and boos from the audience.

It was here that Butler finally lost his cool. "A good friend of mine, Dave Anderson, minding his own business, good dude, upstanding citizen, bland as white toast, got an organized crime guy angry at him. Case of mistaken identity, if you want to call it that. So the Paulie Walnuts buys a dirty FBI agent who hires a bunch of dirty cops to take Dave out. Dirty SWAT cops gunning for an innocent kid. When that didn't work the Corleone hired mercenaries. I'm not kidding, ex-Special Forces ninja deathstalker types, to take on a kid barely out of college. And the kid won. Barely. The skills he got from participating in the action pistol sports you're trashing are the only reason Dave's still alive. That and having some of those 'automatic rapid-fire guns' on hand to defend himself with."

"That sounds like a bit of a tall tale," Bill Parr said, jumping in.

"Horseshit is what it sounds like," the professor spat. As it was HBO the profanity wasn't bleeped.

Butler stared at him. "I can send you the links to the newspaper articles. And the YouTube video interview with Sheriff Osterman in Arizona, one of the shootings happened in his jurisdiction. It was big news six months ago, you can find links all over the web. But maybe we should ban the internet. After all, if the Second Amendment doesn't apply to modern guns, the First Amendment doesn't apply to TV or the internet, right?"

"I think I remember that, actually," the comedienne said, perking up in her chair. "It sounded crazy. Big gunfight in the desert, right?"

The professor was shaking his head at Butler. "Your comparison isn't valid at all. Anyway, even if that story about your friend is true—which I doubt—that's a sad thing for everyone involved, but I still don't think he should have been allowed to have that kind of training. Even if, sad to say, he might have died without it. The good of the many outweighs the good of the few, or the one, after all."

"You're just an ignorant flaming jackhole, you know?" Butler told the professor. Then he looked at Parr. "And you're a douche for lying to me about why you wanted me on your trash show. I remember when you used to be funny. What happened?" The roar from the audience was deafening.

Dave sat back from his computer as the video ended. He'd had no idea something like it was out there in the world. He glanced down at the view counter below the video—23,141 views in just under eighteen months. He'd known Osterman had given a press conference while he still been laid up in the hospital, recovering from his wounds. He'd seen a bit of it after the fact, and that press conference seemed to have been more about throwing corrupt government agents under the bus than detailing Dave's story. In fact, the Sheriff had been deliberately vague about the "young man targeted by criminals". And that was before Dave had told the Sheriff the truth about why he'd been targeted.

Frowning, Dave spent some time online, and finally found a bit of one news conference Osterman gave right after the incident. His memory had been accurate, the Sheriff never mentioned him by name, and laid the blame for the deaths at the foot of "a corrupt FBI agent and a known Detroit Mafia kingpin, in bed with each other".

"Jesus," Dave said. He sank down in his chair and stared unseeing at the screen. Two years since the press conference. A year and a half since Taran mentioned him by name on HBO. How many people had seen that at the time, live? A hundred thousand? More? Plus the twenty-three thousand views this video had on YouTube. He'd disappeared, but what he'd done hadn't. His name hadn't vanished either.

And...nothing.

Dave sat for almost an hour, thinking. Then he roused

himself and looked around. It was dark outside, and he checked the time on his watch.

Lori answered just a few seconds after his knock. He hadn't seen her or talked to her in close to three weeks. She stared up at him, her face devoid of expression. Behind her he could see the kitchen light was on, and hear some movement.

Dave sighed, then looked her in the eye and told her, "You were right. About...shit...probably everything. I'm sorry." He frowned, and opened his mouth, but couldn't think of anything else to say. She stood in front of him, one hand still on the door, her face impossible to read.

After a few seconds Dave nodded, and turned to go. "Where are you going?" he heard from behind him. He turned, and saw the corner of Lori's mouth turned slightly upward. "We need a third for euchre."

Chapter Fifteen

Ramos stood on the sidewalk and looked around. There were people everywhere. Young people, old people, children and dogs and motorcyclists and bicyclists and even a few homeless vagrants wandering about wearing too many clothes for the mild weather. "Is it always like this?" he asked Gabby.

His young lieutenant smiled. "On the weekends, during the summer, yes. Or so I've been told. Prescott is a tourist destination." They were standing in Courthouse Plaza, in the center of the old downtown. It was mostly well-manicured lawn, with an old stone courthouse in the center of the block. Ramos eyed two teenagers throwing a Frisbee back and forth. Gabby gestured to the businesses lining the street to their west. "That's Whiskey Row. That bar there, they advertise that Wyatt Earp drank or gambled or whored there."

Ramos smiled. "Probably not whored. Well, probably, but I doubt they advertise that."

Gabaldon shrugged. "Men are men."

The two men began walking along the sidewalk. When they reached the north side of the square, which bordered Gurley street, they turned east. "Tourists from where?" Ramos asked, curious.

"Mostly Phoenix," Gabby told him. "The real estate agent we used to rent the house liked to talk. Apparently all the wealthy people from Phoenix come up here to escape the heat in the summer. We are at a mile elevation, so whatever temperature it is in Phoenix, it is twenty degrees cooler here."

"Twenty degrees Celsius?" Ramos said in wonder.

"No. Fahrenheit. I don't know what that would be in Celsius. Five degrees? Ten?"

They walked up Gurley, watching the tourists go in and out of the restaurants and art shops and the locals just enjoying the nice weather. Ramos spotted one man wearing a handgun openly, and two others who were carrying theirs concealed, but badly. He did not think they were police officers, just more Americans in love with their guns and Wild West history. Two blocks further up, at a corner, Gabby nodded at a building set back further from the road than the others. "And that, of course, is the Sheriff's Department."

Ramos looked at the big square building, then looked around. "Not as many tourists here," he observed.

"No, but still many people walking around. Still a tourist area, there is a steak house right there." Gabaldon pointed at the low building on the opposite corner. "And this street, it is one of the main ones in the city. If you wanted to do something distracting, right here in front of the *policía* would work very well. The whole town would run over here."

They'd been walking uphill as they moved away from the old downtown, and Ramos could see a good chunk of the city below him as he looked back in that direction. He nodded at the police building. "Is he in there?"

His lieutenant shook his head. "Not at the moment. David and Francisco are on him today, being extremely careful as you instructed. Do you want to talk to them?" He reached into his pocket for his phone.

Ramos shook his head. "Until we know where she is, we can't do anything." He took one more look around, then set his eyes on the steak house. "Are you hungry?"

"Yes, but it is a tourist town. You'll be shocked at the prices."

Ramos clapped the man on the shoulder. "Not much shocks me these days, Gabby, and I'm hungry. Let's eat."

Kling opened the door leading into the house from the garage and waited while Osterman climbed out of his Mercury.

Osterman had made a point to not be in uniform, and told the deputies to have the overhead garage door open so he could pull right in. He stood in the middle of the garage and peered out at the street and neighboring houses. The street was asphalt with a concrete sidewalk running along the far side—not much too look at, although "East Desperado Drive" sounded pretty impressive, very Wild West. The houses were sprawling ranches, with gravel front yards for the most part and small decorative (and hardy) shrubs.

The subdivision was on Glassford Hill Road just south of 89A on the north side of Prescott Valley. It was only a few years old, and the houses were large and pricey. And local real estate prices kept going up, as Prescott and

Prescott Valley became the go-to destination for Phoenix residents looking to escape the heat or retire.

"You can go ahead and close that," Osterman said to his deputy with a nod.

Kling hit the button and the overhead door rumbled down. Osterman followed him into the house. Kling was tall and blonde and resembled a lumberjack in his jeans and plaid shirt. The shirt was unbuttoned in front and untucked to cover the pistol at his waist while providing easy access.

The ranch home had an open floor plan and the provided furnishings seemed somewhat stylish, although Osterman knew he was a bit of a Neanderthal when it came to furniture and fashion. He waited with Kling in the kitchen. The Sheriff smiled and nodded as the witness shut off the TV and then came over to see him. Dino Saunders, the other deputy on duty, followed. He was short and lean and dark.

"It's been a while, so I thought I should check on you myself," Osterman told the young woman. "You're being treated well? Getting enough to eat."

"*Sí*, thank you very much," she told him almost shyly. Physically she seemed healthy, there was only a hint of color still on her face from her beatings, but he observed that she almost seemed to cower whenever she got close to anyone else. "Too much food. I'm getting fat." With no more bruising on her face there was nothing to conceal how beautiful she was. Only the fear clouding her features tempered her beauty, and for that he hated the men who had done this to her.

He smiled. "You're still seeing the counselor at the hospital? She's helping?"

Her hint of a smile disappeared. She blinked, swallowed, then nodded. "*Sí*."

"I know how difficult this all has been for you," Osterman told her. "You've been through something that most people can't even imagine. It might have broken some women, but not you. I can see that. I can see how strong you are."

Reina had been through a lot to get to America, but once across the border the worst trouble she'd had was working double shifts. Until this. "This is taking so long," she told him.

He nodded in agreement. "Our justice system is not as fast as it could or maybe should be, but we will get justice. With your help." He smiled. "Could I talk to my men for a few minutes? Alone?"

"*Sí*, of course." She walked over and sat back down in front of the TV while Osterman and his two deputies retreated further into the kitchen. Osterman glanced at the expensive stainless steel appliances and expensive tile accents on the backsplash.

"The Princess holding up as well as she seems to be?" he asked quietly.

"Princess, sir?" Saunders said with some confusion.

"Doesn't Reina mean 'princess'?"

Tim Kling shook his head. "Queen."

Osterman frowned and waved a hand. "Whatever. She holding together?"

"Seems to be," Kling said. "Talking to the counselor on a regular basis, and she's had several meetings with Shelly Hernandez. Hernandez has explained the local justice system to her, when she'll be required to testify, all that. She hasn't backed down at all. And Hernandez doesn't tend to sugarcoat things."

Osterman nodded. The Assistant Prosecuting Attorney was known for her bluntness. "Hernandez coming here?"

Saunders shook his head. "No sir, we bring the witness to her office in an unmarked vehicle, and check to make sure we're not being tailed every time we leave a meeting, whether it's with the counselor or Hernandez."

Osterman nodded. "Any trips recently to the station to sit down with the feds, answer questions?"

"Not in weeks."

"Hmm." His detectives hadn't found anything new examining the bodies of the suspects, and DHS Special Agent Joe Clark with his strange questions had not made a reappearance.

"She wasn't lying, we're all eating too much," Kling said.

"And watching too much horrible TV," Dino Saunders added. "Daytime TV causes brain cancer. But she seems to be handling things."

"Any issues I should know about?" Osterman asked his men.

"These twelve-hour shifts are getting a bit old," Saunders said with a shrug. "Although the overtime is really padding my comp time account. When this is over I'll have weeks in the bank. Wife'll want to go on another cross-country road trip to visit her relatives in Cali." Out of uniform he liked to keep his black hair slicked back, and it reflected the light in the room. Osterman didn't care for the look on a man in uniform, but since his men were in plain clothes, trying to keep a low profile, he didn't have an issue with a questionable overuse of men's hair care products.

Osterman had done the math. Bringing in a few more men would have been cheaper than the overtime, but he was doing everything he could to limit the number of people who knew the location of the witness. The fewer people in the know, the safer it was for the witness. He trusted his men, but he wasn't blind—cartels could offer a fortune in money to someone experiencing a weak moment, or simply torture them for the information. Best to keep her location as secret as could be, known to the fewest amount of people as humanly possible. And not stay in the same place more than a week or two. Speaking of that…

"How long have you been here?" Osterman asked, looking around. "It's a bit swanky."

"Nicer than my house," Kling agreed. He checked the date on his watch. "Not quite three weeks, I think."

"Just about time to move again, we only secured this house for a month. And I can't guarantee your next accommodations will be as palatial. We got a deal on the rental rate here…but not that much of a deal." In fact, between the overtime and the house rental fees the department was hemorrhaging cash.

"You got a place in mind?"

"Maybe." The Sheriff saw both his men had their sidearms at their waists and glanced around. "Where are your carbines?"

"One stationed at the front door, one staged at the back," Saunders told him. He tilted his head toward the witness in the other room. "She doesn't like seeing guns lying around, I think it gives her some bad memories. Maybe from what happened. Maybe from Mexico. So they're out of sight, mostly, but easily accessible. Has the cartel made any threats concerning her or their head honcho we've got in lockup?"

Osterman shook his head. "No, nothing. I've been keeping in regular contact with the DEA and the FBI and the U.S. Attorney's office. No death threats, no car bombs, no Mexico-style shenanigans at all." He paused, then frowned. "I'm not sure if that makes me more or less worried. I know this isn't exactly a grand assignment, and you might be inclined toward boredom, but keep on your toes. Because if they do try something, it won't be throwing rocks and shouting insults."

The sound startled him, and Detective Billy Dixon reached for his phone reflexively. He had it in his hand before he realized it was his alarm going off and not a phone call. He glanced at the screen. SHITHEAD SEARCH was the name of the alarm.

He shut off the alarm and rubbed his eyes, then checked his watch, even though the alarm went off at 3 p.m. every Thursday. Then he sighed. He was in the office, and not in the middle of something, so he didn't have an excuse, and he hadn't had time the week before...but this routine was getting a bit old. How long had he been doing it, almost a year? Still, it had been a month or more since he'd talked to Anderson's stripper ex-girlfriend and his trailer trash ex-partner, shaken that tree. Maybe something had finally come loose.

He wiggled his mouse to wake up his computer, and then first did a simple internet search—Dave David Anderson Michigan Arizona. If only the kid had a less common name...

It took him half an hour to look through the first ten pages of Google results, but he didn't find anything new linking back to his vanished shithead. That done, he went to AR15.com, which he'd learned was one of if not the largest gun-related forum on the internet. While it was named after one specific rifle, the website and the accompanying forums discussed just about everything that pertained to firearms. The "locals", as they were, called it "Arfcom", and as he clicked in he saw that there currently were just under ten thousand people on the site. At least ninety percent of them crazy or dangerous, near as he could tell, but that description seemed to fit Anderson to a T.

He perused various forums, just checking the subject lines of the threads as there were far too many threads to read every single reply. Heck, the "AR Discussions" forums alone contained 2.4 million replies to posts stretching back years. He was only interested in newer posts, luckily, but still it took him close to an hour just to skim the headlines of the site forums. He found nothing that mentioned David Anderson either directly or otherwise.

Dixon had spent so much time investigating him over the years that he knew as much about Anderson as any other suspect he'd ever investigated, even though Anderson had never so much as sat down for an interview with him. Anderson had been a competitive shooter, and a member of the United States Practical Shooting Association. Dixon went to the members area of the USPSA website and after signing in (he'd long ago bought a membership specifically for this reason) checked through the classifieds and what little other info there was there. No luck.

After a bathroom break and a quick check of his watch, Dixon sat back down at his computer and visited the final stop of his weekly (more or less) online David Anderson search, the Brian Enos forums. Near as he could figure it out, Brian Enos was a former professional shooter, and the forums on his website seemed to be the most popular among active USPSA shooters. Dixon was a member of the Enos forums as well, as being a member gave him unrestricted access to the posts and what information there was on the people posting, and as he logged in he saw that there were just under five hundred people cruising the forums.

Fighting boredom, Dixon clicked through the various folders and forums and skimmed the subject headers. His hand stopped and he blinked, then he rolled the mouse wheel back up. In the Miscellaneous section, in the *Hell, I Was There* forum, was a posting entitled **The Legend is Back and Kicking Ass**. Hmm. On a hunch, he clicked on it.

The original post, written by Enos forum regular FoulMouth1 just four days earlier, made Dixon's heart race. "Guess who came to dinner? Dave Anderson showed up for a match at none other than Rio Salado and engaged Beast Mode! Gunfighter shot Limited Division with a Glock 19 and won, even beating Angus Hobdell. Apparently you can't keep a good man down."

The first reply was someone wondering who the hell Dave Anderson was. The next poster wrote, *He's living proof that the tactards who say that competition will get you killed don't know what the hell they're talking about. He's the guy Taran Butler defended and used as a pro-2A example on FacePalm with Billy Parr.*

Two posts later FoulMouth 1 posted a link to a YouTube video. Dixon clicked on it, only to see it was the clip of the Billy Parr show from several years earlier where Anderson was mentioned. Dixon had seen it when it was new.

The name 'Rio Salado' was vaguely familiar and Dixon Googled it. He discovered it was Rio Salado Sportsmen's Club, a shooting range in Arizona, outside Phoenix, and that several USPSA-affiliated clubs with odd names such as Hosemasters and Grandbaggers held matches there. He double-checked the date on the original Enos post, then went on the USPSA website and checked the results for the pertinent matches.

Heart racing, he skimmed every Limited Division results page, but didn't see Anderson's name anywhere. Frowning, he relaxed, thought for a second, then quickly Googled the name Agnus Hobdell, learning he was a somewhat famous professional shooter and gunsmith. Then Dixon went back in and looked for Hobdell's name in the match results. He found it in just a few minutes.

Hobdell had come in second place at a recent match, beaten very narrowly by…Jack Burton? Why was that name familiar? There was no USPSA member number listed for Burton, just "pending". Still frowning, Dixon Googled the name "Jack Burton" and a dozen photos and video clips of Kurt Russell from Big Trouble in Little China popped up. Dixon instantly remembered Anderson had been a big sci-fi movie fan and he nearly jumped in his chair.

He stabbed a finger at his computer monitor. "Found you, fucker!" he nearly shouted, smiling. Okay, maybe not yet, but he had an honest-to-God praise Jesus slap your momma Goddamn solid lead on Anderson, for the first time in forever.

He had Anderson's current alias and a last known location which was only a few days old. His fingers flew over his keyboard as he started running checks on the new name, focusing his search on the Phoenix, Arizona area.

Chapter Sixteen

"Yessir, we're here now. Just checked in. Well, grabbed the key from the manager, we didn't actually fill any paperwork out, she went straight from the car to the room. I presume you handled that?"

"Oddly enough," Osterman told Deputy Kling, "Max Leopold and I, he's the owner of the Pima, we go back thirty years or so. His father opened that motel back in the fifties, when Prescott Valley wasn't much more than a wide spot in the road east of town. It didn't incorporate as a town until…seventy-seven? Seventy-eight? Somewhere around then. For the time a sixty-room motel seemed a bit ambitious, but now it's a tiny inn in a town filled with giant chain hotels. We're getting a good deal on those rooms. Although not as good as you might hope from a police booster." The Sheriff sounded slightly put out about that.

Tim Kling looked around the small motel room. The décor was dated and kitschy, but it wasn't actually old. Between the wildly patterned carpet and bedspreads and drapes it appeared the owner had deliberately been going for a retro '70s look to the place…and it kinda worked. He stepped to the curtain and peered out. The sheet metal and neon sign at the far edge of the parking lot for the Pima Motor Lodge was original and painstakingly maintained. It was brightly lit at night, greens and red and blues. Beyond it traffic whizzed by on 69. "He's got a whole retro look going on here. Not sure if it's my thing."

"Tourists love it," Osterman told him. "Always makes me think of *North by Northwest* when I see the front of that place."

Kling looked left and right, then let the curtain fall back across the window. "We've got two adjoining rooms on the third floor, three-ten and -eleven." The door between the rooms was open and the witness was on the bed in the next room, reading the provided Gideon Bible. "Almost in the middle of the place. Anyone in the parking lot can see us if we leave the room, but we've got a perfect view of the whole lot out the window and the manager knows to call us if he sees or hears anything hinky. He's got brand new digital cameras up all over the place." The hotel was designed in a shallow U, the arms facing south toward 69. All of the rooms opened on the inside of the U. There was a short roof to keep Arizona's nonexistent rain off the textured concrete walkway on the third floor, and a waist-high iron railing on the second and third floor walkways to keep drunk guests from falling to the parking lot below. There were open steel staircases in both the 'elbows' of the U.

Kling didn't like the cheesy tourist motel as much as the expensive house they'd just vacated, but he had to admit that the motel rooms would be a lot easier to defend. With them positioned on the third floor, the only way in was through the front door. Or the windows in the front of each room looking out onto the walkway, he supposed. They'd told the witness to make sure the thick curtains were closed at all times, and she'd just nodded. She'd been no trouble at all—she'd gone through hell, but she was determined to do the right thing, and not dumb about what that meant.

"Dino Saunders there with you and the Princess?"

"Princess? Oh, the witness." The Sheriff continued to think her name Reina meant princess when it actually meant queen. In Spanish, princess was easy to remember—*princesa*. "No, Dino's off today, I'm here with Flintstone. Uh, Brian Talbot. Well, actually, he's making a run to Del Taco, but he'll be back in just a few minutes."

He heard someone walking outside and his eyes instinctively darted to the M4 carbine leaning against the front wall under the window. Then he looked out the curtain in time to see his partner returning with several bags of fast food. Kling opened the door, pointed at the phone in his hand and mouthed 'Osterman'. Talbot nodded and set the bags of food on the small round table. It was stained a dark brown and made of some low-grade pressed wood. Reina came in from the other room and helped Talbot remove the food from the bags.

Osterman knew quite well just about everybody in the department called Brian Talbot Flintstone for his uncanny resemblance to the cartoon character, but as Sheriff he refrained from using any nicknames. Beneath the head that looked as if it belonged on Barney Rubble's friend the former Arizona State defensive lineman was built like the proverbial brick wall and was just a hair under six foot four. "I know I don't need to tell you, but I will anyway. I know she's still making trips to see the counselor, but keep her out of sight as much as possible. And keep a low profile."

"Yes Sir. Sir, any idea how long we might shackin' up here at the No-Tell Motel? Not that I don't love shag carpet as much as the next guy." As authentically retro as the owner of the place had gone, Kling was surprised there wasn't a coin-operated "Magic Fingers" ready to shake the bed.

Osterman snorted. "Two to three weeks is my guess," he told Kling. "Goodness knows I'd hate for one of my men to be offended by garish décor. I'll look into putting you up at the Prescott Country Club next, I'm sure the taxpayers won't mind footing the bill for that."

"I'll get my tuxedo ready, sir," Kling said, deadpan. After he disconnected the call he turned to see Reina staring dubiously at the food she'd chosen off the menu they'd looked at online.

"This is not Mexican food," she said, poking at her 'Street Tacos Plato'. To Kling she sounded both offended and insulted, and he fought back a smile.

Around a huge mouthful of food Talbot said, "No, but it's delicious."

"Wow". Lori sat back and stared at the credits rolling. She hadn't seen the entire series, but Dave had assured her starting in the middle of the second season as she had (backtracking a bit for him) would be fine, and they'd binge-watched the last three-plus seasons over the course of two weeks. And he'd been right, it had been great. "You know I haven't watched the whole show but that was really good," she said. "There were a lot of great songs they used too."

"Yeah, I got a lot of my workout playlist from watching this show," Dave agreed. They were sitting on his bed together as the credits rolled on the series finale of *Person of Interest*. They'd watched the last four episodes in a row, unable to stop. "The gun stuff wasn't that accurate, but I could look past that because of the story and the characters. It just kept getting better. And they knew the show was getting cancelled, so they wrapped up everything in the last season. Perfectly."

"The idea of an artificial super intelligence is scary. I don't know how believable that is. Maybe someday. The government corruption and collusion seemed a little over the top."

"You'd be surprised."

She glanced at him, opened her mouth, closed it, then said, "I loved Shaw and Root. And Fusco, everybody was great. I'm just sad that he had to die at the end," Lori said after a while, referring to Jim Caviezel's character.

"I'm not surprised," he told her. "You didn't see, but in the first episode he was homeless. And maybe suicidal. He tried sacrificing himself a number of times during the show, but it never took. From the beginning of the series he was almost like the walking dead, looking for a purpose in his life. He found it, and a family of sorts. If he had to sacrifice himself to save everybody he was more than happy to do it." She glanced at him, and saw he was staring off past the laptop, eyes unfocused. Again. While she had seen a definite change in him, a definite uptick in his mood, he was still the same guy most of the time—closed off and silent.

"Okay, so, what's the deal with all the books?" she asked him, jumping off the bed, trying to change the mood, and the direction of the conversation.

"What?" Dave's eyes focused and he looked at her.

She gestured at the bookcases lining every wall of his bedroom, every shelf stuffed with books, mostly old hardcovers. "You've got like five hundred books in here. Mostly old. I can't imagine you reading most of them. Where'd you get them?"

"Garage sales, Salvation Army," he told her.

"You reading them?"

"I've read a few."

She put her hands on her hips. "So what's up?"

He sighed. "Improvised cover. No way I could afford actual steel plates. Besides, I don't think the walls in this place are strong enough to support it."

"What?" She frowned.

He pointed at the shelves thick with hardcover books. "To stop bullets. In case someone showed up, if I had a chance to retreat, I could last longer in here with some cover. Probably only stop handgun rounds, but that's better than nothing."

Lori just stared at him, blinking. "Do I need to start calling you Doctor Doom again?" she said, her mouth wrinkling.

Dave snorted. "No, I..." He shook his head. "After two years, and that circus at Rio Salado last month, if something was going to happen, I'm pretty sure it would've." Still, he'd spent two hours the day before drawing from and working around improvised cover in his house, doorways and furniture and tables. A quick draw was fine, but the first two gunfights he'd ever been in had been in and around cars. Learning how to work a gun around cover—objects that could stop incoming bullets—was a very good skill to have.

"Pretty sure?"

He shrugged. "Nothing's ever a hundred percent. We could get hit by a meteor just sitting here." He looked at her with an innocent face.

"I'm going to punch you in the nose," she growled, and they both laughed.

"Where'd you go with your mom yesterday?" he asked

her. He'd seen them leaving the house. Plus, he wanted to change the subject. He wasn't sure how he felt about a lot of things—his safety, his future—and he didn't want to think about that. Not right now. Even after the big blow up with Lori and the debacle at Rio Salado he wasn't feeling bad. He wasn't quite sure how he was feeling, but there was something there. Something new. Something that had taken him over a week to finally identify, and that scared the hell out of him. Hope.

"I've been going to church with her. She's been wanting to go more than once a week, and I'm trying to spend as much time with her as possible. I haven't burst into flame yet walking through the doors, so…so far so good."

Moro parked the nondescript sedan at the curb, behind another vehicle, and quickly cut the lights and the engine. The men sat inside the car, windows cracked, listening.

The night air was cool, and there was a hint of cedar on the breeze. Their night vision had been wrecked by the headlights and the streetlights, and they couldn't sit there for too long, but every second they waited and listened could make all the difference in the world.

They waited for what seemed a long time but probably wasn't much more than a minute. Ronaldo hadn't heard anything other than the sounds of nature—the hiss of a breeze and the clicking of some insect. No human sounds at all. Just as to be hoped at two-thirty in the morning.

"*Vamanos*," Ronaldo hissed, and the men quickly and quietly exited the car and then softly pressed the doors shut behind them. The interior light had been removed so the car didn't light up like a Christmas tree when the doors were opened.

Ramos had put him in charge, and Ronaldo took a quick look around the neighborhood before striding across the street and plunging into the darkness between two houses. The others followed him just as silently.

There were porch lights and security lights here and there, but most of the houses were sheathed in shadows. The moon was a waxing crescent that provided no real illumination. If his eyes had been fully adjusted to the darkness he could have gone much more quickly, but Ronaldo found he had to slow down not just so his feet made less noise on the gravel that passed for yards in front of most of these houses but so he didn't trip on anything.

Ronaldo had chosen one of the AK-47s, as he had the most experience with them. He had it on a sling, down along the left side of his body, holding it with one hand to keep it from swinging. In his other hand was the long heavy pry bar, also held close in to his body. The other men all had rifles as well.

They walked swiftly between several houses, crossed another asphalt street that was dark as an ink river in the night, and then passed between two attached garages. At the far side of the yards Ronaldo paused and studied the back sides of the houses nearest him. They'd looked at satellite photos and done two drive-bys separated by quite a bit of time so as not to raise any suspicion, but everything looked different in the dark. Still, he was expecting that, and this was far from his first mission. He spotted the correct house and pointed.

The men spread out around him as they all moved cautiously forward. The diminutive Moro went to the right corner of the house, his AR-15 up and pointed at the dark windows. Francisco covered the left corner of the house, rifle up, while Daniel stood behind Ronaldo, covering his back.

The house was dark, no lights visible inside, and in that way it was similar to most of the ones on the block. There was a big sliding glass door off to one side, and as always glass was easy to break, but Ronaldo had chosen the standard door at the rear of the house for their point of entry.

It appeared to be a standard wood door. He knew he could kick it in easily with one, maybe two well-placed hits of his boot, but doorkicking was noisy. Not as noisy as breaking glass, but still.

He glanced left and right. The men were looking all around, not just at the neighboring yards but through the windows into their target house. Nobody was signaling him, so he assumed everything was clear.

With a grunt he wedged the angled tip of the pry par into the crack between the door and frame just above the dead bolt. He pushed the tip in as far as it would go, then wrapped both his hands around the far end of the four-foot bar, braced a foot against the house on the far side of the door, and began pulling. Ronaldo didn't jerk on the bar, he just exerted steady pressure, using all of his two-hundred and fifty pounds and not inconsiderable muscle.

He heard a creak and then a crack, and then suddenly there was some play in the bar as the dead bolt shaft popped out of its receptacle in the frame. In the quiet night all of the men heard the sound and knew what it meant.

Daniel moved up and pressed his body against the door while Ronaldo still kept pressure on the pry bar. Francisco and Moro moved in close.

Ronaldo traded a look with Daniel, then the younger man shouldered the door open as Ronaldo stepped back. By the time he'd set the pry bar down on the ground and gotten his hands on his AK Daniel and Francisco were already inside.

He tapped Moro on the shoulder and they moved into the house. They heard the other two men off to the right so they went left, first encountering a large room that seemed black as pitch compared to the moonlit yards outside. There was a large TV just visible as a dark rectangle on the pale wall. Past that room were the bedrooms, but after less than thirty tense seconds of searching it was clear that the house was empty.

The four men met in the kitchen at the center of the house. He'd heard no shooting, so he assumed everyone had come up empty, but Ronaldo waited for their shaking heads before heading out of the house the way they'd come in. He bent and without even slowing down grabbed the pry bar off the ground.

Less than four minutes after leaving the car they were back in it. The headlights seemed nuclear-blast bright to their eyes, which had just started adjusting to the dark. As Moro pulled away the men hid their rifles on the floor as well as they could, and Ronaldo pulled out the disposable cell phone.

"Yes." Ramos' voice sounded tense.

"It was empty, as you suspected," Ronaldo told his superior. "We're heading back now. Less than ten minutes if we don't run into any problems."

"It was worth a look," Ramos told him. "A little practice, if nothing else. Good job. We will see you soon."

Ramos ended the call and turned to Nelson, who still looked half asleep. "It was as you suspected, the house was empty."

Nelson shrugged, then yawned. "I told you."

They'd had a loose tail on Osterman since Nelson had successfully linked into the Sheriff's cell phone, because knowing where the man was could be an important piece of the puzzle when listening to his calls. They'd lost him inside that new Prescott Valley subdivision full of large houses, the man had made a turn and then simply disappeared into a garage (presumably), and just a few hours later Osterman had made a call which seemed to indicate that he'd been visiting the witness while in that neighborhood.

It had taken Nelson, and Leo with his computer skills, two days to narrow down those two blocks of potential locations to one probable address. An address that belonged to a house with a history as a rental property. When Nelson called the agent, inquiring about renting that specific house, using his best Midwestern white guy voice, he'd been told that the house was in the process of being cleaned but would be available to be shown to potential renters the next day.

So the witness and her guards had already vacated the premises...most likely. Still, they were there to do a job, and Ramos had sent four of his best men to check out the house. Because you never knew.

Nelson yawned again, and Ramos smiled. "Go on, go back to bed, I know you have to get up in just a few hours."

Nelson nodded and shuffled back to bed. He was recording every conversation the Sheriff made on his phone, but monitoring the Sheriff's calls in real time was essential, and the *cabrón* insisted on rising with the roosters every morning, ahead of the sun. So Nelson did as well.

So far the Sheriff hadn't provided any hard details about the witness over the phone, but it was inevitable. They'd discover her new location, he was sure of it. As he climbed onto his soft mattress, Nelson thought, *Not this one, but it is only a matter of time. And then I will be one huge step closer.* The thought made him smile, and then he was asleep.

Chapter Seventeen

Dave checked through the window first, then opened the front door. The Sheriff was standing on his front porch in a dark blue suit, his personal vehicle visible on the street.

"I didn't do it," Dave said with a smile.

"Funny. Never heard that before. Not once." The Sheriff forced down a grin. "I apologize for not calling ahead of time, but I know how you are about phones. I was in the area, and I was wondering if you would like to go out to breakfast. Or brunch, actually, it's a bit late for breakfast. Uhhhmm?" The Sheriff's eyebrows crawled up his forehead in an almost comical manner as the door opened wider and a girl appeared.

"Sheriff, this is Lori," Dave said, nodding to her. "Lives next door, with her mother." He was in a good mood. He'd woken up after four hours of sleep but hadn't felt tired. He'd put in a six-mile run before dawn. Then—making sure not to use the timer, as its beep was too damn loud for six-thirty a.m.—he practiced his draw and shooting on the move for about an hour and a half. He'd taken a shower, and then Lori had come knocking on his door, and they'd spent a very pleasurable morning together. If Osterman had shown up five minutes earlier... Dave smiled at that thought.

"Ma'am," Osterman said, inclining his head slightly. "John Osterman, Tohono County Sheriff. I think I've seen you once or twice." Osterman's eyes moved back and forth. Half a second was all he needed to tell from their body language that they were more than just neighbors. He fought back a smile, thinking that Dave might find it condescending, but he was glad for the boy. Glad he was coming out of the self-imposed wilderness. And the girl was a cute one. Blonde hair and curves in all the right places; she looked like a good all-American girl, maybe a former cheerleader. He cleared his throat. "The invitation extends to you as well. I'd love to take both of you out to eat. Maybe talk a while. I was thinking Cracker Barrel, it's just up the road."

Dave looked at Lori, not sure what to say. Lori treated the Sheriff with a wide smile. "Sheriff, I would love to go out to eat with you. Love to ask you all sorts of personal, embarrassing questions about what's-his-name here, about the headlines you've made, about all sorts of things. But I honestly don't think you want to be seen in public with me."

That surprised Osterman. He straightened up and blinked. "And why would that be?" He glanced at Dave, who didn't seem surprised by her comment.

"You're an elected official. And pretty religious, right? I don't know if you want to be seen in public with an adult film actress. Porn star."

"Former," Dave felt obliged to add. "Retired."

Osterman blinked several more times. Wasn't life just the damndest thing sometimes? "Is that a fact. How long did you...er, were you..."

"Ten years," she told him. "Made a lot of money. Was very successful. And became well known, or so I'm told." She glanced at Dave, then looked at her house. "Then my mom got cancer, and I quit to spend time with her."

"Oh, I'm sorry to hear that," Osterman said with sincerity, using the time to think. "How is she doing?"

"She's dying. It's inoperable. But she's lived three times longer than they said she would, and she still has good days."

"Well, then, you are blessed. Enjoy every minute you have with her. Glad to hear she's a fighter." He studied her. "You've got clothes on now, which is a good start. I'm thinking...if you can assure me you won't start flinging your clothes off and filming a sex tape during our impromptu brunch, I would love to have you join us. I have questions for you as well. Life, in all its facets, has always intrigued me."

That was not what she was expecting to hear, that much was plain. Her mouth opened, then closed. Dave had the same surprised expression on his face. "You're sure?"

He smiled. "I am a Christian, that much is true, but I am no hypocrite. John 8:7, 'He that is without sin among you, let him first cast a stone at her.' My first name is not Jesus, so I've got all sorts of sins racked up on my tab, going back way before you were born. I assume I will have a lot of explaining to do when I get to the Pearly Gates." He looked steadily at her. "I imagine our Lord and Savior will have more of an issue with me and the lives I've taken than with you and what you might have done with your clothes off. And I'll say the same to anyone who asks. So what do you say?"

"I'll get my purse."

Ronaldo pulled the creaky Chevrolet into the parking lot and stared across the sea of glass and steel and asphalt. The big man watched closely for thirty seconds, then called Ramos on his cell phone. He made sure to speak English.

"He just arrived at a restaurant. It looks busy. So he should be here for half an hour or an hour, maybe more. I haven't been inside, but it should work for what we plan." He gave his *jefe* the address and location of the restaurant. Ramos recalled seeing it while driving back and forth through the city.

Ramos closed his eyes for a few seconds and took a deep breath, then opened them. The kitchen of the rented house was crowded with anxious faces. They'd been ready since dawn, just waiting for the right moment, and the room smelled of nervous sweat. He checked his watch. 10:31 a.m. How much time did they really need to get everything and everyone into position? Not much. Everything was ready to go, waiting for just this call. "This is it. Manuel," he said to the man in front of him, "Ronaldo," he added into the phone, "you go at eleven, exactly. You have five minutes to make an impression and draw all eyes and ears to you. Go," he told them forcefully. "You are all trusted soldiers. Solid, proven men. You know what to do." To Ronaldo, he said, "I am sending you Francisco, Nelson, and Daniel, with everything you'll need. Call me immediately if he leaves or something changes. I would prefer to include him in today's activities, but it is not essential."

"*Sí, jefe.*" Ronaldo sounded tense. Ramos didn't correct the big man's use of Spanish.

The Cracker Barrel was crowded. At least a dozen people were standing outside the entrance, chatting, a few others sitting in the large rocking chairs on the covered porch. Country music heavy on twang and banjo played from hidden speakers. Osterman got a few doubletakes as they walked in, but no one said anything. Dave and Lori exchanged a look and followed the Sheriff inside.

The gift shop/lobby area was relatively crowded with people as well, and the three of them waited in the short line before the hostess' podium by the wide doorway leading into the restaurant proper. There was very little empty space in the room—the registers lined the wall to the left, where diners paid before departing, and the room was so dense with shelves and counters and displays of jewelry and toys and candles and hats and gospel music CDs that there were few places where two people could stand side-by-side.

"Three for breakfast," Osterman said politely as he stepped up to the busy hostess.

"It should be about a ten-minute wait." The hostess blew a stray hair out of her face but didn't look up from her seating chart. "Name?"

"Osterman."

She started writing the name, then Dave saw her pen stall and she looked up. Her eyes went wide. "Oh! Sheriff. Um, waitaminute, I'm sure I can get you in there right away. Three you said?"

"Now hold on young lady," Osterman said with a smile, raising a hand. "You go on ahead and put my name at the bottom of that list, and when you get to me, in order, you get to me. The last thing I want to do is cut the line. And I truly despise those people who do."

"Um, are you sure? It's no problem."

"It will absolutely be a problem if you give me special treatment," he told her gently. "I work for you, not the other way around." He nodded, then took a step off to the side. "Just call us when you've got a table ready."

Dave heard the sounds around him change as people recognized the Sheriff. He took two steps to the side to distance himself from the Sheriff, for a better view, and just watched as the man drew people like gravity. In less than a minute Osterman had a crowd around him in the gift shop three deep. He never stopped smiling and shaking hands and making eye contact. Even when the person who leaned in was not happy, Osterman nodded and smiled and listened.

"Damn, he's good," Lori observed, standing close enough to Dave for their shoulders to touch. It was a bizarre feeling for her—out in public, in the middle of a crowd, and she might as well have been invisible. She watched the Sheriff work. She'd met a few real celebrities, and so far the Sheriff was anything but a disappointment. He seemed to be the person he played on TV, which was very rare.

"He's been Sheriff as long as we've been alive." Dave glanced down at her and the corner of his mouth curled up. "Well, maybe not you."

She opened her mouth to say something appropriately spicy in response, then her eyes darted to the Sheriff just a few feet away. Half the people pressing in to shake his hand were retirees, dressed as if they'd just come from church, and there were a few parents with young children as well. "I'll get you later," she promised, eyes narrowing. Dave just smiled, and she was glad to see it.

Manuel parked the sedan at the curb in front of the police headquarters and frowned.

"*¿Problemo?*" Moro asked him from the passenger seat.

Manuel shook his head and gestured at the automobile they were in. "This auto runs perfectly well, I hate doing this to it." There were a few other vehicles in the angled parking spots, so they wouldn't attract attention. It was late enough in the morning that there was already some traffic on the downtown streets, and people out walking their dogs or riding bicycles. Not as many people as they'd expected, though.

Moro laughed in surprise at the former mechanic. "That is what is on your mind right now? The car?" The small man clapped Manuel on the shoulder, then checked the time on his watch. He pulled the disposable cell phone from his pocket and checked the display, just to make sure he hadn't somehow missed a call while they'd been driving. No missed calls.

"Six minutes," Moro said. They'd arrived a little early, even with Manuel driving the sedan as slow and careful as a grandmother. Still, better early than late. Their instructions were to make no calls unless something went wrong and they couldn't get into position on time. If they received no call, they were to proceed.

Manuel reflexively checked his watch as well. He fought back his nervousness. "The Ford was where we parked it, yes?" he asked suddenly. He'd looked over and checked to see if the hatchback they'd parked nearby the day before was still there, but now his mind was blank. Had it been there?

"*Sí*, relax. Do not worry. We have the easy part. The fun part," Moro told him. This was not the first mission for either man, but Moro was known to be a cold man, good to have in a fight. Manuel did what needed to be done, but he always sweated through it.

"You and I have different ideas about fun," Manuel said quietly, his knuckles white on the steering wheel.

"Sheriff. Sheriff!" The hostess nearly had to shout to be heard over the crowd in the gift shop. Osterman politely pushed his way toward her. "We've got a table already, no cuts in line, I promise. But—it's right inside the door." She gestured at the doorway beside her. "Everyone who goes in and out will be walking by you. Do you want to wait for another one, maybe in the back?" There was a chunky waitress standing next to her holding several menus.

"Up front will be just fine," he told her. "That pretty much describes how I live my life anyhow."

"Yes sir. Enjoy your meal."

"She wasn't lying," the waitress told the Sheriff. "I would say 'follow me', but we're already there. Here." She walked through the doorway and then pointed. The country-style wood table was just inside the doorway to the left. "Will this work?"

"Just fine," Osterman assured her. He moved to the far side of the table and sat down facing the door. Then he patted the chair next to him for Lori. Lots of things to talk about with her, he'd been plain about that. Dave was left with the seat closest to the doorway. When he sat his back would be half turned toward the entrance. He wasn't happy about that, but the Sheriff had seniority when it came to choosing seats. He glanced around the packed restaurant, then sat down. The dining room was one huge room, packed with people, but tall wood lattice partitions divided it into smaller, more familial-feeling spaces.

"I'll be back with some biscuits in a jiff," the waitress told them. "Don't know if you're rushed for time but they've been rockin' it out this morning so your food shouldn't take long at all to come out. How about something to drink to start. Coffee? Orange juice?" She was dressed in a light blue button-down shirt and khakis, over which she wore a brown apron.

Nelson was back in the car two minutes after he'd left. He was sweating, but not because he was scared or even worried, just tense—the 'before' was always the hardest part of it for him. And this mission was riding on intelligence he'd collected. He wiped a hand across his forehead and leaned forward so Ronaldo and Francisco could hear him even with his voice low. "He's in there. Sitting at a table, just inside the door to the left. Past the lobby shop."

"Alone?" Ronaldo asked him.

"No, but I saw no other police."

"Good."

"It is *muy* crowded in there. Every table full."

"Even better," Ronaldo said. "They can watch and learn." He checked the dashboard clock, then his wristwatch. "Two minutes. Load up." He reached inside the bag beside him. The magazine was already inserted into the AK-47, and he retracted the bolt slightly to see if there was a round chambered. There was not. Without removing the rifle from the bag he worked the bolt handle, chambering a round. The men with him all did the same, the metallic sounds loud inside the car.

"I'm surprised you're not at church on a Sunday," Lori told the Sheriff.

He nodded and finished chewing his bite of biscuit and

gravy before answering. "Normally I would be, but my better half felt a bit under the weather this morning, and after getting her settled in front of the idiot box with a hot cup of tea I discovered service had already started. She didn't like my 'hovering', so I went out looking for trouble. And found the two of you. How long have you been dating?" His eyes sparkled with interest as he leaned in.

"A couple months I guess," Lori told him. "My mom and I were living there when he moved in, but it took quite a while before we started…talking." She glanced at Dave. She wasn't sure what the Sheriff meant by 'dating', but she figured whatever their relationship was, 'dating' was as good a description as any.

Osterman nodded, leaned back, and used the time needed to sip some water to decide what to say. He glanced around the restaurant. There were ancient farm implements, old sports equipment, and random antiques mounted on the walls, sometimes at dangerous heights. Horribly kitschy paintings and sepia-tone photographs of people presumably long dead. "So…adult film. I admit I am more than a little curious, but if you don't want to talk about it I am perfectly fine with that as well." He nodded at Dave. "It is, apparently, not a secret."

Lori smiled. "Not to him. Not to my mother. And I get recognized from time to time. It's part of who I am. Of what I've done. Nothing will change that, and I'm not ashamed of it. I enjoyed it, and was good at it…but I'm glad that part of my life's over. So ask away."

Moro looked around. "I wish there were more people. Not like this. Few cars, few people. Maybe in a couple of hours there would be more." Some of the downtown businesses were just starting to open.

"We're not here for the people, we're here for them." Manuel nodded out the windshield at the Sheriff's Department headquarters.

"One and both," Moro said flatly. He checked his watch. "Time."

The two men exited the vehicle and anyone watching would have seen how carefully they closed the doors. Then, each carrying a small duffel bag, they walked across the street and halfway down the block to an artisanal candle shop that had just opened its doors for the Sunday morning crowd.

Chapter Eighteen

Moro led the way down the sidewalk and turned the corner to the front door of the candle shop, which was open to the cool morning air. He stepped inside the shop and looked around. There was one slender young woman behind a register at the back of the shop, and about half a dozen other customers wandering aimlessly about. Every few seconds one of them would bend over to sniff a colorful oddly-shaped candle. Even with the front door open the store smelled as strongly as a perfume factory.

The sidewalk had sloped downward as they'd walked away from the Sheriff's Department building, and Moro saw that the windows on the sidewalk side of the candle store were a bit higher than was usual to accommodate the sloping ground outside. He moved inside the store and stood close to that wall. Manuel stepped in next to him, and both men set their bags on the floor.

Manuel glanced at Moro, feeling the sweat popping out all over his body, but the small man's stoniness buoyed his own courage. Manuel dug the cell phone out of his pocket.

The two men looked around, then squatted down over their duffel bags. Manuel typed in a number, looked it over to make sure it was correct, then glanced once more at Moro. Moro was intense as usual, and nodded. His eyes glinted in the light coming in the windows.

Manuel hit the small green phone icon on the display, then set the phone down on the floor. A pair of shoes appeared just beyond the phone.

"Can I help you two gentlemen?"

They looked up to see a woman in her thirties staring down at them quizzically. Her long black hair was pulled back in a ponytail, and her makeup looked perfect. Her eyes moved from the bags on the floor to the phone and then back to the faces of the men squatting inside the store for some odd reason.

Moro said nothing, he just remained there, elbows on his knees, waiting. Manuel opened his mouth, wondering if he should say something, when every window in the store exploded. The floor shook with the blast and suddenly the store employee was on the floor in front of them, screaming. Her face and arms were laced with cuts from flying glass that began bleeding profusely.

The concussion was greater than either man was expecting. Manuel fell backward onto his ass, and Moro had to catch himself with a hand. Their ears were ringing, and beyond that they heard car alarms and screaming. Several of the store patrons had been hit by the flying glass, but none as badly as the woman in front of Manuel. He forced his eyes off of her as she writhed in pain, shrieking, clutching her face where a piece of her cheek was gone.

Manuel found the zipper of his duffel bag and pulled it from one end to the other. He pulled out the AR-15 and chambered a round. Moro already had his rifle out.

The inside of the candle shop was filled with dust and glass particles catching the slanting morning sun like party glitter. Several of the people that had been inside the shop staggered outside, stunned, looking for the source of the explosion. There was a huge tower of smoke casting a shadow over the street.

Moro shot the shopwoman still shrieking on the floor, just to shut her up, then shot the two people standing in the doorway, blocking the way. The sound of the rifle inside the store was huge, but still it seemed quiet compared to the explosion. Or maybe his ears hadn't recovered from the blast. Manuel joined Moro on the sidewalk outside the store and they walked together toward the Sheriff's Department building, firing their rifles at anyone they saw. Every window in sight had been shattered by the explosion. Ahead of them cars were tumbled around the street like toys, some bent and folded as if they'd been made of paper. As they drew close they saw a crater ten feet wide where their car had been.

"*¿Esta loco?* How much did he use? I think I have a concussion," Moro spat. And to think he'd ridden in a car stuffed with that much explosive.

"Moro!" Manuel called out, his ears ringing violently. He saw the deputy in his brown uniform running out of the front of the building. Manuel raised his rifle. He fired until the man fell down, then he and Moro emptied their magazines through the fractured glass doors of the police building.

Francisco was in the lead, the AK hidden inside his untucked and unbuttoned canvas work shirt, underneath his arm. Six inches of muzzle hung below the edge of the shirt as he quickly walked between the parked cars, but he doubted anyone would notice. Daniel was right behind him, his rifle in a bag. Ronaldo had his tucked inside his shirt, but he was so big only the tip of the AK showed at the bottom. Nelson brought up the rear, his rifle wedged into a duffelbag.

The men walked in a line between the parked cars, heading for the front door. Ronaldo looked around as they drew close. There were at least a dozen people standing outside, and from what he could see the inside of the place was packed as well. Nobody was paying them much attention, but it was too late for that to matter. With this many people here, no matter what happened their mission would be a success.

"It's a job," Lori told the Sheriff. "Where you're using your body, sure, but you do that if you're a garbageman, or a cop, or a gymnast. Except normally people have a lot—a *lot*—of emotion tied up with this physical act. Because it can feel so good, or because it's so intimate—you're up against or inside another person, after all. Naked. And the act can create another human being. So people end up confusing the physical sensations with the emotions. Or tying the two together. Having sex for a living, with strangers or people you are not emotionally tied to, in front of cameras, you end up with a different perspective. You're performing sex for the cameras, you're not having sex, if you get what I'm saying. You can separate the physical act, and the physical pleasure, from any emotions you feel toward the person."

This was not the conversation Osterman thought he would be having this morning, that was for sure. It was far more interesting. "You don't subscribe to the idea that something as special as sharing your body with someone else should be reserved for a…what's a good modern politically correct term?" Osterman thought for a second. "Life partner, let's go with that."

"Nothing new about what I was making, only the media has changed. Pornography has been around for at least three thousand years. Since before Christianity. But if you want to talk about religion I'm going to need more coffee."

"Not a believer?" Osterman kept any tone of judgment out of his question. He smiled neutrally.

"In a God?" Lori cocked her head to the side. "Honestly, I don't know. I hope there is one, it means there might be something more for us after we die. But I know if there is a God, he's not the misogynistic vengeful overburdened-with-hang-ups one from the Bible. The idea of a God that would make us in his image, give us all these parts and the hormones to make us want to use them the way they were designed, and then tell us using them is evil, is complete jackassery if you ask me."

Dave winced and shook his head. This brunch might have been a very bad idea. Maybe not as bad as heading to Rio Salado and getting recognized, but close. And Lori was far from done. "Organized religions were the original governments," she told the Sheriff. "Like all governments they want to control people. Religions did it with rules about what you could or couldn't do with your body, among a lot of other things. And they did it in the name of God. The idea that sex is evil unless done under a narrow set of circumstances that have nothing to do with biology or nature smells strongly of people to me, not a God. People who want control."

Osterman hid a smile, worried that she'd take it as condescension. Quite the opposite, actually. His young ward had found a pretty girl with a past, yes, but a brain. He didn't agree with her, of course, but he appreciated that she could think. "Intellectually I can't find many faults with what you're saying," he told her. "But remember, in ancient societies they often had no other way to regulate the birth rate and ensure stable family groups than by proscriptions on relations between men and women. But religion is about faith, and faith is something you have that is independent of evidence. I have faith—I have to have faith that the tenets of my religion, while written down by men, were written down by men speaking to and inspired by God." He gestured at Dave, who had a pained expression on his face. "How about a lighter topic? We seem to be giving him a headache."

Matt Fagel had been with the department for two years, Brion Sanderson for twelve. Which meant any time Fagel had nothing to do and the phone rang, Sanderson sat there and looked at him pointedly. Fagel took it, but not quietly.

"Two years. Twenty-four months. One hundred and four weeks on the job. Seven hundred and whatever days. At what point am I no longer a rookie?" the deputy asked Sanderson as the two of them sat at the front counter of the Sheriff's Department. Desk duty was something everyone got stuck doing once a month or so.

"I'm not sure," Sanderson drawled laconically. He rolled his eyes toward Fagel. "But avoiding answering stupid phone calls from idiot citizens isn't a rookie thing, it's a seniority thing. And I'll always have more seniority than you. I'm not even sure why you're complaining, we've gotten all of three calls in the past hour. Which is par for the course for Sunday morning."

Fagel crossed his arms over his chest, which was made bulkier by the Kevlar vest under the brown uniform shirt. "Oh, so you're counting them? Glad to see you're doing something. Although I'm surprised we haven't had any civilians walk in yet."

Sanderson shook his head and waved a finger. "Nope, see, this is why you're answering the phones. An FTO's job is apparently never done. What's the Sheriff's pet peeve?"

Fagel frowned. "I don't know. There's a hell of a lot more than one. Liberals. Illegal aliens. Guys with long hair. Guys with earrings."

"No. Well, yes, but specifically I'm talking about the misuse of the word 'civilian'." Sanderson waved a hand toward the front door. "Those people out there are civilians, yes, but so are you. The Sheriff wants us to be correct in our verbage. Or nounage. Or whatever."

"What the hell are you talking about?"

Sanderson smiled. "You're either in the military or you're a civilian. Which makes us civilians." He pointed toward the front doors. "And them citizens."

The blast shook the building and turned the security glass in the front doors white with fractures. Fagel found himself on the floor, the air filled with dust. The lights flickered but didn't go out.

"The fuck was that?" he wondered. His voice sounded odd to his own ears, blurry and distant.

Sanderson pulled him to his feet and ran for the door. "Call dispatch!" he yelled over his shoulder. "Get EMS rolling this way."

Fagel was on the phone to dispatch upstairs as his partner went through the shredded front doors. He heard gunfire outside a few seconds later. He instinctively ducked, then ran for the door back around the corner that opened onto the lobby. He'd just opened it when more loud shooting erupted, and bullets began whanging around the lobby. Two hit the door next to him and he dove behind a concrete column. "Shots fired! Shots fired!" he shouted into his radio. "In front of the station."

A thought occurred to him. The gunfire had ceased—for the moment. He pushed himself up and ran to the front doors. Through the splintered security glass in the doors he saw something on the pavement outside, and a second later realized it was his partner in a spreading pool of blood.

The deputy had his pistol in hand as he ran outside. There was a pall of smoke hovering over the nearby buildings and a haze in the air from the explosion. Fifty car alarms were warbling and blaring. He saw one car upside down, smoking, but his eyes were locked on his partner as he ran up. He was so focused on Sanderson he almost didn't notice the two figures on the sidewalk about thirty yards away. At the last moment he looked up and saw both the men had rifles. Rifles they'd just reloaded.

Fagel dove to the concrete just as they began firing again. Bullets whizzed over him and skipped across the pavement near his head. The deputy shoved his pistol over the top of his injured partner and began firing, pulling the trigger as fast as he could until the slide of his pistol locked back. He saw the two men duck, then run off, but he couldn't be sure he'd hit either one of them.

"Officer down! Officer down!" he keyed into his radio, trying not to shout and blow out the speaker. "In front of the station main entrance. Two suspects with long guns, on foot, heading west on Gurley." He heard more shooting nearby, and screaming, and reloaded his pistol with shaking hands. He stared toward the sound of gunfire, then down at Sanderson, torn by indecision. The senior deputy was pale, unconscious, and lying in a huge pool of blood.

"You've met the President, right?" Lori asked Osterman. "What's he like?"

"He said lighter topic. You want to ask him about politics, I should have brought my earplugs," Dave said. "And we'll be here all day. Aren't politics and religion the two topics you're *not* supposed to talk about with strangers?" Not to mention sex.

The Sheriff shot Dave a look, pretending anger, then gave him a small smile. "You, young man, are not entirely incorrect. But I often dive in where others fear to tread. Some think it's my raison d'être." He addressed the question. "Are you 'just' a former adult film actress?" he asked Lori. "Does that define you? For the rest of your life?" He pointed at himself. "Am I just a Sheriff? Our current President had been an adult for the better part of fifty years before finding himself elected to the highest position in the country. In those fifty years he's been at the highest levels of business, traveled the world, been on television shows, been married more times than I'd like, and is the father to a number of children. So who is he? Businessman, father, reality TV star? President? He's all of those, and none of those." Osterman raised a finger. "But I'm guessing your question is more whether, in person, he is anything like he comes across during his speeches and press conferences."

"Yeah," Lori said, nodding.

Osterman smiled. "If you listen to what he says, and more importantly watch what he does—not what the deranged media who hates him with every fiber of their being reports that he says and does, mind you, twisting all they can—then you should have a pretty good idea of who the man is, both in public and in private."

The Cracker Barrel dining room was still full, and the hum of conversation was constant. Waitresses zipped back and forth from the kitchen. As she looked around Lori saw their table, or more specifically the Sheriff at the end of it, was still getting a lot of attention. Some of it overt, with pointing fingers, but most people were trying to be subtle with their sidelong glances. Doubletakes and subtle stares were nothing new for her; having someone else be the subject of that attention was. Across the aisle a young married couple ate their breakfast. Between them in a high chair was a little girl in a pink dress with a giant white bow in her hair. The sight of it made Lori smile. She ate a bite of chicken, then put her fork down. "Okay," she said to the Sheriff, "now tell me about *him*." She tilted her head toward Dave.

"Oh. Well…" the Sheriff began. His eyes darted toward Dave and back. It was the first time she'd seen Osterman uncomfortable or less than sure of himself.

"I already told you pretty much everything." Dave told Lori. He took a sip of water from his glass, then looked at the Sheriff. "Apparently that's not enough."

Osterman was a bit surprised at the revelation, and leaned back, studying the young man's face. "If there's one thing I've learned about women," he began, smiling, then his eyes darted up and past Dave.

Dave physically recoiled at the explosions next to his head, jerking back so violently he almost fell out of his chair. Then he was up, on his feet, turning, suddenly immune to the flinches as adrenaline sang through his body.

He bumped the muzzle of the AK-47 with his shoulder as he stood, that's how close it was. It jumped again and again and

Dave felt the burn against his face, the concussion, the burning particles of gunpowder, saw the flash. He shoved the rifle away, toward the wood-paneled wall, and the gun discharged again. The man behind the rifle had time to lift his eyebrows in surprise before Dave was firing, pulling the trigger on his Glock almost as soon as he'd cleared the holster, the draw instinctive.

He rode the Glock's recoil up, firing over and over into the man too close to miss, putting the last round between the man's eyes, seeing other men with rifles behind the first. The rifles slow to maneuver in the crowded doorway that was too narrow for so many people.

Off-balance but the Glock now in a good two-handed hold Dave pushed his pistol out, drove the muzzle right and continued firing almost without a pause, putting three bullets into the face of the next guy. He was right behind the first man, too close actually to even bring his rifle up. He died on his feet, his fingers twitching, the rifle firing into the floor as he collapsed.

Behind the collapsing terrorist or whoever he was more men began shooting through the doorway. They were aiming at Dave, but Dave was going down, the first man he'd shot a dead weight hitting him in the hip and chest. As the ceiling swung into view the rifles hammered and the room filled with rising screams and shouts.

Dave hit the floor hard, half under the dead man. He immediately kicked out from under the weight and jumped up, seeing empty brass cases from the rifles bouncing crazily off the tile floor. He was on his feet before he realized he'd lost his Glock, but there was a man right in front of him, pushing through the doorway into the dining room, a huge guy, the AK-47 in his hands looking like a toy. There was no time.

As the man began to aim the rifle Dave charged him with a roar, body-slamming the man so hard he took several steps back. Dave grabbed the AK in both hands and tried to wrestle it away.

Nelson had said he was sitting just inside the door, but Ronaldo hadn't realized just how close the man would be. Francisco was first through the doorway and started firing before most of them even saw the Sheriff, before Nelson even had his rifle out of his bag. Then something was happening, there was more shooting, not a rifle, and suddenly Francisco was down, Daniel as well.

Ronaldo saw a man come up from the pile of bodies on the floor and charge him with a yell, and the impact sent them back into the gift shop. The American grabbed at the AK in his hands but Ronaldo had it by the pistol grip and forend and wasn't about to let go. They smashed into a display rack, sending crockery and glasses falling to the floor, fighting for possession of the rifle. People around them screamed and scrambled for safety.

Ronaldo slammed the man against a postcard rack, then lifted him off the ground by the rifle and pounded him backward into a display of hard candies. The man still wouldn't let go of the AK, and Ronaldo couldn't turn it enough to get the man in front of the muzzle. He'd lost track of Nelson—he didn't think the man had been shot, but he was nowhere to be found.

Ronaldo didn't want to let go of the rifle to hit the American; instead he tightened his grip on the rifle and slammed the steel receiver into the man's bearded face. Blood flew. He pounded the man's head with the side of the rifle, hit him over and over, trying to beat him down, hit him until he loosened his grip.

Dave felt his head fly back as the AK smashed into his face. His face went numb and burned, all at the same time. The guy he was fighting was big, and hugely strong. Dave had tried, but he couldn't seem to get the AK away from him. Still, he knew that if he let go of it the man would turn the rifle on him, and he'd be dead. He kicked out, and his foot hit something, maybe a leg, but it felt like kicking a tree trunk, it had no effect.

His head snapped back as the man punched him in the face with the side of the rifle again. Dave felt the steel bolt handle rip into his cheek. His feet slipped on fallen candies. The big man punched him in the face again and again with the rifle. The room was a blur, his head snapping back with every impact. He saw the ceiling, the floor, flying blood. The steel receiver slammed into his skull again, the sharp end of the bolt handle a spike into his flesh. Dave felt something in his face crack, and his grip on the rifle loosened. The sudden fear as he felt his fingers slipping off the bloody wood filled him with a panicked rage.

With a primal roar Dave lunged forward in desperation and buried his teeth into the man's surprised face, clamping down until his jaws creaked, feeling his teeth sink deep into flesh. The big man reared back, eyes wide in near terror, and tried to shake Dave off like a dog. Dave's feet slipped out from under him and for a second he hung there by his teeth. Iron-coppery blood was all he could taste. The big man's eyes just inches from Dave's own were wide in a combination of terror, pain, and rage. Then Dave felt the flesh under his teeth give and he went down, ripping most of the man's nose, upper lip, and half of one cheek off as he fell. The rifle was slick with blood, and Dave's hands slipped off it.

The back of Dave's head slammed on the hard floor as he landed. The gunman fell atop him, hitting Dave in the face again with the rifle. Bright spots appeared in Dave's vision and then everything flickered as if someone was jiggling the power switch to his eyes. There was blood everywhere. Then the big man straightened, a look of fury on his butchered face, and he punched Dave with his big fist.

Dave's head rocked to the side under the blow, and everything dimmed again. When his vision cleared he saw the big man kneeling above him, blood running from the huge ragged hole torn in his face. His nose and upper lip were mostly gone, his teeth bright white and crimson both, jutting from unnaturally bare gums. He raised the rifle, stuck the muzzle right in Dave's face. Dave knew he was dead.

Osterman stepped up behind Ronaldo, pressed the muzzle of his pistol against the back of the man's head, and pulled the trigger. The man's head changed shape, and one of his eyes popped out of the socket as he lifelessly fell sideways, bright red blood jetting from the ruin that had been his nose.

Parts of his body felt numb as Dave struggled out from under the heavy dead body. Osterman was down on one knee but waved a hand to say he was okay as Dave got to his feet. Gradually Dave became aware of the screaming and shouting. There was pain—no, not pain, agony, but he didn't have time for it as he looked around.

"Wasn't there another guy? I think there was another guy," Dave said, although his voice didn't sound right. And his face didn't feel right. His lips weren't working correctly.

A terrified looking man stuck a hand out, pointing at the door. "He ran outside," he told Dave, staring.

Dave grabbed the AK from the pool of blood and ran out the front door of the restaurant. There were still people outside even after all the shooting and screaming. They didn't seem to know what to do. "Where is he?" Dave shouted. "Where'd he go?" he nearly screamed, not noticing the blood flying from his lips.

A shivering woman huddled behind one of the rocking chairs jerked at Dave's shout, her eyes wide as she stared at him. She pointed toward the parking lot and Dave ran in that direction.

He waded into the parking lot, running between the rows of parked cars. There were cars...but nothing else. A few vehicles driving off, too far away to tell who was in them. Dave had the AK stock at his shoulder, sights up, looking left and right, spinning, but there was no one to shoot. He ran back and forth, looking for a target. There was no one.

With a frustrated curse Dave jogged back toward the front of the restaurant. As he drew close the front door opened and Osterman staggered out. His pistol was still in his hand, and there was blood on the Sheriff's shirt. As Dave reached him the man fell. Dave dropped the AK and tried to catch Osterman but was only halfway successful.

The Sheriff was wheezing loudly as Dave lay him on his back and opened his suitcoat. Osterman had a confused look on his face. Underneath his shirt was bloody, and Dave ripped that open as well, as wide as he could. He counted three bullet holes, bleeding heavily.

"Somebody call nine-one-one!" he shouted, looking around. He found himself suddenly surrounded by people, diners exiting the restaurant in a rush. Most of them were running in a panic for their cars.

A slender man in his sixties, wearing a peach-colored polo shirt, knelt on the opposite side of the Sheriff. "I'm a doctor," he said. He pointed at one of the bullet wounds in Osterman's abdomen. "Put pressure on that." He looked around and saw half a dozen of the quickly growing crowd members on their cell phones and presumed they were calling emergency services. He took hold of Osterman's bloody hand. "Sheriff, we've got help on the way. Can you squeeze my hand?" He glanced at Dave and then did a double-take at his savaged face. "You're injured as well. Are you shot? Maybe you'd better lie down. Can I get more help over here?"

Dave was looking around and saw Lori emerge from the front door of the Cracker Barrel, helping a woman whose leg was covered in blood. Lori appeared terrified, and there were smears of blood on her shirt, but she wasn't moving as if she was injured. She looked around until she saw Dave, then she gave an involuntary cry. He couldn't hear her, but her lips were easy to read as she saw his face: "Oh my God."

Dave looked around and saw several of the customers standing around had produced pistols. Three of them moved close and formed a circle around the downed Sheriff, as if they were standing guard over him. They looked ready —eager—to shoot someone, but the only people in sight were panicked, crying, covered in blood, or some combination thereof.

"There's people shot inside," a frantic female diner said to the doctor leaning over the Sheriff.

"There's another doctor in there helping the wounded,"

Dave heard someone say. He could also hear a dozen phone calls, everyone apparently on the line with 9-1-1.

"Come help me, put pressure on this wound," the doctor told the woman. He looked down at Osterman. "Sheriff, can you hear me? How about you squeeze my hand?" he repeated.

Osterman ignored the doctor and grabbed Dave's sleeve with his free hand. "Cartel," he said, his voice wet and wheezy. He looked straight at Dave, his focus clear. "Had to be. But why would they come after me? I'm not testifying." He lowered his head to the sidewalk and stared up at the sky. "Just to spit in my eye?"

"Don't worry about it now. Just relax," Dave told him. His mouth felt strange. So did his face. His whole body was aching piercing pain but he ignored it, forced it down. He was dripping blood on Osterman and leaned back, but then it ran into his own right eye. He couldn't breathe through his nose. All he could taste was blood. He wanted to touch his face, to see if it was as bad as it felt. Instead he blinked his vision clear and put his hand on Osterman's, trying to ignore the rising voices all around them, the crying, and the blood that was everywhere. "Maybe as a fuck you, for daring to go after them?" he volunteered, to distract the Sheriff from the pain. "You're really good at pissing people off." He didn't pay much attention to the news, local or otherwise, but had heard there'd been some kind of cartel murder nearby a few months back, typically brutal, only this time there'd been a witness willing to testify.

Osterman lifted his head. It seemed a huge effort for him. "Yes, but they wouldn't do that until after they'd gotten rid of the witness, she's the real problem for them, going after me is just…" Osterman's eyes opened wide and his hand tightened on Dave's forearm like a vise. "A diversion," he hissed, his voice failing. "They're going after the witness." His eyes darted wildly all around, then fixed once again on Dave. "Right now, they're going right now, while everyone's distracted by this. You have to save her, if it's not too late."

"What?"

"Pima Motor Lodge. Room three-eleven."

"I'm not going to leave—"

"You're seriously injured yourself," the doctor said to Dave with concern. "You need to lie down before you pass out."

Osterman let go of Dave's arm and gave him a weak shove. "You have to go now," he said, his voice weak. "You have to save the witness."

"I don't even know where that is." Dave didn't notice the blood drops flicking from his lips with every syllable.

"Pima Motor Lodge? That's right down 69 from here." Dave looked up and saw one of the guys standing guard over the fallen Sheriff had spoken. "Cartel's going after a witness? This was cartel?" The man's hand flexed around the pistol he carried, pointing at the ground.

"Maybe, I don't know."

The Sheriff sat up halfway and pushed at Dave with a shaking hand. "Go!" he shouted roughly. "You've got to save her!" He coughed, and blood sprayed from his mouth. "Go save the witness," Osterman said one last time, his voice faint, and to Dave's ears it almost sounded as if he'd said *princess*.

Suddenly Lori was beside him, hands flat on the Sheriff's chest, putting pressure on one of the bullet holes. Dave stared at her. "I don't know where the hotel is," he told her, nearly crying with frustration. She gaped in horror at his face, in disbelief at everything that had happened, was still happening, unable to find words.

"I do."

Dave looked up and saw it was the same guy who'd spoken earlier. He looked to be in his sixties, fat, with a gray beard and a black leather vest over a striped shirt. He held a small revolver down along one leg. They traded a look. Dave looked from him to the Sheriff, who was now unconscious. Lori had half her bodyweight on her hands which were pressed against the rifle wound in Osterman's upper chest. It looked to him like she was in shock, and just kept staring at the blood oozing from between her fingers.

Dave dug in Osterman's pants until he found the car keys, then grabbed the bloody AK off the concrete. He looked at the stranger with the revolver in his hand. "Then let's go," he said, and took off running.

Ramos sat in the back seat of the big truck, staring out at the face of the motel. Staring up at the third floor. He couldn't see the numbers on the doors, he was too far away, but knowing he was so close…

The men in the truck with him shifted with nervous energy. He glanced out his open window at the car full of men parked next to the truck. His men. They all looked anxious as well. Intense. Eager. He smiled, then frowned as he looked west down the main street. He hadn't heard anything unusual, no gunfire, or explosions, but he supposed he was too far away.

Every man with him stiffened as they heard the siren. It was faint at first, then grew in volume rapidly. Seconds later the police vehicle flew by them, never slowing, siren wailing, lights flashing, travelling at what seemed an insane speed. It was out of sight in seconds, the siren gradually fading.

Ramos smiled, and checked his watch. 11:05 a.m. "It is time," he announced. "Let us finish this."

Chapter Nineteen

Dave ran through the parking lot. When he reached Osterman's Mercury and unlocked the doors he found they'd been joined by a third man, one of the others who'd stood by the downed Sheriff with a pistol in his hand, looking around for somebody to shoot.

Dave jumped behind the wheel, dropped the AK onto the seat beside him, and didn't bother with the seatbelt. The Mercury started with a roar and Dave chirped the tires backing out of the spot.

"Where am I going?" he yelled as he roared down the row of parked cars toward the parking lot exit.

"Turn right on 69, it's about a mile down," the guy in the front seat with him said. "Fuck!" He grabbed onto the door as Dave took a corner way too fast.

Dave got the car up to fifty miles an hour in the parking lot, hit the brakes, and then roared out onto 69 in a sliding turn. Horns blared behind him as he punched the gas.

"Jesus!" the guy in the back seat cursed as they were thrown around.

Dave hadn't driven a fast car in quite a while but he'd owned one for years, and had a lot of experience dealing with Detroit traffic. He slewed the big sedan around slower moving cars, and where they blocked the road he veered into the center left turn lane to pass them. When he found a clear spot on a straightaway he floored it. The big V-8 roared.

"It's on the left, maybe half a mile down. Um, I'm Carl," the man in the front seat next to Dave shouted over the noise, suddenly very nervous as he realized what he was doing.

"Jack."

"Larry," the guy in back said. "Those fuckers cartel back there? The Sheriff going to be okay? Jesus. There was so much blood." Dave glanced quickly at the rearview mirror at the guy in the back seat. Larry was in his forties and wearing a Hawaiian shirt. Both of the men were wide-eyed, in apparent disbelief that they were actually doing this.

"Are you okay?" Carl asked Dave, staring. "Holy shit, Jack. Your face is hanging off your face."

"It's not my blood," Dave growled, staring out the windshield as he slalomed down the road. He didn't notice his words were slurred from the blood and his shredded lips. He wiped blood out of his eyes with the back of one hand.

Staring at the blood not dripping but running down Dave's neck and chin, the flaps of skin waving with every movement of his head, the blood covering almost every inch of him from his hairline to the middle of his chest, Carl's mouth opened and closed a few times. Then he looked questioningly at the guy in the back seat. "Umm...?"

Larry just shrugged. "You a cop?" he asked Dave,

having to shout to be heard over the sound of the engine and tires. "Fuck, watch it!"

"I see them," Dave shouted back, jinking the Mercury around a slow-moving minivan. The tires howled. Once past he pounded the accelerator again and leaned the car into a curve. A Sheriff's Department squad car blew by them racing in the other direction, lights and siren bright and loud and then gone in an instant. He glanced down at the speedometer. He was keeping it near eighty in a 45 MPH zone. "Where's this hotel?" Dave demanded, hunching forward to peer out over the steering wheel. They'd gone more than half a mile, and still nothing.

"I think it's right around this curve," Carl said, pointing, then grabbed onto the door frame as the blood-smeared driver slalomed around slower-moving cars. His heart was hammering painfully in his chest. Sixty-two years old and fat, he knew he was fat. This was the most exercise he'd had in years. The most stress he'd had in… well, ever. He hoped he didn't have a heart attack before they even got there. Or throw up in the car. Those three biscuits with honey and butter were now a lead weight in his gut.

"This is crazy, this is fucking nuts," Larry muttered from the back seat. He felt his SIG P365 in its inside-the-waistband holster digging into his kidney with every jink of the car. One small pistol, and a spare magazine, and he was going after Mexican cartel guys? What the hell was he thinking? But it was too late to back out now, he was in the back of a car going a bazillion miles an hour, driven by a dude who looked like Freddy Krueger'd been hacking on him.

Suddenly Carl thrust his arm out and pointed. "There, turn in there." Dave locked the tires up, throwing everyone in the car forward, and slid the Mercury between oncoming cars. Horns blared.

"Shit, no, it's the next driveway," Carl cursed almost immediately. "We can cut through the parking lot though, they're connected. Watch that lady!" He jabbed a finger.

"I see her," Dave shouted. He stomped the brakes and the chirping tires startled the pedestrian into actually paying attention where she was walking. Dave had to come to almost a complete stop to keep from hitting her, and she scowled at the three of them in the car before scuttling out of the way. Dave accelerated past her and into the motel parking lot. They swung around one end of the motel and Dave stopped the car in an empty spot. As the car rocked back and forth the three men looked out the windows, everyone panting.

"Is that?" Larry asked, pointing to the left.

"Shit, there too," Carl said, pointing right. He looked at Dave. "What do we do?" His voice shook. His knuckles were white around the grip of his revolver.

Dave stared out the windshield. There was a group of men going up the left stairway, already halfway to the third floor. A second group was going up the stairs on the right. All in regular clothes, no uniforms. The faces he saw looked Hispanic. And in their hands, Dave saw a shitload of poorly concealed guns. Maybe eight guys total? There was no time to count.

"Find some cover and shoot those fuckers," Dave spat, throwing the car into park. He didn't know who the witness was, or even exactly what the woman might have witnessed, but he doubted the witness would be armed. Which meant it was up to him, and the guys who'd jumped in the car with him, because one way or the other it would be long over before any cops showed up.

He hadn't fired a rifle in a few years, and it had been even longer since he'd shot an AK, but he knew how to work the safety, and the sights were simple. Half the battle was being willing to pull the trigger. He was more than willing.

He swung open the driver's door, grabbed the blood-soaked AK off the seat, and crouched behind the open door. As he raised the rifle he was vaguely aware of Larry and Carl scrambling out of the far side of the car.

The two groups of men hadn't noticed the Mercury pulling into the lot—they were focused on their mission, charging up the stairs to the third floor. The group on the left was farther away, maybe forty yards, but they were farther up the stairs, closer to the witness. Dave only had eyes for them. As the front sight settled into the rear notch of the AK Dave started pressing the trigger, aiming for the man in the lead.

The first round from the AK blew out the window on the Mercury's open door in front of him and Dave felt the muzzle blast as it bounced off the door. Everything was moving in slow motion, the glass glittering as it flew through the air, the front sight of the AK coming up in recoil, then down, the group of men on the motel stairs freezing. Then Dave fired again, and almost as one their heads snapped around toward him.

He was aware of movement to his right, in his peripheral vision, either the men he'd arrived with or the second group of cartel soldiers, but only had eyes for his sights and the men he had targeted. He fought the recoil of the AK, firing again and again at the men on the exposed metal staircase, the front sight post bouncing up and down over the men, ejecting cases flying over the roof of the Mercury, sparks flying from a bullet hit on the metal railing next to one of the cartel soldiers. Dave saw one man go down, then he was taking incoming fire as they began shooting back. He ignored it, ignored the bullets peppering the windshield of Osterman's sedan, thunking into the pavement around him, blowing chunks of plastic off the Mercury's door as they punched through. There was yelling off to his right but he tuned it out, doing nothing but pouring rounds at the men now shooting back at him. Front sight, press. Front sight, press.

Dave saw a second man go down. One man jumped off the stairs to the second-floor walkway and ran left, firing a handgun wildly in Dave's direction, either trying to get an angle on Dave or trying to make himself harder to hit by moving. Dave let him go and focused on the guy at the top of the stairs, at the third floor, nearer the witness' room. The man had a black rifle up to his shoulder and was ducking and firing back. Dave felt something whip by his ear but kept his focus on the front sight, and saw the man fall to a knee.

A huge amount of gunfire erupted to Dave's right, pistols and rifles. Bullets hammered the ground around Dave, spanged off the open door, punched through the Mercury's roof like it was cheese. He ducked down behind the car, rolled behind the rear wheel, then felt a searing pain in his thigh.

The Mercury's rear tire at his back Dave looked up and saw the man who'd run left firing a pistol down at him from the far end of the second floor. There was a huge pop and a jolt against his back as the tire behind him blew out. The bullets were landing all around Dave and he got the AK up and hammered half a dozen rounds at the man, who did an odd dance and fell over the railing to the parking lot, landing bonelessly.

Dave shoved himself up onto a knee and glanced right. He saw one cartel member facedown on the stairs and another on hands and knees shaking his head slowly. Two others were on the second-floor walkway, scrambling in opposite directions as they fired downward, muzzle flashes bright. Dave caught glimpses of Larry and Carl as they crabwalked behind cars and popped up randomly to fire their pistols at the men. They looked terrified but determined as they kept shooting, dodging bullets that blew out car windows and dimpled steel.

Using Larry and Carl's efforts as a distraction Dave stood, shouldered the AK, and fired at one of the moving men on the right. The man stumbled, then fell, dropping his handgun. The second man over there raised his AR and fired a volley at Dave. Dave ducked back behind the Mercury but not before feeling a sharp pain in his chest. He gasped as glass flew all around him, landing in his hair.

Pushing the pain away Dave glanced left again, saw the last man of that group on the third floor. He was holding onto the big steel railing, and limping badly, and seemed to have lost his rifle, but he was still moving. Moving toward the motel door. Moving toward the witness.

Dave fired at him but the shots went wide, he felt it. His hands were getting shaky, and his vision a little dark around the edges. With a roar he pushed himself to his feet and started running toward the man, trying to get his attention, trying to get him to slow down, to stop. His left leg wasn't working right and he found himself limping badly and hopping more than running but he forced himself faster and faster, firing another couple of shots from the AK that went nowhere near the man on the third floor but made him flinch and slow down. Then Dave's rifle was empty.

Someone started firing a rifle off to his right and Dave

fell down. It felt as if someone had shoved a spear that was both burning hot and ice cold into his hip. His forehead smacked into the asphalt but his face didn't seem to be capable of registering any more pain.

He levered himself up with a gasp, using the now-empty AK as a cane, as a burst of handgun fire off to the right silenced the rifle. There was screaming and shouting everywhere, but it all seemed distant. The parking lot was getting dark, the light seemingly fading to the black of the new asphalt under his feet.

Dave reached the stairwell and started up. He dropped the AK and used his hands and feet to climb, like a child. It seemed forever before he found the first body. There was an AR-15 next to the man and Dave grabbed that. He somehow found the energy to get back on his feet and stumbled up the clanging metal stairs, wheezing, having a hard time seeing in the waning light.

There was blood everywhere on the stairs, making them slick. He tripped over more bodies, none of them moving. He found himself at the third floor by surprise and looked around drunkenly. Twenty feet away the cartel soldier was on all fours, crawling toward the room. The smear of blood under him was a foot wide. Dave stumbled after him, raising the rifle.

"I blame you." Tim Kling shook his blonde head as Reina giggled and wrote down the points.

"What?" Dino Saunders gave his partner an innocent look.

"You're the one who taught her to play." Kling took a look at the gin rummy score on the notepad and made a face. "Thank God it wasn't poker, she'd own my house."

The round table was stained a dark walnut color, ugly and cheap, but at least it was off-balance. Saunders had needed to stuff some McDonald's napkins under one leg to keep it from wobbling back and forth.

"I am just lucky," Reina told them with a smile. Then her face fell. "Today," she added, in a lifeless voice. The two deputies exchanged a look, able to guess exactly what she was thinking about.

"You want something to drink?" Saunders asked her, trying to disrupt her thought process. There were several cans of Sprite on ice in the sink.

The gunfire was hugely loud, and it seemed to come from everywhere at once. Dino found himself on the floor without any recollection of having ducked. He looked over and saw his partner had tackled the witness out of her chair and was now lying on top of her protectively as she shrieked and shuddered.

"Fuck!" Saunders said, then belly-crawled to the front of the room. He grabbed the stock of the M4 leaning against the front wall and pulled it down to him. The gunfire continued, echoing to the left and right. He could hear shouting and screams and bullets hitting metal and brick. The window above his head shattered as a bullet blew through it, rippling the curtain, and shards of glass rained down on his back. There was a loud thunk and he rolled onto his side to see plaster dust falling gently toward him. A bullet had punctured the door and holed the ceiling above his head.

"What the shit is going on out there?" Kling shouted. It sounded like a war. But whoever it was, they didn't seem to be shooting at their room.

"I don't know," Saunders said, confused. "Stay down. Get on the phone and call this in, get us some backup."

Their decision not to have prep radios with the guard detail now seemed very ill-advised. He was crawling backward, carbine up and trained on the door.

Those were rifles out there, and maybe a few handguns. Half a dozen, maybe more. The cascading reports echoed between the wings of the motel, rolling in waves. But as loud as they were, they weren't close. Except for what seemed to be a few stray rounds, nobody was shooting at their room. Dino Saunders couldn't figure it out. If this was an attempt on their witness it made absolutely no sense. They'd heard thirty, forty, maybe fifty shots already, but only two rounds had banged into their room. Could it be some kind of random gang violence happening in the parking lot down below? What were the chances?

Kling had his pistol out as he lay atop Reina. He heard her talking fast, her voice low, and at first thought she might be praying. Then he realized she was cursing, cursing at the men outside that she assumed had come for her, using the roughest, crudest profanity he'd ever heard. It shocked him. Then made him smile. She definitely was a fighter.

When Dino got back to him he tossed Kling the carbine, then quickly low-crawled to the other carbine positioned at the front of the connecting room. Dino took up a defensive position in the other room, covering the second door. He wanted to head outside, find out what the hell was going on, but had to force himself to stay put. His job, their job, was to protect the witness. Period.

The gunfire ebbed and flowed, sputtered, and then stopped. Kling knew it had probably lasted barely a minute, although it had sure felt a lot longer. He pushed the witness behind him, against the wall, and waited, with his M4 pointed at the door one-handed. With his other hand he'd dug out his cell phone and was calling 9-1-1. Saunders positioned himself on one knee in the other room, behind the bed, rifle up, safety off. He felt as much as heard a thump, and a wheeze, from somewhere nearby. Close. Maybe right outside the door. Then…nothing.

No more gunshots. Just shouts and yelling in the distance. Dino moved up until he could see his partner through the connecting door. "Stay there!" he told Kling, keeping his voice low. Crouching, he moved toward the front of the room. He flicked the curtain open with the muzzle of the M4 but didn't see anything. The motel echoed with the sound of running feet, shouts to call the police, someone crying. But all those sounds were distant.

Taking a deep breath, Saunders undid the lock on the door, grabbed the knob, turned it as stealthily as he could, then charged out onto the walkway with the rifle up, spinning left and right.

Ten feet away there were two bodies, facedown, in the biggest pool of blood he'd ever seen. He forced his eyes away from them, rifle following, and swept left to right and back again. He saw bodies nearby on the stairs. On the far side of the hotel on the second floor. There were people running back and forth in the parking lot. And between two cars whose windows were blown out he saw a pair of men on the pavement. An old guy in a black leather vest holding onto another guy in a Hawaiian shirt, and one of them was bleeding. A lot.

"Somebody call nine-one-one!" the guy in the vest was shouting. "Somebody fucking call nine-one-one!"

Sam Wheaton couldn't park anywhere near the Cracker Barrel. None of the witnesses had been allowed to leave, of course, and all of their cars were blocked in by the emergency vehicles anyway. As he jogged up between rows of vehicles one of the ambulances spun up its siren and slowly pulled away, heading for the nearby Yavapai Regional hospital.

The first one of his men he met was Norm Hill, who'd been shopping at the nearby Academy Sports when the shooting had started. The detective was wide-eyed. His pistol was in his hand, seemingly forgotten. "Sam, what the fuck?" he said.

"Yeah, I know," Wheaton said, not even slowing down.

"They hit the station?" Hill called after him, sounding lost.

There were still-wet pools and smears of blood on the pavement outside the front of the restaurant. Paramedics were loading an elderly woman with a leg wound onto a stretcher. A man her age was holding her hand. Two uniformed deputies stood outside the restaurant, M4 carbines in hand, scanning the area, looking furious and eager to shoot something. One had blood smeared down one arm. At least fifty people stood around, most of them in apparent shock, but Wheaton was glad to see they'd been moved back from the front of the Cracker Barrel enough for the medical personnel to be able to do their work.

"Jesus, sir," one of the rifle-toting men said to Wheaton. Wheaton patted his shoulder as he went inside.

"Make sure you keep a perimeter," Wheaton called over his shoulder.

There were four deputies inside the small gift shop, two of them with shotguns in their hands. Half of the displays in the small shop were overturned, and there was a lot more blood.

"The Sheriff?" one of the men asked him.

"At the hospital, being prepped for emergency surgery,"

Wheaton told them tersely. "Or maybe he's already under the knife. Multiple gunshot wounds, that's all I know. His wife's been called."

"Shit."

"The fuck happened at the station?" someone else demanded.

"Car bomb, followed up by a couple guys with rifles shooting anybody and everybody. Got two dozen wounded there and two dead, including Brion Sanderson. What exactly happened here, anybody know yet?" He wanted to look around, but he couldn't move much more than two steps in any direction without stepping in blood, and he didn't want to destroy any more physical evidence. Although the floor was already covered in bloody footprints. And in the middle of the room a bloody pile of meat that had once been a man. A big man.

Jesse Ferguson was a Sergeant with the Sheriff's Department, and had been ranking man on scene until Wheaton showed up. He gestured as he talked. "We've got eight wounded, two critical, including the Sheriff. He was having breakfast when a bunch of assholes came in shooting. Cartel, from the tattoos on one of the dead guys. There's two of them dead, right around the corner there, plus this guy here." He stuck a thumb at the body on the floor in the middle of the gift shop. "Right now I think the only fatalities here are bad guys. Haven't touched the bodies. You should see all the empty cases on the floor in there, I don't know how we don't have more dead." He shook his head. "None in the dining room, but there are cameras here in the gift shop. Footage gives you a pretty good idea of what happened."

"Show me."

Ferguson led him to a room in back, where a still pale

restaurant manager was waiting for them. There were speckles of blood on her neck. "Roll it back to the beginning," Ferguson told her. She nodded and bent to the computer.

Another deputy looked at Wheaton. "Sanderson? Shit. What about the assholes that hit the station?"

Wheaton shook his head. "Fagel might have tagged one. Got a description of the car they took off in, but that's it so far. Entire state's been alerted, feds on down."

"This is it, this is where they walk in," the manager said, nodding at the computer monitor. She enlarged the view from the camera until it took up the whole screen. The display was black and white but the camera was digital, and the image was clear, although it had some sort of electronic twitch every few seconds. The other deputies crowded close to watch and Wheaton cursed.

"What are you doing?" he demanded of them, his emotions making his tone harsh.

"Sir, I've seen the video, you won't believe—"

"I believe there are all sorts of witnesses to interview and a big ass perimeter to secure and we're shorthanded as it is." He glowered at the men.

"Yes sir. Sorry." Everyone but Ferguson left. A siren started up outside and slowly faded as another ambulance departed.

Wheaton turned back to the screen. The shot was from a camera high up in a corner of the gift shop. The opposite corner from the entrance to the dining area. The video rolled.

"You've got it running at half speed, right? Okay." The Sergeant pointed. "This is them. Four of them, looks like. Most of the shooting took place in the dining room and you can't see any of that beyond a few legs. The

Sheriff reportedly was sitting just inside the door on the left."

"Back that up, run that again," Wheaton told the manager. Four men, one of them tall and thick with muscle. Hispanic looks. Unremarkable clothes. One had a duffel bag that swung as if it was heavy, and he'd seen what might have been the muzzle of an AK. Then the four men—who definitely had that hard cartel look—walked past the hostess station and entered the dining room, stacking up in the doorway. At that point they were visible only from mid-thigh down.

There was no sound on the video. Wheaton watched, tense. He wasn't sure exactly when the shooting started, but suddenly there was a blur of motion, and one of the likely cartel soldiers, the big guy, was backpedaling into view, an AK in his hands. He'd apparently been tackled by a diner, and they were wrestling for control of the rifle.

The cartel soldier was built like a Hollywood lumberjack, and Wheaton watched as he tossed the smaller man around like a rag doll, smashing him into displays left and right, scattering glasses and toys and mugs and postcards everywhere. But the skinny guy refused to let go of the rifle. The cartel fighter began hammering the face of the smaller man with the side of the rifle, hard and fast and over and over like someone tenderizing a difficult piece of steak with a studded mallet. With about the same results.

The diner's face was nothing but blood and pulp and when it looked as if he was finally about to lose the fight over the rifle he lunged forward and bit the big man's face, sinking his jaws deep into the man's nose, his eyes wide and crazy.

"Jesus hell," Wheaton said.

"Guy's a fucking pit bull," Ferguson said in admiration.

"Getting rag-dolled around and just refuses to let go. Watch this though."

The fighting diner bit through the cartel hitman's nose and ripped it off and most of his upper lip as he fell to the floor, where he was pounded a few times. Both men were covered in blood. Just when it seemed as if the valiant diner was about to die, Osterman moved into frame, stuck his pistol in the cartel soldier's ear, and killed him.

"I thought the Sheriff was done adding notches to his belt, but I guess not," Ferguson said with respect.

Sam Wheaton had known John Osterman for thirty years, give or take. In that time the man had killed before in the line of duty, but none of those gunfights had been caught on film. What Wheaton saw was his friend of thirty years angrily striding up and executing a man by shooting him in the back of the head without even a hint of hesitation. And without remorse. It was a sobering thing to see.

The brutalized diner with his face in shreds clambered out from under the dead body and then ran out of view. After a few long seconds staring at the dead man before him the Sheriff headed for the front door as well, moving slowly.

"I think he was already shot here, although it's hard to tell," Ferguson said, meaning the Sheriff. The manager paused the playback.

"There were four assholes," Wheaton said. "When these two started fighting over the rifle you see one bolt toward the door, but what about the other two?"

"Those are the two dead inside the dining room. Just inside the door. Haven't touched them, rolled them over, nothing, if you want to look at the bodies. Sheriff shot them."

"No, I don't think so," Wheaton said, frowning. "Roll this thing back," he told the manager. "To where Osterman just comes into view." He waited while she used her mouse to find the spot in the video. Wheaton pointed. "No, see, he's just drawing his gun as he comes into the gift shop from the dining room. Somebody else shot them. Go ahead and let the footage run, full speed," Wheaton told the manager. He wanted to see it all happen in real time.

At actual speed the beating the diner took was just as brutal and hard to watch, if not more.

"You heard a bunch of citizens traded shots with the cartel guys at the Pima, right?" the Sergeant said to Wheaton as he watched the video.

"I know there were shots fired, but I thought it was her protective detail," Wheaton said.

"No," Ferguson told him. "I talked to Tim Kling. They never fired a fucking shot, they just listened to it happen. I think it was all citizens. He said it sounded like a war, and the parking lot looks like Detroit. You haven't been over there yet?

"Jenkins and Floyd are on scene there," Wheaton told the Sergeant, naming two of the department's four Division Commanders. He looked at his watch. "This thing's not even an hour old, we're still trying to figure out what the hell happened." He turned to look at Ferguson. "I think the Sheriff was just a target of opportunity. Same with the station. A distraction, while they went after the witness."

"Well they fucked that up."

Wheaton grunted, and turned back to the security video. The manager had paused it right after the Sheriff had fired his shot. The Sheriff was staring at the diner whose face had been brutalized, the man who was turning toward the front door of the restaurant right before he charged out. From the side, the damage to his face didn't look so severe.

Wheaton blinked, then leaned in close. "Roll this back again," he told the manager, "I want to see this guy, the punching bag. Slow mo."

She backed the video up and let it play again. Wheaton leaned in close, watched the brutal fight inside the gift shop once more. "Pause it, here!" he said suddenly.

The blood-soaked and battered diner was a blur, heading toward the door, and the Sheriff was right there, watching him go. With a strange expression on his face. Wheaton recognized the look on his friend's face. And that wasn't all he recognized.

Wheaton stabbed a finger at the monitor. "This guy, right there. Where is he now?"

"I don't know," Ferguson admitted. "He went charging out the front door. Maybe the hospital? He was in pretty bad shape. Can't believe he's still conscious. Osterman made it outside too before he collapsed."

The chatter on the radio had been tense and constant the whole time, but Wheaton heard his name and grabbed the prep off his belt. "Yeah, Wheaton." He recognized the voice of one of the Division Commanders.

"I've got five, maybe six dead over here and half a dozen injured, including two who probably aren't going to make it. Nobody can tell me what the hell happened, and to top it off I've got the Sheriff's personal vehicle here in the Pima parking lot," Jenkins said. "Door open, steering wheel covered in blood." The Division Commander sounded confused. "You got any clue what it's doing here?"

Wheaton grabbed Ferguson by the shoulder. "Nobody else in this building until the detectives get here. Nobody touches the bodies." He pointed at the desk with the computer holding the security camera feeds. "And you secure that footage," he shouted, running toward the door.

Chapter Twenty

Dave didn't slowly regain consciousness; he was asleep, then he was awake. But everything was blurry. His vision, the pale room around him, his thoughts. It felt like his head was stuffed with cotton. Stuffed so full it was lumpy and misshapen and numb. He wasn't sure how long it took, blinking slowly, before the room around him came into focus. After another minute he realized he could only see out of one eye, his right.

He didn't recognize anything. Not the bed, not the walls. It was quiet, although he heard a soft beeping. He rolled his head to the left and finally saw something he recognized. He opened his mouth to speak, but his tongue felt dry as a wool sock. His breath wheezed and he tried to lick his lips, but his tongue didn't seem to be working right.

Sam Wheaton looked up from his phone and saw that Dave was awake. "Hold on a second," he told Dave, and got up from his chair. He walked around the hospital bed and picked the cup of water off the small bedside tabletop. It had a bendable straw in it. Wheaton stuck the straw between Dave's lips and held the cup while he sucked at the straw.

Dave's mouth was so dry it seemed as if his tongue and throat had soaked up all the water before it got close to his stomach. Wheaton looked down, saw the cup was empty, and set it back on the table.

"I'll get you some more in a bit," he said. He walked back to his chair and sat down. After the water Dave's tongue felt close to normal, and he used it to explore his mouth. His teeth were there, but something seemed seriously awry with his lips.

Gradually Dave became aware that Sam Wheaton was looking at something in his hands, turning it over and over. Finally he looked at Dave over the object.

"This looks real," he said, waving it.

Dave blinked a few times. Finally he was able to discern what was in the Captain's hands. A driver's license. He could guess whose.

"It is," he said, his voice a croak, the words barely intelligible.

"How'd you manage that?" Wheaton tilted his head to the side.

"Sheriff," Dave told him, the word a slur. His lips wouldn't work properly. Barely at all. He'd also gotten a Social Security number to go along with the new driver license. An authentic one, tied to his new name. He wasn't sure quite how the Sheriff had managed that, but he supposed after forty years in law enforcement and contacts now all the way to the White House he had a few close friends in the business willing to do him favors.

Wheaton made a face, then shook his head. He stared at the far wall. "Been so many years, thought I knew all his secrets. Apparently not." His gaze returned to Dave. "Last time I saw you, you were in a hospital bed. Right in this hospital, on this very floor in fact, although at the other end of the hallway. Not sure if that's irony, fate, coincidence…" His voice trailed off.

"How long?" Dave asked, his voice barely louder than a whisper.

Wheaton looked at him. "You? Here? Two days. It's Tuesday."

"Sheriff?"

Wheaton's face grew dark. "He's alive. Barely. Still in critical. On a ventilator. Was on the table for twelve hours. Shot three times in the chest. Collapsed lung. What do they call it? Pneumothorax." His eyes rotated to the ceiling as he tried to remember the specific terms for the Sheriff's injuries. "T10 transverse process fracture—that's his vertebra, but they think his spine is undamaged. Broken ribs. Bullet fragments punctured his liver and intestines." The cop sighed and peered at Dave. "Although he looks better than you. I've seen corpses that looked healthier than you." He stood up long enough to grab the chart at the end of the bed, then sat back down in the chair. He flipped through the pages. "Technically you are currently in stable condition," he told Dave. "But if you haven't realized it yet, you're doped to the gills on the good stuff. For good reason."

"Witness?" Dave croaked.

Wheaton's frown grew deep. "She's alive. They tried to murder the Sheriff and set off a car bomb at the station just to distract us while they went after the witness. If we were the feds we'd blame it all on a YouTube video nobody'd seen, but somehow everybody already knows it was the cartel going after our girl." He sighed and wandered over to the window, peered outside at the news vans. "Not counting cartel I've got six dead and twenty-seven wounded, including one of the two idiots you roped in on that jackass stunt. Caught a bullet." He jerked his head. "He's down the hall with everybody else, we've taken over the whole floor."

"Cartel?"

Wheaton turned around. "There were at least fourteen involved. We can only account for ten of them, so until that shit gets straightened out everything's on lockdown. And in case they want to take another run at the Sheriff, just for shits and giggles." He sighed, and suddenly looked tired. "This is the worst thing that's ever happened in the county."

"Ten." Dave repeated the number. "Dead?"

"Eight. Well, nine now, one of the guys coded out yesterday, and the last guy we've got died on the table three times before they got him stable. Shot six times." Wheaton huffed and growled at him. "What the hell were you thinking?" he demanded. Dave just stared at him with his one bloodshot eye.

Finally Wheaton shook his head. "Well, from the security camera footage and witness interviews and physical evidence it looks like you, Larry, and Curly killed seven of the eight cartel soldiers that showed up at the motel. Found one behind the place, next to the Dumpster, it's a good bet he tried to make a run for it but bled out. Gutshot. Didn't even find him for an hour, otherwise he probably might have made it. One got clean away, and the last one is down the hall looking like spaghetti with all the tubes in him. The other Stooges can't stop flapping their gums 'bout how you charged the assholes at the motel with your liberated AK." Sam leaned forward. "What the hell were you thinking?" he repeated. "Were you trying to get yourself killed?"

Dave didn't say anything for a long time. After a silence that stretched so long Wheaton wondered if he'd fallen asleep with his eye open, Dave quietly asked, "Am I blind?"

Wheaton started at the question. "What? No, you're not blind. Jesus, kid. Your left eye seems to be fine, but your face is swollen up like a handstitched basketball over it. Trust me, don't ask for a mirror, not for a while, you're a goddamn horror show, gives me the heebie-jeebies just looking at you." He looked down at the medical chart in his hands. "Well, at some point the doc's going to come in and give you the rundown, but I don't see why he should have all the fun. You passed out from blood loss is the best guess, as when the paramedics finally fished you out of that pool of blood and figured out you were alive your blood pressure was about sixty over nuthin'. You've got a concussion. Sixty-seven stitches to close up every rip and tear and hole in your head and body, along with a good amount of that glue they use. You might think sixty-seven stitches is a record for this hospital, but I'm told it's not. You've got a fractured orbital bone." He gestured at his own face. "That's your eye socket. Broken nose, which they set for you. I doubt you'll be able to breathe or smell out of it until next month. Maybe a cracked tooth? I think they're waiting for a dental expert to look at your X-rays." He leaned back in his chair. "And you managed to get shot three times. Although, as gunshot wounds go, it could be worse. You got hit in the left thigh, but no bone, no femoral artery. Docs recovered a handgun bullet. Something, I'm guessing a rifle bullet, tore a nice hunk out of the bottom of your left pectoral muscle. And you got shot in your right hip bone, the part at the top. Hmm." He went searching through the papers in front of him. "Iliac crest. Guess that's the top half of the hip bone? Sounds like a stinky flower or expensive retirement community. Bullet went in, ricocheted off the illy whatever and went out almost the same way it came in, tearing up a bit of muscle. You've got a lot of inflammation there, but no actual fracture to the bone. Either way, you're going to be here for a while. As soon as you think you're up to it, I'll want to have a couple of detectives come in and get a statement from you."

Wheaton looked up when Dave didn't respond, and he saw the young man's one good eye was closed.

Sam Wheaton stared at the sleeping figure for a long time. Finally, he stood and put the chart back. He looked down at Dave. "Get some rest, kid," he said softly. "You earned it."

The man sometimes known as Department of Homeland Security Special Agent Joe Clark pulled his nondescript SUV into the cell phone lot of the Phoenix Sky Harbor International Airport. The sun had just set, but the parking lot wasn't simply well-lit, it was crowded. There were cars everywhere, and dozens of people sitting in those cars, standing around, sitting in the beds of their pickups enjoying the cool night air, walking to and from the numerous Port-A-Johns. Every car was parked facing an electronic billboard that reminded Clark of a drive-in movie screen, although this screen wasn't showing a movie but rather the status of all incoming flights. First the airline, then the flight number and origination city, then the plane's status—EN ROUTE, ARRIVED, DELAYED, etc.

There were cars constantly coming and going, turning their lights on and off, people getting out of their cars and stretching, more than a few people drinking and eating. It was closer to a tailgate party at a football game than a drive-in movie theater. It was a crowded, busy scene…and a completely anonymous one. He drove up one aisle of cars and down another, finally pulling in beside a dusty Chevy.

No one even glanced in his direction. He kept the vehicle running and the windows up.

He'd deactivated the ceiling dome light, so when the passenger door opened the interior of the midsize SUV stayed dark. Clark waited until the door was closed before speaking.

"Marty, what the fuck?" he said with some exasperation. "Eight months? Eight months you've been dark. Not a peep. No signal, no sign. We weren't even sure you were still alive." While Clark was case officer, there were only so many things he could do in a situation like this. He'd done them all. Then a few more, such as talking to that pretty witness being held by the Sheriff's department. It had been a borderline stupid move, but after eight months with no word he was pretty sure his man was long dead and buried in the desert somewhere. Then he'd gotten the call.

The man known to the *La Fuerza* cartel as Nelson Santiago was unapologetic. "Deep cover is deep cover, Joe," he said in English with a Midwestern accent. "I couldn't risk it. It's been over four years of my life getting here, so it's not like you have anything to complain about. 'Operation Tentpole is expected to last twelve to eighteen months', remember that briefing? Shit. I knew it was BS when I heard it, but I still didn't think it'd take four years to get in deep with these bastards. Finally, though, I think I'm golden after this job. Provided I can get back south without getting killed. Look, I understand you were worried, but this is the first time I've been completely off on my own in close to a year." He was wearing a baseball cap and was growing out his beard, just in case anyone at the Cracker Barrel had gotten a good look at him. Martin Cabrera had been born and raised in the United States—Kansas City, in fact—but raised by his grandparents, who had immigrated from Guatemala in the seventies. His parents had died in a car accident when he was eight, and when he'd been taken in by his grandparents he'd learned they spoke Spanish at home. He'd never even heard the language before, but his *abuela* had been patient, and children seem to pick up languages rather quickly. In just a few years he'd been speaking fluent Spanish with a Central American accent, and spoke English with a Midwest accent. One thing had led to another, which had led to the CIA....

"You tech support for that Prescott circus?"

"Among other things."

Clark sighed. "Not to get all dewy-eyed and Disney on you, but we stuck an agent with specialized skills—you—in a position where he hopefully would get noticed by a cartel. When a cartel did notice you, it was a young upstart one, which worked even better for our plan. Namely to do everything we could to foment civil war between the cartels. What's bad for the cartels is good for America, etcetera etcetera. Participating in what effectively is one of the biggest terrorist attacks on American soil falls a little outside the lines, don't you think? Tad of a gray area. Dark gray. Charcoal."

"Don't give me that shit. You just want to make sure none of it can blow back on us. It can't."

Clark sighed. "If they were looking to make an impression, they did. Press is acting like you assraped the baby Jesus when you went after Osterman."

"Messy and ugly and big was what they were going for, so that should make them happy. Although we lost a lot more guys than Ramos was expecting, not sure how many, and they'll probably be pissed Osterman's not dead. Unless he died since I last saw the news?"

Clark shook his head. "As pissed as they'll be the witness is still alive?"

"Probably not. But that's not on me. I was there to get them her location and provide some gear. Ramos was in charge of the mission, and he was there with the team that was supposed to take her out. If they failed, that's on him. I've got to hit the safehouse in Tucson tonight, see how many others have made it back." From what he'd heard on the news, a lot of the men who'd snuck up from Mexico wouldn't be heading back.

"Eight months, Marty. We need to get you debriefed. We've got a vague idea of the cartel's activities through signint and surveillance, but that's not enough. You've been in the middle of it. We need to sit you down in a room for about a week."

"Not going to happen. I've got to get back. You have no idea the tapdancing I've been doing that last few weeks." Ramos thought Leo was their 'computer guy', but in fact the kid didn't have a fraction of the skills 'Nelson' did, although he kept his computer skills very closely hidden from *La Fuerza*, just in case. No one in the cartel knew he was able to do much more than watch porn online, which was how he was able to fly under their radar and spoof some email addresses. He'd placed digital clues in front of the right people, which ultimately convinced his cartel superiors that the meeting in Prescott with representatives of *Los Zetas*, ostensibly to arrange a cease-fire, was actually a setup, a planned ambush. "Did you check that sterile Gmail account? I sent you something encrypted a couple hours ago. Rough summary of everything I've been doing, all the players involved." He'd had the forethought to take his computer with him to the Cracker Barrel, leaving it in the backseat of the car. As soon as things had turned to shit in the restaurant—according to the news it had been citizens shooting back? What a mess—he'd ran back to the car and taken off. He'd spent six hours in a Starbucks chugging espressos and typing like a madman, then used their Wi-Fi to upload the coded document to the sterile email account. Then he'd wiped the computer and tossed it in a Dumpster.

"You sure they're not going to take it out on you, just a little bit, for failing?"

"I was there to locate her using my technological expertise, and maybe build a bomb or two if needed. I found her, check. The news can't stop showing that bomb crater outside the sheriff's department, check. If the trigger pullers fucked up and let themselves get shot by some local yahoos, that's on them. I can't do everything. Either way I should have proven myself to the top leadership. Which means I'll finally be put where I can get the intelligence you needed. And the leverage you wanted to influence their decisions."

Clark thought the man was being naively hopeful, but he didn't want to say that out loud. Cartels had never been known for forgiveness or leniency if they thought you screwed up.

"How are you holding up? I know it's gotta be stressful." He wasn't going to offer to pull him out. If the cartel didn't put any of the blame on 'Nelson', then after this mission he'd truly be in the inner circle. Finally.

The undercover agent shook his head. "It's like riding with Genghis Khan, man. Beheadings, gunfights, drugs, booze, sex slaves..." Clark's eyes went up. His man jabbed a finger at him. "That's in the coded brief I sent you. They're getting involved in human trafficking too. Every day's an adrenaline roller coaster. It's like living in a different world.

A different time." He paused. "Listen, there is one thing you could do for me. I got the hell out of there as soon as things started going sideways. I'm trying to make my place with them using something other than a gun, they've got enough soldiers. From what I saw and heard on the news it sounds as if it was regular people who jumped in and fucked everything up for us at the Cracker Barrel and the motel. Can you look into that? Find out exactly what happened? If it was citizens or an off-duty cop or whoever?"

"Why?"

"Depending on what you find, maybe I can use it to my advantage with the cartel. Just in case they want to blame me and whoever else made it out. Whatever you find, just park it in that Gmail account."

"So you can look at it in eight months?"

Marty/Nelson frowned. "I don't know when I might be able to access it. Or when I'll next be able to check in with you. I think I'll be heading back to either Mexico City or Guadalajara. If so I'll be able to use our old dead drops if not the Gmail account. One way or the other, after what happened, things are going to change."

The next time Dave woke up Wheaton was standing at the foot of the bed talking to a man who, from his white coat, was most likely a doctor. They were talking quietly, but the voices had been enough to wake him.

"Water?" he asked in a croak.

The doctor grabbed the cup and held it while Dave drank slowly from the straw. "I don't know if you remember me, but I remember you," the doctor said as he put the empty cup down. "Or rather, I remember your hands. Your face is another matter." He reached down and took hold of Dave's chart. "As is the name on your chart. No record of ever treating a 'Jack Burton', not that I could find." The nametag on his white coat read BRENNAN.

"That's the name he's here under, and it's not going to change," Wheaton said warningly.

The doctor raised his hand and gave a little wave. "I'm not here to rock the boat. I've already got enough headaches, hospital looks like we're in a war zone, I'm not going to make trouble I don't need." He looked down at Dave. "You've got some serious injuries young man. Your recovery is going to take a long time. And you're going to be in a lot of pain. Luckily you're young, and in good health." He smiled. "I'm actually very pleased to see that your hands have healed as well as could be expected, last time I saw them they were still raw. How long was your recovery? Was your physical therapy extensive?"

Dave just stared at him balefully with his open eye. Wheaton and the doctor glanced at each other. The doctor frowned. "Well, we've got time to talk about that later."

Wheaton fixed Dave with a thoughtful look. "I wanted to tell you that we're not releasing any of the details of the incident to the media. As far as they're concerned you're just another innocent bystander. They're going to keep digging, and eventually a few things are going to come out, incident this big. I've already done one press conference, and I'll probably have to do another tomorrow, but we're not releasing any names. I remember you drew heat last time from some organized crime types. Apparently all those bodies in the desert didn't fix the problem if the Sheriff's got you living here under an alias. He's not prone to whimsy."

"Thanks," Dave said quietly.

"In case you're wondering, the suspect we had down the hall died this morning, so that's ten dead soldiers out of the fourteen they sent. Fourteen that we know about. Reviewing the video from the motel, it looks like the guy that got away might be wounded, but we haven't tracked him down yet. I'm going to tell my detectives to come in tomorrow to get a statement from you. And the feds might show up too, they're all over this like ticks on a hound. At this point a statement from you would be more of a formality than anything, we've gotten statements from everyone else who was there. Reviewed all the video. And on that note…" He looked at the doctor.

"Are you up for a visitor?" Brennan asked Dave. "Because there's a very concerned young lady outside who's been waiting to talk to you since they wheeled you in three days ago. She says she's your girlfriend, but until we verified that with you…"

Dave blinked twice, then nodded stiffly. Dr. Brennan smiled, then headed for the door. Sam Wheaton looked at Dave over his moustache. "I'll be around," he told him, then followed the doctor.

She'd been escorted in to see him once, when he was sedated. So she knew how he looked. Still, she had to blink back tears when she came into the hospital room and saw him looking at her out of his one good eye, sunk inside a swollen mass of red tissue crisscrossed with stitches.

She forced a smile out of a mouth that wanted to whimper and moved to the side of the bed. She took his hand in hers and just stood there for a long time, not saying anything.

"Do I look as pretty as I feel?" he whispered.

Lori laughed, tears running down her cheeks. He looked

absolutely horrific. His face was unevenly swollen and red, the stitches black zippers running everywhere, turning his face into a patchwork quilt. They'd had to shave half his head, and it was shiny and gooey with all the antibiotic ointment they'd smeared all over his wounds. He had so much damage to his face the doctors were worried about infection that could spread quickly to his eyes, to his brain, and they were trying not to cover him in bandages so they could keep a closer eye on every stitch, every incision.

"You're going to have a few more scars, but I hear chicks dig guys with scars," she told him.

He tried to smile, but his face wouldn't move. So he just looked up at her. "What's going on out there?" he asked.

She blew out a big breath and sat in the chair next to him, still holding his hand. "It's, well, do you want to talk about this now? Aren't you pretty doped up? You gonna remember any of it?"

"I'm okay."

"Yeah." She shook her head. "It's a circus out there. Car bomb at the police station—you heard about that? Okay, car bomb, people shot up all over a sleepy Arizona town by terrorists, and Shotgun John Osterman near death because of an assassination attempt. Gun fight at a Cracker Barrel." She still had a hard time believing it had happened, even though she'd been there. Everything had happened so fast she wasn't even sure what she'd seen. One minute she and the Sheriff were talking, the next everyone was shooting and she looked over just in time to see Dave shoot a man between the eyes. No hesitation whatsoever. The pure look of insensate rage on his face was burned forever into her memory. Then he'd tackled a guy with a rifle and driven him out the door.

"Terrorists?"

"That's what everybody thought it was, at first. And it had the same effect as a terrorist attack, only difference was what they were trying to do. So a lot of people are still calling it that, even though everyone knows it was the cartels, trying to kill a witness. The hospital is circled by news trucks, and they're still doing live remotes in front of the Cracker Barrel, which probably won't reopen for another month, if ever. There was so much blood…" She shuddered. "Plus the whole block in front of the Sheriff's Department downtown with the crater is roped off. CNN, Fox, even international channels are all wandering around town, interviewing people, taking pictures of the bomb crater. Cops, feds, everybody is going apeshit, arresting everybody they know who even has the slightest connection to the cartels. Border patrol got in a huge gunfight down near the Arizona/New Mexico border with who they're saying is smugglers, but CBS is saying they were just migrant workers trying to find jobs. CNN and MSNBC are scheduling townhalls to talk about gun control. A host on NPR apparently said the Sheriff brought this on himself due to his stance on immigration. Or calling Black Lives Matter a domestic terrorist organization. Or both. Fox News is ranting about illegal aliens and MS-13. It's a shitshow."

He wet his lips, as well as he could. "Are you okay?"

Her eyebrows crashed together over her nose. "Am *I* okay?"

"I saw blood on you. At Cracker Barrel."

"It wasn't mine. There was blood everywhere. I'm fine." She couldn't close her eyes without seeing it. Couldn't sleep without having nightmares. "I mean, I'm not hurt."

"How's your mom?"

She laughed and wiped away a tear. "She thinks I

should marry you, that's how she is. Word got out that it was a bunch of regular people, not cops, who fought off the cartel hitmen at the Pima, and she guessed you were involved even before I told her. The owner of the motel made like half a million bucks or something selling footage of the gunfight there from his security cameras to MSNBC. Cops are furious and filing injunctions to keep it from getting airtime, but I don't know that they'll win, the motel owner gave them copies of everything he had. Like I said, it's a shitshow."

"The guys I was with?"

"That drove away with you?" The fear she'd felt watching him take off in the Sheriff's car returned, and she pushed it away only with difficulty. "They're down the hall. Well, one of them is. He got shot, but I don't think he's too bad. The other one got banged up but I think they released him a few days ago."

"I want to go see them. And the Sheriff," Dave told her. He looked around the room with his one good eye. "Can you find me crutches or something?"

"Hell no. You can barely talk, I know you can't walk. You stay right in that bed. And the Sheriff's still unconscious, wrapped in an oxygen tent or something."

"They rode with me," Dave told her. "They didn't have to. They didn't know me. But they backed me up. Ran toward a gunfight. Not many people would do that. And they got shot."

"One of them did. And he should be fine. He's in a lot better shape than you."

Dave pulled the sheet down with his arm that didn't sport an I.V. The bandage around his left thigh was thick. So was the one on his right hip. He could feel the bandage on his chest underneath the cotton gown. Even through the heavy painkillers his whole body ached. "I want to go talk to them," he told her. He started inching his legs toward the edge of the bed.

"Hold on. Stop. You shouldn't be moving, much less getting out of bed. Dammit, okay, hold on, I'll find you something." She saw there was no arguing with him. She got up and disappeared.

She returned two minutes later, and she'd been half hoping he'd fallen back asleep. No such luck. He'd gotten his legs over the edge of the bed and was sitting up. He'd pulled out the I.V. She had a wheelchair, and set it next to the bed, almost underneath him. After two years of helping her mother she was a veteran at moving bodies, although he weighed a lot more than a woman wasting away from cancer. Still, she was able to get him into the wheelchair with only one sharp intake of pain from him.

"You're an asshole," she told him. "Did you tear your stitches? You've been shot, you know."

"Can you wheel me down to their room? His room? The guy who was with me?" Dave asked. He was panting and exhausted even though she'd done all the work getting him into the chair. It had hurt so much he'd almost cried out. Hurt more than when he'd actually been shot. Probably because he didn't have adrenaline filling his veins with liquid fire. Wasn't focused on killing everyone he could before he died.

"Is abusing hospital patients a crime?" she wondered aloud. "Because this probably counts. They're going to kick me out, and then you won't see me until you get released."

He didn't respond. She sighed, then made sure his feet were on the chair supports. Then she grabbed the blanket off the bed and draped it over him, since all he wore was the cotton gown that barely came to mid-thigh.

At the end of the corridor, not too far from Dave's room, a deputy stood guard at the door to the stairwell. He was in full tactical gear; hard armor, helmet and rifle. He stared at Lori as she wheeled Dave out but didn't say anything.

"They've got the whole floor sealed off," she said quietly to Dave as she pushed him down the corridor. "Afraid the cartel is going to make another attempt on the Sheriff or something. Everybody who got seriously injured is up here, and they've got cops stationed at all the elevators and stairs, and down in the lobby too. They've been looking in on you from time to time." She snorted. "They've caught a couple of reporters trying to sneak up here, but that's it. I think this is it."

A nurse hurrying past them gave Dave a curious look but didn't say anything. Lori stopped the wheelchair in front of a room door and knocked softly. "Yeah?" they heard.

Lori pushed the door open and Dave leaned over in the chair to see inside. Larry the Hawaiian shirt aficionado was lying in the hospital bed wearing the de rigueur gown. He looked pale and had a bandage on his forehead. A middle-aged woman was standing on the far side of the bed and was obviously very unhappy. Carl was at the foot of the bed, dressed in jeans and his apparently ever-present black leather vest. There was a puffy bandage on his elbow. A true look of horror crossed the woman's face when she saw Dave.

"Holy shit, what are you doing even awake?" Carl said in total surprise. He winced involuntarily, staring at Dave's face. It looked worse than when he was covered in fresh blood and flaps of skin. He blinked, and frowned. "Didn't you get shot? Shouldn't you be in bed?"

"Welcome to the chorus," Lori said to Carl, pushing Dave into the room.

"Honey, this is Jack, he drove the car," Larry said to the woman standing next to his hospital bed. "Jack, this is Mary, my wife."

"What the hell were you doing dragging my husband into a gunfight?" she demanded of Dave.

"Mary," Larry said, sounding tired.

Dave could see she was scared more than anything, and the anger helped her shove the fear away, so he didn't take it personally. Plus, the painkillers helped keep him mellow. Still, he had an idea of how bad he looked, and was in a lot of pain and didn't know how long he'd be able to stay vertical even in a chair, so he stared unblinking at the woman with his one good eye until she looked away. Then he smiled at Larry. Or tried to, his face still wasn't working. "I heard you got shot. Wanted to check on you," he said quietly, his words more than a little blurred due to his misshapen lips.

"I'm fine," Larry said, smiling wide. He gestured at his side. "Bullet went in and out. Muscle, cracked a rib, but didn't go into my...whatever they call it. Abdominal cavity. So it's not life-threatening, it just hurts, even with the good stuff." He pointed at his head. "Flying glass."

"You're not fine," his wife protested, on the verge of tears. "You got shot! What's wrong with you?" Carl stood silently at the end of the bed. This wasn't the first time he'd heard this conversation.

Dave looked at Carl. "You okay? Elbow?"

Carl looked down at his bandaged arm and lifted it. "Not used to moving around while ducking. Not used to moving fast, period. I'm old and fat. Kept falling on my ass while trying not to get shot, and banged it up real good.

Pulled a muscle in my back. Nothing compared to either of you guys."

"Why are you smiling?" Larry's wife demanded of Carl. "You almost died doing something stupid. For strangers."

"Mary," Larry said firmly. "Could you give us a minute? I'd like to talk with him. Alone. Privately."

"I'll head down to the waiting room with you, if you want," Lori told her. "The coffee from the machine isn't too bad."

Larry's wife scowled at Dave, but she went. Dave waited until he heard the door close behind him.

"I'm sorry I got you shot," he told the man on the bed. "Seriously." He glanced at Carl, including him.

"Buddy..." Carl began.

Larry laughed, then winced and grabbed his side. After a careful breath, he said with a smile, "Dude, are you fucking kidding me? I was scared shitless, sure, but you didn't get me shot, I volunteered. And Jesus Christ and pass the mustard, we went screaming across town in the Sheriff's muscle car all gunned up like Delta Force, got into a no-shit firefight with flying glass and blowing tires and saved a witness from cartel hitmen. And probably saved the lives of a couple of cops. I can't believe it and I was there. We're big damn heroes. Hell, you did all the heavy lifting anyway. You're a fucking animal."

"Everybody was so busy shooting at you they barely noticed us," Carl told him.

"That's not exactly..." Dave began.

Carl was shaking his head. "I had a six-shot revolver. How long do you think my ammo lasted? Shit, mostly all I did was make noise. Although I think I tagged one of those assholes."

"And I think I got at least two," Larry said. "Although

it's not like the movies. You shoot someone, they keep shooting back. For a while. Mostly." His smile disappeared as flashbacks of the gunfight popped into his head. He'd been having nightmares every night. And flashbacks when he was awake bad enough to give him the shakes.

"Unless you shoot them with a rifle," Carl agreed. He nodded at Dave. "I should have grabbed another of those commie rifles at the Cracker Barrel like you."

"I ran out of ammo too," Larry admitted. "Two magazines, twenty-three rounds of ammo sounds like a lot until you're in the middle of a goddamn war. Although it lasted until you went charging toward the stairs. The last guy close to us was shooting at you and I dropped him with my last shot. Christ." He shivered at the memory, then laughed. "I've been in a gun fight," he said in disbelief, looking between the two other men in the room. He looked at Dave. "Did you really eat some dude's face in the gift shop?"

"Not exactly."

Carl worked his injured arm and snorted. "I thought I was going to have a heart attack. That's the most scared I've been. Ever. But I did it. We did it. And we didn't die." He looked at Dave. "I'll ride with you any time."

Lori was back a few minutes later, without Larry's wife. "I don't think she wants to see you," Lori told him as she wheeled Dave out of the room.

Dave nodded. Getting into the wheelchair had hurt an indescribable amount, and simply talking to Larry and Carl for three minutes had exhausted him. Still, he wasn't ready to go back to his room yet. "Osterman?" he said weakly, looking up at Lori.

"He's still unconscious," she reminded him.

"Where?"

She sighed and began pushing him down the corridor.

"Where do you think?" she asked, and nodded ahead of them. A doctor Dave didn't recognize walked past them, talking on a cell phone. He smiled politely as he went by, focusing on his conversation.

There were two deputies stationed outside of a private room in full tactical gear. Their helmets and tactical vests were desert tan. Their carbines were slung cross-body. They watched doctors and nurses walking back and forth, their faces stern, their hands on their carbines. He recognized the look. They were half hoping the cartel showed up and tried something. Maybe more than half.

"How'd you even get up here?" Dave asked her.

"Twenty people saw us eating brunch with the Sheriff," she told him.

The deputies' heads moved as one as Lori came close with the wheelchair. The deputies were big men, made even bulkier by their body armor and gear. Dave felt small and shrunken in the chair, and it seemed as if he was staring straight up at the ceiling when he looked between their blank faces. "I just wanted to check on the Sheriff," Dave croaked. "See how he was doing."

The two deputies exchanged a glance, then looked down at Dave expressionless for a while. Then, finally, one of them said, "I don't know how you're sitting there in that chair, balls that big."

Everyone in the department had seen or heard about the video of the fight in the gift shop, and just about every second of the gunfight at the motel had been captured by the owner's new HD full-color cameras. Which was why MSNBC had been willing to pay so much for the video. Charging toward the motel stairs, AK in hand, his face a torn bloody ruin, blood streaking his arms and chest and covering the rifle, the man in front of them had looked like something out of a gory horror movie. And that was after he'd eaten a guy's face. And when he very obviously got shot, and fell down, he got back up, grabbed a different gun, and kept coming. Between the Cracker Barrel and the motel this secret personal friend of the Sheriff's had killed at least five Cartel soldiers, maybe as many as seven. And saved who knew how many lives. Biggest question any of them had was who the hell he was. Sam Wheaton seemed to know, but the Captain wasn't telling.

"I am in a lot of pain," Dave admitted, and the two deputies broke out in laughter, then immediately sobered up.

"He's in bad shape," one of them told Dave. "Shot three times, collapsed lung, one of the bullets hit his liver... it's just a mess."

"And he's not exactly young," the other deputy added.

"I'm sorry," Dave told them sincerely. "I just wasn't fast enough."

The deputies exchanged another look, surprised at the comment. The one on Dave's left frowned and studied his sewn-together face. "Don't know that anyone could have done much better, Cujo," he said finally.

"What in God's name are you doing out of bed?" they all heard. The voice was surprisingly loud.

They all turned to see a senior nurse standing in the middle of the corridor, hands on her hips.

"He was—" Lori started to say.

"I was—" Dave began to croak.

"I don't care," the graying nurse nearly shouted. She shooed Lori away from the wheelchair handles. She pulled the blanket off Dave and gave him a quick onceover, noticing how pale he was, then pulled up the edge of his gown. The bandage on his thigh was showing a spot of blood. So were the ones on his hip and chest. Her glare at Lori was accusatory and venomous. "You've reopened all of his wounds. He's going back to his bed and staying there even if I have to get these deputies to handcuff him." She looked over at the nurse's station. "Marcy! Help me get this suicidal idiot back into bed."

Chapter Twenty-One

When Dave woke up he was happy—and a little surprised—to see that he wasn't handcuffed to his bed. He was pretty sure he'd passed out from the pain as the two nurses were getting him back into it. He was also surprised to see Aaron sitting in a chair next to Lori.

"What are you doing here?" he croaked.

Aaron looked up from his phone. "It's called moral support, asshole." The sharp comment was followed by a grin.

"No, I mean...they said they weren't releasing my name."

Aaron rolled his eyes. "Biggest gunfight in the state since the O.K. Corral? Shotgun John Osterman in the middle of it? And private citizens getting into a shootout with cartel fuckheads." He gave Dave a dirty look. "Seriously, what are the chances you weren't involved? But then I saw the clip, and I recognized you."

"Clip?"

Lori told him, "MSNBC started playing the security

camera footage from the motel. You're in it, but..." She shook her head and bit her lip.

Aaron said, "Nobody'd be able to recognize you. Nobody who didn't know you already. You look like something out of a Clive Barker movie. Like somebody threw a ruptured placenta in your face."

"Aaron, Jesus!" Lori said, horrified, hitting him on the arm.

"What? It's true," he said defensively.

Dave couldn't frown, his face couldn't move enough to show that expression, but his confusion was evident in his tone. "Okay, but how did you get up here? I thought they had the floor on lockdown."

Aaron pointed at Lori with a thumb. "I hung around your place until the porn princess showed up, and she brought me over."

"Still." He had the impression security was tighter than that.

Aaron snorted. "It's not cuz she's your girlfriend. It's because she's your girlfriend and knows the Sheriff...and every one of them fuckers recognized her from her, um, previous career. She's a celebrity."

"Oh."

"You should see their brains smoking when they try to figure out why their Bible-thumping Sheriff was sitting down to eat with Jizzabelle Porksnorkle. Fucking hilarious." Then he grunted. "But they wouldn't let me wear my gun up here. Assholes. Listen, just shut the fuck up and lay there and heal," Aaron told him. "You look like you got tossed in a wood chipper."

"Stop it," Lori scolded him. "What do you need your gun for anyway, there's cops with rifles all up and down the hall." She moved to the bed and took Dave's hand in hers. Aaron stepped up on the other side of the bed.

"How long's it been?"

"We went on our field trip yesterday," Lori told him. "Today's Thursday."

"Sheriff?"

"Still alive. Still in critical condition." She fought back tears.

Aaron said, "He's a tough fucker, but I guess he is a senior citizen. I'm going to be here for a while. You need clothes from your house, phone, tablet, Snickers, Diet Coke, whatever, I'm on it. I know the food here probably sucks. Least I didn't have to pull you out of a fucking fire this time." Aaron remembered back to when his mother had been in the hospital during the last rounds of her fight with cancer. He turned around and saw the bathroom door right behind him. "Although I'm guessing I'll be helping you on and off the john for a while. I'm not wiping your ass, though," he said with mock seriousness, jabbing a finger at Dave.

"I haven't been cleared to use the toilet yet, they don't want me ripping anything. I'm still bedpanning it," Dave told him. Which was both humiliating and disgusting.

"Hospitals suck," Aaron agreed. "You need anything, you let me know."

"I've got a Glock 19 in a fanny pack at my place," Dave told him. His voice sounded as tired as he felt.

Aaron made a face. "A fanny pack? You mean a nut sack. I look like a dude who'd wear one of those?"

Dave looked at Lori. "They checking your purse when you come up to visit?"

Her sigh spoke volumes.

Aaron and Lori were absent, eating dinner in the hospital cafeteria when Dave heard a soft knock at the door. "Come in."

He didn't recognize the woman who pushed open the door. She was old, at least in her seventies, the cruel teamwork of gravity and time compacting her into a short stout fireplug. She walked with tiny, quick steps. Before the door closed he saw a rifle-toting deputy standing in the hallway outside, watching her intently. She stood at the foot of his bed and regarded him with moist, gray-blue eyes, one hand plucking at her sweater.

"Can I help you?" Dave asked finally.

"They tell me Johnny for sure would be dead if you hadn't been there," she said finally, in a surprisingly rich voice. "I'm Lillian Osterman," she added as an afterthought.

"Oh! Uh, nice to meet you."

She grabbed the arms of the nearest chair and dragged it closer to the bed, then sat down carefully, with a sigh. "We've never met, but I've heard a lot about you. Not by name, of course, Johnny was good with secrets, but when I heard about your burned hands I knew you had to be one and the same. His special project."

Dave wasn't sure what to say to that. She reached out and took hold of his closest hand, turned it over. Her hands felt very soft and warm. She peered at the scar tissue. "So much pain," she said. "Does it still hurt?"

"Not my hands. How is your husband?"

"Fighting," she said flatly. She paused, then said, "I've got detectives volunteering to tell me all about physical evidence and bullet trajectories and timelines. Witness statements. Sensational video of some of it, apparently." She shook her head quickly, then cocked it to the side. "Did you kill the man who shot my husband?"

"Yes." He paused. "Not soon enough."

She heard the remorse in his voice. After a few seconds, she patted his hand, then let go of it. She nodded at his wounds. "Not for lack of trying, by the look of it." She sat for a few moments. "They're surmising that if I hadn't been under the weather, and we'd gone to church like usual, that they'd have come for him in church." She met his eye steadily. "Three hundred people, men, women, and children, sitting in pews. Babes in arms." Her eyebrows went up. "You think that's an accident? That he was with you, there, when they came for him?" She tsked and shook her head. "And people say there's no evidence of the Lord."

"I'm sorry I wasn't able to do more."

She waved a small hand in dismissal, then looked at him sideways. "And the young lady dining with you two?"

"My girlfriend."

"Hmm. I hear she's got a colorful background."

"Don't we all."

Lillian Osterman snorted. "If I had to guess, I'd bet my Johnny talked religion with her. He was always trying to save everybody." She gave Dave a pointed look.

"It did come up," Dave admitted.

"Hmm." Without warning she stood up. "You get better," she told him, and patted his hand again. "I'll pray for you." Then she was out the door.

The nurses acted as if the room didn't have a door. Not that Dave would have locked it or was doing anything other than watching TV or sleeping, but still he would have appreciated them knocking more often. The senior nurse, the gray-haired one who'd yelled at him in the hall and gotten him back into bed after his field trip, came in one morning with some paperwork in her hands. Her nametag said MacDonald, and he'd heard other nurses call her Ginny. She at least had knocked once on the door, although she hadn't waited for a response.

She was fierce-looking, he had to give her that, but from what he'd seen she was very good at her job. She stood at the foot of his bed, frowning at the forms, then looked up at him. "And how are you feeling this morning?" she asked.

"Like I got shot. And hit in the face a lot."

Ginny nodded. She glanced at the I.V. next to the bed. 'Pain management' was a big focus these days, but in her professional opinion for the wrong reasons. Doctors and insurance companies were so paranoid about getting their patients addicted to their pain killers they weren't giving them as much as they should, or for as long. "If you had to describe the intensity of the pain you're experiencing," she asked him, the standard question long ago memorized, "on a scale from zero to ten, with zero being no pain whatsoever and ten being the worst pain you can imagine, how much does it hurt right now?"

Dave shrugged. "Five."

She frowned. "Five?" she said dubiously.

Dave blinked his good eye. "Was there a right answer?" It's not as if he hadn't earned it. All of it.

Ginny pursed her lips together. "Like you said, you got shot. Three times. And hit in the face a lot." She walked around the bed and peered at the I.V. setting. He was still on opioid pain medication, but at a very low dose.

"It's a subjective scale, right? Ten is the worst pain I can possibly imagine?" He held up his horribly scarred hands and worked them like claws. "I can't imagine anything hurting worse than this did. For weeks. Months. I think it's shifted my pain tolerance. Or my frame of reference."

"And you've been shot before."

"And I've been shot before," he agreed. He thought he'd recognized her. "I was treated here."

"Yes, you were. And I remember your hands." She was in silent agreement with him; burns were worse. In every way. She sighed and gave him an appraising look. "You're sticking with a five?"

"Yeah."

"Five it is." She wrote it down. Keeping her eyes on the forms in her hands she said, "The Sheriff is a friend of mine. Everyone says he'd be dead if you hadn't been there." She swallowed. "So thank you."

She turned and hurried out of the room without looking up from her paperwork. It wasn't professional for the patients to see you crying.

Two days later Sam Wheaton came to visit again. Dave had been expecting it. The day earlier Larry and Carl had sat down with Mindy Tonaka and given an exclusive interview about their "GUNFIGHT WITH THE CARTEL!" or so the headline went. He'd seen a rerun of it. They showed the motel security footage, with "VIDEO COURTESY OF MSNBC" plastered all over it. It had been bizarre watching himself, not that even he could recognize his face under all that blood and ripped skin. He hadn't realized he'd been bleeding that much, it had soaked his shirt down to his belt.

It seemed so fast—when he'd been in the middle of it, everything was happening in slow motion, and the gunfight seemed to last forever. From arrival to last shot the gunfight at the motel actually hadn't lasted ninety seconds. Less. He was interested in seeing how his two impromptu partners had performed under fire. In the video it was obvious they were terrified, but they kept popping up from behind cars and firing. When the back window of a Prius blew out in Carl's face he fell backward, then got back up, his elbow dripping blood. He emptied his revolver in short order. Larry didn't take much longer to run through the first magazine of his SIG, then Carl stood watch over him as the man fumbled through a reload and then got back in the fight. As the slide of his little pistol locked back for the second and last time Larry looked down at himself, then fell down, suddenly realizing that, at some point, he'd been shot. Dave nodded. They never ran away, and they never stopped until they ran out of ammo, and then, luckily, it was over. Courage was doing what needed to be done even if you were afraid.

During the interview Carl and Larry—back in a Hawaiian shirt—had given most of the credit to Dave. He didn't care about that. He was just happy they kept referring to him as 'Jack'.

"I'll be giving another press conference this afternoon," Wheaton told Dave. He wasn't looking forward to it, that much was clear. "FBI and ICE and DEA all one big happy behind the podium, each of us taking a turn. The department's still refusing all interview requests on your behalf," Wheaton said, frowning behind his moustache. "Want that to continue? Or do you want to get in on that strokefest Tonaka's got going on? They've already given you a nickname, 'Pima Jack'."

"I'll pass."

"Smart man."

"You track down the cartel guys who got away?"

Wheaton shook his head. "Probably long gone by now,

deep in Mexico. They rented two houses in town to operate out of. Been here for two months, that should tell you what kind of planning went into this. Still not sure how they found the witness, but we're working on it. So is the FBI, DEA, Department of Justice, ICE, CIA...probably the Coast Guard too, just in case." He looked at Dave. "The President called me inquiring about his personal friend John Osterman. Things don't get much bigger than this. Not on American soil. Wish I had an excuse for staying out of sight. I shouldn't even be here, all the shit I've got to do, but I come to see him every day." He glanced around the hospital room.

"Osterman?"

Wheaton sighed. "Sheriff's still in critical condition, but improving." He peered at Dave's face. "The swelling's gone down a lot, but you actually look worse with the bruising coming up to the surface."

"So I've been told. Hurts just as much. Hurts to talk." He was trying to move his lips as little as possible. Not that they could move much anyway. The swelling had subsided enough that he could almost see out of his left eye. Almost. "If you're going to stand on that side of the bed, can you talk louder? I can't really hear out of this ear." He gestured at the left side of his head. "Just ringing." The muzzle of the AK had been maybe six inches from his ear when he'd jumped up.

Wheaton's eyebrows went up, then he nodded.

Dave told him, "I'm told the stitches are coming out tomorrow. I guess if they leave them in any longer they might cause scarring on their own."

"Sounds like fun." Wheaton turned to Aaron, who was sitting in a chair in the corner, uncharacteristically quiet. "I knew I recognized you, but it took a while. You were here last time he was, right?" the Captain asked Aaron, gesturing at Dave.

"Yeah. I was there in the hallway, when you and the Sheriff were facing down the government guys trying to drag Dave off. I thought for sure there was gonna be shooting. Then you started singing. Stomping your feet. Freaked them the fuck out."

"That was the point of it." Wheaton turned back to Dave. "Doc Brennan says the specialist who put your face back together, Maureen Tiernan, is an artist. You'll have some scars, but her hope is that they'll be minor and not that noticeable, long as they can keep them from getting infected. Although she won't tell you that, not this soon. Under-promise and over-deliver. Doctors." He shrugged.

"I'm on antibiotics by the bucket. They won't be my first scars. She or Doc Brennan say anything about when I can go home?"

"Not officially. A week, maybe? Apart from the fractures in your face it's all soft tissue injuries. Still, you've got a bullet hole through your thigh." He smiled. "Ginny tells me they've started weaning you off the painkillers already. Don't want you getting addicted. How's that going?"

"I've got sixty-seven stitches in my face, and was shot three times. What do you think?"

Wheaton snorted, then checked his watch. "You up for a visitor this afternoon?"

"I'm not going anywhere."

"No you are not. Or Ginny'll have me handcuff you to that bed." He shot Dave with thumb and forefinger and turned to leave, then stopped. "Don't know if you've been worrying much about it, but they got the blood test back the other day."

"Blood test?"

Wheaton pursed his lips. It made his moustache wriggle like a caterpillar. "On the fellow you chose to nibble on. He didn't have anything. No Hep C, no HIV, nothing. So you don't have to worry about coming down with anything."

"Oh. Okay."

Wheaton could see from Dave's expression that the boy hadn't even considered those potential repercussions for what he'd done. The captain shook his head and left with a wave.

"The one time spitting is better than swallowing," Aaron observed profoundly.

Dave looked over at him. "I don't know what you're talking about, that fanny pack looks good on you."

"Everything looks good on me."

It was late in the afternoon when he heard a knock on the door. "Come in," he called out. He was doing a better job figuring out how to enunciate with lips that couldn't and shouldn't move. And the swelling had finally gone down enough for him to open his left eyelid a slit. Enough to see out of, at least.

The door opened. Three people Dave didn't recognize filed in. There was a big pale guy and a small fierce-looking middle-aged Latina. Both of them were wearing suitcoats over guns, the guy in a tie, and Dave pegged them as cops immediately. Between them was a young, very pretty woman. Who threw her hands up to her face in surprise when she saw Dave.

"Maria Flores, Norm Hill," the older woman said, gesturing at herself and the big guy. "Detectives, with the Sheriff's Department." Flores was trying hard not to flinch or make the kind of horrified expressions that seemed natural seeing this citizen's chewed-up face. She threw a questioning look at the guy sitting in the chair against the wall. She didn't recognize him, but he looked like he could be a cop.

"I'll go get some coffee," Aaron told Dave, standing up. He nodded at the newcomers. "Officers." He gave the pretty woman an appraising gaze as he went by.

When he was gone, Flores gestured at the young woman next to her. "This is Reina. The witness in the cartel case. She wanted to talk to you."

Reina moved to stand beside the bed. "I am so sorry," she told Dave in accented English. She had to force herself to look at his face.

"Bad guys did this, not you," he told her.

"But you didn't have to," she told him. "You don't know me. You are not *policía*."

"It was the right thing to do. I'm glad you're okay."

"We'll leave you two alone," Hill said. He held the door open for his partner and they moved down the hallway where they wouldn't be overheard. Hill's eyes went wide.

"Man, I saw the footage from the motel, but I thought it was just blood all over his face. You know how head wounds bleed. Guy looks like he went face-first through eight windows. He's stitched up like a baseball."

Flores asked him, "Didn't you watch the footage from Cracker Barrel? The shithead there was hitting him in the face with an AK like he was a piñata, until the Sheriff put a Saigon-style end to the conversation."

"I read his statement. All the witness statements. I think that guy has some serious anger issues. From the ballistics report it looks as if he killed at least six guys, four of them after that happened to his face." He frowned. "It kinda reminds me of that thing about fifteen years ago. In the

Midwest, right when I was coming on the job. Beheading. Because it got caught on video too. You remember that?"

"Beheading? I think I would remember that."

"Well, it was Detroit. And they yanked the footage off the news almost immediately and you never heard about it again. There was something weird about it, terrorists or private contractors were involved or something. It wasn't too long after nine-eleven."

Flores shook her head. "Not a clue."

Norm glanced at the closed door then back at his partner. He hid a smile as he said, "You gonna ask him out? Seems like the two of you have a lot in common."

"What? Oh, because we both bit people? Norm, you've got to watch that video from Cracker Barrel." She shook her head, still slightly in disbelief. "I was panicked and scared when I bit that suspect. On his arm. Barely broke the skin." She tilted her head toward the closed door. "That guy in there? He went for the guy's face, and he looked like he was trying to eat that motherfucker. Down to the bone. And that was after he shot two people in the face, so fast that by the time the witnesses looked over the bodies were hitting the floor. Then he drove over to the motel with his face hanging off and started a crowdfunded gunfight, killed three more guys, maybe four, got shot three fucking times and the only thing that stopped him was running out of blood. Half the guys in the department want to have his baby, get his name tattooed over their hearts. It's embarrassing."

"Well, they say the crazy ones are always better in bed." He smiled innocently, then asked his partner, "Any idea how the Sheriff knows this guy? Pima Jack." He rolled the nickname around his mouth, trying it on for size. "He a former cop?"

"Jack Burton isn't a former anything," Flores told him. "I ran him." She saw Norm's look. "Hey, look, I'm the lead on this case, and I wanted to know who this guy was, if he had any ties to our witness. Jack Burton doesn't exist if you go back more than two years. There's absolutely no record of him even being alive before he got his driver's license. I'd run his prints, but you saw his fingers, he doesn't have any. Which I find interesting as well. When I brought it up to Wheaton, he told me to drop it. Not 'Hey, don't worry about that, you've got better things to do,' but 'Stop that shit right now,' which means he knows who this guy really is. Undercover, I'm guessing, but for who? Because he's not ours."

"He was having Sunday brunch with the Sheriff. With a retired porn star, too, you hear that shit? So who the fuck is he? A fed? Some military spec-ops guy?"

"That's what I'd like to know."

"Who's that lady I've seen at your house a few times?" Dave asked Lori. "Sort of chunky, big round blonde hair."

"That's my aunt Kimberly, my mom's sister," she told him. "They've never really gotten along, and they don't have a lot in common, and she hates me, thinks I'm a disgusting slut, has actually said that to my mom more than once…but now that my mom doesn't have too much longer she's trying to spend some time with her. And not spit venom at me. Lives in Phoenix."

"You guys have much family?"

"I've got an uncle who lives in Turkey, of all places, and Kim married into a big family, but mostly it's just me and Mom." She looked at him and debated whether to ask him a question, and reworked it a few times in her head before she said, "What about you? You told me about your parents. Any brothers, sisters, uncles?"

He shook his head. "Well, a few aunts and uncles, but they were all older than my parents, and I barely knew them. Rarely saw them when my parents were alive. Growing up it was just me and them."

"And Aaron."

Dave snorted. "Only known him about five years. Good thing I didn't grow up with him, I think we would have ended up doing something stupid and getting arrested. He's not a bad influence, not really, but he's not exactly an angel. Are those your mom's friends I see, what, every Friday?"

"Yeah, her little book club. These days she struggles to keep up with the reading, but they all pretend like everything's just fine with her."

She'd been living next to him the same amount of time, and had never seen anyone other than the Sheriff visiting Dave. If he had any friends other than Aaron, they hadn't come to visit. And he never talked to anyone on the phone. Never emailed anyone. She wasn't sure what to make of that. Then there was the Mickey issue. She was pretty sure Mickey was the name of the FBI lab guy who'd died in the shootout a few years back that had almost killed Dave. Twice now while she'd been sitting in the hospital room, watching him sleep, Dave had had a nightmare, and both times she was pretty sure he'd said "Mickey". He'd just been in a life-and-death struggle, and yet he was having nightmares about something that had happened two years ago? She wasn't sure what to make of that.

She stared at the big piece of blue construction paper propped up on the small dresser, folded once to make an oversize card. A big flower on the front, with a yellow sun and wiggling rays shooting out from it, drawn in crayon. All sorts of notes on the inside in crude block writing. Above the flower, on the front, was the only adult writing she saw —*From Mrs. Miller's 3rd-Grade Class*.

"Who's Mrs. Miller?" she asked Dave. He shook his head. He had no clue.

From where she was sitting, she could only read one of the many notes on the inside of the card. *Thank you for saving my Mommy.* Jesus. She looked over at Dave, but he was back reading his book. She casually wiped the tear from the corner of her eye, hoping he wouldn't notice.

The knock on his door was polite, and when he called to come in Dave was pleased to see it was Larry and Carl. They'd both been by to see him in his room a few times already.

"I'm getting released here in an hour or two," Larry told him, almost apologetically. He was in a wheelchair, with Carl doing the pushing.

"Good, I'm glad," Dave told him sincerely. "Go home. Eat some real food."

"I'm taking him out for a beer. Or eight. If I can pry him away from his wife," Carl said with a grin. Then it faded. "Look, Jack, um...we've been asked to be on *Hannity* tonight. On Fox News?" He and Larry traded a glance. "They really really would like to talk to you, too. You're the guy who did most of the stuff anyway, we wouldn't have even been there if it wasn't for you."

"You were there. And you did as much as I did," Dave told them. "Thanks, tell them thanks, but I'll pass." This wasn't the first such media invitation he'd gotten since the motel footage had aired. Wheaton had brought interview requests from MSNBC, CNN, Fox News, all three of the big networks, and half a dozen newspapers and magazines from The New York Times to Esquire. Dave had said no to everybody.

"You're sure?" Larry said. He traded another look with Carl. Dave got it then.

"Look, don't feel guilty talking to these people without me. You kicked ass. You are big damn heroes. You've got every right to talk to whoever you want, whether or not I'm there. But other than what's already out there, on that video, I don't want to add anything. Tell 'em I'm shy or whatever."

"I thought Aaron was yanking my chain, but you do look like a raccoon was eating your face while you were asleep."

Dave had been dozing, and opened his eyes to see Arlene, Aaron's girlfriend, smiling at him. Aaron was standing next to her, the corner of his mouth curled up in a smile. She was built like a wire coat hanger wrapped with muscle, with a big mop of hairsprayed blonde hair on top. "Arlene? What are you doing here?"

"I took a few days off to see the Grand Canyon, and got lost. Should have taken the left turn at Albuquerque." She shot him a dirty look. "What do you think I'm doing here? You're our friend, and I haven't seen you for two years. Then this happens. So I took a couple days off to see you. Then Aaron and I have to head back."

Aaron shrugged. "I can't afford to take too many more days off," he admitted.

"No, that's fine," Dave said. "I love the company, but I'm pretty set for security."

"Yeah, I saw," Arlene agreed.

"You missed all the news trucks," Aaron told his girlfriend. "Place was crazy last week. I wouldn't have been able to get you up here." He looked at Dave. "Now it's just you, the Sheriff, and a couple of other people who were seriously injured still up here. Flying glass from the bomb fucked a lot of people up."

"How is he doing?" Arlene asked Dave.

"The Sheriff? Better," Dave told her. "Well, not any worse, the nurses never want to give specifics. He's healing. They're hoping he regains consciousness soon, but they're not trying to rush it." He smiled at her. "It's great to see you." And he meant it. He hadn't realized how much he'd missed everyone from his old life.

"They still got you on the serious painkillers?" Aaron asked him.

Dave shook his head. "They offered, but I'm down to nothing but ibuprofen. So everything hurts all the time, but my brain doesn't feel like someone's trying to smother it with a pillow. I can actually think." He couldn't remember what it was like not being in constant pain. But he'd lived that before, with his hands.

"You got health insurance?"

"Me? No," Dave told him.

"Then it's a good thing you're here under an alias, so it'll be easier to skate out on the bill. Wouldn't be surprised if it was six figures by now."

"You want to play some cards?" Arlene asked Dave. Maybe it would help get his mind off the pain. And his medical bills.

Dave would have given her a wide smile if his face could move that way. "That'd be great," he told her. "And, at some point," he said to Aaron, "can you grab me some books from my house? I think watching daytime TV actually kills brain cells." He paused. "Which would explain a lot of things in this country."

Wheaton had stopped by for a visit. He checked on the Sheriff several times a day, and usually at least once a day popped his head in to check on Dave.

"I don't want to get your people in trouble," Dave said, "but isn't it a little dangerous for them to be bringing that witness here, even with the firepower in the hall?" Working as a private investigator he'd followed people through horrible homicidal Detroit traffic, and knew following the witness and her security detail from the hospital to wherever she was currently hold up in Prescott's light traffic would be child's play.

Wheaton frowned. "You didn't hear?"

"Hear what?"

"Those three cartel suspects we had in custody. Two of them were just muscle, but the third, Muñiz, was a hotshot. A known guy to the DEA and a lot of other people, someone high up in the cartel. Nobody knows quite how high he was."

"I'm hearing a lot of past tense," Dave observed.

"He was found dead in his cell, two days after the attack." Wheaton still looked angry about it. "Hung. With his own pants. Tentatively ruled a suicide."

"Tentatively? Don't you guys have cameras in the cells?"

"Electrical's been twitchy all over the station since the car bomb. Intermittent outages. We've got a backup generator, but still. Power went out to the cameras in the jail for ten minutes or so. Not for the first time. When they came back on he was swinging from his neck."

"That timing sounds awfully convenient," Dave observed.

"Yeah." Wheaton sighed, and looked out the window. "Lot of people here love the Sheriff. They got the message the cartel sent, loud and clear. And I'm pretty sure decided to send one back. We're looking into it, actually the Department of Justice is looking into it, but with the cameras out there's no evidence it was anything other than a suicide no matter the suspicious timing. Unless somebody confesses, and that's not going to happen." Wheaton shook his head. "So the witness, she'll still need to testify against the two suspects we've got in custody, but these two guys, they're just soldiers, nobody special."

"You've had a busy week."

"Christ, you have no idea. I'm attending three funerals tomorrow."

Nurses came and went on a regular basis. They gave a perfunctory knock, then entered before he even had a chance to respond. So when the tapping at the door wasn't immediately followed by a nurse bustling in he knew it wasn't one of his usual visitors. He checked the clock on the wall. Just after seven-thirty in the evening. Aaron and Arlene were out running errands, and Lori was home taking care of her mother. Dave glanced at the fanny pack on the bedside table, then pulled it into the bed with him and stuffed it under the sheet and blanket. Next to his hand. "Yeah?"

The woman who entered was slim and brunette, wearing a cardigan to fend off the cool air. Dave guessed she was maybe forty years old, although she had one of those faces that was hard to read.

"Mr. Burton? I'm Emily Pendleton. I wonder if I could talk with you for a few minutes." It didn't sound like a question, and she moved to the chair next to his bed without waiting for an answer.

He had to give her credit. She hadn't even blinked when she'd seen his face. "Who are you?"

She smiled, and in an instant he realized why she wore glasses with big clunky black frames instead of contacts—she wanted people to take her seriously, and the glasses were the only trick she could use to hide how pretty she was. Especially when she smiled. Which meant she worked in some sort of professional field. Lawyer, maybe, or…he looked at the cardigan. "Let me guess," he said, without waiting for her to answer. "Shrink."

She gave a little nod. "I am a counselor, yes. And I've been talking to a lot of people in Prescott this past week. Many in this hospital. Some very horrible things have happened. People have died. Been badly injured. Yourself included." She crossed her legs, and laid her hands on her knee. "And you had to take a life." She paused a beat. "Several." She looked at him earnestly.

"My only regret is I wasn't quicker to do it."

She cocked her head. "What do you mean by that?"

Inwardly he cursed at himself for even opening a dialogue with her. "Don't waste your time," he said.

"What, by talking to you? You are absolutely not a waste of my time," she assured him. "You suffered more than most. Seen some horrible things. Even highly trained soldiers are bothered by the things they see and have to do, and you're not at war." She sat patiently and met his gaze. He knew this game. Most people would want to talk, to fill the silence. With what he'd been through, after all he'd been through, he was pretty sure he wasn't like most people. And this woman, for all of her good intentions, had no idea who he was. What he was.

After what he guessed was two full minutes of silence, she finally spoke. "I watched the video of what you did. Well, some of what you did. It might appear to some people that you were doing everything you could to get yourself killed."

He snorted. "There are a lot easier and less painful ways to commit suicide," he told her.

"Yes, there are," she said agreeably, letting the sentence hang in the air. Then she sat and patiently waited again. Until it was clear he wasn't going to respond.

She held a hand up. "Please, I don't want you to feel any pressure. You don't have to talk to me. But the things you've gone through, you should talk to someone. Some sort of support structure. Friends, family, pastor. It will help you process them."

"I've processed them just fine," he said flatly.

She smiled indulgently. "Most people need far more than a few days to process such a traumatic event. To even recognize the emotions they're feeling. Grief, rage, everything in-between. That's all I want to do, help you work through what you've experienced. Because it will affect you for the rest of your life. And I deal with these kinds of things all the time." She paused, and waited. When he didn't say anything, she tried something else. "Biting another human being is a very extreme act."

Dave stared at her, unblinking, for several long seconds. "I've said no, politely, twice," he finally said, his voice flat. "Don't make me show you to the door."

"No, of course, sorry to bother you," she said, standing. "If you change your mind, I'm on staff at the hospital, and any one of the nurses or doctors has my contact information." She paused, but when he didn't say anything, just stared at her, she smiled self-consciously and left.

Aaron was in the chair in the corner, hitting his phone with his thumbs as if he was angry at it and occasionally grumbling. After a while he shut it off and tossed it onto the table. Dave looked up from Neal Stephenson's *Cryptonomicon* —it was one of his favorite books but hugely long, so he was using the occasion of his forced bedrest to give it a fresh readthrough—and saw Aaron looking at him.

"Between the Cracker Barrel and the motel they sent twelve guys," Aaron said. "Twelve fucking guys, man. Jesus." He peered at Dave for a long time, then seemed to fold in on himself. He sat that way for a long while. "You know I've never shot anybody," Aaron volunteered unbidden.

"You've also never been shot," Dave was quick to point out. The response didn't seem to satisfy Aaron. He sat for a long while, staring at nothing, then picked up his phone and began hitting it with his thumbs again, the tapping loud in the small room.

"Sweet baby Jesus, my Lori said it was bad, but you actually look worse than I feel," Grace Hoskins said, looking down on Dave. She appeared frail, but had shuffled in under her own power. "I'm sorry I didn't visit earlier."

"Soon as I can get out of here I'm just going back home. And that would have been a shorter trip for you."

Lori's mother smiled. "And when you get home Lori's going to take care of you."

"Umm…" Dave's eyes darted from Lori to her mother and back.

Grace Hoskins tsked. "Hospitals these days always release people before they're healed, because it's gotten too expensive to stay here. You're probably already off painkillers. I'm surprised they don't have you sharing a room, too. You're going to need help changing your bandages, getting in and out of bed." She glanced at her daughter. "She's gotten pretty good at that. Do you know how much longer they're going to want to keep you?"

"It's been over a week. I'm ready to get the hell out of here. But they want to keep an eye on my face for a few more days at least. I appreciate the offer, but I don't need—"

"Nonsense," she cut him off. "Lori told me you can't even walk yet without worrying about ripping your wounds open. So when we get you home, you just shut up and don't try to be the big tough guy, you let her take care of you."

Dave looked at Lori, then her mother. His face twitched, which was the closest he could get to a smile at the moment. "Yes ma'am."

PART IV
CHECK

Chapter Twenty-Two

Lori pushed the wheelchair up to the edge of the bed. She and Dave looked at Osterman for a long time without saying a word. The Sheriff was pale and seemed to be sunk into the mattress, as if it had begun absorbing him. He was still sedated, and on a ventilator, although the doctors hoped to get him breathing on his own soon. One bullet had torn up his intestines. Another had punched through his liver and busted off a piece of the Transverse Process of his T10 vertebra on the way out. A third fractured two ribs and punctured a lung. His recovery would take months even if everything went well and he didn't suffer any setbacks.

"He looks so old," Lori said, fighting back tears.

"He is old," Dave said, then flashed her a grin to cut the sting. Still, shot three times with an AK at point blank range and the man had gotten up off the floor, charged into the next room, and killed another man to save Dave's life.

The machines monitoring the Sheriff's vital signs made muted noises, and they could hear the faint hiss of the ventilator feeding Osterman oxygen. The technology was there to keep him healthy, and yet Dave couldn't shake the irrational thought that the machinery, squatting in the corner, was alive, somehow counting down the heartbeats left to the man.

"You okay?"

Dave blinked, then looked up. Lori was eyeing him with concern. He wondered how long he'd been sitting there without saying anything. "Yeah. Just been in this place too long. Ready to go home."

They'd gotten approval for this road trip down the hall. In fact, Ginny the head nurse had insisted it be her and her people who got Dave into the wheelchair as, she eloquently explained, 'We know what the hell we're doing'.

Lori stepped out from behind the wheelchair and moved to the side of the bed. "I'm not praying for you," she told the still figure. "You know I don't believe in that stuff. But we weren't done having our conversation. So don't you—" her breath caught in her throat, and she swallowed noisily," don't you dare go anywhere."

She put her hand on his. His hand was short and wide, with thick fingers. It felt cold to her. She gave it a squeeze, then looked at Dave. "Do you want to sit with him a while? Alone?" Then Dave saw her jump, just a little, and make a small sound. "He squeezed my hand!" she said in surprise.

They looked and saw Osterman's eyes were half-open. His eyes were wet, his gaze vague. Before they could say anything to him his eyelids fell once more as if they were too heavy to keep up for long. They waited, intently watching his face for any signs, but he didn't regain consciousness.

"Sounds like you've got a deal," Dave told her. They traded a grin.

Aaron pushed open the hospital room door without knocking. Which would have bothered Dave if it had been a nurse, but Aaron was, well, Aaron. He had Arlene in tow. They stopped next to the bed.

"Dude, I just wanted to let you know we've got to take off." Aaron seemed apologetic and genuinely upset. Arlene smiled at him, then reached over and squeezed Dave's arm.

"That's okay, I know you've got to get back to work."

"Not that I'm going to miss lowering your ass onto the shitter, but I was hoping we could stay around long enough to take you out for dinner or something. A nice steak. Or at least get you home." The latest word from the hospital was they wanted Dave to stay another two to three days.

"That's okay. You'd just order a fancy steak and put ketchup on it anyway," Dave told his friend.

"Yeah, so?"

"Putting ketchup on steak is the culinary equivalent of a mullet," Dave told him.

"I like ketchup on steak. Besides, I used to have a mullet," Aaron said proudly. "I live in a trailer. I smoke Marlboros. Do you not notice a trend?"

Dave laughed.

"Speaking of that, kinda, you might want to wash your sheets when you get back home," Aaron told him, with a sly smile curling up one corner of his black moustache. He and Arlene had been staying at Dave's house while in town. "Not everything we did in your bed was sleeping, and not everything in Arizona is dry."

Arlene hit him in the arm. "I changed the sheets," she told Dave. "Dirty ones are in the laundry." She scowled at Aaron. "And I made him smoke outside, so your place doesn't smell like cigarettes."

"Thanks for coming. Seriously. Both of you."

Arlene was blinking away tears. She leaned forward and kissed Dave on his forehead as Aaron said, "Dude, that's what friends are for."

"You see that, right?" Dave said, pointing at the TV mounted high up on the wall.

Lori glanced over at it. Fox News was on, the sound down low. "See what?"

He'd been flipping through channels and just had to stop and gawk at Shepard Smith. Once again the newsreader resembled nothing more than a poorly colored caricature. "The makeup. That's not me seeing things, right? One of my eyes isn't messed up? His makeup's that bad?"

Lori peered at the talking head. His makeup was pretty damn horrible, layers upon layers, with a lot of orange. "No, it's not you."

"He looks like a Ken doll in funeral parlor makeup. Can't he see that? He's got to be able to see that, there are probably monitors showing the view from the cameras where he can see them. I don't get it."

She shrugged. "Maybe he's color blind. Or that's the way he wants to look. Everybody has different tastes."

"He looks like that old ventriloquist dummy. Howdy Doody. Or an Oompa Loompa." Dave sighed. "How's your mom doing? I'm surprised you haven't brought her by." As soon as the words left his lips he noticed just how tired she looked, especially around the eyes. Maybe not tired. Drained.

"Not so good," she told him. She plopped into the seat next to the bed. "Lot of bad days in a row. Vicki's been over a lot."

Dave couldn't think of any question to ask that wouldn't

make Lori feel worse. Her mother, after all, had a terminal condition. She wasn't going to get better. They only thing Lori was hoping for, she'd told him late one night a few weeks back, was for a quick end. "Preferably in her sleep," she'd admitted to him. It almost felt like a betrayal to her to say it out loud. "The tumor's putting pressure on some nerves, and she's been getting a lot of twitches and jerks, left side of her body. I guess it can get a lot worse. Everything can get a lot worse."

With that in mind, Dave was hard-pressed to come up with a question that wouldn't make Lori feel worse. "I'm sorry I'm not there to help," he finally told her.

"You've got a pretty good excuse." She looked around the familiar hospital room. "You still getting released tomorrow?"

"Unless they change their mind, or I fall out of bed and rip something open. I'm so ready to get the hell out of here."

If he laid in bed, not moving, distracted by something interesting on TV or a captivating part of a good book, the pain faded into the background. With the help of 800 milligrams of Motrin every four hours. The rest of the time, however, his wounds ached and throbbed. Still, for getting shot three times and beaten nearly unconscious he supposed he was in pretty good shape.

"You're not going to do the stupid macho thing and try to walk out of here, are you?" Ginny MacDonald said to him as Lori helped Dave get dressed in real clothes for the first time in nearly two weeks.

With the chunk taken out of the bottom of his left pec Dave wasn't sure he could stick a crutch under his left arm and put weight on it without tearing something, and he told the head nurse as much. With his hip injury there was no way he could wear a belt or even tight pants, and Lori had brought a pair of his sweatpants from his house. He made sure to tie the drawstring very loosely around his waist. He was standing on his good leg, leaning against the side of the bed, Lori right there in case he had some balance issues. And the wheelchair standing ready, within reach.

"Maybe some sense is seeping into your head," she told him. She eyed his face, and the stiff way he held his left leg. The one they'd dug a bullet out of. "What's your pain level now?" she asked him.

"Two," he said. He saw her expression and changed his answer. "Three?"

She shook her head. "Forget it. Doc Brennan gone over aftercare with you, changing your bandages, schedule a follow-up visit?"

As Lori helped him carefully sit in the wheelchair, he told the nurse, "Yeah. Gave us a thick folder of papers. All I have to do now is sign my release forms, I think. Those them?" He nodded at the forms in her hand.

"Yep. And then I think you've got an escort waiting to take you downstairs." The nurse watched the girlfriend—with a notorious past, Ginny had heard all about that, but she was too much of a professional to say anything—put a bulging fanny pack on the boy's lap as he sat in the wheelchair. Probably stuffed with his wallet and car keys and whatever else guys carried around.

"Escort?" Dave said in confusion.

In her heels Mindy Tonaka was six inches taller than Lillian Osterman, but she never felt as if she was towering over the woman. In the small waiting room just off the side entrance of the hospital Tonaka knew that she looked like an Asian Barbie doll posed next to a gray-haired fire hydrant...and that it made absolutely no impact on the elderly woman, who put no stock in appearances. When it came to sheer force of will his wife was the equal to the Sheriff, even though everyone's first impression of the diminutive woman was that she seemed shy. That impression was soon shredded, even though she never raised her voice, never uttered a profane word.

"You've been up to see him," Lillian asked her. It wasn't a question.

"Yes. Twice now. And talked to him for a while. But I don't know if he heard any of it."

"He heard, Mindy," Lillian Osterman told the reporter confidently.

Mindy wished she had that kind of confidence. That kind of faith. In spite of what a lot of her fellow media types might think about her reasons for visiting the hospital, she truly cared for the Sheriff. Considered him a friend. Their politics were miles apart, of course, but he had always been polite and fair to her, ever since granting that first interview request some fifteen years before. He'd never lied, never misrepresented anything he'd done or said. And she'd tried to do the same, doing her best to be objective and impartial when reporting every story, whether or not it involved him. After over a decade she'd come to know Osterman as a person, not just a public figure. "How are you holding up?" she asked the elderly woman.

"Praying a lot, but the Lord gives me strength," Mrs. Osterman told her. She glanced around. "I am reminded that a hospital is no place for anyone who isn't sick."

"It is a bit difficult to keep cheerful," Mindy agreed. She

peered down at the woman. "This isn't the first time you've been at his bedside after he's been shot."

"Vietnam? We were practically teenagers then," Lillian Osterman said, the memories taking her back. "So young. So stupid." She snorted. "Although it was interesting, visiting the Philippines. That's where he was flown for follow-up surgery." She glanced at the glamorous reporter. "My parents paid for that ticket, there was no way I could afford it. I was surprised at the time, that they'd spend so much money. They weren't happy about me marrying so young. But my father saw something in Johnny. Something he liked." She snorted again. "Something that reminded him of himself, I imagine."

"Your husband is the closest thing to a national treasure this state has," Mindy Tonaka told her sincerely. "I truly hope he recovers quickly."

"I'm amazed at how old I've gotten when I wasn't paying attention," Lillian Osterman observed. "Johnny too." She peered upward at the beautiful young woman. "At this point it's not just the wounds that concerns them, it's what effect the stress of the wounds has on his body. Heart attack. Or infection. Or pneumonia." She sighed and looked around again. "I've been practically living here. And you're right, it is difficult to stay positive, but I can't help but think God has a few more challenges for Johnny down here before he's ready to wave him through the pearly gates. Why else save him?"

They heard the distant sound of an elevator opening, and the two women looked over to see four uniformed deputies walking in formation toward the hospital's side entrance. At their center was a man in a wheelchair, being pushed by a pretty blonde.

"Will you excuse me?" Lillian Osterman said quickly,

touching Mindy's arm so lightly it was like a butterfly landing on her wrist. Then the short woman was off, across the floor on her tiny feet, bending down to quietly talk to the man in the wheelchair while the deputies—all of them in body armor and carrying rifles—stood patiently by, waiting.

Tonaka stared at the figure in the wheelchair for ten seconds, blinking, then yanked her phone out of her purse. She turned her back to the group and moved a few steps away from them. Her cameraman answered on the second ring.

"Rabbit! Where are you? How fast can you get a camera up and running, trained on the west exit?"

"West? Oh, the side exit. 'Bout thirty seconds, why?"

"Because I think Pima Jack's getting released. He's in a wheelchair, surrounded by cops. Sheriff's wife is talking to him right now. It's gotta be him, with that face."

"No shit? Damn. I'm on it."

Mindy felt a light touch on her elbow, and turned around. The Sheriff's wife was looking up at her, mouth set in a firm line. But the elderly woman also looked vulnerable, somehow. She was shaking her head, just a tiny bit.

"Please," she said softly. "As a favor to me. Leave him be."

Mindy glanced at the crowd moving toward the doors, then back at the Sheriff's wife. The decision wasn't a hard one to make. "Rabbit," she said into her phone. "You still there?"

"Yeah." She heard heaving breathing as he jogged through the parking lot.

"Forget it."

"What?"

"Forget it. No video."

"You're sure?"

"Yeah. I'll be done in just a couple, meet me in the van at the front entrance."

"Okay, Tones, you're the boss."

"Thank you," Lillian Osterman said, a brief smile touching her lips. The two women watched the deputies escort the couple out the side door. The blonde left the wheelchair right outside the door and headed quickly for the parking lot. The deputies stood around the injured man, talking quietly to him. The blonde pulled up in a Toyota a few seconds later and Mindy watched the deputies shake his hand, one by one, then the young woman helped the rawboned bearded man from the wheelchair into the front seat of the vehicle. He moved slowly, as if he was still in a lot of pain.

"Who is he?" Mindy asked as the Toyota slowly pulled away. She must've watched the incredible footage from the Pima Motor Lodge shootout fifty times while preparing for the interview with 'Pima Jack's' partners, and while she hadn't seen the security camera footage from the Cracker Barrel—no reporter had, the police had refused to release it, citing evidentiary concerns—she'd heard about it. Talked to a lot of people who were there and had witnessed the incident. Had the scene described to her in gruesome detail.

Lillian Osterman stared out the windows and watched the vehicle drive away. "Someone who's sacrificed enough."

Lori parked in her driveway. She pulled the wheelchair from the back of her Toyota and unfolded it for Dave, then opened his door. He didn't move from the seat, not at first. Just stared out the windshield, hand on the fanny pack in his lap.

"You want to come in?" she asked him. "My mom would like to see you."

Dave looked at the front of her house, then forced a smile at her. "I think I'd just like to be alone for a while, you know? At home. My place." Osterman showing up at his door unannounced, inviting them to brunch, now seemed a lifetime ago. "Sorry."

"Sure, no, I get that. Don't be sorry, Jesus. Here, give that to me." He handed her the fanny pack, and she was surprised by the weight even though she knew what was in it.

Very carefully, almost moving in slow motion, Dave turned in the car seat and lowered his feet to the concrete. He took a deep breath, let it out, then slowly stood.

Lori watched his face. She saw how much standing had to hurt him—but just for a brief second. Then he buried the pain. Covered his face with a blankness. He took half a step, turned, and slowly sank down onto the wheelchair.

"I got you," she said and after setting the pack in his lap quickly bent down to lift his feet onto the chair's fold-down rests. She popped off the brake with the toe of her shoe, wheeled him backward to the sidewalk, then pushed him toward his place.

"How do you want to do the stairs?" she asked him, eyeing his porch. She didn't wait for an answer. "Do you think you should get a ramp?"

"No," he said firmly, the word out of his mouth even before she was finished with the question. "I won't be needing the chair that long."

"Hey!" she said sharply. She stopped the chair so quickly he almost fell out. She walked around in front of him, mouth tight. "Don't be an idiot and reinjure yourself doing too much too soon. I know you're a badass." She waved a hand around the neighborhood. "Everyone knows you're a badass, they've all seen the video even if they don't know it's you. So take a victory lap…in your fucking wheelchair." She sobbed suddenly, sucked it back in, and angrily wiped away a tear.

"Okay," he said. He looked at her face, then away. "Sorry."

She nodded, not looking at him, then walked around to grab the chair handles again. She pushed him up to the porch. There were only two steps. "How do you want to do this?" she asked him, pretending like the last twenty seconds hadn't happened. "I'd turn you around and pull you up backward, but I don't think I'm strong enough."

"I'll walk 'em," he said. He held a finger up. "Carefully," he said. "Slowly." He paused. "In a non-badass manner."

She snorted. "Where are your keys, in the pack?" She found his front door key and opened it wide. She set the fanny pack on the small table by the door with a resounding thunk. Dave pushed up on the arms of the chair and slowly stood. His right hip ached from the ricochet. His left thigh burned from the bullet wound. There was a constant twinge in his chest from the near-graze. His entire head throbbed and pulsed like an infected tooth. He reached up and took hold of the porch posts, lifted his right foot to the first step, then lifted his left foot to the second. His right foot joined his left and he stood, still holding onto the posts for balance.

"Hold on, let me slip by you." There was just enough room for the chair on the porch beside him. He sank back down onto it. She was strong enough to get him over the sill, with him helping a little bit, hands pulling back on the wheels.

"You sure you're good?" she asked. The chair was a few feet inside the room, facing out the door.

"I'm fine," he assured her. "Go see your mom. Tell her I said hi."

"Okay. I'll be back in a couple hours to check on you. If you need anything, you call me. You've got your phone, right? Heck, or you could just yell, I'll probably be able to hear that."

"I'll be fine, go."

"Okay." She took half a step, then came back and kissed him. "I want to visit the Sheriff. Maybe not tomorrow, but soon," she told him.

"Definitely."

"You want the door open?"

"Close it."

"Okay." She paused, little more than a silhouette in the bright doorway. Her eyes caught a glint of light, a reflection from somewhere. Her hand was on the doorknob, and she hesitated. But just for a second. "I love you," she told him, then pulled the door shut behind her before he even had a chance to respond.

Dave sat in the wheelchair in the dim room, staring at the closed door, his mouth hanging open just a little bit.

Chapter Twenty-Three

"Is this as good as I think it is?" Lori asked Dave, as the credits rolled on the fifth episode of the first season of *Stranger Things*.

"I think so," he told her. He turned to her mother. "I can't believe you guys haven't seen it before, I know you're really into eighties stuff." The supernatural series was set in 1983.

"Didn't know what it was about," Grace told him. "You haven't seen it before?"

He shook his head. "I'd been meaning to watch it, heard great things about it, but never got around to it. It's even better than I'd heard."

"I want to watch the rest of the episodes straight through, but I think I've got to take a break," Grace said apologetically. "I'm fading fast. Probably should head to bed."

"You and me both, sister," he said, checking his watch. Not even eight p.m., but Lori said her mother's internal clock was all screwed up. So was Dave's. He was sleeping off and on during the day and awake half the night. He grabbed hold of the wheels of his wheelchair as Grace carefully got to her feet. "Race ya."

She snorted, then shook a finger at him. "Don't you go tearing anything. You haven't even been home a week."

"Yes ma'am."

"Let's get you to bed," Lori told her mother. Her mother made a raspberry sound.

"I can get myself to bed," Grace told her daughter. "Doing just fine tonight. You get your wounded warrior back home, spend some time with him. I'll do some reading in bed, if I can get the book cracked to the right page before I nod off. Go, shoo."

"Yes mom."

Trading a smile Lori grabbed the seat handles of Dave's wheelchair. If she tilted the chair back, and leaned back herself, and he helped a little with the wheels, she could bump him up and down the porch stairs pretty smoothly.

"You want to watch TV, or surf Facebook while I read, or...?" Dave asked as she wheeled him into his front room. She went back and closed the door behind her.

"What I'm thinking is that you're long overdue," she told him. She walked around behind the chair and set the brake, then moved around in front of him and knelt down.

"For...?" he asked.

"A hero's welcome home," she said, and explained by removing the fanny pack from his lap, setting it on the floor, and undoing the drawstring on his sweatpants.

"I'm no hero," he said reflexively. "And not that I'm not interested, but I'm still not supposed to be doing anything that'll open a wound. I'm considering it a victory that I'm finally able to get on and off the toilet by myself."

"You won't need to do a thing," she assured him. She

was getting good at reading the expressions on his healing face and saw his dubious expression. "Trust me," she told him. "I'm a professional."

"Ha ha. Um. Uh. *Ooooohhhhh.*"

"I came here right after it happened, maybe a day or two later. Just to see. It was roped-off, for evidence or because it was still a crime scene then," Lori told him. "Looked like half the town was standing around staring. Now I think it's just for safety, so people don't drive into the crater." As she spoke Dave gazed out at the street.

As craters went he had to admit it didn't look like much. He'd been to Meteor Crater east of Flagstaff in Arizona as a kid and that was almost a mile across, something close to five hundred feet deep. It was actually featured in the 1984 movie *Starman* starring Jeff Bridges, which he'd watched recently with Lori and her mother as Grace raced to watch every movie made in the 1980s. Maybe before it was too late? He didn't want to think about that.

That was a crater. What he was staring at out the open window of Lori's Toyota was just a shallow bowl in the road barely ten feet across and a foot or two deep. Smaller than some Detroit potholes. But he could imagine the kind of explosion needed to create it and wondered how many cars had been tossed about. What the blast and concussion had done to anyone walking nearby. Half the windows he could see from where he sat were still boarded up, and the rest were obviously filled with brand new panes of glass, some with manufacturer's stickers still affixed.

"They shot a deputy out front and a bunch of people up and down the sidewalk before they took off," she added. "I think the two assholes who did this are some of the ones that got away." She looked over and saw Dave was just shaking his head. "What?"

"All this just for a distraction. Going after the Sheriff too. Just a distraction to keep the cops occupied while they went to kill the witness." He made a sound halfway between a grunt and a growl.

Lori put her vehicle in gear and slowly pulled away. Looking around, Dave saw that it was more than just physical damage to the town. He noticed the way the residents kept glancing over at the sheriff's department, at the crater, around themselves. He'd seen people staring at the Cracker Barrel in the same way when Lori had driven past it. Their sense of safety had been ruptured. They felt violated. The town didn't feel the same to them anymore. Because of that Dave hated the men who'd done this even more.

He sighed. "Can we get a coffee?" he asked her. "I haven't had a good cup of coffee in forever. And I need to get up out of this seat and move around, my hip is getting stiff." Actually, it was hurting like hell, but he didn't want to tell her that because he knew she'd make a fuss and try to take care of him.

"Sure. Where do you want to go? There's a couple of Starbucks not too far from here. I know you dig that place by the Cracker Barrel, but I don't know if you…"

"No, let's go there," he said.

She supposed he wasn't as stubborn as he could have been, and he hadn't done anything stupid which had reopened any of his wounds, but he definitely didn't let her help him as much as she would have liked. It had been a bit of trial and error, this new physical relationship they had. Maybe once she might have thought helping to take care of him was a lot of work, but after two years of dealing with her mother's deteriorating condition Dave's infirmities didn't seem like anything new.

She stood a few feet away and watched patiently as he pushed open the car door and fished his crutches from the back seat. She glanced across the huge parking lot at the Cracker Barrel a quarter mile away. The parking lot around it was empty, and she could still see the POLICE tape fluttering in the breeze.

Dave awkwardly stood up and got the crutches nestled in his armpits. "I know you want to help," he told her, clenching his teeth against the pain. He wasn't looking at her, but he could sense her standing there, waiting. "If you can just get the door, though, that's all…that's all I need."

"Sure," she said. She closed the car door behind him as soon as he was out of the way, then walked ahead of him to the coffee shop and held that door open for him. She was pretty sure he was still supposed to be in a wheelchair, but she didn't try to correct him. She was just glad he was willingly using the crutches and not trying to walk on his own.

The Aloha Snackbar wasn't too busy, with only a handful of patrons sitting at tables, and Matt had just finished emptying the trash behind the counter when the door opened. Matt didn't recognize the guy at first, not with all that damage to his face, but he recognized the girl with him. Oh, he definitely recognized her, and then recalled the face of one of the guys she'd been with on her last visit and realized he was the same one with her today.

"What the hell happened to you?" he asked as the guy clanked up to the counter on his crutches behind the girl.

"Gremlins," Dave told the redhead, happy that his lips were now working in a near normal fashion. They'd watched the movie just a few days before.

"Those little bastards," Matt agreed without missing a

beat. Having spent months of his life in VA hospitals after losing his foot he knew all about guys who didn't want to talk about their injuries. He was guessing a car wreck. Windshield glass could to that to a guy's face. Or maybe he was drunk and fell through a glass patio door.

Lori turned and saw Dave struggling to get his money out of his pocket without dropping one or both of his crutches. "I can pay for yours," she told him.

He made a sound deep in his throat. "I'm a bit broken, but I'm not broke." He successfully tugged the cash out of his pocket and held it up for her to see.

"You're a stubborn bastard is what you are," she said. That got a little smile out of him.

"You don't pay," Matt told the porn star. They'd meant it when they said she could drink for free, anything. "Put your money away. What can I get you?"

"Neither does he," they heard. His business partner Mike came out from the back office. Matt looked at his friend and co-owner with one eyebrow raised.

"You don't recognize that face?" Mike said in disbelief. He turned to Dave. "Didn't you get shot too?" he asked. "A lot? How the hell are you even walking around?"

"Slowly," Dave replied honestly.

"That's fucking Pima Jack," Mike said to his partner who still hadn't placed him.

Matt blinked and looked back and forth from Mike to Dave. Then he took a good long look at Dave's face. "Oh. Dude. *Duuuuude*. Nice work. Holy shit. How are you doing?"

Dave took a deep breath before answering. "I really just want to get a cup of coffee," he told them.

Even though the expression on his healing patchwork face was impossible to read, both men recognized the strained tone in Dave's voice.

"That's definitely something we can get for you," Mike said cheerfully, dropping the matter instantly. "What's your pleasure? Regular or unleaded? Flavored or straight as it comes from nature? For sweetener you want calories or cancer? Cowjuice or no?"

"I can take your order Ma'am," Matt said with a smile at Lori, moving a few steps down the counter.

She glanced over at his business partner efficiently and professionally whipping up a latte for Dave, then turned back to Matt. He knew exactly what the smile she flashed at him meant.

Thank you for changing the subject.

"So I heard you stole my car." His voice was weak and raspy, his face pale and unshaven, but he was smiling.

"Borrowed," Dave told him. The sight of the Sheriff awake, the sound of his voice, however reedy, filled Dave with a warmth he hadn't felt in a long time. "But I know what you're doing, and I guess it means you're feeling better. Isn't the first rule of politics knowing who to blame?"

The Sheriff shook his head in a small arc. There was a clear tube under his nose feeding him oxygen. "No, that's the second rule of politics. The first rule of politics is getting reelected."

"I don't think you have to worry about that. Not ever again." On his crutches Dave moved slowly and sat down in the chair next to the bed. Lori set his crutches out of the way before she took Osterman's hand in hers. He smiled up at her warmly, then his eyes moved to Dave and stayed there.

"You saved her," the Sheriff said to Dave. Peering at him intently.

"Barely," Dave replied.

Osterman just looked at him for a while not saying anything. He wasn't up for much talking but since he'd regained consciousness Sam Wheaton had been in several times a day giving him updates on everything. And everyone. The feds' progress, or lack thereof, on tracking down the remaining cartel members. The media circus. The in-custody death of Muñiz. The car bomb and the damage both physical and psychological to downtown Prescott. And what Dave and his impromptu posse had done to save the life of the witness.

"Your wife is wonderful," Lori told the Sheriff, jumping in.

"She's definitely earned her place in Heaven after everything I've put her through," Osterman agreed.

"Oh, you be quiet," she told him.

"How is your mother doing?" Osterman asked her.

Lori glanced from the Sheriff to Dave and back again. "Better than the two of you," she observed.

A small wry smile crept across Osterman's face as he looked at Dave. "I hear Sam sent one of the talking doctors to visit you."

"The shrink? Wheaton was behind that?"

"It's required for every one of our officers who get involved in a deadly force incident. I hear you weren't, ah, especially forthcoming."

"I'm not one of your officers," Dave reminded him. "I'm your 'special project', remember? At least according to your wife."

Osterman lay still with a small smile at his face on his face for quite some time. Dave was quiet as well. "So are the two of you going to talk about what happened?" Lori finally asked. Both of them had killed people, in especially ugly ways. And nearly died. She looked back and forth between the two of them. Dave frowned at her.

"Us tough guys are a taciturn lot." Osterman drily replied.

She blew a raspberry, shaking her head, and in that moment looked and sounded just like her mother. It made Dave smile.

Pietro Bufonte sat on his patio and sipped at his espresso, staring out at the rear of his property. Nearly two acres of lawn, the grass as green and flat and featureless as a billiard felt. A tall concrete wall ran down both sides and across the back of the property but it was shielded from his view by thick privet hedges to either side and a row of tall ornamental cedars in back resembling green fence posts. He couldn't hear or see his neighbors. For what he paid in taxes, for what the property was worth, he would damn well hope for a little privacy.

He was wrapped in a thick velvet robe but was still chilled even in the warm humid morning air. Behind him, a sprawling custom cantilevered two story that could have been designed by Frank Lloyd Wright's cousin, heavy on windows, sat quiet and dark. The morning sun was behind the house, the brick patio still in shade. The shadow from the house stretched deep into the grass.

There was nothing to be heard other than the chirping of a few birds and, very distantly, a lawn mower. It was peaceful. Serene. He hated it.

Having led a bigger-than-life existence for so long, to be reduced to little more than a prisoner in his own house was humiliating, and it galled him. The feds for sure were onto half of everything he was involved in, the deals and businesses and shady people, and he couldn't be sure about most of the rest. Couldn't be sure there wasn't a rat or three somewhere, ready to flip on him to avoid lengthy jail time. And there was nothing he could do about it but wait and see if the cancer killed him before some overeager young FBI agent showed up with handcuffs after finally—finally, after years of harassment and investigation and intimidation—finding enough evidence to charge him with something, anything.

He heard the sliding glass door behind him open and close, and he turned. Anthony, who'd been with him forever, who was one of the few people he trusted completely, was walking toward him across the patio, cell phone in his hand. One of the cheap disposable ones they kept handy. He held the phone out without saying a word and Bufonte took it.

"Yeah."

"You where we can talk?"

Bufonte glanced back at the house. Even if the feds had managed to bug his house, he didn't think the microphones could pick him up out here. And they didn't know about this phone. "Yes."

"I've got a location for that hard-to-find item you've been looking for," Detective Billy Dixon said into his burner phone. He was sitting in the parking lot of a Home Depot, in his personal vehicle, on his day off. He'd told his wife he needed to run to the hardware store to buy some drill bits, and that much was true, but he also needed to make this call where he knew no one could overhear his end of the conversation.

Bufonte sat up in the chair, wincing at the sharp pain in his abdomen. "Well," he said. "That's long overdue."

Dixon didn't rise to take the bait. "I've got a current name and address."

"Local?"

"No. Arizona."

He'd actually located Anderson almost two weeks earlier and had delayed telling Bufonte for as long as possible. For a whole host of reasons, not the least of which the former boss of bosses seemed to be growing desperate. Desperation led to mistakes, and Dixon had a lot to lose. But by finding Anderson for Bufonte, he had a lot to gain as well. Still, the situation wasn't so simple.

"He found himself in another dust-up. He's got a lot of eyes on him at the moment. A lot of law enforcement presence all around him, although I can't imagine it lasting for very long. I'll get you the details." He paused, then took a deep breath. "I know how long you've been waiting for this information, but I would urge restraint. Patience."

Bufonte stared out across his lawn toward the bright green cedars, the blue sky beyond, seeing none of it.

"Would you now."

"Shouldn't you be in a wheelchair?"

Dave looked up at the man in his tailored suit. "You sound like my…everyone."

Richard Roberts, Esquire, hid a smile as he retrieved the crutches from the back seat of his Lincoln. He would have preferred his new client arrive for this meeting in a wheelchair solely for the dramatic effect, but he'd learned very quickly upon meeting Dave that the young man was decidedly bullheaded. In that way he was just like the client who'd recommended him.

The attorney waited patiently as Dave grunted himself to his feet. He then handed Dave the crutches, grabbed his briefcase out of the back seat, and led the way toward the entrance at a pace Dave could match.

Roberts held open the first door for Dave, then the second, then strode past him to the front counter of the Sheriff's Department. "Richard Roberts and Jack Burton," the attorney announced them through the security glass to the two deputies. "I believe they're expecting us."

The man all the deputies called "Ricky Bobby" behind his back was a familiar face to everyone in the department, as he'd been John Osterman's personal attorney for close to twenty years. Richard "Screaming Eagle" Roberts could trace his family's Indian heritage back to their dealings with Spaniards in the 1700s. In his blood were traces of the Yavapai, Pima, and Quechan tribes. He had a slightly hooked nose, long black hair in a ponytail, bronze skin, was just over six foot three inches tall with an athletic build (even at 62 years of age) and was so handsome he'd been dubbed the "Native American Tom Selleck" by People Magazine ten years earlier when they'd done a profile on him.

Deputy Chet Henley had been with the department for over a dozen years and had met the Sheriff's attorney several times. He got up, leaving his partner manning the desk, walked past the two loaded M4s staged where the rifles could be quickly accessed but not visible to anyone in front of the counter, and hit the buzzer to unlock the door leading back into the bowels of the Sheriff's Department headquarters. He met the two men just inside the door.

"I'll take you down," he told them. He'd met Ricky Bobby before, but he'd only seen video of Pima Jack. He eyed the slender man leaning on his crutches. His face looked absolutely wrecked.

Dave cleared his throat. "Ummmm, not sure about your rules," he told the deputy, "but I'm carrying a gun." He tugged up at the waistband of the khakis—they were several inches larger than he needed, bought specifically for this meeting, loose so they didn't interfere with the bandage on his hip, and worn without a belt for the exact same reason. They were so loose Dave was surprised they hadn't fallen down around his ankles yet. He gestured at the fanny pack hanging low around his hips. Arizona had constitutional carry, which meant any citizen legally allowed to own a gun could carry a firearm concealed without a permit, but he figured inside the Sheriff's Department headquarters might be another matter.

Roberts turned to his client, his eyebrows raised. "Don't you think this is something you should have discussed with me first?"

Dave's voice was flat. "There's a crater in front of this building. Fresh glass in all the doors. At least four of the cartel guys got away, some of whom might have seen me shooting their friends." He looked up at Roberts. "Assume I have a gun." He looked back at the deputy.

Chet Henley looked from the fanny pack to the attorney to Dave. "If you trust your attorney to hold onto that for you while you're here, I don't think anyone here today will have a problem with it," the deputy told Dave. He lowered his voice and leaned in, so close their foreheads were almost touching. "And if the cartel does show up, I'd appreciate it if this time you let us kill some of those fuckers before you jump in. Brion Sanderson was a friend of mine."

Their interrogation rooms were too small for this, so the meeting was being held in one of the classrooms usually reserved for in-service training. Henley opened the door, and Dave clacked past the deputy on his crutches. A bemused Richard Roberts followed, briefcase in one hand, fanny pack in the other, the straps dangling. He was surprised by the weight of it even knowing what was inside. He wasn't, however, surprised by the number of people in the room, or at the cameras set up to record everything.

"We have quite the full house here today," he observed. He pulled a chair out for his client, and watched with concern as the young man slowly and painfully lowered himself into the seat. Then he set the fanny pack on the table and his briefcase on the floor before looking around the room. "I recognize representatives from the Sheriff's Department, the FBI, the DEA..." His eyes drifted over the two dozen or so people in the room, and settled on an athletic blonde guy in a suit. "I don't believe I know you," Roberts told the man.

"Special Agent Joe Clark, Department of Homeland Security," the man said with a smile.

"Ah, of course. The agency which couldn't have been named more appropriately by George Orwell," the attorney said drily.

"That's not quite the suit I would have expected on someone with the name 'Screaming Eagle'," Clark shot back. "Although the ponytail doesn't disappoint."

"It comes from my time with the 101st Airborne Division. Screaming Eagles," Roberts told the man, not rising to take the obvious bait. "My hair was a bit shorter back then."

"I understand your being nervous, but you are not a suspect in any crime," Norm Hill told Dave, ignoring Ricky Bobby and the federal agent. "No one here thinks you did anything wrong. Far from it. And, honestly, most of the incident was captured on camera. But we've never talked to you, you've kept putting us off, and we're just looking for clarification on a few things."

Even though it seemed to hurt Wheaton's feelings, all

Dave would say to the cops or federal agents repeatedly stopping by his hospital room was, "I was eating at Cracker Barrel when some guys came in shooting, and I responded accordingly. I will be happy to give you a full statement as soon as I consult an attorney." The truth was he didn't want to talk to them until he'd spoken to Osterman, and it was Osterman who'd provided Dave with an attorney.

"I know you didn't do anything wrong," Osterman had said quietly to Dave. "Consider him insurance against saying something stupid that will come back later to bite you in the ass."

Roberts set his briefcase on the table and popped the lid, then looked at Norm Hill. "Can you guarantee me that nothing my client says here today will be used as evidence against him in any kind of legal proceeding? Ever?" He moved his eyes from the Sheriff's Department detective and looked around the room. "Guarantee that in writing?" He waited a good twenty seconds, looking around the room, just seeing how many people would meet his gaze. A lot of them stared back at him unflinchingly, but nobody said a word. "That's what I thought."

Roberts pulled a yellow legal pad and pen out and set them aside. He withdrew a small digital recorder from his briefcase, placed it gently on the table, and turned it on. Then he nodded at the two video cameras on tripods aimed at his client, and turned his famous brilliant smile on Norm Hill. The attorney gestured at the seats all around the four tables that had been pushed together in the center of the room. "So…shall we begin?"

Chapter Twenty-Four

Dave struggled to get out of the passenger seat of Lori's Toyota. After two hours in the car his wounded hip and thigh were stiff and aching, but he'd finally traded in his sweatpants for a pair of jeans, sized to fit him, unlike the clown-pants khakis he'd worn to the recorded statement at the Sheriff's Department. He wore them loose because of the bandage on his hip, no actual belt, but he had the fanny pack carefully secured around his waist. A small victory was still a victory. And he was getting good with the crutches. He had his crutches staged and was already levering himself to his feet inside the open door by the time Lori walked around the SUV.

He was actually capable of walking without the crutches, although every step hurt. He was using the crutches as slip-and-fall insurance. Falling down would definitely rip something open. He'd been back to see the doctors twice on follow-up visits since being discharged from the hospital, and they were very pleased with his progress. He and Lori sat and talked with Osterman nearly every day. The visits were short, as the Sheriff didn't have the energy for long conversations.

Lori glanced around the parking lot, then at the front of the strip mall. The whole area was nice, the residents obviously had a lot of money, and the small retail area reflected that. The parking lot was dotted with ornamental trees that were probably a gigantic pain to keep alive in the Arizona heat.

"Why did we drive all the way down here? Aren't there gun stores a lot closer to Prescott?" she asked Dave once he was on his feet. She closed the car door behind him, then walked beside him as he crutched his way toward the front door of the business. The signage for the Scottsdale Gun Shoppe was classy and subdued, but the gun store seemed to take up most of the building. She hadn't been expecting such a big place, but then again she couldn't remember if she'd ever been to a gun store before.

"Think of it as customer loyalty," Dave told her. "I bought a bunch of Turnerite here a couple of years ago and it saved my life, so I guess I'd rather spend my money here."

"What's Turnerite?" she asked, opening the door for him.

"Binary explosive," he told her.

"Explosive? Are you serious?"

The look he gave her told her he was. Once inside she stopped and looked around. She was expecting...well, she wasn't sure what she was expecting, but it wasn't this. The interior of the Scottsdale Gun Shoppe was all brand new, almond and cherry wood with subdued chrome trim, and expensive-looking laminate flooring. It was also much brighter than she was expecting. There were a few customers browsing, and a number of employees behind the counter clad in matching polo shirts. She smelled fresh coffee brewing somewhere nearby. Good coffee.

"Not what you were expecting?" Dave asked her, seeing her expression. "Ever been in a gun store before?"

"I was just thinking about that. I don't think so."

"Well, this one's a little nicer than most, but they're not all shacks filled with fat rednecks who have a thing for beer and banging their sister and drinking beer while banging their sister and playing the banjo." He stuck the crutches back under his arms and made his way toward the counter, the crutches giving a metal clack each time he set them on the floor.

Two of the employees behind the counter saw him coming and instinctively moved closer together. Crutches, extensive facial injuries...this guy had obviously recently been in a serious incident. Which was a potential red flag. Bartenders weren't supposed to let people too drunk to drive head out the doors with keys in their hand, and gun stores had an ethical and legal responsibility, beyond the questions on the requisite federal paperwork, to make sure a potential customer didn't have evil intent. If somebody showed up and looked or acted like a terrorist, or seemed as if they were making straw purchases for a third party, they had a duty to report it to the ATF. This guy looked like he'd just survived a prison riot. Probably not a potential terrorist or gang member, but he perhaps might be someone who was looking to get revenge on whoever did that to his face.

"Good afternoon, sir, how can we help you?" one of them asked.

"Looking for your Glocks," Dave said, scanning the handguns inside the brightly lit glass cases.

"You look like you had a rough week," the other

salesman said to Dave. His nametag read TONY. "If you don't mind my asking, what happened?"

Dave gave him a wry smile. "Do you know that the most dangerous thing most people ever do in their lives is drive a car on public roads?" Lori glanced at him but didn't say anything.

Tony relaxed at the man's smile and easy tone and nodded. "Yep, I hear you. More cops are injured in accidents than by bad guys. Actually, a hell of a lot of cops are hit by drunk drivers. They're drawn by the flashing lights like moths."

"Really?" the other salesman said, jumping back into the conversation. He looked back and forth from Dave to his co-worker. "I would think wrestling with drunks and assholes would cause more injuries—pardon the language," he said to Lori. She flashed a smile at him.

"No, it's car accidents," Tony said. "Cops are driving all the time, they only wrestle with idiots occasionally. Unless you're in some sort of high-risk occupation, driving's the most dangerous thing you can do. It's pretty bad around here." He waved a hand. "Not people driving fast. All the old people come out here to retire—it's all them driving slow. I call them rolling roadblocks. Never get into an accident, but totally oblivious to how many they cause." He moved a few steps down and gestured at the guns on display in the counter there. "These are our Glocks. This case, and the next. You interested in a particular model?"

"Nineteen, Gen 3," Dave told him, clacking down to the indicated display. "Preferably with something better than the standard shitty factory sights."

Tony nodded appreciatively, then paused. He squinted at Dave. "Hey, I know you," he said.

"Yeah?" Dave's heart sank. He really didn't want to talk about the Prescott incident.

"Yeah. You're the guy who beat Angus at Rio Salado last month, right? With a Glock 19." That's what had keyed it in his memory. "I shot the match too. Production Division."

Dave relaxed. "Oh. Cool. I was having a good day."

"Looks like you won't be shooting a match for a while, though, that sucks. I've got a few Gen 3s in the case, but hold on a second, I've got something I want to show you, maybe you'll be interested. I know you'll appreciate it." He held up a hand, then strode off purposefully.

Lori leaned over. "Don't you already have a gun?" Lori asked him, glancing down at the fanny pack strapped loosely around his waist. She kept her voice down, not sure of the legalities carrying a loaded gun into a gun store.

"Yes," he responded, "but you always need a back-up, somewhere. Gun number two is always Plan B." The Glock he'd used in the Cracker Barrel had been taken as evidence, and he assumed he'd never see it again.

Tony was back a minute later and set a plastic Glock pistol case on the counter. "Just got this in from a regular customer. It's new in the box, unfired, but he needs cash quick because his wife just filed for divorce." He opened the case and let Dave look. Lori stepped up too. To her it looked just like all the other pistols in the counter, black and vaguely L-shaped.

"Wow," Dave said.

"Glock 17, Gen 3," Tony said. "I know you're looking for a 19, and this is bigger, and a bit pricey, but it's just so pretty I thought I'd show you. TTI did their Combat Master package on it. They're a custom shop, trick out ARs and shotguns and Glocks. The grip on this is stippled, the slide's been contoured, trigger job, carry mag well, the works. This is actually the gun that Keanu Reeves used in *John Wick 2*, the catacombs shootout. Well, not this gun, he had this package done on a Glock 34, which is a bit longer, but this one looks just as nice. TTI's run by Taran Butler, a pro shooter, and he actually did some live fire training of Keanu for the movie. Posted it on YouTube. Reeves can actually shoot pretty damn well in real life, it's not your typical Hollywood magic-of-editing B.S."

Dave stared down at the pistol. It was beautiful, or at least as beautiful as Glocks got. It was also twice as much as a standard Glock 19 would cost even priced to sell fast. But what were the odds, the salesmen bringing this particular gun out to show him? Priced almost exactly to the dollar with the amount of cash he had in his pocket? "Well, that's serendipity or fate or destiny or whatever you want to call it," Dave said, carefully scratching at an itch on his face.

Tony looked at him strangely, then the light went on behind his eyes. "Wait, didn't somebody at the match say you know Taran?"

"Yeah, we go back."

"You're friends with someone who knows Keanu Reeves?" Lori said, frowning at him. The things he didn't talk about were astounding.

Dave took a deep breath, then unzipped the front pocket of the fanny pack and pulled out his wallet. He withdrew the Jack Burton driver's license and set it on the counter. "You only live once, right?" he told Tony. Beside him Lori made a small sound.

"Absolutely," Tony said, beaming. "Let me get the paperwork," he told Dave. He headed down the counter.

"Well, now we find out just how good this ID is," Dave muttered.

Waiting for the Kick

"Why didn't you just buy it at a gun show?" Lori asked him.

Dave was confused at first. "What? Oh, you've been watching too much garbage news. All firearm dealers in this country have to be federally licensed. And any time they sell a gun, new or used, handgun, rifle, or shotgun, out of a store or at a gun show or out of the trunk of their car, the buyer has to fill out the same federal form and undergoes the same federal background check. Or they lose their license and could go to federal prison."

"Oh. Really? You're sure?" That's the exact opposite of what she'd thought was the situation.

"The term 'fake news' exists for a reason," Dave told her. "The 'gun show loophole' isn't a real thing. Never has been. You probably don't know that machineguns and silencers are legal to own in over forty states, either. Including this one."

"Seriously?"

"All those hours a day on Facebook are rotting your brain. Honestly, it's nothing but public masturbation using a keyboard."

"I'm okay with public masturbation no matter what you're using," Lori told him with a smile.

He sighed loudly. "No, seriously, you know Sarah Palin never said she could see Russia from her house, right?"

"All I know about Sarah Palin is that Lisa Ann played her in that movie. Totally boosted Lisa's name recognition. And her paychecks."

"Movie? Wait, are you talking about that porn movie? What was it, Nailin' Palin?"

"Something like that."

Dave rolled his eyes and shook his head. "You know, this might take a while." He jerked his head toward the fancy doors past the counter. "You should check out the VIP area. I hear they have a rectal scanner." He laughed at his own joke.

"What?"

"Sorry. Retinal scanner," he explained. "I heard somebody mispronounce it once."

The corner of her mouth twitched. "I thought you were my rectal scanner."

Tony returned with the multi-page form. He set it on the counter, then looked at Lori. He cocked his head. "You know, you look kinda familiar too."

She smiled innocently. "I get that a lot."

Dave was limping down the shoulder of Old Fain Road not too far from the Glassford Meadows entrance when a Sheriff's Department cruiser pulled up next to him and he heard the window roll down, the tires quietly crunching gravel.

"Sir, everything all right?"

He didn't pose much of a threat, one lone slender man limping along the side of the road, but he supposed his presence on the road at 3:52 a.m. might raise a law enforcement eyebrow or two. He'd seen the lights behind him coming close a while back and caught the reflection off the light bar on the roof, seeing it was a cop car. He wasn't surprised the deputy stopped.

"Having trouble sleeping," he told the officer. Inside the vehicle, through the open window, the man was only a silhouette.

As Dave stopped the squad car stopped as well and suddenly he found himself blinded as the officer keyed a handheld flashlight in his face. "Whoa, what happened to you?" the officer asked upon seeing Dave's face. He'd noticed the limp and had assumed the figure was a senior citizen. Wandering about this early, there was a chance the man could be suffering from dementia, considering the average age of a GM resident. But this was no senior citizen. And his face was a lot sweatier than it should have been on such a cool night.

Under other circumstances Dave would have brushed off the inquiry with a joke, deflecting concerned inquiries with smart-ass comments as he had been doing for weeks, *cut myself shaving, my wife was driving, Velociraptor attack*, but he just wasn't in the mood. "I'm Pima Jack," he told the officer flatly, "although I'm not real fond of the nickname. Nightmare," he added, which was the truth. He hated sharing his personal problems with anyone, much less a stranger, but he figured it was the quickest way to satisfy the deputy. The man's face was unreadable inside the dark car.

There was no response from the officer for a few seconds, then the flashlight beam moved down from Dave's face to his hands and the fanny pack at his waist and then back up to his face. "You live around here?"

"Inside GM," Dave answered.

"Aren't you supposed to be in a wheelchair or on crutches?" he asked Dave.

"Yep," Dave answered simply. After another couple seconds the flashlight shut off, leaving Dave with dark after-image globs in his vision. He blinked to clear them, but it didn't help.

"Looks like you're limping pretty bad, dude, you want a ride back to your place?"

"I'd like one," Dave answered, "but I'm not out here walking because it feels good."

The deputy didn't say anything for a long while, then he put the squad car in Drive. Before he pulled away he told

Dave, "Take it easy Cujo, don't blow an O-ring. I have a feeling if you end up back in the hospital because you overdid it, the Sheriff will somehow make it our fault."

Dave supposed it was a bit like a baby learning to walk. First he'd hobbled across his front room touching furniture and the walls as he went to help keep his balance, the crutches nearby. He drunkenly weaved back and forth. He knew Lori would get stressed out if not yell at him for exceeding the doctor's recommendations and be worried about him tearing something, but he was tired of the crutches, tired of being weak. That first trip across the room hurt. A lot. But he made it and after standing there for a few minutes, panting heavily, he walked back to his crutches. The round trip from one side of the room to another took over a minute, but he did it without falling down or reopening any wounds.

He started doing that trip several times a day until he could walk across the room and back without needing to pause, needing to touch the furniture, needing to catch his balance on anything. When he was sure he could walk short distances without losing his balance he began walking up and down the street in front of his house.

He only did his walks at night when he couldn't sleep and he knew Lori was asleep, just so she didn't get worried and didn't hover around him.

Back and forth in his front room became two doors down and back, then grew to the end of the cul-de-sac. The first time he made it all the way to the end of his street and back seemed like a triumph. It took him ten minutes and he had to stop several times, but he made it. Every step hurt, hurt both his left thigh and his right hip, but he didn't let the dull aching pain stop him. Although he did let it slow him down; he did not want to reopen his wounds, although he wasn't as militantly paranoid about it as Lori.

Slowly limping back home after the encounter with the deputy Lori finally caught him. He was two houses away when he saw her stepping out her front door. At first she stared at nothing, then she spotted him limping up. She didn't seem surprised to see him out there. It wasn't until he drew close that he saw she was crying silently, the tears silver streaks down her face in the moonlight. He knew immediately what that meant and glanced at the quiet house, then back at Lori.

"Whatever you need, just let me know," he told her. "I'll help however I can."

She nodded, then hugged him, burying her face in his neck. He could feel the wetness of her tears on his skin.

The funeral was a modest affair, at a small local cemetery Dave supposed he had driven past a dozen times without ever noticing. The priest from Grace's church did the eulogy, saying some very nice things about her. Dave was actually surprised at the number of people at the graveside service, and at the reception afterward in the nearby church's semi-detached "activity center". He spotted a number of his neighbors including Mrs. Leslie, all of Grace Hoskins' book club friends, and a number of other elderly men and women he ultimately learned knew her through the church.

Lori and her aunt had apparently put aside their differences, at least long enough to arrange the funeral. The meeting room was well-stocked with drinks and a shocking number of dishes baked by Grace's friends and neighbors.

While he saw a few tears, the death was far from unexpected, and mostly the attendees seemed to be sharing funny or heartwarming stories about Lori's mother, which was what was supposed to happen at a wake. For the funeral and the get-together afterward Dave had left his crutches at home and was actually using a cane that had belonged to Lori's mother, although he'd rarely seen her use it. He didn't need it to walk, it was more an insurance policy than anything else, especially if he got tired. Which he did, often, and far more quickly than he liked, but he was getting better, every day.

He was sitting in a chair, alone at a table against one wall, when Lori excused herself from a group of their neighbors and came over to him, wiping a tear from her cheek. "How you doing?" she asked him, nodding at his leg.

"I ate too much," he told her, gesturing at the plate in front of him. Between the goulashes and cakes and pies and casseroles and 7-layer dips the food table looked like it was sagging in the center.

"I'm going to have leftovers for a month," Lori sighed, staring at all the food. She looked at Dave, and jabbed a finger at him. "You have to help me eat it," she told him. "Or I'll get big as a house."

"I'll do what I can. I'm not exactly burning many calories hobbling around. How are you doing?" he asked, peering up at her.

She looked around at all the people standing around eating and talking animatedly, and a bittersweet smile slid into place. "Sad. Relieved. Angry." She sighed. "We knew it was coming, and talked about it a lot, but still…" She shook her head. "She'd be so happy to see all these people here."

"And she'd be chatting them up a storm," Dave said with a smile.

"Yes she would."

"I'm really glad I got to watch the end of *Stranger Things* with her," Dave told Lori. "With the two of you together. And that awesome popcorn. That was a good night." Her mother's second-to-last night on Earth, he declined to point out.

"Yes, it was." She cocked her head at him. "Why does Rose Leslie think you were in a train accident?"

Dave blinked. "Train accident? I have no idea. What does that even mean? Like a train on the tracks train?" He looked across the room at his neighbor. She was in a group of other GM residents talking animatedly.

"I don't know, I asked you. Probably something got lost in translation somewhere. Nice lady, but her, um, record skips a lot if you know what I mean. You need a drink or anything?"

He shook his head. "I'm good."

"Okay. I've got to mingle some more."

"Go do what you need to do. I'm not going anywhere."

He poked at his food a little bit, then stood up as his hip was aching and looked around the room. For the second time he noticed a group of people off to one side who didn't seem to fit in. Four women and two guys, his age or a bit older, although one of the women was in her forties, with dark hair. The women wore dark-colored dresses and heels, the guys khakis and ties over button-down shirts, and they were all in shape. He'd seen them drive up in a new Cadillac Escalade with Nevada plates that cost more than his house. Most of them looked vaguely familiar, especially the older woman with dark hair. They were glancing around disinterestedly and drinking from beer bottles. One of the guys saw Dave looking over, and headed straight for him.

"Saw you talking to Lori," the guy said. He was maybe

five-ten, wiry, wearing a white button-down Oxford shirt over khakis, with a thin black tie. He'd rolled up the sleeves of the shirt, revealing forearms corded with muscle and covered in tattoos. "You're one of the few people here not on Medicaid. You know her, or her mom?"

"Both of them, actually. Live next door."

"Ah. I'm Danny." He took a sip of his Corona.

"Jack. What about you?"

The guy seemed surprised at the question. "I, uh, knew her when she was in California," he said, peering at Dave, trying to read his expression. Then he gave a little shake of his head and looked around the room. "I'd never even heard of Prescott until that terrorist attack last month."

"Cartel," Dave corrected him.

"Yeah, dude, whatever. Fucking wild west."

"So I heard."

"No fucking thank you, know what I mean? Didn't sign up for that shit. But then I figured, what the hell, might as well make the trip, lightning never strikes the same spot twice, right?"

Didn't sign up for it? Dave pointed at Danny's exposed forearm. "Isn't that an Army tattoo?"

Danny glanced at it. "Yeah, from like World War II." He looked around and then jerked a thumb over his shoulder at the other thirty-something guy he'd traveled with. "Pete over there, he's the vet. Did a tour in Iraq. Even got a Purple Heart when his convoy was attacked." Pete was a serious weightlifter and had his hair buzzed short. He was talking to Lori's aunt, a big smile on his face, and it looked like she was blushing.

"Man, I gotta ask," Danny said. "What the hell happened to your face?"

"Slipped in the shower," Dave told him.

Danny's eyebrows slid up his forehead and he took another sip of beer. "Damn."

"I'm really glad you guys came out. I haven't seen you in forever."

"We were going to be in Vegas anyway, and it's a quick drive down," the pretty dark-haired woman who'd arrived in the Caddy was telling Lori as Dave limped up. Most of the other guests had left, and the group who'd had arrived together in the Escalade was standing in front of the building entrance.

"Thanks Lisa, it was great," Lori told her.

"I haven't been around this many geezers since the AARP convention," the youngest woman in the group said, now chewing gum. She looked Asian and even in heels was short. She blew a bubble and looked around the parking lot distractedly.

"Jesus, Chichi, show some class," one of the other women said. She had burgundy streaks in her dark brown hair, and JUDGE ME NOT just visible, tattooed across the tops of her sizable breasts in large letters. There were a number of tattoos visible on her arms, mostly flowers. She looked directly at Dave. "Lori said not to bother you in there, but I wasn't going to leave before I talked to you." She held a hand out and Dave shook it. "I love love love the Sheriff. You're amazing. Thank you so much, and I hope you get better soon, I can't imagine how much getting shot hurts."

"Anna, what are you talking about?" Danny said, frowning and confused. He looked back and forth between Dave and the woman. "He fell in the shower. Didn't you say you fell in the shower?" he asked Dave. Dave just shrugged.

"He took the bullets meant for the Sheriff," Pete, the big guy, corrected him. "Personally I think the man's a grandstanding ass, but standing up to those crazy cartel motherfuckers takes some serious balls." He held his hand out, and Dave shook it.

"Didn't you say he shot a bunch of them?" burgundy-tressed Anna asked Lori.

Lori shot Dave a look out of the corner of her eye, then stepped close and put her arm through his. "Yeah, but we don't really talk about that. Some of them got away." On the side away from Dave, where he couldn't see, she held her hand up, all five fingers splayed, mouthed the word '*five*', and gave her friend a pointed look. Pete caught the exchange.

"Okay," Dave said, with some force. Lori looked at him guiltily, but he wasn't looking at her but rather everyone else in the group. "It's been bugging the shit out of me, but I finally figured it out. Who you are. The context screwed me up, I'm not used to seeing you dressed up for a funeral. But I got it now."

Lori looked surprised. "It took you 'til now? Didn't you used to be a detective?" The other women were trying not to laugh.

"The tits and tattoos didn't clue you in?" the one blonde in the group said with a smile. Dave had heard someone call her Thea.

"Gimme a break, I've had a rough month. And I got a concussion too, you know?" He looked at the women, then the two men. "You guys worked together. With Lori. Nice to meet you. Glad you could make it out." The corner of his mouth curled up as he looked back at the four women, his eyes coming to rest on Lisa. He borrowed a line from Aaron. "I've enjoyed your work."

Osterman-loving Anna gave Dave a big smile. "We're running back up to Vegas tonight, but if you're ever in town, you look me up. You deserve a good time. On the house," she clarified for him, in case he wasn't getting the message. She glanced at Lori, and smirked. "You can bring her along too, we always worked great together."

"You got shot?" Danny asked Dave, still trying to figure things out. "So you didn't fall in the shower? And what the fuck is up with your hands?"

Chapter Twenty-Five

"Humunurr?"

Dave smiled in the dark and glanced back at Lori. She was a featureless lump under the covers. "It's okay, go back to sleep," he said quietly. Sitting up in bed had been enough to disturb her, apparently, even though she was a sound sleeper. They'd been sleeping together every night since her mother had passed, half the time at her place, half at his. He reached back and gave her a comforting squeeze, then pulled the comforter back up. Her skin was warm under his hand. He wasn't sure what part of her he actually touched in the dark, as she slept nude, but the touch seemed to settle her down.

Trying not to jiggle the bed any further he felt around for his pants and then stood up. Not smoothly, or quickly, or without pain, but he was doing it, and getting healthier and stronger every day. He still wasn't having much luck sleeping, though. Not that he was tired, he just couldn't sleep. Or, rather, stay asleep. Sometimes it was nightmares, and flashbacks, but not always. And once he was awake, that was it.

He dressed in the dark room, then carefully moved out into the kitchen. The floorplan of Lori's house was reversed from his, and altered even from that, so he put a hand out so he didn't run face first into something unexpected until the glow from the night light and oven clock in the kitchen swam into view.

5:12. He tilted his watch to reflect the blue glow coming off the night light and saw the same time as displayed on the oven. Not too early, not compared to some mornings, but Lori wouldn't be up until seven, at least. He moved to the counter, opened the cupboard door and near blindly felt around for the bottle he knew was there. When his hands closed around it he pulled it out and held it up to the clock so in the dim illumination he could make sure it was ibuprofen. Dave swallowed four pills, washed them down with a drink from the tap, then headed out the front door.

The morning air was cool and he shivered. There was a hint of light in the east, but overhead were a few stars. Not as many as usual, though, so he suspected there were clouds up there, although they were invisible at the moment.

He took the two stairs carefully, then set a steady pace; not fast, but not slow. Down to the end of the street, left toward the front of the subdivision, then north on Old Fain Road. His feet kicked up dust with every step but in the near dark he heard it more than saw it. His leg and hip ached with every step, but it was a background ache, not a "you're about to tear something" ache.

It had been two weeks since Lori's mother had passed. Was she going to sell the house? Should he sell his house and move in with her? What were her long-term plans? She'd mentioned that once her mother died she'd probably have to get a job. But he didn't have a job either...

Dave knew those questions were out there, floating in

the ether at the edge of his conscious thought, but he was doing everything he could not to look at them, think about them, acknowledge their existence. For over two years he'd been living his life one day at a time, never thinking much more than 24 hours ahead of where he was. But that era seemed to be drawing to a close. He hadn't addressed that yet. Hadn't consciously sat down and thought about it. Even with all the time he'd had to himself in the hospital he'd studiously fought any and all urges to think about his future. And he still hadn't made any plans. But he was gradually becoming aware of the fact that, someday soon, he might have to start thinking about the rest of his life. Because it appeared that "the rest of his life" wasn't going to be measured in weeks or months.

He'd been cold and shivering when he started his walk —even at the height of summer there was no humidity in the high desert air to retain the sun's heat—but between the light exercise of walking and his body reacting to the low-grade pain he was warm before too long. Lost in thought— he couldn't say about what—Dave paused and looked around. The sky was starting to light up, and he'd spent enough time jogging up and down Old Fain Road to know he was about a mile, maybe a mile and a half from the entrance of Glassford Meadows. Not far at all, in the grand scheme of things, but his hip and leg were starting to throw out distress signals. Unless he wanted to actually reinjure himself, it was time to turn back.

With a sigh he crossed over to the other side of the road and headed back. He could actually see the edges of the road now, although the land around him was still nearly dark. The sky above was much lighter, and he saw he'd been right, there were more than a few wispy clouds streaked across the sky. They were charcoal shadows thrown across the black of the late-night sky, past them a few bright stars twinkling.

By the time he made it back to the Glassford Meadows entrance the sky to the east was lit up orange and pink, as were the cotton candy clouds above, but the sun was not yet visible, and the neighborhood itself was still gray and dark. His hip was starting to throb, and his thigh was burning. He'd gone too far, maybe half a mile too far, and as he turned the corner onto his street his barely noticeable limp was very noticeable. If Lori was up and saw him limping as he was she would not be happy.

His plan was to go inside, swallow some more ibuprofen even though it hadn't been nearly four hours, and sit in one of Grace's nicely padded chairs until his body stopped ringing alarm bells. It was then that he saw the cop car parked in front of his house, facing out, toward him, passenger side against the curb.

Dave sighed and limped down the street toward the car. It wasn't a marked unit, there were no lights on the roof of the dark-colored four-door sedan; more likely it was a couple of detectives, maybe federal agents, back to ask him "a few follow-up questions". It had already happened twice, in spite of Ricky Bobby's admonitions to not attempt to talk to his client without him being present. Couldn't blame them for trying. As Dave drew close the front passenger-side door opened. A guy in a white polo shirt climbed out and stood inside the open door.

"What's up?" Dave asked tiredly, stopping right in front of the car.

The man was tall, with dark blonde hair. He smiled. "Man, do you get up early." He reached down and leisurely produced a large silver pistol. He held it loosely in his hand, not quite pointing it at anything, while continuing to smile.

"Mr. Bufonte would like a word," he said, enunciating very clearly, seeming to relish every syllable. "Let's go for a ride."

As soon as the blonde had produced the pistol Dave's heart had thudded once in his chest, hugely. It felt like a door slamming. Then the adrenaline hit and his brain was running at a thousand miles an hour, the world around him moving so slowly it might as well have been standing still. His brain processing information at lightspeed—the relaxed body language of the man standing, someone not expecting any resistance. The fact that he was about ten feet away. The type of pistol in his hand—a stainless steel Smith &Wesson 3rd generation semi-auto. Dave's mind had taken all of this detail in before the man had even finished speaking—then his eyes flicked right, as the man behind the wheel of the car drew his attention by shifting in his seat.

The driver's hand appeared, moving slow as a snail, and he set a pistol on the dash in front of the steering wheel. It seemed a clear message. The guy behind the steering wheel was in dark clothes, some sort of gray smudge on his left sleeve. The pistol he'd placed on the dash was an old Army 1911. Then the car rocked slightly. Both rear doors unlocked and he saw the vague shadows of men inside starting to get out.

As the word "...ride" left the blonde's lips Dave ripped the false front of the fanny pack down with his left hand as he'd done a thousand times in practice, the Velcro loud in the still morning air. Eyes locked on the blonde Dave's right hand grabbed the Glock, pulled it out of the holster in one smooth motion, his left hand joined his right as he pressed the gun out, the tritium-powered night sights glowing green in the dim morning light.

The blonde barely had time to react, his eyebrows rising, hand holding the gun twitching up, before Dave started firing, the front sight dancing in front of the man's face in slow motion, everything crystal clear, the gunshots distant thumps. Seeing the hits in his face and throat, knowing the man was dead on his feet, Dave swung the Glock right and began firing through the windshield even as he stepped to the right and moved forward past the bumper, his limp forgotten, his pain forgotten. There was nothing in the world for him but the front sight of his Glock. His brain was running at lightspeed and everything around him seemed to be standing still.

The windshield safety glass frosted white around the bullet holes, glittering particles of glass spraying outward, the driver jerking left and right as if he was being hit with electric shocks. Dave kept moving forward down the car and continued firing without pause, sweeping his gun from the driver to the man sitting directly behind him, just a vague shape in the backseat pushing his door open, empty cases ejecting from the top of the Glock so slowly it seemed he could read the headstamps on the brass. Dave fired, fired, kept firing at him, then smoothly bent down and fired past the twitching silhouette to where he knew the fourth man in the car had to be. Then the slide locked back on his Glock.

Dave sidestepped to the rear of the car, dropping his spent mag, reaching down for the spare mag he always kept inside the fanny pack, doing a reload through sheer muscle memory, smooth is fast, never taking his eyes off the car. Fresh mag in the gun he found himself at the rear bumper of the vehicle which a distant corner of his mind identified as a Dodge Charger, dropped the slide of his pistol on a loaded round and proceeded to empty the second fifteen-round magazine through the back windshield of the vehicle at anything and everything as fast as he could pull the trigger.

Pistol empty a second time he stood panting, staring at the car. The air was hazy with gunsmoke. Every window in the car was blown out or spider-webbed with bullet holes. The doors hung open, unmoving. Hands starting to shake, empty gun still pushed out in front of him, he retraced his steps along the driver's side of the car, staring at the interior.

The men inside were bloody and misshapen, slumped over in the awkward poses of death. Nobody was moving. He pulled the empty Glock back, staring at the corpses. At the men he'd killed.

"Fuck you," he said. "FUCK YOU!" he shouted at the dead men, seriously starting to shake from the adrenaline dump.

Belatedly he realized that his ears were ringing violently, but beyond the ringing he could hear someone yelling. He turned and saw Mrs. Leslie standing on her porch in a pink nightgown, staring openmouthed at the scene before her.

"Jackie!" she cried in horror. "What did you do? What did you *do*?"

When the first Sheriff's Department squad car arrived not quite four minutes later the street was filled with people, but Dave had made it explicitly clear none of them were to approach the Dodge or touch the bodies. His empty Glock was on the hood of the car, slide locked back, and Dave was standing in the middle of the street thirty feet in front of the Dodge, fingers interlaced atop his head. Lori was standing on her porch, hands covering her mouth, eyes wide and glistening. He'd made it clear she needed to stay there no matter what happened.

The deputies exited their vehicle guns drawn, but seeing

as the street was filled with chattering senior citizens they rightly deduced that the chance of immediate danger was low.

"Call Sam Wheaton," Dave called out to them, carefully kneeling in the middle of the street. He did not move his hands from atop his head.

The two deputies carefully moved toward him, their eyes moving back and forth between Dave and the shot-up car behind him.

"Who are you?" one of them asked.

"Look at my face," Dave replied flatly.

The deputies' eyes had been scanning the vehicle, the bullet holes, Dave's hands for weapons, the area for anything or anyone that looked threatening, but at Dave's words—and his tone—both deputies' eyes slid to his face and locked on. The morning sun had crested the horizon and there was more than enough light to see all there was to see. As the recognition dawned in their eyes Dave said, "There's four guys in the car. I'm pretty sure they're all dead but you might want to make sure. I saw at least two guns. That's my Glock on the hood."

Sergeant Jesse Ferguson stood on the curb and briefed Wheaton and the two detectives.

"My guys finished canvassing the neighbors. None of them saw anything. Most of them were still in bed. The few who were awake, it was over before they could get to their windows and look outside to see what was going on. But they heard it, and they're all saying mostly the same thing, including crazy cat lady over there." He gestured at Rose Leslie standing on her porch, Mr. Bigglesworth in her arms.

"Which is what?"

"Somebody shouting and then shooting a machine gun. Or shooting a machine gun and then shouting."

"Machine gun?" Wheaton looked over at the perforated Charger, then at Dave, sitting on his girlfriend's porch, then back at the car. "It was a Glock. Wasn't it?"

"They said it sounded like a machine gun." Ferguson paused. "Apparently he's a mite quick on the trigger," the sergeant said drily. "Color me unsurprised." The two men exchanged a look, then Wheaton glanced at his detectives. He'd called in Maria Flores and Norm Hill, as the incident involved "Pima Jack" and was undoubtedly cartel related. Or so he'd thought.

"Thanks," Wheaton said distractedly. He wandered over to the Charger again, Flores and Hill following, and peered at it for maybe the twentieth time. All the bodies had been removed, but he could still smell the blood. He walked around to the curb side of the car and stared at the blood trail in the dirt. It was a foot wide. The man who'd been in the back seat, on the passenger side, at some point had fallen out of the car and crawled across the kid's yard before dying around the corner of his house. Face down in the dirt.

Dave had spent the better part of an hour in cuffs in the back of a squad car but for the last two hours he'd been sitting on the steps of Lori's porch. Lori had been sitting next to him the whole time. They'd barely exchanged a word, she just held his hand as the detectives and evidence techs processed the scene and talked to his neighbors. He knew it was more than a bit unorthodox, the cops just letting him sit there, but he understood he presented a... unique challenge. His front yard was roped off with yellow tape. One of the guys he'd shot had crawled away while

Waiting for the Kick

Dave had been shooing senior citizens away from the car. The blood trail he'd left in the dirt was massive.

The street was roped off with plastic evidence tape, and all of his neighbors—apparently everyone who lived in Glassford Meadows—was standing in the nearby yards and at the end of the street, staring and pointing and shaking their heads. Dave watched Sam Wheaton pacing back and forth along the curb. Wheaton was on a phone call, his fourth or fifth in the last half-hour, and he hung up looking angry. He consulted briefly with the two plainclothes detectives on scene—Dave recognized both of them, they'd brought the cartel witness to visit him in the hospital—then Wheaton turned and marched up the sidewalk, the two detectives in his wake. He stopped a few feet in front of Dave.

"Rental car out of Vegas," Wheaton said. He jabbed an angry thumb at the vehicle in question, as if its very existence irritated him. "Everybody in there was whiter than white. This wasn't a cartel hit."

"I never said it was," Dave replied. His left ear was ringing, badly. It had never stopped, after the Cracker Barrel, but now it was a lot worse.

The detectives traded a look. Wheaton frowned, glanced back at the detectives, down at his boots, and took a deep breath. It looked as if he was mentally counting to ten. "They had four guns in the car," he told Dave. "Three handguns and a shotgun. And a roll of duct tape. Michigan IDs. Every one of those guys has a criminal record. And links to organized crime, according to the Detroit detectives I spoke to not too long ago."

Wheaton paused, then jabbed an angry finger back toward the car again, nearly poking Maria Flores in the eye. "Four dead guys," he shouted. "Four more fucking dead guys!" His voice echoed off the housefronts, and caused a lot of the residents standing at the edge of the tape line to look over.

"Sir?" Norm Hill said cautioningly.

Wheaton held a hand up, closed his eyes, really did count to ten in his head, then looked back at Flores and Hill. "Give me a minute with him," he said.

They didn't like the sound of that but he was the boss. After another glance at Dave, Flores and Hill walked back toward the shot-up vehicle. Wheaton watched them go. When he turned back he glanced at Lori, then at Dave, his question unspoken but clear.

"I've got no secrets from her," Dave told him.

Wheaton took a deep breath then stepped in close and leaned down so that his face was less than a foot from Dave's. "Are the Mexican cartels hiring the Detroit mob to do their dirty work now, or is this something else? The other thing."

"It's probably something else," Dave told him. He licked his lips. "Who's their boss in Detroit, do you know?"

"Peter Baffoni or something like that," Wheaton said.

"Then this is that other thing," Dave told him.

"God dammit," Wheaton cursed. He stomped in a circle, then came back to Dave. "If this was a hit they're really shitty at their jobs. Doesn't look like any of their guns were fired."

"Attempted abduction," Dave told him.

Wheaton gave him a sharp look then shook his head. "Jesus H. Christ on a popsicle stick son, you're not even all the way healed from the last time. This other thing that got you all shot up and burned?" Wheaton frowned and tried to remember the details. "The crime boss who thought you killed his son, or blamed you for his son's death?"

"Something like that." Lori looked from Dave to Wheaton and back, but didn't say anything.

"Fuck," Wheaton cursed under his breath. He turned and stared at the car full of bullet holes for a while. "They even get a shot off at you?" he finally asked.

"I don't know," Dave responded truthfully, "I was too busy shooting."

They both looked up as a helicopter flew by overhead. A TV news logo was visible on its side.

"Right now everybody thinks this was the cartel making a run at Pima Jack," Wheaton told him, "and I'm overdue in correcting that misapprehension. But I will. Probably within the hour. I can't have the citizens thinking the cartel are back and wreaking havoc in their town again." He paused. "Although they might not believe me come to think of it. We are not going to release any details on the deceased until we have notified their next of kin. And we're not going to release any background info on exactly what happened here today. But eventually their identities will become known. Their criminal associations. And everybody, apparently, already knows you were involved. Pima Jack." He glanced up and down the street at the residents who were staring in rapt joy at the scene, this shooting being the most exciting thing most of them had ever experienced. He sighed again. "That mob guy really has this much of a hard-on for you after all these years?"

"Apparently," Dave said.

Wheaton dug in his pocket and pulled out Dave's flip phone. "Call Ricky Bobby," he said pointedly. "I've already talked to him this morning. He's expecting your call."

"You call the Sheriff yet?"

"What? Christ no. Probably try to climb out of bed and drive down here himself." Wheaton walked back toward his two detectives, who were waiting for him in the middle of the street. And they did not look happy.

"Every one of these guys had a felony record," Maria Flores said to him, jabbing her finger at the now-empty car. "So simply getting caught with a gun, one gun, would put them all back in the big house for some serious time. But they had four guns, all of which are stolen according to our friends at the ATF, and drove four hours across the desert in the middle of the night to get here."

"With duct tape," Norm Hill added. "Fresh roll."

Wheaton stared at his detectives. "And?" He looked back and forth between Flores and Norm Hill, who looked like he'd eaten something sour.

"Vegas, and Detroit? This has shit-all to do with the cartels," Hill said. He stared at his supervisor. "You know it." He stabbed a finger at Dave. "And he knows it too. Knew it. He burned those four guys down before they even had a chance to get out of the car."

"Sir," Flores pleaded. "Can you please stop blowing smoke up our asses and tell us what the hell is going on?" She turned and eyed Dave. "Who is that guy?"

John Phault sat in the front seat of his Ford Expedition and watched nothing happen. He'd been watching nothing happen for the better part of five hours, which meant it had been a pretty typical work comp surveillance. He'd made half a dozen phone calls, listened to several talk radio programs, and used the restroom, which for a male on surveillance meant a resealable plastic bottle—in this case a wide-mouth bottle originally filled with washing machine detergent. He expected a lot more nothing to happen over the next few hours.

He was in northeast Detroit, near Seven Mile and Gratiot. There were a lot of nearly empty neighborhoods in Detroit but this area was still heavily populated...which meant it had a high crime rate. Not before noon, though. All the troublemakers stayed up late and slept in. His client didn't care about that, they wanted to make sure this claimant wasn't working a second job when he was supposed to be off due to an elbow injury.

His phone rang, the volume on the ringer so low it wasn't audible outside of the car. He checked the display but didn't recognize the number. 928 area code, wherever the hell that was. Somewhere out west, probably.

"John Phault," he answered, keeping his eyes on the front of his claimant's house halfway down the block.

"John, hey, it's, uh, Dave Anderson."

A smile exploded across Phault's face. "Dave! Wow. Hey. Long time."

"Yeah, I know, sorry about that."

"Hey, before I forget, did your partner every get ahold of you? Ex-partner. Mullet Man. Aaron?"

He heard Dave snort. "Yeah. Yeah, I talked to him."

"Good, I...hold on, I've got a citizen walking up on me," John told his former employee, and rolled his window down half way, lowering the phone. He'd seen the guy come out of one of the nearby houses. Thirty-something black guy in a tank top and shorts, wearing flip-flops and a confused expression.

"What are you doin', man?" the man asked Phault.

"What do you mean what am I doing? Didn't you get the notice?"

The man's look of confusion deepened. "What notice?"

Phault did his best to look earnest and sincere. "They

sent out a notice to everybody living on the street," he told the guy. "Both sides," he added.

Flip-flop guy made a face. "Well, I don't actually live here, I'm just stayin' here with my girl," he told Phault.

"She didn't tell you about no notice?" Phault said in astonishment.

"No," the man said, now looking concerned.

"Hmmmm," Phault said, giving the guy a pointed look. "Sounds like you need to talk to your girl."

"Shit." The guy looked up and down the street, maybe looking for one of the notices. "So what did it say? The notice?"

"Man, I can't tell you that, you don't even live here," Phault told him. "You need to talk to your girl." And he rolled up the window on the man's confused face and put the phone back up to his ear. He could hear Anderson laughing.

"You're still doing that 'notice' bit?" Dave said.

"Why not? It's hilarious. And works every time." Phault waited a few seconds for the confused resident to wander away from the SUV back toward his house. "So what's going on? How are you doing?"

Dave sighed. "Well, that's why I called. And it's a dick move, only calling because I need something."

"What do you need, name it," Phault said without hesitation.

"Pietro Bufonte," Dave said, sitting on Lori's porch and staring at the rented Dodge Charger getting loaded onto the back of a flatbed tow truck. Wheaton was in the middle of the street, on his phone again, one arm waving as he made a point. "I'm hoping you can run a comp report on him. Or whatever else you need to run. I'm looking for addresses in Vegas. Places that he owns, addresses associated with him, anywhere he could be. Anything and everything."

"In Vegas," Phault said, thinking.

"Yeah."

Phault blew air out his mouth loudly, then said slowly, "You know, if I'm doing work for you, you're a client, and I protect my clients. But if I run him, there's a record of me running him. And you and I are, as they say, 'known associates'."

"If anyone ever asks why you ran him, tell them you did it at my request," Dave said flatly. "I'm okay with that." He paused. "If you'll do it, I'm hoping for sooner rather than later."

"Do I want to know why you…no, no I don't," Phault answered his own question before he'd even asked it. "Just…try not to do anything extra stupid, okay? Let me get to work and I'll get back to you ASAP. Hour or two, maybe. Call you on this number?"

"Yeah."

When he got off the phone Lori was looking at him strangely. "This bullshit has gone on long enough," Dave told her. "I'm going to finish it one way or the other. That is, if I'm not in jail." He looked down at the phone in his hand. "Guess I better call Ricky Bobby." He started punching in the number from memory.

Lori watched him. He'd just killed four people. Four *more* people. And once the adrenaline shakes had left him he'd been cool and calm and, what, resigned? as a retiree picking up a prescription at CVS, even when the responding deputies cuffed him at gunpoint. The only time any strong emotion colored his voice, animated his features, it was during the phone call to some guy she'd never heard of before. Who apparently was some sort of detective. And when Dave was on the phone with him, trying to track down the mob boss, she could have sworn he seemed relieved. Perhaps happy. Maybe even eager.

Aaron was sitting in the back of The Beast—1551, the armored car, built sometime back in the Paleolithic, that would never die—watching the overhead door roll up, when the radio above Eddie's head crackled. "Base, fifteen fifty-one, you've got Abruzzo, in there, right?"

Eddie glanced over his shoulder at Aaron in the captain's chair as he reached for the handset. "Christ, what did I do now?" Aaron said.

"Fifteen fifty-one base, that's a roger."

"I know he can hear me. Abruzzo. Come to the vault soon as you can."

"He heard you," Eddie said into the mic before hanging it up. He looked back at Aaron. "So what'd you do?"

"Shit, I don't know." Aaron glanced around him. He wasn't bringing back any cash to store in their vault overnight, so he normally could have just walked out the door to his car after punching out. He frowned, trying to think of what he'd done the day before. Had he screwed up some paperwork? Transposed a number on a deposit? Or was some money missing? Shit. "Drop me off inside the door."

Aaron hopped down from the armored car as soon as the metal overhead door closed behind them. He pushed his way through the door into the small narrow room outside the vault room, which doubled as the office for Absolute Armored. Leo was on the other side of the armored glass, frowning. The glass was four inches thick and had a permanent orange-brown tint due to decades of cigarette smoke.

Waiting for the Kick

"What'd I do?" Aaron asked. Leo wore thick black-framed glasses over a greasy moustache, and was one of the few people Aaron knew who smoked more than he did.

Instead of replying the vault manager on duty crooked a finger at Aaron and reached below the counter. Aaron heard the electronic buzz as the steel door leading inside unlocked. Aaron pushed the heavy door open and walked inside. There were security monitors lining the counter to the left, and to the right was the vault itself. Sporting a giant steel door a foot thick, it was a state-of-the-art bank vault... for 1951. Still, it worked, and was surrounded on three sides by an additional four feet of reinforced concrete. Nobody was getting in without explosives.

Aaron nodded at Ernie, who was at the counter filling out logs, then turned to Leo. You didn't get called into the vault unless you'd fucked-up big time. "What, Leo?"

"Abruzzo." Leo was looking at him strangely.

"Yeah?"

"You know I didn't say shit about shit about your last-minute vacation to Arizona, but we're not all as stupid as you like to think we are. Dave Anderson had a place out there and he was involved in that gunfight there a couple of years ago, and then you go down there right after that big terrorist attack."

Aaron frowned. This wasn't the kind of conversation he'd been expecting. "Yeah? And?"

"And did you catch the news today?"

Aaron's frown deepened. The question made a cold knot form in his guts. "No, why?" he said slowly.

Leo spun on his stool and pointed at the small tube TV on the counter behind him. Aaron stepped next to Leo and stared at the TV. CNN was on, the headline at the bottom of the screen NEW CARTEL TERROR ATTACKS?

"Motherfucker," Aaron breathed, staring.

"Same place as that last attack," Leo told him, "Prescott or whatever. Buncha people got shot."

Aaron didn't need to be told that, he recognized the trailer park from the helicopter footage being played over and over. Recognized that all the yellow police tape was in front of Dave's house. As was a dark-colored car with what appeared to be bullet holes in the windows. Cop cars filled the street halfway back to the neighborhood entrance. "What happened? When did this happen?"

"Sometime this morning," Leo said, staring at the TV, then he turned to look at Aaron. Just a quick glance at the expression on Aaron's face made him ask, "So does this mean you're taking another trip?"

Chapter Twenty-Six

Richard Roberts rubbed his eyes, then glanced at his watch. Nearly two and a half hours. Longer than he'd expected, but...he looked over at the man sitting next to him. His client was still out of jail. Free. Not in cuffs. And the cops across the table were highly irritated. Sometimes the small victories were the sweetest. Everything else aside, this was definitely one of the most interesting clients he'd ever had.

"So...are we done? For the moment?" the attorney asked. He stared across the table. Sam Wheaton sat next to Maria Flores, who was scowling. Norm Hill was at the end, arms crossed over his big chest. The two detectives traded a look, then turned to Wheaton.

"For the moment," Wheaton said, after a long pause.

The attorney stood up and buttoned his suitcoat, then grabbed his briefcase. He held the door for his client, who limped out of the room. The two detectives watched the men leave, and the door close. No one said everything for several minutes. Finally Norm Hill laughed, a sudden bark. Wheaton and his partner looked at him.

"So a guy in witness protection walks into a Cracker Barrel…"

"Jesus Norm." Maria Flores shook her head.

"Detroit mob after him? Shot him up twice already? No wonder he's so quick to go to gun. Christ. You ever shoot anybody?" Norm asked her. He glanced at Wheaton. "I know you have."

"Just that guy I bit," she admitted. "In the leg. He was out of the hospital in two days."

Hill was shaking his head. "This guy's taken more of a pounding than his pornstar girlfriend. And killed more guys than I've arrested. Fuck." He looked at Wheaton. "I helped collect evidence at the scene two years ago, empty shell casings and shrapnel from that bomb. I can still smell the bodies that burned inside that cabin. Looked like a war zone. Sheriff was all over Fox News for a week with that recording of that dirty FBI agent hiring the hit. One of the hits. Attempted hits," he corrected himself. "Don't know that I ever even looked at a picture of the kid of the time, not that I would have recognized him after that beatdown in the Cracker Barrel. And you didn't know he was here? That the Sheriff had him squirreled away?"

Sam Wheaton shook his head. "Not until I saw him on the videotape."

"Anybody else killed four people they'd be in lockup just on general principles while we figured shit out. I don't like this. Not one fucking bit. Sir," Flores added. "We're going to need to talk to the Sheriff," she said, her mouth a thin line. She glanced from her partner to Wheaton. "Does he even have the authority to get someone a new ID?"

Wheaton didn't answer.

"If that's an official avenue you seriously want to

pursue, that's a question for a courtroom, and you'll be facing off against Ricky Bobby," Hill told her. He glanced at Wheaton, who held up his hands.

"Right now I'm just in damage control," Wheaton admitted.

"Have you ever known Osterman to do anything illegal?" Hill asked his partner. "Or what he thought was illegal?" Numerous left-wing advocacy groups had sued the Sheriff's Department over the years because of policies they claimed were illegal and unConstitutional. "If he did it, I'm sure he could explain to you exactly why it was legal and/or within his power to do so."

Flores was not happy. "And the four bodies from this morning? He killed four people, Norm. Shot 'em dead in their car. None of them fired a shot. Assholes, yeah, probably there to kidnap and do heinous things to him, but still, seeing him walk out of here, no cuffs…"

Hill grunted. "He's Pima Jack, the mysterious hero of Prescott. Saved the Sheriff's life. Saved the witness' life. Saved the lives of who knows how many other people, cops included. All while mortally wounded, his face looking like a bowl of spaghetti with extra sauce. What we have here is four illegally-armed professional bad guys going after him. Felons from out of state. With ties to organized crime. Doesn't matter why, everyone is going to assume it was some sort of revenge for the cartel thing, even if they find out who he really is. Was. I know you were pissed off he wasn't in cuffs on scene, but just arresting him would make us look bad, I'm with the Captain on this. You see how many of those bystanders had their phones out, trying to get good video of him sitting there on that porch? Couldn't believe Pima Jack lived in their neighborhood. He's practically a folk hero." Hill sighed and waved a hand. "Look, we investigate, and arrest or not, but it's up to the county Prosecutor as to what happens afterward. What he's actually charged with, if anything. Even if Ricky Bobby wasn't his lawyer, you think the county Prosecutor is going to waste time filing any charges when she knows she won't get a conviction? When we don't have any evidence that contradicts his story? Which I happen to believe, by the way."

"So do I, but that's not the point," she snapped.

"Any defense attorney not legally brain dead would position him close to the jury box, so they can see those scars on his face. And then it's over. Guy's got a permanent Get Out Of Jail Free card in this town."

"I know, I know," Flores said in exasperation.

"Governor called me yesterday," Wheaton told them. "She was thinking of awarding him the Order of the Silver Crescent, for saving the witness, and Osterman, and everybody else that didn't die in that attack because he was there." It was highest civilian award in Arizona. "Wanted my opinion." He sighed. "I still have to call her back."

"So what are you going to say to the press?" Flores asked Wheaton. "You figure that out yet?"

"I need to talk to the Sheriff first."

"That ID, that Jack Burton ID, that's a real Arizona Driver's License," Hill said slowly, thinking. He looked back and forth between his partner and Sam Wheaton. "We've got nothing written down anywhere that says we know any different. You told us a few things. The lawyer told us a few things too, but he's bound by client confidentiality. And our little meeting here was not recorded, by mutual agreement. So the question is, what would you like us to put in the report?"

"Jesus, Norm," Maria Flores said to him, shocked he'd even hint at such a thing. "We can't ignore this. Not with everything we know. We know who the dead guys worked for, so when we talk to Bufonte we can't claim ignorance about why his guys were in Prescott. His beef with this guy is well known, apparently."

"Don't book that flight to Detroit just yet. We won't get within a hundred feet of Bufonte," Hill argued. "The FBI's been after him for decades. He probably has lawyers around him five deep. We'll be lucky if we can get his lawyers to pick up the phone long enough to tell us to pound sand."

She looked between the two men. "Yeah, well, we have to try. And don't forget something. How many times has—allegedly—Bufonte tried to kill this guy, over how many years? Doesn't seem like he's given up." She scowled. "And the kid's still alive. Who's to say he's not going to try again? Maybe next time it's when the kid's walking through Courthouse Square downtown, surrounded by babies and dogs and tourists throwing Frisbees. We can't sit on this." She looked at Wheaton. "You going to call the FBI?"

Wheaton looked sick to his stomach.

"Not that I blame you for keeping your background private, given what you've told me, but...is there anything else I should know?" Richard Roberts asked his client.

Dave leaned against the wall, wincing. Sitting for two hours hadn't done his leg or hip any good. "Like what?" He worked his leg a few times, then they resumed walking down the corridor.

"Well, that's the question, isn't it?" The attorney studied his client carefully, waiting for an answer.

"When there is, I'll let you know," Dave told him.

Roberts pursed his lips. "I'm not sure you understand just how unique your situation is. Anyone else, after shooting four people to death, justified self-defense or not, would be behind bars while local law enforcement did their investigation. But because of the earlier incident, with the cartel, you have quite a bit of...store credit? Good will? Perhaps benefit of the doubt, with the Sheriff's Department." He put a hand out to stop Dave and leaned in close. "Don't squander it." He leaned back. "Are you going to talk to the Sheriff? I don't think he's been informed of what happened today. Probably better if he heard it from you."

"I will. But not right away. I've got to," he paused, "do some thinking first."

For all of his client's level-headed behavior and matter-of-fact answering of questions during the interview with the detectives and Wheaton, Roberts had to remind himself that the man had been through a life-or-death situation just hours before. He probably still hadn't processed the incident fully. Was probably still in shock. He nodded and patted Dave on the shoulder comfortingly.

The two parted ways outside the front door of the Sheriff's Department. Dave stood on the curb outside and dug his phone out of his pocket. He thumbed the ringer on and looked around. The new concrete filling the crater was starting to darken, to blend in, but it was easy to spot if you were looking for it.

He blinked when he saw his phone's display. Eight missed calls. Eight, in not quite two and a half hours, and four voicemails. He scrolled through them and saw seven of the calls were from Aaron. "Shit," Dave cursed. Apparently bad news traveled fast. The last call was from John Phault.

Dave called his voicemail and listened to the messages.

He could have scripted the messages from Aaron ahead of time—his friend worried and panicked and wondering just what the hell happened, using typically colorful language. The last message was pure Aaron: "Motherfucker, you better call me. You better not be fucking dead. Am I going to have to come down there, lift you on and off the shitter again? I swear to God, how does one guy get shot so much? Didn't your mother ever teach you how to duck? Christ. Shit. Call me. Fucker." There was a long pause. "Dammit."

The last voicemail was from John Phault. "Call me, I think I've got what you're looking for," Phault said. That was the entirety of the message.

Dave called Aaron back first, and the call went straight to voicemail. Dave smiled as he told Aaron's phone, "I'm not dead. And I'm not in jail, either, which is a pleasant surprise. Not sure how long that will last. I was in a meeting with cops for hours, I wasn't ignoring your calls. But… uh…" he looked up and down the sidewalk, but there was nobody near him. "Don't call me for a while. I've got some things to do. I'm not blowing you off, I promise. I'll give you a call when I can."

Dave waited until he was back in his Jeep before he returned Phault's call. The private investigator answered on the second ring. "Okay, you ready to take some notes?"

"Yeah, what'd you find?" Dave asked him.

"I've got three addresses associated with Pietro Bufonte in Las Vegas. Here, let me give you the first two." Phault rattled them off, and Dave wrote them down on a scrap of paper he found in a cupholder. "The first is in a light industrial area. I did a little Google-Fu, and it looks like that address is in the middle of a building. Roll-up doors, some signage. Machine shops, maybe. That's in northeast Vegas. The second address…well, I can't tell if currently it is a gas station or a vacant piece of property. And what records I have are a little confusing, I can't tell if Bufonte just bought it or just sold it. But it definitely is just a gas station."

"Okay," Dave said, scribbling notes quickly.

Phault took a breath. He wasn't an idiot. There were only a few reasons Anderson would want this information, and most of them were bad. Well, maybe not bad, but maybe not legal. Dave, however, was an adult. He could make his own choices. And be responsible for his own actions. "It's the third address that might be what you're looking for," he told Dave. "1523 Champion Hills Lane. It's a private residence. House. Big fucking house, actually. In Summerlin."

"I thought it was in Las Vegas."

Phault snorted. "Kids. Summerlin is a neighborhood in Vegas. One of the oldest. Probably the richest. Northwest of the Strip. Named after Howard Hughes' mother or grandmother, something like that."

"Howard who?"

Phault sighed. "Jesus, I swear—"

Dave cut him off with a laugh. "No, I know who he is. Leonardo DiCaprio did a movie about him."

"That's how you know who he is? Christ, pop culture is going to be the death of us all. Those who are ignorant of history are doomed to repeat it. Anyway, I found a real estate listing for it that's about five years old, and I think that's when Bufonte bought it. Six thousand eight hundred and nineteen square feet—"

"Damn," Dave said.

"Yeah. I think Justin Timberlake owns a house down the street, it's that kind of neighborhood. I'm actually surprised the FBI hasn't seized it for one reason or another. Six bedrooms, six baths, pool in back, even its own putting green. Ooh, and a hot tub, for those chilly desert nights. Mountain view, isn't that nice. And it backs up to a golf course. Maybe TPC Summerlin?"

"What's 'TPC'?" Dave asked.

"I don't know, I don't play golf. If you search the address online you should be able to find that old real estate listing, and all the photos are still there, inside and out. Looks like just the kind of place a Detroit mob boss would buy. Way too much white marble for my taste, but whatever. Mortgage isn't even six grand a month, so quite a bargain. What is that, less than a dollar a square foot a month? Three-car garage, on point three-nine acres, so out here it'd be called a McMansion. No yard, no lawn, because you'd have to be insane to go outside six months out of the year, Vegas is an oven." Phault paused. "If he's got a home away from home in Vegas, it's got to be this place, because it's too damn big and expensive for anything else. For anyone else. No way he'd buy it just to stash a mistress there, that's what condos are for."

"Great, thanks."

"Dave."

"Yeah?"

Phault's voice was flat in his ear. "I didn't get those addresses from a comp report. Didn't use my computer for any of this. I called in a favor from an old friend who wouldn't open his mouth if he was on fire. And I'm not exaggerating even the tiniest bit, which is the scary part. So all this is off the record, and will stay that way. There's no record of me researching him. For you or for anyone. The only record there is of anything are these phone calls between us. Just two old friends who haven't talked in a while, catching up."

Dave stared at his notes, then looked up and stared at Prescott out the window. "Right. Thanks."

"Be careful." Phault told him. "Be smart."

"So...not in jail," Lori observed, standing in Dave's open front door.

"No." He checked his watch. Just after three p.m. Everything had happened at dawn, around six in the morning. He wasn't sure whether or not there would still be cops posted on the street, or evidence tape up, but apparently they'd photographed and collected everything they needed. The only thing he saw on the street when he got home was a tiny glitter of glass. And the blood trail across his gravel front yard, that was still there, now more brown than red.

She watched him grabbing things. Stuffing tools into a backpack, which seemed weird. The ibuprofen she understood, but what did he need with screwdrivers and a hammer? The new gun he'd bought, the expensive one, was on his hip. The cops had taken the one he'd used to shoot all those guys in the car, which to her didn't seem right. "So where are you going? In case anyone asks. When will you be back?"

He stopped and looked at her. She was biting her lip. Lori wasn't dumb, which was one of the reasons he liked her. "Tell them I didn't want to sleep here, because of what happened. But you don't know where I went."

"And you'll be back tomorrow?"

Dave tried to decide how to answer. "That's the plan." He hefted the backpack, took a step toward the door, then stopped and looked at her. He opened his mouth, closed it, then said, "I love you too."

Aaron turned his phone on as soon as the wheels hit the runway in Phoenix. Before they'd reached the terminal he'd heard the voicemail from Dave, and the huge weight on his heart lifted. Dave hadn't managed to get himself killed. Hadn't even been injured, apparently. Must be following up on that New Year's Resolution, "Stop getting shot."

Even though Dave had said not to, Aaron called him. It went straight to voicemail, but that was okay. Dave was alive. Still, though...

Every news channel had been worthless, with few details on what exactly had happened other than a bunch of guys had been shot. After an hour of pacing at home Aaron had cursed loud enough to rattle the windows in the trailer, then booked a ticket on a flight he'd barely made. He'd had flown out to Arizona in a panic, thinking Dave was back in the hospital, shot up or dead. That wasn't the case, but Aaron was still in Arizona. And Dave wouldn't be answering his phone? Had "things to do"? What the fuck did that mean? It sounded to Aaron that Dave was thinking of doing something stupid. Exactly what, he had no idea. And maybe Dave was just fine, just needed some time alone, but he'd be damned if he was going to turn around and go right back. Besides, he needed to know what the fuck was going on.

Fuming, he waited to collect his briefcase-sized gun case from the Delta luggage office. Not only weren't they putting gun cases on the luggage carousel anymore, they were putting giant zip ties around them so nobody could easily get them open in the airport. He already had two damn padlocks on the thing.

"Here you go, sir." Aaron had heard the woman putting the black zip ties on the case right around the corner out of sight.

Aaron took the gun case from her, walked over to one of the lobby chairs, slid one of the metal arms between the thick zip tie and the case, and twisted. The zip tie snapped with almost no resistance. He couldn't use his pocket knife to cut the plastic tie, his knife was in there with his pistol.

"Hey, you can't do that!" the Delta employee said, watching.

"You're the only airline which zip ties gun cases at baggage claim, which means it isn't a law, it's just a pain in my fucking ass," Aaron told her.

"I'm going to call the cops," she warned him.

"You go right ahead. I'm heading for the rental car place," he told her. "While you're waiting for them, why don't you pick that up." He pointed at the broken zip tie on the floor. "Nobody likes a litter bug, and it's there because of you."

In a slightly better mood, he headed toward the door and the shuttle to the remote rental car facility. Another goddamn rental car. He was going to max out his credit card, but fuck it.

Dave exited I-40 in Kingman, Arizona, when he saw the sign on the freeway for a Starbucks. He could have used a coffee, but that wasn't why he was there, and he never entered the coffee shop. Instead, he parked in a space close enough to the building to pick up the free wi-fi, after looking around to see if there were any external security cameras. Nope. Then he pulled out his tablet. The sterile one, that he'd never used to search anything personal on himself, that was in no way connected to either one of his names.

The wi-fi signal was strong, but still he spent almost two hours online. Researching. Making notes on the map of Las

Vegas he'd bought in Prescott. Before leaving town he'd also stopped at a gas station. He'd filled up his tank and bought a six-pack of Gatorade, beef jerky, and four king-size Snickers, all with cash. Also a fresh burner phone. The one he'd been using, that now was known to the Sheriff's Department, that he'd left at home, on his kitchen counter.

He'd searched the house address and found the Zillow real estate listing Phault had told him about. Studied all the interior photos and done his best to memorize the layout of the house. Used Google Maps to view overhead shots and Google Streetview to study what he could of the areas around each of the three addresses.

As he sat there, working, the sun slowly sank in the sky. Dusk was approaching as he pulled out of the parking lot and headed two blocks north to the Safeway grocery store. He parked as far from the building as he could, then put on a baseball cap, pulled down low. That was one of his pet peeves with the Jason Bourne movies—the guy's supposed to be this world-class spy on the run from every government agency in the world and he can't figure out a hat would hide his face from the all the security cameras everywhere.

He was in and out in less than ten minutes, paying cash. Once he was back in the Jeep he jumped back on I-40. Less than two miles later he exited onto US-93 north. The sun was setting off to the left, turning the sky a lovely combination of pink and orange.

He was ninety minutes from Las Vegas.

Aaron pulled the shitty rental Kia up in front of Dave's trailer and hopped out. The shot-up car he'd seen on the CNN helicopter footage was nowhere to be found, but there was yellow police tape fluttering from a post stuck in Dave's front yard. There was a big black stain in the dirt there, near the curb, visible even in the dim light of dusk. Aaron could guess what it was.

Dave's Jeep wasn't in the carport, but Aaron banged on his front door anyway. "Dude! You there?" He banged some more, and not quietly. After a second he spun halfway around, hand going to his pistol which he'd uncased, loaded, holstered, and covered with a flannel shirt open in the front before making the two-hour road trip up from Phoenix. He'd seen something out of the corner of his eye, but it wasn't anyone close, it was Lori, standing on her porch next door. They stared at each other for a few seconds. She wasn't surprised to see him.

"What happened? Where is he?" Aaron said. He clenched his fists. "Is he okay?" He paused. "Is he doing something stupid?" He was getting a bad feeling.

Lori glanced across the street. The loud knocking had drawn out Rose Leslie and she was standing on her porch, watching the two of them. Lori looked back at Aaron and jerked her head. "Come on in," she told him.

Dave took US-93 to I-11 and rode that northwest into Las Vegas. The city was laid out before him, the tall hotels of the Strip lit up in the distance like a backdrop from a science fiction movie. The interstate curved north and the Strip moved off to his left.

Dave exited at E. Flamingo Road. Instead of turning left, which would have taken him to the Strip four miles west, he turned right and zigzagged northeast for a few minutes, checking his hand-written notes for directions at red lights. It brought back memories—he'd spent two years working for John Phault, doing surveillances in and around

Detroit, nearly every day tasked with finding a strange address on which to set up surveillance. Finally he arrived in the area and studied the address from a distance. His old boss had been both right and wrong—it was a gas station, but it was in the process of demolition. Most of the building had been gutted, and the pumps had been removed.

He drove around the block, just to make sure he wasn't confusing the derelict gas station with something else, but he had the address correct.

The second address, the one Phault had said was some sort of light industrial building, was close, just a little north and east of the gas station. It only took Dave a few minutes to drive there. Phault's description—presumably gleaned from various online sources, maybe Google Streetview—had been accurate. It was a small unit in the middle of a low commercial building.

There was a large roll-up steel door, and a pedestrian door beside it. No signs of any sort on the unit. No windows, so he had no way to know who or what was inside it. But there were no cars present. Looking out at the building, at the small, empty parking lot, it didn't feel right. If Bufonte was anywhere in Vegas, it wasn't here.

Which left just the one address, the fancy house.

"So what the fuck happened?" Aaron really wanted a cigarette. He stuck his hands in his pockets instead. He looked around the house. Nice place, nicely decorated. It still smelled faintly of antiseptic, an odor very familiar to him after dealing with his mom's cancer.

"A carload of guys showed up and tried to grab him when he came home from a walk," Lori told him.

"Cartel?"

"No. Detroit."

"Shit."

"Working for some guy named Buffalo or something like that."

Aaron was shaking his head. "Yeah, yeah, I know. Shit. Shit shit shit." He turned in a circle. "He's not hurt at all?" He peered worriedly at her.

"No. None of them even made it out of the car. Except that guy who crawled away. I don't think they thought he had a gun." She shivered. She'd been asleep in bed when the gunfire erupted, and found herself on her porch without any memory leaving her bedroom. She hadn't realized she'd been naked until Dave, standing by the shot-up car, looked over, did a doubletake, and told her to put some clothes on.

"And he didn't say where he was going?"

She shook her head no. "Just that he wanted to finish it."

"Shit," he said with renewed force. Aaron knew his friend wasn't driving to Detroit, which meant he had no idea where Dave was going or what he planned to do.

"He called somebody," Lori told him.

"Somebody who?"

She shrugged. "Some sort of detective, I think. Dave asked him to run some sort of records on the mob guy." She squinted. "Maybe his name was John?"

"Goddammit." Aaron pulled out his phone and made the call. It went straight to Phault's voicemail, which made him suspect the P.I. was dodging his call. Aaron waited for the beep, then said, "You run some records for our mutual friend? I'm out in Arizona. And he's not. I'm hoping he's not out doing something stupid. Alone. Call me."

"You know who he called?" Lori frowned at him.

"Maybe. We know a P.I. in Detroit. Dave used to work

for him." Aaron made a face, then called Dave again, hoping in vain that his friend would pick up this time. As he waited, in the distance he heard a neighbor's phone ringing. After a few rings he realized it was coming from Dave's house. He could hear Dave's cell phone ringing next door.

"Son of a bitch," Aaron sighed, putting his phone away. If he'd left his phone behind Dave was definitely up to no good.

"You want to stay here? Wait?" Lori found she was actually wringing her hands together, like someone on a soap opera. She forced herself to stop.

Aaron looked around the house and then down at her. He knew she desperately wanted company, but...he shook his head. "No. I'm going to...I don't know what I'm going to do, but I've got to do something. If he calls you lemme know right away. You got my number?"

She nodded. Aaron wasn't quite sure what to do, and finally reached out and squeezed her shoulder before heading out the door.

Aaron stomped over to the post stuck in the dirt of Dave's front yard. He scowled at the fluttering yellow tape, then at the bloodstain in the dirt. With a growl he ripped the tape off the pole and threw it high. The breeze caught it and it sailed over Dave's house. Aaron watched it go, then got into his rental with a curse.

When he said he didn't know what he was going to do, he meant it. Aaron drove up and down the main drag of Prescott Valley three times looking for Dave's Jeep and thinking. He didn't spot the car, and couldn't think of what to do. It was while driving through the huge mall parking lot looking for the Jeep that he spotted the coffee shop that he remembered from his first trip.

The guy behind the counter looked from Aaron's face to

the big stainless Colt Delta Elite 10mm on his hip and back up, then waggled a finger at him. "Detroit, right? Was it zombies you were hunting?"

"That's half the population of Detroit," Aaron said sourly. "Give me something big, and dark, with a lot of caffeine."

"You got it."

The redhead only took a minute to fill a big cup and slap a lid on it. Aaron took a seat at a table facing the door, sipped at his coffee, and fumed.

Dave's hours spent on the tablet outside the Starbucks hadn't been wasted. He didn't have to check his map once driving north and west from the small industrial space Bufonte owned.

The retail area was on the north side of Vegas. Actually, it was in the city of North Las Vegas, which he hadn't even been aware existed until he'd spent some serious time studying a map of the area.

There were strip malls lining both sides of North Decatur Boulevard just north of Interstate 215, a Game Stop and Bank of America and a dozen other stores on the right, a Walgreens and Chili's restaurant and another fifteen businesses on the left.

The buildings were right up against the sidewalks on North Decatur. He wasn't interested in the buildings, he was interested in the huge parking lots behind them. On the far side of the west parking lot was a Costco and a Best Buy. On the far end of the gigantic east side parking lot was a Walmart Supercenter. The Costco was just about to close for the evening, the Best Buy soon afterward, but the Walmart was open 24/7. There was a Bed, Bath, and

Beyond, Sally Beauty Supply, and a few other stores in the strip mall attached to the Walmart Supercenter. Just eyeballing the overhead image of the parking lots on Google Maps he'd guessed there'd be hundreds of cars in the parking lots, even at that hour of the evening, and he'd been right.

Dave drove slowly through the Costco parking lot, not seeing anything that looked right. He waited at the traffic light, then drove across North Decatur into the Walmart parking lot, and it was there he found what he was looking for.

The Jeep Wrangler was parked a good distance away from the Walmart itself in the angled spots, with space all around it. The lot was pretty well lit with lights, but Dave didn't see any security cameras on the light posts, only on the Walmart itself, and he knew their resolution wouldn't be good enough to see detail any distance into the parking lot, especially at night.

Dave pulled up past the other Jeep, so the rear bumpers of their vehicles were nearly parallel. He kept the headlights of his Jeep on and looked around. There was nobody nearby, and what people he did see on foot leaving the building, even if they headed in his direction, were at least a minute away.

Moving with feigned confidence, baseball cap still pulled all the way down on his head, Dave jumped out of his Jeep, screwdriver in hand. He opened the back of his Jeep as if he was loading some groceries. The open tailgate also gave him a little bit of cover from curious eyes. Then he bent down and as quickly as he could, he used the screwdriver to remove the license plate from the neighboring Jeep.

He closed his tailgate and was back in his vehicle and out of the lot in twenty seconds. He drove south for five minutes and took several random turns before pulling into the parking lot of a Lowe's. Replacing the license plate on his Jeep with the stolen plate took him less than a minute, then he was back in his vehicle and heading southwest, toward the third address.

Chapter Twenty-Seven

Intelligence was everything. Well, almost everything. Intelligence was the bones upon which every operation was built. Reconnaissance was a valuable and usually necessary part of intelligence, and Colman had done a lot of it when he was new to the game, but it had been a few years. Still, those hard-learned lessons stuck with him even after all this time.

Before he ever stepped foot inside the state he spent hours poring over maps, both hardcopy and digital. He would have loved real-time satellite imagery of the target's house, or even photos, but to get those would have meant breaking emcon, and it had been made clear to him that the mission was more important than whatever new operational morals the fresh administration might foist upon them. To contact anyone at the Agency would be to risk getting shut down. Besides—and he had no problem admitting it to himself—he had a personal investment in this one. He wanted to see it through for a number of reasons.

One of the items he'd requisitioned upon receiving the assignment was a sterile vehicle. A bland sedan registered to a corporation in Maryland with an eminently forgettable name. Apart from a few hidden compartments that wouldn't show up under any kind of scan the two-year-old silver Chevy was dealer lot stock, with the OnStar system removed so there was no GPS tracker. After four days spent examining the data on the flash drive and doing his own investigation online, and studying maps of the area, he headed out. Driving from Virginia to central Arizona was a thirty-hour-plus trip, and he spread it out over three days. Flying was quicker, but driving provided him complete anonymous freedom of movement, with no restrictions on equipment. Not that he had a lot, but most of it would definitely not get through TSA screening.

After a second very long day on the road he stopped in Albuquerque and spent the night at a chain hotel right off I-40, using a credit card tied to the eminently forgettable corporation listed on his vehicle's registration. The free breakfast offered in the lobby wasn't suitable for dog food, and he got directions from the clerk at the desk to a nearby diner.

The diner was a five minute drive away. The food was good, but something about the place kept nagging at him. It looked familiar, but he was sure he'd never been there before. Only when he Googled the place on his sterile smartphone—Loyola's Family Restaurant—did he realize it was the diner featured in the *Breaking Bad* prequel series *Better Call Saul*. Which made him snort, and relax.

From Albuquerque to Prescott was just over a six-hour drive, and he arrived in mid-afternoon. The first thing he did upon arriving in the AO was recon it. Not the immediate area of the target, not at first, but anywhere and everywhere he might end up in the operation. Main traffic arteries that would be likely escape routes. The locations of police headquarters and hospitals. Looking at a map was never the same thing as eyeballing everything in person.

It was Anderson's visit to the shooting match outside Phoenix, or rather the mention of it in an online forum, that had finally put him on the radar, nearly three months before Colman got the assignment to track him down. Colman figured out that David Anderson of Troy, Michigan was now Jack Burton of Prescott Valley, Arizona, and it took him only another few minutes of investigation to discover this Jack Burton was the same "Pima Jack" who had been in and out of the headlines after having gotten involved in an incident that had made front-page news all across the country.

After everything he'd seen Colman believed in both luck and coincidence. He just didn't count on them working in his favor. Apparently the kid couldn't keep out of trouble, which actually made things a bit tougher for Colman. Driving around he noticed an increased police presence in the streets of Prescott and Prescott Valley. Some of the residents, who like most Americans tended to sleepwalk through life, actually seemed to be displaying a rudimentary grasp of situational awareness. When he stopped to fill up at a gas station he overheard someone at a nearby pump mention the word cartel, months after the attack.

After he'd done all he could to memorize the surrounding metropolitan area, he focused on his target, first rolling in near six o'clock in the evening. Anderson lived in a small new trailer park, on a dead-end street. Not the best set-up for surveillance, but not the worst he'd ever had to deal with. Once Colman had learned Anderson's new name it hadn't taken him long to learn everything he could about him, even without access to the Agency's resources.

Anderson only owned the one piece of property. One vehicle. For once the desert climate worked in Colman's favor—Anderson, like so many people in Arizona, didn't have a garage but rather just a covered parking area, so all Colman had to do to determine whether or not he was home was drive down the parallel street and sneak a quick peek between the trailers, where Anderson's parking spot was just visible.

Over the course of an hour he'd done two drive-bys—once down Anderson's street, turning around in the driveway across the street, and once down the parallel street. Anderson's Jeep had not been present either time, and Colman pulled back to think, parking in the lot of a nearby gas station.

Direct surveillance of Anderson's house from inside the trailer park just wasn't practical. Neither was sitting on the single exit to the trailer park. Residents could head north or south once they left the trailer park, but examining maps of the area Colman rightly assumed most traffic would head south, so taking a position in or near the Maverik gas station where he currently stood was a good bet to spot Anderson's Jeep. However, he hated waiting, and sitting still even more. Driving around town he'd noticed that seemingly eighty percent of the stores in nearby Prescott Valley appeared to be lining the one main drag.

In ninety-minutes he was pretty sure he'd checked every parking lot of every store in the small town, with no sign of Anderson's Jeep, but he kept at it until the sun was well and truly down. His plan wasn't high speed or even scientific—he was going to drive around until he spotted Anderson, then play it by ear. If that didn't work he'd surveil Anderson's neighborhood from the area of the gas station until he saw Anderson head out in his Jeep. He'd then follow him in hopes he'd get a good look at his hands, or maybe be able to retrieve something Anderson had touched and examine it for prints. He had a portable fingerprint kit with him, one of the pieces of gear he'd grabbed upon getting the assignment.

If a loose surveillance didn't work, he'd just go into Anderson's house at night, gas him, and examine his hands at leisure. A lot of things could go wrong with that kind of frontal assault, though, so he was keeping that as his fallback plan if the casual surveillance didn't pan out.

He stopped briefly for coffee then turned his vehicle back toward Anderson's neighborhood, checking the same parking lots a second time but without much hope of actually spotting the Jeep.

Summerlin was northwest of the Vegas Strip, which had so many futuristic lights in every color of the rainbow dyeing the night sky Dave wouldn't have been surprised to see spacecraft taking off and landing. The pricey neighborhood was halfway between the Strip and the Red Rock Canyon National Park. Even at night, driving in, he could see the houses get bigger and bigger. Interestingly, though, they all sat on small pieces of property. No one was interested in giant rolling lawns around their houses. No one in Vegas had lawns.

The neighborhood was on the west side of N. Rampart Boulevard. Rampart was three blacktopped lanes in each direction separated by a raised median covered in red rocks and spotted with the occasional pine tree and hardy shrub.

The house was in a gated community, Tournament Hills, he'd seen that in the Google Streetview photos. A cement and tile gatehouse squatting between the entry and exit drives. The photos online even showed the Guard on Duty sign, and a glimpse of an actual guard in something that resembled a brown police uniform. Undoubtedly the guards were all retired cops.

In the photos there was a turnaround past the gatehouse, right before the gates themselves, which were wrought iron and eight feet tall. Connected to a stone or cinderblock wall at least six feet tall. Still, he had faint hopes that the photos were out of date, the residents had removed the gates and gatehouse because they were inconvenient, or the gatehouse was unattended and the gates were left open.

He peered out the side window of his Jeep as he drove by the first time. Nope, still there, gatehouse and gates both, and the gates were closed. A place with this much money, he was sure the residents had in-car remotes to open the gates so they didn't have to demean themselves by talking to the guard. As a sign of just how ritzy the place was, there were raised berms on either side of the entrance covered with beautiful emerald green grass.

He went past, looped around the median and came back, then pulled into Bruce Trent Park which was across Rampart from the secured neighborhood. There was a soccer field, tennis courts, and a baseball diamond with actual grass in the outfield. He parked in one of the spots across from the entrance to Tournament Hills and studied the view for a bit. It looked just like the photos he'd seen, which meant he wasn't going to be able to drive in and ogle Bufonte's house. At least, not from the street.

There was only one other car in the park lot at that time of night. Dave backed out of the space less than a minute after parking and headed north on Rampart. Past the T-intersection with Vegas Drive, past the small subdivision, he'd seen something on the right when doing research. He drifted the Jeep over into the right lane and slowed down to a crawl. His eyes darted back and forth.

Nothing but scrub on the right. As he passed over a short bridge there were some peach-colored walls close together, running out from under Rampart to a complex coming up on the right. Then he rolled past a driveway, and more featureless wall. On the right he'd seen a big building, a trailer, and a lot of equipment and vehicles. Exactly what he'd been hoping and expecting to see, down to the signs on the peach walls on either side of the driveway—GOLF COURSE MAINTENANCE.

Dave increased his speed and checked his watch. It was dark, but it was early. He still had several hours to wait.

The PVS-21s were far from the best night vision goggles in the government's inventory, but he had a lot of time behind them. Compared to what Hollywood put in movies, or kids saw in video games, the view through most modern night vision goggles sucked. Narrow field of view, no depth perception, and a narrow focus range. Everything shades of green. The latest generation of NVGs that used some sort of white phosphorous technology were a lot better, but each set ran about the cost of a new Cadillac, there weren't many of them, and they were rather closely monitored. Much smarter to use PVS-21s which had been in service for years.

He set the focus close so the ground in front of him was as crisp-edged as possible and made his way slowly across the scrub field. The ground was uneven and he didn't want to turn an ankle.

There was more than enough starlight to see by, not that he would turn on either of the IR illuminators the NVGs were equipped with. While the not-visible-to-the-naked-eye flashlights worked very well, every camcorder and DSLR sold between Karachi and Kansas City was capable of picking up IR—infrared—lights and lasers on the right setting. The chances of anyone looking out where he was with the right equipment was low, but he hadn't gotten old by being sloppy or leaving things to chance. And his target had proven to have a lot of luck, both good and bad.

The panoramic quad NODs the Seal Team Six guys used were so heavy they required a weight mounted at the back of the helmet to counterbalance the damn things, and still they caused neck strain. On SEALs. The PVS-21s, by night vision goggle standards, were featherweights, but that didn't mean they were light. The head harness included a chin strap, and padded braces against his cheeks to support the weight hanging in front of his face. He thought it looked a bit like an abbreviated catcher's mask.

People who'd never operated at night thought you needed black clothing for "camouflage". Too many ninja movies. The truth was any color clothing that matched your surroundings in daylight and didn't have a shine to it worked quite well at night. And the human eye detected movement faster than color, so the trick was to either not move at all, or to move with the flow of traffic so you didn't stick out. In khakis and a medium-blue windbreaker he knew he blended into the background of the desert at night, especially if he wasn't moving.

He had no specific plans to do anything other than watch, but he'd been at the game long enough to know anything that could go wrong often did, so he had an HK pistol in a holster on his right hip. He figured there was a better chance of having to shoot a rattlesnake than anything else, but better safe than sorry.

The pistol had an extended threaded barrel. He had a sound suppressor for the pistol in his pocket and could thread it on in the dark in less than thirty seconds. With the silencer attached the pistol was over a foot long, impossible to conceal and awkward to carry. But again, better to have it and not need it.

The suppressor was polymer. Freshly 3-D printed from a machine in the supply room where he'd picked up the NVGs and the rest of his equipment. Because it was polymer instead of metal it wouldn't last much more than 60 rounds before melting or disintegrating (or both), but that should be more than enough. As a bonus the polymer suppressor was light and completely untraceable.

Other than two non-electrified wire fences there were no obstacles in his way, so he made good time. Twenty minutes after starting out he saw his destination up ahead.

He picked his way carefully across the ground and stopped about 150 yards out. Colman looked around, then moved twenty feet to the right and went to sit on the big rock, then stopped, halfway bent over. He hissed, clicked, then kicked gravel at the rock first on one side, then the other. There were no answering rattles, no sound of slithering, but still he squatted down to peer at the base of the rock before claiming it as his own. A rattlesnake bite wouldn't kill him, but he'd suffered enough odd injuries throughout his career and didn't wish to add to the list. He set the paper bag on the ground next to his feet.

The resolution on the NVGs wasn't that great, but there wasn't a lick of cover between the rock he was sitting on and the object of his interest. Even if he accidentally made a noise and someone swung a flashlight his way he was far enough out that they wouldn't see him.

He frowned, then flicked up the goggles. He blinked his eyes a few times, then looked around. Lots of stars, bit of a moon, and some surprisingly good streetlights down there. Brand new LED ones, but the look of it. He raised the binoculars to his eyes and peered through them, fiddling with the focus ring.

The rear and south side of Anderson's residence sprang into view, which included his driveway. One light shone inside the trailer, but Colman didn't see any movement through the windows, and Anderson's Jeep was still gone. He probably wasn't home...but time spent doing surveillance on a target was rarely wasted. You didn't just learn your target's patterns but the patterns of those living around him, which could be just as valuable.

Colman reached down into the open paper bag at his feet and withdrew a bottle of Gatorade and a Snickers. Just because he was sitting on a rock in the middle of the desert didn't mean he couldn't enjoy the benefits of doing that surveillance in America.

Dave didn't go sit in a Burger King, didn't go wandering around the always-open Walmart, didn't go anywhere or do anything where he'd get noticed or his face would end up on security camera footage somewhere.

Without a destination in mind he headed east, toward the Strip, but never got there. Driving down a road he saw a big parking lot off to the side, nearly full of cars, even at that time of night. As he rounded the corner he saw the marquee—an AMC movie theater. Perfect. He found an empty spot close to the building, angled so his license plate wasn't visible to whatever security cameras might be mounted on the building, and leaned his seat back.

Heading in to see a movie, to keep his mind off everything, or at least try, was actually what he wanted to do. But he couldn't risk it. Dave didn't want a record of him being in Las Vegas if at all possible. There were sure to be cameras inside the theater lobby. So he sat in his car, and waited. He didn't even try to sleep, he knew it would be a waste of time. Instead, he did everything he could to not think of what he was doing. Of what he planned to do. He tried to clear his mind, and not think of anything at all. With very little success.

Absolutely nothing had happened, but that was just fine with Colman. He wasn't cold, or hot. The rock was a little hard, but he could stretch or stand up and walk around any time he wanted. He had a grocery bag full of the best gas station food money could buy. As he was a male the world around him offered unlimited urinal access.

And, best of all, he was outside at night with night vision goggles. One of his favorite things in life was staring up at the night sky while wearing NVGs.

Out in the middle of nowhere about three times as many stars were visible to the naked eye when compared to what could be seen near cities with their light pollution. Slap on a pair of night vision goggles and the number of stars twinkling in the night sky multiplied by a factor of ten, at least. He couldn't stretch his arm up and stick his thumb out and find a spot of darkness so small he wasn't covering up a star or six with his thumb. The sky was a sea of glittering light. The planets were as bright as the moon. Even a crescent moon seemed vivid as a searchlight. A green searchlight.

He knew the planets, knew the constellations, knew the map of the moon from the craters to the maria and could point out all the Apollo landing sites in his sleep. Unfortunately, the goggles weren't that great for studying the moon, their resolution wasn't fine enough. Where they shined was in bringing out normally hard to see features in the night sky. In most cities around the world the Milky Way was just a name, not visible to the naked eye. In the middle of the high desert, wearing night vision goggles, it was a glittering carpet of diamonds.

The technology wasn't there yet, but he looked forward to the day when night vision goggles would show the world in its true colors, with resolution as fine as the human eye. Then he would find a remote spot somewhere in the world, lie back, and study the stars all night.

Dave could use every brain cell he had trying to guess the exact right time to check out the house, but the fact of the matter was, with surveillance, unless you were willing to devote endless man hours to the watching, you had to rely on experience. And luck.

The question wasn't if Bufonte was at the house, the question was—what if he wasn't? Dave didn't want to waste his time sitting on an empty house, or worse, a house occupied by people who'd never heard of Bufonte. The mob boss could have sold the house weeks before and the info might not show up in whatever database Phault's contact had used.

Show up too early and he might get spotted by neighbors walking dogs or doing whatever rich people did at night outside their houses Swimming? Tennis? He had no idea. Too late and the house was guaranteed to be dark and quiet. The last thing he wanted to do was blindly enter a residence that could just as easily be home to a retired New York dentist as a mob boss and his retinue.

He drove south down N. Rampart and stared down the driveway when he went past. He circled around the median, then when the driveway came up he pulled down it without hesitation, right past the GOLF COURSE MAINTENANCE signs.

Earlier there'd been a few cars parked along either side of the short driveway, but now there was just a small pickup at the far end, a tank of liquid fertilizer mounted on the back. It was brightly lit by his sweeping headlights. Dave pulled in quickly, turned left at the end of the drive, heard his tires hit the gravel, and parked next to the Dumpster that was located between a construction-type trailer on the left and a big pile of dirt on the right. He shut off his lights, then waited. Both his front windows were cracked. He could hear traffic, and the night air felt cool on his sweating face. There was one lone light above the porch on the trailer and it silhouetted the Dumpster. Ten feet from the passenger side of his car was the five-foot tall pile of dirt—no, it would have to be sand, wouldn't it? Golf course maintenance, sand traps, etc? He was surprised he hadn't realized that earlier.

The lot was shielded from view by anyone passing on Rampart by a six-foot wall that looked charcoal gray in the dark but was actually a medium pink in color. On the far side of the driveway he'd come in on, out of sight as he sat there, was a larger building. A maintenance garage, he assumed.

No one came to investigate his headlights or the sound

of his engine. After two minutes Dave got out of the car, quietly pressed the door closed, and moved across the lot and the entrance drive.

There was no gate or anything—past the drive he found himself in the parking lot of the golf course maintenance garage. There were a few security lights illuminated on the front of the building, but no lights on inside, no cars, and no movement.

He kept walking. Past the building the asphalt parking lot angled down and closed in, and the narrow walls he'd seen earlier driving along Rampart sprung up. The blacktop path was maybe eight feet wide, and it curved slightly right as it went under N. Rampart Blvd. Dave heard car tires humming across the bridge overhead and music that quickly faded.

Past the bridge the walls to either side of him disappeared, but the path continued on. In the darkness he couldn't see much, but he could smell the grass. Wet grass, actually, nothing else smelled like it, and he could hear the sprinklers. The air was cool, but he was sweating profusely. His leg and hip hurt a bit as he walked, but he thrust the pain away to a distant corner of his brain.

The ground to his left rose sharply, the decorative boulders just suggestive shadows in the dark, but the terrain to the right was open. He couldn't see the fairways and the greens, not really, they were just darker patches of ground. Across the fairways, to the north, were more houses, but they were at least a hundred yards away and except for a few lights here and there he could make out no details on them in the dark.

He followed the golf cart path, walking slowly. The houses to his left loomed above him, squatting past their fences atop small rises so they had scenic views across the golf course in daylight. The short slope blocked most of his view of them but even in the dark he could sense just how huge the houses were.

Dave counted, and past the third house he moved off the cart path and carefully and slowly climbed up the fifteen-foot slope. He squatted behind a bush and stared at the fourth house from the end, and compared what he saw to the images in his mind. Even at night the lines of the mansion were distinctive. This was the place. Bufonte's house.

Ten feet ahead of him a six-foot wrought iron fence ran the length of the property. Past the fence the entire backyard was paved, either with textured concrete or stones, he couldn't be sure. Directly across from him was a small dark oval that, as his eyes continued to adjust, he saw was a putting green. A short palm tree towered over it. Farther off to the right was a small swimming pool shaped like a stepped-on kidney bean.

The house itself sat barely ten yards back from the fence. After the darkness of the golf course the six thousand square-foot residence seemed as brightly lit as a space shuttle launch. Seemingly every window on the ground floor was lit up, and he saw at least one light on in the second floor. From his angle he could even see the flickering blue of a TV screen somewhere just out of sight.

The slope from just outside the fence to the golf cart path below was three terrace-like steps made of large stones and gravel, spotted with bushes. Dave looked around, but he didn't see a better place from which to study the rear of the house than from the shadow of the surprisingly fragrant bush. It smelled herby, like good dough from a gourmet pizza. He was wearing his long-sleeved dark blue canvas work shirt over faded blue jeans, which he hoped helped him blend into the shadows.

Colors always looked different at night. Eyeing the house Dave would have bet that the exterior was gray, but he knew it had a peach stucco exterior, with blood red tiles on the roof. There were a lot of windows on the back of the house. Through them he could see there was some sort of dining room on the left side, with a big glittering chandelier. A door sat in the center of the house, most of it window, and to the right was a room with a lot of overstuffed leather furniture. It was from that room where he could see the glow of a TV. To the right of the TV room were darkened windows, and if he remembered the floor plan of the house well enough there was another door leading into the house just around the dark corner to the right, for convenient access to the pool. The lights weren't on in the pool, it was just a dark shape cut into the concrete to his eyes, but he could smell the chlorine in the water.

Occasionally Dave could hear a distant car, maybe driving past on Rampart. Very far away, maybe on the other side of the fairway, he heard someone laughing. The only noises close to him were the clicking of bugs and the occasional skittering of the small darting lizards that were everywhere.

After twenty minutes of kneeling on the cold ground his thigh was killing him and he had to sit down. Not long after that he saw movement, and a fat guy in a maroon polo shirt walked into view in the TV room. Not Bufonte, not anyone Dave recognized, but there was nothing about the man's heavy features that told Dave he had the wrong house. He moved back out of sight and Dave fought the urge to move, to get a better angle. Five minutes later the man stepped into view again, holding a plate filled with food. Dave saw him laugh, and disconcertingly heard the sound off to the left, then he realized the sound had bounced out the closest open window. The man laughed again, and turned away from the window as he gestured to someone out of sight. The object stuck into his waistband at the small of his back was very clearly a pistol.

Dave didn't need to see anything else to confirm, in his mind, that he was at the right place. Pietro Bufonte was in the house.

Chapter Twenty-Eight

Aaron was taking a sip of his coffee when the guy came into the coffee shop, and he frowned behind the paper cup, his thick eyebrows coming together. The guy's face was familiar. Slender, plain face, maybe in his mid-forties, mostly forgettable...but Aaron definitely knew him. Recognized him. His face. From somewhere.

The guy didn't see Aaron, he only had eyes for the menu board on the wall behind the counter, exchanging a few words with the redhead co-owner as he placed an order. Aaron set his cup on the table and made a face—where the fuck did he know that guy from? It was really bothering him. It seemed like he should know who he was...except he didn't know anybody in Arizona, so how could that be? Other than Dave and the porn princess. Hell, Aaron had only been to Arizona on a few occasions as an adult, most memorably arriving just at the last second to pull a shot-up Dave out of a fire. Man, he'd almost been cooked, and if Aaron and the DPD detective had arrived even a minute later it wouldn't have been a hospital they'd have taken Dave to, it would have been—holy shit!

Aaron jerked in his seat, nearly knocking over the cup in front of him. Nobody else in the restaurant noticed. The familiar face was just getting his change back from the redhead and he didn't turn around, didn't apparently notice the small choking sound Aaron made.

Motherfucker, Aaron thought, staring at the guy's back, his eyes wide. Then he forced his stare away, looked down at the table in front of him, and furiously tried to think while keeping the guy in his peripheral vision. He could feel his heart pounding in his chest. It was the guy, the asshole, the government agent who'd tried to steal Dave out of the hospital two years ago. He'd shown up with a bunch of guys in tactical gear, DHS plastered all over their chests, and waved around a federal warrant or something, but the Sheriff had refused him. Threatened him, in fact, with his shotgun. Aaron had been right there, just a few feet away, heard the loud-as-balls click as the Sheriff took the safety off on his shotgun, and he'd been so sure there was going to be a gunfight in the hospital hallway he'd flicked the safety off on his own Colt.

But the Sheriff had backed the guy and his team down. Immediately after the agent and his team left Aaron had heard the Sheriff talking to Wheaton about how the guy was obviously a spook. Aaron figured for sure the Sheriff would get in trouble with someone, maybe the governor, for basically flipping off the feds, but that had never happened, so it sure seemed the Sheriff had been right about the man being a spook, and up to nothing legal.

The realization chilled him to the bone. Aaron didn't believe in coincidence. Dave's cover hadn't been blown because of the cartel thing—he was using a fake name and was unrecognizable on the video. No, his cover had been blown by Aaron flying down and visiting him. He was Aaron fucking Abruzzo, known associate of Dave Anderson, and how many times had he flown to Arizona in the past few months? Didn't take a goddamn genius to do that math. He'd blown Dave's cover identity.

As the man headed toward the door Aaron's eyes tracked him. The guy had never looked around, and even if he had Aaron wasn't sure the guy would recognize his face. That standoff had been over two years ago, and he'd been behind Ringo, the Detroit detective, and next to a huge uniformed deputy holding a rifle. C-something, that was the guy's name. Aaron couldn't remember exactly, but he'd introduced himself as Agent C-something with the Department of Homeland Security. Agent Cockface had a nice ring to it. So many possibilities.

Agent Cornholio stepped off the curb and walked to the left, moving out of Aaron's view. Aaron took a deep breath, counted to ten, then stood up and headed toward the door himself.

"You have a nice night, Detroit," the guy behind the counter told him.

Aaron didn't respond. He pushed out the door and kept walking without hesitation, angling left. He saw the guy moving between cars, then opening the door of a vehicle. Something newer, white, boring, domestic. Impala, Malibu, maybe a Buick, all the cars fucking looked alike these days. Aaron moved up the row, slowing down a bit, and then cut between the cars, popping out into the same lane just as the spook was backing his car out of the space.

Aaron glanced over, all casual like, as he kept walking. Between more cars. Behind him he heard the Malibuick pulling away, down the aisle. As soon as he was out of sight of the departing sedan Aaron ducked and ran back in the other direction, toward his rental. He'd caught the first four digits of the license plate on the agent's vehicle and repeated them to himself as he darted between the parked cars.

Aaron darted his eyes over as he opened the driver door of his rental. Agent ChoadSmoker's bland sedan was nearing the stop sign to leave the parking lot for the main road, right turn signal on. Aaron didn't bother with the seatbelt, he drove like his ass was on fire through the parking lot to the exit, where he hung a right in front of some oncoming traffic, earning him an angry horn.

He spotted the spook's sedan up a quarter mile up, in the right lane, just a few cars in-between them. Aaron floored the car, then five seconds later had to stand on the brakes as the cars in front of him slowed for a traffic light turning red. The government agent sailed right through the yellow light and kept on going.

"Shit!" Aaron looked for a gap, intending to run the red light, but there were cars in every lane, and before he could decide whether or not to ram someone out of the way the cross-street traffic began flowing through the intersection. Aaron watched the spook's car roll out of sight as the road curved around to the left.

"C'mon, c'mon, c'mon!" Aaron said a few more choice words before the light changed. Then, hitting his horn, flashing his lights, and revving his engine he bullied the car in front of him out of the way.

He roared around the corner, but of course the car was nowhere in sight. Aaron zigzagged around traffic, even darting into the center left turn lane to pass of few slow asses apparently asleep behind the wheel, but after he'd gone at least three miles without catching sight of the agent's car Aaron knew he'd lost him.

"Goddammit," he swore, swinging his rental around in an illegal U-turn. He raced back to where he'd lost Agent C-Word, eyes scanning all the passing traffic just in case, but it was hard as hell to see shit at dusk, heading into the sun, the cars were little more than headlights until they were almost past.

Once he was back to where he'd lost sight of the agent's car Aaron started checking the parking lots, working his way back east. Shopping centers, big box stores, even a few restaurants—although that wasn't likely, the guy had just grabbed a coffee. But where was he going?

"GODDAMMIT!" Aaron roared at himself. He was an idiot. He nearly clipped a fender peeling his rental out of the parking lot and drove as fast as he could toward Dave's trailer park. That was the direction the spook had been heading, after all. Dave wasn't there, but the spook didn't know that. Probably.

Aaron hit eighty on the dirt road leading to the trailer park entrance, feeling the tires dancing over the gravel, wanting to lose traction and send him into the ditch, but he held the car in line and hit the trailer park entrance in a power slide that was a thing of beauty. The rental's engine boomed as he hit the accelerator, hiccupped as he jogged left and right, and then he turned down Dave's street. And —nothing. No movement. No sign of the spook's car, or the man himself.

Aaron slid the car to a stop in front of Lori's house, the tires chirping. She opened the front door before he got there. His face was sweaty, his eyes darting back and forth. "What is it?" she asked worriedly.

"Anybody been here? Anybody stop by Dave's house in

the past twenty minutes? Or just drive by? Skinny middle-aged white guy? Driving a white four-door?"

Lori shook her head. "Nobody's gone to the house. Not sure if anyone drove down the street. Why? Who is he?"

Aaron huffed out a nervous breath. "Government guy. Seen him before, and I saw him in town, but I lost him. I think he's here for Dave." He kept moving his head, looking left and right.

"What do you mean, here for him? To do what?"

Aaron shook his head. "I don't know. But I don't think it's good." He saw the look of worry on her face. "Look, I don't know who he is. Maybe it's not a big thing. Or trouble. Last time he was here he talked to Osterman about Dave, maybe that's why he's back. But you see him, see anyone that looks like him, or if anyone stops by Dave's place, you call me. Don't talk to them, don't answer your door, don't even let anyone know you're home, but you fucking call me, okay?"

She nodded. "Yeah, yeah. What are you going to do?"

The guilt was eating him up, but he shoved it away. "Keep looking for him. If he's not here, maybe he is at the hospital visiting the Sheriff." He jumped off her porch, putting a hand on his Colt to keep it from bouncing out of the holster. Walking backward toward his rental, he pointed a finger at her. "Anyone, anything, you call me," he nearly shouted.

Lori nodded. "Okay," she said, her voice quiet and quavering.

It took him twelve minutes to get to the hospital, and over ten minutes to check all the lots around it. No sign of Agent CockBlocker's Malibuick. He let loose a long rambling string of creative profanity, then headed over (what the hell, it was possible, wasn't it?) to the Sheriff's

Department. Maybe the agent was here on an official visit. There were a lot fewer spaces around the police building, and it only took him a few minutes to circle it. No sign of the white car—well, he saw two lookalikes, but their plates were wrong.

Since he was already there he checked all around the touristy downtown, which featured angle parking on all the city streets. All the blocks were simple squares, and none of the streets were one-way, so it didn't take him too long. Success free, he headed back to the main drag through Prescott Valley, State Route 69, and checked every likely parking lot between downtown Prescott and the turnoff to Dave's trailer park. That took him almost an hour and a half.

After it all, he had nothing. Zero. Zilch. Fucking nada. It was not just dark, it was getting late, and he was growing even more stressed out because he hadn't been able to find the guy in what was a small fucking hick town. At least compared to Detroit.

Lori had promised to call him if anyone showed up, but he drove back up to the trailer park anyway. Nothing—no sign of the guy, or his car, nobody at Dave's trailer, and no new vehicles had parked on the street since he'd been by the last time.

Aaron did a U-turn in the street and headed back to the entrance to the trailer park. He pulled to the curb where he could see Old Fain Road. What should he do? He'd checked everywhere he could think of in town, the hospital, the Sheriff's Department, the parking lot of every mall, restaurant, and hotel in town. Where else was there? Wait—

He blinked. He was forgetting something. Some local attraction he'd meant to go visit, and never got around to. What was it? He tried to remember. He'd wanted to go with

Arlene, when she was in town, but instead—casino! That's what it was. A big casino, and hotel, at the top of a big hill or small mountain on the north side of SR 69 near the Prescott/Prescott Valley border. It wasn't right on the main drag, you had to take a side street and head up the steep hill to it, that was how he'd managed to drive right by it half a dozen times already that evening. Could the spook be up there? Gambling or whatever?

Aaron couldn't remember if it was an Indian casino or not, and he supposed it didn't matter. He threw the rental in gear and headed south down Old Fain Road again, the tires throwing a big plume of dust behind him. Five minutes ahead was the small industrial park on the right, and past that the traffic light with the Maverik gas station on the far side lit up like the landing pad from Close Encounters of the Third Kind.

As he passed the low industrial buildings he glanced over...then slammed on his brakes. The car skidded to a sideways stop in the middle of the road.

Aaron shifted the car into reverse and slowly backed up, looking over into the parking lot of the heavy equipment rental business. There, parked along the fence, mostly hidden behind a flatbed trailer, was a car. A white four-door sedan.

He pulled into the lot, and his headlights splashed over the car. It was the right make, model, and body style, Generic Motors all the way. Aaron stopped his rental twenty feet away and stared at the parked car. It appeared empty. He looked around but didn't see anyone. There were security lights at the top of the building faintly illuminating the lot, but the business appeared to be closed for the day.

Was it the same car? Shit. Aaron got out and walked toward the car, his headlights throwing his shadow around.

The car was definitely empty. He walked around to the rear and squinted at the license plate hidden in shadow. The first four digits were the same. This was the spook's car. He bent down and peered in the windows, cupping his hands around his eyes to shield them from the headlights.

Nothing.

Not nothing as in gum wrappers and gas receipts and spare change in the cup holders, but actually fucking nothing. The car was as spotless as if it had just been detail cleaned by a dealership. There was no indication a human being had ever sat inside it.

Growling, Aaron stood up and looked around again. He knew he was a big target, standing there in his headlights, but he didn't care. He didn't see anyone, and there were no other private cars in the parking lot, just a few pieces of rental equipment. He walked around the rear of the building, then around the far side. Nothing. He checked, but there were no security cameras on the outside of the building anywhere, which made sense if the spook was parking there. There was a lot of larger power equipment—front-end loaders, motorized wheelbarrows, even a dump truck—crowded behind an adjacent locked gate, topped with razor wire.

The glass door at the front of the building was locked, the interior dark. No lights on inside. He didn't think the guy was here. And a heavy equipment rental place seemed a weird choice for a CIA cover business.

So where was the guy?

Aaron went back to his car and drove around the rest of the small industrial park. It only took him three minutes. None of the other businesses were open either. He parked in the lot of a paper recycling facility just behind the equipment rental place. He had a clear view of the spook's car fifty feet away, and the open ground to the north. He reflexively looked up to check for security cameras above him, then sat back in the seat, lit a Marlboro, and thought.

He'd just been at Dave's trailer. The guy wasn't there. Unless he'd walked there and broke in, was waiting inside. Could he have done that? How far of a walk was it? Aaron guessed it was at least a couple miles. He almost started his car and zoomed back to Dave's trailer, but then stopped himself. He'd just found the fucking car, he hated to go running off, then come back only to find the car gone again.

But finding the car parked at the end of the road leading to Dave's trailer park? That couldn't be coincidence. No fucking way. Was the guy on foot? Or had he just parked his car here and jumped into another ride? Maybe someone had picked him up. There was just no way to know.

He called Lori. She picked up on the first ring. "Hello?" She sounded worried.

"Any changes? Anybody come by?" Aaron asked her, chewing on his moustache.

"No."

"You're right next door, right? Would you hear it if someone was inside his trailer?"

"You think someone's inside his trailer?"

"I don't know. I don't know anything."

He heard her walking. "His windows are open," she told him. "If anyone was in there and did anything more than cough I'd hear them. I haven't heard anything. And there's no more lights on than when he left."

"Okay. It was probably a dumb idea. But...keep an eye on the place. Any strange cars parked on the street. If you see or hear anything, you call me."

Aaron hung up and stared at the spook's car, hearing the engine of his own vehicle clicking as it cooled down. Shit.

He didn't know what to do. Should he sit on the car and wait for the guy to come back? Or sit on Dave's house?

All he knew for sure was that the government agent, in town after all the excitement, hiding his car walking distance from Dave's trailer, was up to no good.

Chapter Twenty-Nine

Dave got back up on his knees, feeling the ache in his thigh and the twinge in his hip. The sweat was drying under his arms in the cool night air, and he shivered. He studied the wrought iron fence in front of him. He wasn't too far from the left edge of the property, and the fence ran unbroken to the neighbor's property line. Narrow six-foot posts, with pointed tops, cross bars at the top and bottom.

He crept backward, easing down over a large boulder to the middle level of the terraced slope. Squatting, only the roof of the house was visible. Dave moved to the right in a deep crouch, his feet kicking up dust he smelled more than saw, carefully picking his way over the boulders and rocks and small spiny bushes.

He hadn't crossed any steps or path, but when he straightened up Dave ran his eyes back along the fence line, looking to see if there was any gate leading from the yard onto the golf course. Nope.

The far right edge of the property, near the pool, was darker. However, there were no conveniently located bushes for him to hide behind, nothing between him and the fence other than the slope. The top layer of the terrace was waist high on him, but he sank down until just his head and shoulders were above it.

He studied the back of the house from his new position. He could see a corner of the giant flatscreen TV, which seemed to be tuned to ESPN. No one was visible inside. One last time he peered at the back of the house, looking for trouble—security cameras, motion-activated exterior lights, dog bowls, a sleeping alligator on a leash, whatever. He didn't see any of that.

He felt as much heard the whispers of a light breeze. Far off in the distance so faint as to be a mere suggestion was the sound of a motorcycle travelling far too fast on a city street. Closer was the metronomic tsk-tsk-tsk of sprinklers keeping the golf course grass alive.

From his pocket he pulled out one of the pairs of latex gloves he'd brought and slipped them on his hands, being careful to move slowly and make as little noise as possible. When he was done there hadn't been any change at the house.

Taking a deep breath, Dave moved up the slope to the corner of the fence, the spot in deepest shadow, and climbed over it. Before his injuries he could have hopped it easily, but getting over it in his current state took him quite a bit of effort. And it hurt. A lot. But he didn't make much noise.

When he was finally over the fence he laid on his stomach on the cement. He was on the far side of the pool from the house. He waited to see if anything he'd done had been noticed. The TV continued to flicker inside the house, and he caught the faint hint of conversation. But no one opened a door or pressed their face against a window.

Climbing to his feet, Dave remained hunched over and crept around the edge of the pool to the shadowed side of the house. The windows were all dark and closed, and he couldn't see past the venetian blinds. He tried the knob of the door, but it was locked. He swore silently and looked around.

He couldn't see any of the windows in the neighbor's house, which meant they couldn't see him. The side of the house remained dark and in shadow all the way to the front corner, near the driveway, but heading in that direction would expose him to other houses and anybody passing by on the street or sidewalk. And none of the windows in that direction appeared open.

Sweating heavily, his heart thudding in his chest, Dave edged to the back corner of the house and peered around it toward the brightly lit windows. After the shadows of the pool, the windows seemed bright as searchlights.

He took a half step and then another, slowly moving an eye past the frame of the window. The TV was a huge thing, with a screen that had to be close to six feet wide. It was tuned to ESPN SportsCenter, but the sound was low. Facing the TV were a leather couch and overstuffed chairs, but they were empty. A plate with a fork on it sat on one of the square end tables. Past the furniture was a wide doorway leading into another brightly lit room.

Dave saw nobody, no movement whatsoever, but he didn't want to take any chances. He got down and crawled across the back of the house, below the windows, the concrete hard on his knees and elbows. He reached the back door, and stretched up with one arm. The knob didn't turn under gentle pressure. Or intense pressure.

He fought back an urge to growl and instead crawled farther along the back of the house, until the sound of the

TV was above him. Dave lifted his head and confirmed one of the windows was open. It slid to the side, and was open about six inches.

Lifting his head a bit higher he saw that the window opened into a large dining room with a huge wooden table in the center surrounded by a dozen chairs. There was one table lamp on in the room. There were two doorways into the room, one on the far side of the table and one to the right.

He waited. He didn't hear anything but the TV. Didn't see anyone. Couldn't think of a better way in, even though the spot provided no cover whatsoever in any direction.

"Shit," he whispered, almost subaudibly. Then he reached down and pulled his knife from where it was clipped to his pocket.

He unfolded it carefully, making sure to muffle the click of the liner lock as it opened fully. Remaining on his knees, he stretched the knife out and pushed it into the screen covering the window. From how little resistance he felt when the knife cut into it he decided the screen was nylon instead of aluminum.

Dave ran the blade sideways, along the bottom of the window frame, then used the knife edge to slide the window open further—slowly, carefully, cutting the screen as it went. Then he brought the knife back and ran it up the screen as far as he could reach. It made a quiet "brrrip" sound as it cut the screen. When he guessed that the opening was big enough he sunk back down, closed the knife with some difficulty (he'd never done it wearing gloves before), put it away, and waited.

No sound but the TV. No movement.

The latex gloves were unfamiliar, and his hands were swimming in sweat. He could feel the sweat dripping down his sides from his armpits, even as the night air felt cool on his face. He wiped his face on his sleeve.

One eye above the window frame, Dave stared at the empty dining room. He didn't want to go in...and yet he did. Knew he had to, in fact.

Slowly, Dave climbed to his feet, drawing the TTI Combat Master G17 from the holster at his waist. It made a slight *snick* as it cleared the Kydex. He lifted one leg and stepped through the cut window screen, paused, then ducked into it and pulled his second leg in after him.

Inside the house it was warmer, and the TV a bit louder. He still didn't hear anyone. It felt strange to be standing in someone else's house. He'd felt odd all evening, as if he was on autopilot, watching someone else do things with his body. An in-body out-of-body experience.

Glock up in two hands and pointed at the closer doorway on the right, he moved slowly forward. The arched doorway accessed a hallway. To the right it led to the back door. To the left, deeper into the house, it opened into a large space, dim on the left, bright on the right. He moved left, one step at a time, gun up, pausing after every step to listen.

Ten feet down the hallway ended. Dave pulled the Glock in tight and slowly peered around the corners, first left, then right. In front of him to the left was a big room, a foyer, with white marble floors and a glittery chandelier hanging between the front door and a curving stairway heading up. The chandelier was dark, but a lamp was lit on a table nearby. There was another hallway on the far side of the foyer. To the right was the biggest kitchen Dave had ever seen, or rather the front half of it, and he could see a small table and a counter with bar stools. The back half of it was concealed by a short length of wall. He could see the corner of what might be a kitchen island but no appliances, not unless he wanted to move right, into the bright light. At his right shoulder was a wide doorway, the one which led into the TV room. He took a quick glance. Still no one in there. No sound in the house other than the TV on low volume. He gripped the Glock tighter, feeling his sweaty hands move inside the gloves.

Dave actually jumped a little as a roar erupted seemingly on top of him. It took his brain half a second to realize it was the sound of a toilet flushing. He looked left, and saw light coming underneath a door off the foyer, maybe six feet away. As the sound of the flushing toilet faded, he heard rustling inside the bathroom. Pants being pulled up?

He only had a few seconds to make a decision. Instinctively he holstered the Glock and reached for the other object hanging at his waist as the bathroom door opened and a guy stepped out into the dim foyer, holding a folded car magazine in one hand. Dave's eyes registered the droopy eyelids and heavy cheeks, then the maroon polo shirt covering his big belly.

The man stopped and blinked at Dave, confused. Before he had a chance to open his mouth Dave hit him in the forehead with the hammer, a brutal blow. The hammer head bounced off the man's skull with the sound of a coconut hitting concrete. The man made a glottal sound and dropped to his butt in the bathroom doorway. Dave hit him again, harder, and this time blood sprayed.

The man fell backward with a thump, his head hitting the tile floor between the vanity and the toilet. Dave lost his balance and caught himself with a hand on the man's chest. Close up he could see the hammer buried at least an inch into the man's forehead. The wound was ringed with blood, and the man's blue eyes were staring up at the ceiling unblinking.

"Lenny?"

At the voice behind him Dave tugged hard twice at the hammer, finally freeing it from the man's head. He turned, bloody hammer in hand, but didn't see anyone.

"You drop something again *stronzino*?" The comment was followed by a snort.

The voice was coming from the bright kitchen, seemingly right around the corner. Dave quickly moved across the foyer and hugged the wall, hammer still in hand. He heard someone moving around. Close. Right on the other side of the wall, sounded like.

Gripping the hammer tightly, Dave darted around the corner into the brightly lit kitchen. There was a marble-topped island with a stainless-steel sink, and cherry wood cabinets everywhere. A man was standing at the stove, turning at the sound, but he wasn't close like Dave had thought, he was ten feet away, halfway behind the island.

"Who the fuck?" he said in confusion, eyes going wide at Dave. He completed the turn, then grabbed at the pistol stuck into his waistband.

Dave charged him with a strangled yell, the hammer coming up as the pistol came out. They slammed together, Dave's weight shoving the man up against the stove behind him and pinning his gun hand between their two bodies. The man was so close Dave could smell his breath, see the capillaries in his bloodshot eyes.

The man grunted and with his free hand shoved at Dave's face, his fingers claws. Dave slapped the man's hand out of the way with his left, then brought his right hand down in a wicked chop, the hammer missing the man's head but hitting him low on the neck.

Bufonte's soldier cried out at the impact, and Dave heard the dull crack as the man's collarbone snapped. Their feet twisted together, and suddenly the man was falling to the side in front of the stove. Dave followed him down, landing on the guy with a grunt, hoping to keep his gun hand pinned. Dave could feel the man frantically struggling to twist the gun free, and his other hand came for Dave's eyes again.

Rearing back to protect his eyes from the jabbing finger, Dave got room to swing even as the grunting man started to turn the pistol toward him. The head of the hammer struck a glancing blow to the man's temple, but it was enough to stun him. Dave shouted in fear and rage and hit him again, and again, only stopping when something wet splashed across his face.

He stopped, panting, staring down at the man. Maybe fifty, medium build, dark hair...with a hammer buried in his left eye socket, the other eye wide and staring. Blood was running down the side of the man's ruined head, pooling inside his ear, dripping to the tile.

Dave pushed off the corpse, grabbing the pistol out of the man's limp hairy hand. It was a Beretta 92, a big gun, the hammer pulled to half-cock in their struggles. Hands working on autopilot, Dave checked to see that the chamber was loaded, then pulled the magazine out of the gun. It felt fully loaded, and a quick glance at the rounds topping the magazine showed they were jacketed hollowpoints. Good enough.

The Beretta up in both his hands, hammer cocked and pointed towards the dim foyer, Dave tried to get his breathing under control. He hadn't been quiet killing the second man. In fact, they'd made a hell of a lot of noise thrashing around on the floor. But he didn't hear anything. No curious voices, or shouts, footsteps, slamming doors. Of course, his left ear was still ringing badly from the gunfire that morning.

He edged forward, slowly pieing the corner into the foyer, Beretta up and steady. The foyer was still empty. The house silent.

Dave pointed the pistol at the empty hallway past the curving staircase and moved forward on bent knees. There were several doors ahead of him, at least one of which was open. The house was huge, with who knew how many rooms. Clearing them would be a nightmare.

The marble tile was smooth under his shoes. The bannister on the stairway curved up from the left, heading to the second-floor landing which gradually slid into view as Dave carefully moved across the foyer. He raised the pistol and swept it across the landing, then moved it back down to cover the hallway ahead of him—then he stopped suddenly. He'd heard something.

He frowned, then lifted the Beretta again. It had been just the faintest whisper of a sound, maybe brushing fabric, maybe shoes on carpet…

An arm shoved out around the corner on the second floor, an eye above it, and before Dave could even react the man began firing, the gunshots huge as they echoed around the staircase. Dave fired back instinctively even as he dove to the side, hitting the marble hard with a grunt. He scrambled off to the side, out of view. The bullets made loud smacks as they hit the marble past him.

He was out of sight past the edge of the stairs but the man continued firing, wood splinters and drywall dust flying everywhere. A dozen shots, more, the bullets pounding through the walls and staircase railing and balusters. Panic shots? Suppressive fire? Dave wasn't sure. Then the pistol fell silent.

Making a sudden decision, Beretta up, Dave moved quickly and silently back the way he'd come across the marble, around the outside curve of the staircase. The second-floor landing was clear—the guy was out of sight, probably reloading. When Dave stopped at the base of the stairs he was almost directly below the second-floor landing and out of sight of anyone upstairs.

Mouth wide open to make his breathing as quiet as possible, gun pointed almost directly above his head, Dave lifted a foot onto the first step. The wood was solid as rock, and didn't even creak. He moved his other foot to join the first, then moved up another step, then another. Then he stopped.

The sights of the Beretta had cleared the bottom edge of the second-floor landing. The balusters supporting the railing up there were six inches apart, but from his extreme angle the gaps were barely more than an inch wide. He peered between them, up into the second-floor hallway, past the corner crumbled by gunfire. He wasn't aiming straight up, but it felt like it.

There was nothing there, no one, but still Dave waited. He was in no hurry, he had the rest of his life to get this right. Any further up the stairs and his head would clear the balustrade and be an easy target to anyone who peeked around the corner. Instead, he willed his body to stillness, tried to silence his breathing.

It felt like forever, but in reality it was probably less than thirty seconds before the gunman edged back to his position at the corner and risked a glance downstairs. He had a shiny stainless 1911 in his hand, no doubt reloaded. He looked both nervous and angry. "C'mon, fucker!" he shouted, then pulled his head back. He'd be out of sight to anyone standing in the marble foyer, but Dave wasn't in the foyer, he was almost directly below the man. He could see a narrow slice of the panting man as he pressed his back against the wall in the second-floor hallway.

From almost directly below, Dave shot the man through the gap in the balusters, just below the thick cherry wood railing. One careful, well aimed shot, at a stationary target at most twelve feet away. He knew the man was dead even before he heard the boneless thump of his body on the carpet, but charged up the stairs anyway.

The man was sprawled awkwardly on the floor, eyes open, one small dark hole in his cheek. Dave didn't even see any blood.

He glanced to the left, but the man had come down the hallway to the right, and at the end of the wide hallway the door was open, the room beyond brightly lit. Dave's steps were silent on the thick white carpet.

He edged up close to the open doorway. The bulk of the room was off to the right, nothing but a green wall and a bland painting visible to him past the doorjamb. He took a deep breath, then darted around the corner, Beretta up, finger tense on the trigger.

Pietro Bufonte was sitting behind a desk at the far end of the room, a disgusted look on his face. He didn't look surprised to see Dave.

"Mr. Anderson, I presume." A look of snarling fury twisted Bufonte's face and just as quickly disappeared, to be replaced with something resembling resignation. Dave gave the room a quick glance. There wasn't much to it—a small bar in the corner, a leather loveseat in front of a flatscreen TV, and the desk. That was it. He approached carefully, stopping six feet in front of the desk.

Both Bufonte's hands were visible above the desk, one empty, one cupping a fluted glass. On the table by his elbow was a bottle of something bright yellow. Limoncello, Dave read on the label. Never heard of it. At the corner of the desk was an antiqued brass lamp with a green shade. Dave didn't say anything, just stared at the man he'd never met, never talked to, yet who had been such a huge part of his life for so many years. Or was that responsible for a huge part missing from his life?

Bufonte jerked his chin at the gun in Dave's unwavering hands. "I got a felony conviction, from way back. I don't dare touch a gun, FBI up my ass so deep I can taste what they had for breakfast."

Dave didn't say anything. Bufonte looked just like his photographs. Big head, heavy features, the beginnings of jowls. Even beyond the green glow thrown off by the desk lamp his color wasn't good. His eyebrows were caterpillar-thick, dotted with a few unruly gray hairs. The Beretta in Dave's hands never swayed from the bridge of Bufonte's nose.

The mob boss growled deep in his throat. "You run over my son, ambush my men, and now plan to murder an old unarmed man in his home." He peered up at Dave through his thick brows. "How am I the bad guy here?"

"Nobody thinks they're the bad guy," Dave told him, finally speaking. "Not even the bad guy."

Bufonte looked like he'd eaten something sour. He poured himself a tall shot of the viscous yellow liqueur and downed it with one perfectly-timed flick of his wrist and head. He smiled at the flavor, and nodded. Then he looked straight into Dave's eyes. "Yeah? So who does that make you?"

Dave was silent for so long Bufonte thought he wasn't

going to answer, although the Beretta in his hands never wavered. Finally, Dave said, "Someone trying to get justice. For my parents. For Mickey." Dave clenched his teeth. "For me." He paused again. "Which makes me the guy who killed your asshole son. And you," Dave told Pietro Bufonte, and shot him between the eyes.

Bufonte's whole body jerked, then his head slowly rolled forward and dropped to the desktop with a soft tap. Dave stared at him, waiting to feel something. Victory. Shame. Remorse. Anger. Mostly what he felt was relief. He and this man had been tied together for so long. Now that was over.

His brain slowly swam upward through the memories into the here and now. No sirens. He still hadn't heard sirens, which meant that none of the neighbors had heard the gunshots, or recognized them for what they were. Or maybe the LVPD was having a busy night and slow to respond to a noise complaint that was "probably just fireworks".

He set the Beretta on the desk in front of Bufonte, beyond the slowly spreading pool of blood, and walked over to the bar. He didn't drink, but he had a pretty good idea which liquors had a high alcohol content, and there were a lot of them lined up in front of him. The first bottle he grabbed was greenish gold and had an unpronounceable name, Laphroaig. He twisted off the cap and emptied the contents over the desk and Bufonte's head. The dead guy downstairs, in the bathroom, he smelled of cigars. Dave was sure he had a lighter on him, somewhere. Probably one of those fancy butane torches. And the stove in the kitchen, it had gas burners.

Surveillance was never a waste. You never learned nothing. Even when there was zero activity, you learned something.

There'd been absolutely no activity at the target's house. No movement, no lights, no arrivals, no departures...but it hadn't been a wasted evening. Colman had been observing not just the target's house but the whole street. Learned there wasn't a whole lot of nighttime activity going on. Saw almost nobody parked on the street. Figured out that the trailers were so close together that sound from one could easily carry to another. All of this information would help his decision-making down the road, could help keep him out of trouble.

Getting close to Anderson wouldn't be easy, but he'd had harder missions. Colman reviewed possible options as he picked his way back across the desert grit and scrub toward his car, the NVGs in place on his face. He hadn't wanted to wait until dawn, because he wasn't sure how exposed he'd be on the walk back. Not that a guy walking through a field was necessarily suspicious, but he preferred to be as close to invisible as possible.

The sky in the east was beginning to light up as Colman crested the last hill and started making his way down the gentle slope to the industrial park. He shut off the PVS-21s and flipped them up on his head. The ground underfoot was still dark, but the lights around the building where he'd parked his car would just blow out the night vision goggles.

Careful not to trip over something and injure himself—stupider things had happened—Colman circled around toward the front of the building, around the chain link fence, and approached his government sedan from the front. He stopped in surprise when he saw the figure standing at his rear bumper.

"Hey there," he said with a smile, and walked a few

more steps. "How can I help you?" Maybe it was the business owner, starting the day early, wondering about the strange car parked in his lot. Except...as Colman drew close, and got a good look at the guy. He didn't seem like a business owner.

"D'you get a good look?" Aaron asked him. He'd spotted Colman as he crested the low hill and was silhouetted against the lightening sky. Aaron was out of the car before he realized he'd decided what to do. Confronting the spook seemed like a really stupid idea, but he didn't have a better one.

"Excuse me?" Colman stopped about a dozen feet from the guy. '70s porn star moustache, hair a bit too long to be in fashion, and he could smell the cigarette smoke on the guy from across the parking lot. Who the hell was he? Local? Plainclothes site security? Not a cop. And definitely not a serious operator.

"Dave. Dave Anderson," Aaron said with sudden vehemence, staring at the guy.

Colman blinked in surprise. Normally he prided himself as being the most informed guy in the room, and once again, working Anderson, he found himself suddenly behind the information curve. But, when in doubt, bullshit, play for time, and try to find out as much as you can. "I think you've got me confused with—"

"Someone whose last name starts with a C?" Aaron taunted him. "Who tried to snag Dave out of the hospital a few years back? Remind me what that C stands for. Crackwhore? Cockgobbler? Cunt?" he spat. A sudden thought occurred to Aaron, staring at what had to be night vision goggles atop Agent Circlejerk's head. "I think you're someone who might be interested in what Dave's fingertips look like now."

Colman froze. Something was very definitely wrong here. He didn't know who the hell this guy was, but the conversation had taken a hard left turn into dangerous territory. This guy knew way too much. Knew more than he possibly could. Was he a friend of Anderson? It couldn't be Winston Elliott deciding to wipe the government's dirty slate clean for the new administration, could it? Reflexively, his right hand twitched toward the pistol concealed on his hip, then he blinked as the giant sound caromed off the building next to them and rolled up the hill.

Colman stared stupidly at the big silver pistol which had suddenly appeared in the man's hand, his draw blindingly fast. Then the world yawed and he was on his back, the graying night sky above him. There was a burning cold ache in his chest. He couldn't catch his breath.

"No," he wheezed. He flopped over onto his side and tried to crawl. "Not like this."

Aaron stared at the government agent scrabbling in the dirt. His jacket concealed the damage to his flesh, but the bloody hole where the ten millimeter slug had exited was in the center of his back, and Aaron could guess what that meant. Colman got up onto his hand and knees, then made a small keening sound and fell over. He took two shuddering breaths, then died.

Aaron found himself standing over the man, Colt forgotten in his hand, staring at the blood soaking the parking lot gravel. Then at the man's face. All his anger at the spook evaporated. The agent's eyes were closed, his face almost peaceful.

Aaron pressed his lips together, the stillness of his body disguising the fact that his heart was hammering in his chest, his mind racing. He reached down with his free hand and flicked Colman's windbreaker back to reveal the pistol on his hip. After another few seconds staring at the man, Aaron nodded, then flicked the safety on and holstered his gun.

He stood, gazing off into the distance, for most of a minute, then thought to look around. Nothing had changed, other than the sky growing brighter as the sun rose closer to the horizon. Aaron turned to head back to his car, then stopped. He looked at Colman's sedan, at Colman's body, where he guessed he'd been standing when he fired the shot, then off to the right. The spent cartridge case was nickel-plated and easy to find on the dark ground next to the building. He picked it up and put it in his pocket.

He was two miles away and very carefully driving the speed limit before he got the shakes. They were so bad he had to pull over.

Lori was sitting on her porch when Dave pulled up in his Jeep. It was just after seven a.m., and the morning sun stretched the shadows sideways. She hadn't slept all night.

When he climbed out of his Jeep he looked exhausted. She met him on the sidewalk.

"Is it over?" she asked him.

Dave didn't respond at first. He was thinking. A major organized crime figure had been murdered. Dave didn't know if he'd be on the short list of potential suspects, but he'd be on a list, somewhere.

Given enough time and resources he was sure the Las Vegas cops would be able to pull up traffic or security camera footage of his Jeep—and maybe him inside it—on the evening of Bufonte's death. But he'd specifically grabbed and used the Beretta because it wasn't his gun. The fire he'd seen raging as he'd driven off had been massive, silhouetting the neighboring mansions, with no fire department vehicles even in earshot yet. The clothes he'd been wearing in the house were soaking in bleach in a garbage bag in a Dumpster miles from Summerlin. Including the shoes.

He was confident there was absolutely no physical evidence remaining that could put him in Bufonte's Vegas mansion. Even if there was, there was no evidence that he had killed any of the men inside the house. And there never would be. The only way he'd ever be convicted of the crime was if he confessed to the police. He was sure that within a day or three he'd be visited by Las Vegas police officers, maybe FBI agents, politely requesting to interview him to "clear up a few details" or "ask a few follow-up questions". They'd be more than disappointed when he'd refuse to meet with them without a lawyer present, and feign anger when he refused to answer any questions about where he was or what he was doing on the night in question. He didn't need to imagine the threats and yelling and intimidation they'd try; he'd gone through it all before with the West Bloomfield detective trying to nail him for the hit-and-run murder of Bufonte's son.

"Is it over?" Lori asked him again, staring at him hopefully.

"Everything but the shouting," he said. To her uncomprehending frown he elaborated, "Not over, not quite." He paused. "But it's the beginning of the end."

She reached over and took hold of his hand. "So what are you going to do now?" she asked him.

He didn't have an immediate answer for her. "What about you?" he asked. He glanced over at her house. "Now that your mom's gone..."

"I don't know." She shrugged. "I never thought about

after. I took it one day at a time. And there were a lot more days than I was expecting."

He looked at her. "I know what you mean." He stood there for a long time, then closed his eyes and turned his face to the warm morning sun. Through his eyelids it was a golden orange glow. Without opening his eyes he said, "I didn't think there'd be an after."

Next in the James Tarr Conspiracy Thriller Series

vinci-books.com/madmen

Dave Anderson thought he was free, but the past never stays buried.

With the mob boss dead and his heroic stand against the cartel behind him, Dave Anderson is finally trying to move on. But in a world where the government never forgets and Mexican cartels never forgive, his troubles are far from over.

Turn the page for a free preview…

Ghosts and Madmen: Chapter One

PART I: OUTLIERS

El Paso, Texas, was situated at the tip of the far-west-jutting arm of America's second-largest state, driven like a spike between Mexico and the American state of New Mexico. It was almost directly south of Albuquerque, the two cities linked by a four-hour-drive along I-25. Across the border from El Paso was Ciudad Juarez, which occupied the northern-most point of Mexico east of Phoenix. It was a sensible spot to cross if you were heading anywhere in America other than California or Arizona.

More than two million people lived on either side of the border there, twice as many in Ciudad Juarez as El Paso. The cities shared nearly twenty miles of border, which followed the winding path of the Rio Grande—El Rio Bravo (del Norte) as it was known in Mexico. The El Paso border crossing was the second-busiest between Mexico and the United States, second only to the San Ysidro crossing between Tijuana and San Diego.

The street was named Broadway, in the Thomas Manor neighborhood of El Paso, in the middle of the city, and it seemed particularly ill-suited to the grandiose name. Barely wide enough for three cars, the asphalt was so cracked and faded it looked like the desert floor. Dry grass sprouted in random tufts along the low curbs and occasionally pushed through the cracks.

The houses lining the street were little better. They were small, single-storied, brick and siding, all done in light colors—white, peach, and various shades of pink—and yet still looked dirty and faded. There were occasional trees, but most of the low roofs were open to the baking sun. A few of the houses had carports, but most of the vehicles belonging to the residents squatted in the short driveways, in full sun, soaking up the heat. If it wasn't clear from the dilapidated condition of many of the houses, or the age of the vehicles parked in front of them, the bars across almost every window told the tale.

Directly behind the houses on the west side of Broadway were the six lanes of Texas State Route 75, Cesar E. Chavez Border Parkway, running nearly north/south, and directly behind that was the Wall. Although, technically, here it was more of a fence, constructed of square steel beams with almost no horizontal cross-supports, so few people short of accomplished gymnasts and mountain climbers could get over it at all, much less quickly.

The Wall wasn't the border; the border was the shore of the Rio Grande some four hundred feet from the Wall. Depending on the time of year, and the rain, the river here was sometimes less than twenty feet wide. Three hundred feet west of the Mexican riverbank was Blvd. Cuatro Siglos, a six-lane highway running along the northern border of Ciudad Juarez. There was a six-foot-high berm running along the shoulder, so the locals driving along couldn't see the river, or the border, but everyone knew it was there.

Clouds didn't keep the moon out of the sky; its gravity still turned the tides.

On the west side of Blvd. Cuatro Siglos were the kind of businesses you would expect—gas stations and industrial parks, for the most part. The Ciudad Juarez neighborhoods sat to the south and further inland, including the Parceles Ejido Jesus Carranza, which stretched for a mile and sat almost directly across the border from Thomas Manor. From the houses on Broadway on the American side to the buildings sitting along Cuatro Siglos on the Mexican side was barely more than three hundred meters in a straight line.

Thomas Manor hadn't been a good neighborhood in years, and with the situation at the border at its worst since The Republic of Texas had been at war with Mexico, For Sale signs dotted both sides of the street.

The house they were interested in was on the west side of the street, near the south end of the block. There was no For Sale sign in front of it, and no vehicles parked in the driveway. Since they'd had it under surveillance there'd been no sign of life.

The drone had been circling over it for hours, so far overhead it was practically invisible to the naked eye. It was equipped with night vision and thermal cameras, both of which were useless in the baking Texas summer heat. The house was a plain one-story that was indistinguishable from its neighbors. The person who owned it was a ghost; the name went nowhere, and the property taxes were paid out of a business account. It was a shell company, owned by another shell company, but the company which owned that one was a known entity. So that gave the intelligence they'd received more weight.

However, it was time sensitive. They'd gotten the drone

parked over the house in the early hours of the morning, minutes before the ground team was even in the air and en route. They studied the real-time feed from the drone during the flight, working up several plans.

There were a lot of ways to do it. All of them had risk.

Pike was lead on the team. He didn't need to tell any of them that. As soon as he identified himself to the group—a formality, as four of the five men already knew who he was, and three of them had worked with him on various missions—he got respectful nods. And a few penetrating, wondering stares.

Pike was a legend, as much of a legend as you could be in a profession where most of what you did was secret, classified at the highest level. The more successful the mission, the less anyone knew about it. It was only massive screwups which made the news. But whether you were talking military, CIA, or private contractors, the top-tier spec-ops community was small and closed-knit, and everyone knew everyone, or you knew a guy who knew the guy. The accepted background story was that he'd started out in Special Forces, before the date Nine-Eleven had any meaning, and he'd been in his current position for at least five years, but between those two postings was over a decade of mystery, rumor and innuendo. Most of the whispered stories about his "greatest hits" were so outrageous that they couldn't be believed...except the people who were telling them had no tolerance for tall tales, not about the shit that mattered.

Pike was, by far, the oldest man still in the field. Most guys his age were in management, sitting behind desks or watching, on monitors, the action taking place elsewhere, usually across the world, directing the action. Not Pike. He was still shrugging on the armor, lacing up the boots, and hitting the skids. Or, in this case, the leather recliners, as they were travelling in style. Nicer than most of them were used to—the G5 was undoubtedly registered to one of the countless shell companies the government had on paper and used whenever it needed insulating layers.

"We don't have anything that can see through that roof?" Fancy asked. It was a rare man on the teams who didn't use a work name. You didn't want to shout a guy's real name during an op, only to have surviving bad guys try to track him down. Fancy was a former Navy SEAL, lean and dark-haired.

Pike shook his big head. His head was nearly square, with a big jaw. His dark blonde hair seemed to be fading rather than turning to gray. He was of average height, and thick everywhere. At his age, most people would assume it was fat. That he was, perhaps, a 'former jock'. "Not on that Reaper. And as soon as that sun's been on that roof for half an hour, the mirage is going to fuck everything up, thermal will be useless. We'll know who's in there when we get inside. For what it's worth, it's supposed to be empty."

That got snorts out of the team members. "That's worth exactly nothing," Cherry said, which is what they were all thinking. He'd started out in the Rangers, and during his first combat tour in Afghanistan had met up with a bunch of trigger pullers from the operations side of the DIA. They'd had very cool toys and been doing some wicked stuff, and it didn't take much to get him to change lanes.

They looked at the slowly rotating image of the house. "There's hardly any back yard. Or front yard, for that matter. Is that a fence or a wall that runs along the back?" Boot asked. He was of Italian descent, but depending on his haircut, facial hair, manner of dress, and how much tan he was sporting (as he got very dark), could pass for Arab, or Israeli, or Greek. Or Mexican.

Fancy pointed at the second laptop, which was displaying an image from Google Earth, taken from the northbound lanes of the Cesar E Chavez Border Highway, running just behind the house in question. "Both. There's a six-foot wall, concrete or cinderblock, that runs along the edge of the sidewalk. But it looks like the city put it there to block noise. It's not the property line. See?" He leaned in and tapped the screen with his finger. "There's a chain link fence that runs along the property line. Of all the houses. But that's, what, two, three feet between the wall and the fence? Should be able to fit between that easy. Completely out of sight of anybody driving by. And that chain link is waist high. Once you're over, looks like you're about twenty feet from the back door."

"Easy to get over," Cherry said, "but you're exposed as fuck to anybody in those houses. We've got to cross behind one or two before we get to the target house."

"Two."

"We're going to get there, what, early afternoon? How long can we wait?" They all looked at Pike.

"We can't."

Boot nodded. That was the answer he'd been expecting. "I can walk right up and knock on the front door. I won't look out of place in that neighborhood. If they're already in the house, there's a good chance, a real good chance, that they'll assume I'm a contact or something. Dropping off, or picking up. Whatever." He looked at Pike. "I'm fluent, and dressed in civvies they wouldn't know I'm not a local." He had on a plaid work shirt over faded jeans and boots.

Pike shrugged his big shoulders. "This is me not saying no. But whether it works or not, we need to get all of us, six guys, into that house. ASAP. Which means not waiting until dark. The only way to do that is to walk right in the front door, or go over the back wall. A next-door neighbor might see us going in the back, but somebody is bound to see us going in the front door."

"Like a fucking chorus line," Tommy said. Tommy was short for Tomboy, or sometimes Tomcat. "And you have to assume there's at least one person on the block paid to watch, if they're not in the target house."

"The mission's the mission," Cherry said, shrugging.

Fancy looked at Pike. "And then once we get in, if the house is empty, we sit and wait? For how long?"

"For a day or a week, until something happens or we're called off. But they're supposed to show up around dinner time, late afternoon to evening. So if we can get in without causing a scene, we shouldn't have long to wait." He crossed his arms around his chest, displaying his huge forearms, and tilted his head down. It looked as if he was trying to nap, but they knew better. After a minute, he looked up. His eyes roamed around the expectant faces. They stopped on Fancy. "*¿Como 'sta tu Español?*" he asked the man. How's your Spanish?

"*No malo*," Fancy responded without missing a beat. Not bad. "*Tengo un poco de acento.*" I have a little accent.

"*¿Como carajo no tienes acento?*" Boot demanded of Pike. "*Eres mas blanco que la leche.*" How the fuck do you not have an accent? You're whiter than milk.

Pike just smiled, and looked at the second-in-command of the team. Dog—named Doug by his parents—had done two combat tours in Special Forces, then started contracting for Blackwater and the companies that came after Blackwater's fall from grace. When the contracting started drying up he wasn't ready to retire, and had run into a number of spooks during his time in country, so he knew who to call. "What kind of vehicles will we have when we get there?" Pike asked the man. "Find out. Make, model, color, year."

Dog nodded, and pulled out a satellite phone. "Not that I give much of a shit for the formalities, but will there be someone from Border Patrol or whoever there when we touch down? FBI? Home game, they prefer to have someone from a domestic agency attached, like the CIA has to roll."

"This is officially a joint operation between CBP and us," Pike told him. "Ask the colonel, he'll tell you the same. The bigwigs are looped in."

Dog frowned. "Yeah, but aren't they supposed to have someone actually on the ground? With us? Participating? Or at least watching?"

Pike gave him a look, and then shared it with the rest of the team. "The rules don't seem to be the rules anymore."

"You can say that again. Okay, well, I had to ask." Dog walked to the other end of the aisle to make the call, grabbing a Gatorade out of the mini-fridge on the way.

The rest of them looked back at the laptops and other intelligence and site data spread atop the table. "What are you thinking?" Cherry asked Pike.

Pike shrugged. "Nowhere to hide on this one. So you work with what you've got. Magicians can't do magic, what they do is make you look over here," he stuck is right hand off to the side, "while they're doing something over here." And he wiggled his left elbow. They saw he'd stuck his left hand in his pants pocket, and while they watched he withdrew it, like he was pulling something out of his pocket, and turned his hand up so they could see him flipping them off.

The car was a small sedan, a tired Hyundai whose paint had faded under the brutal Texas sun until it was somewhere between silver and gold. It pulled to the curb across the street from the target address. Boot climbed out the passenger seat and stretched, looking around, up and down Broadway. He was in no hurry as he walked across the street.

Behind the tint and the glare, Fancy, at the wheel, was little more than a silhouette. Anyone looking at him wouldn't have been able to see more than his black hair, which is why Pike had picked him.

Boot clomped across the street in his boots, feeling the heat through their soles. His thick navy-blue cotton work shirt was untucked, but the collar was buttoned, and the sleeves were rolled all the way down. He had a flat-brim Texas Rangers ball cap—with the reflective sticker still on the brim, of course—pulled down low on his forehead. He walked up the concrete path to the front door without hesitation and banged on the steel burglar door with the palm of his hand. "Yo! *¿Estas ahi?*" You in there? He waited about ten seconds, then banged again. "Hey! *¡Hola! ¡Pendejo! 'Stoy aqui.*" Asshole! I'm here. He tried to peer through the door, but it was too dark. He moved to the side and looked through the front window, which was also covered by bars. "So far I've got nothing," he said quietly into his mic. "No sound or movement."

"Roger that," Pike said into his ear. "We are inbound. Do your thing."

Fancy rolled his window down half way. "*¿Qué carajo?*" he shouted across the street. What the fuck? Boot threw his hands up theatrically in response. He stepped back onto the small square concrete slab that served as a porch and banged at the door again. Half a dozen good hits with the side of his fist, then he kicked the door as well. "*¡Despertar!*" he shouted. Wake up.

"*¿Deberíamos irnos y regresar?*" Fancy called out. Should we leave and come back?

Boot frowned and pulled a cell phone out of his pocket. He angrily punched at it with his thumbs, then held it up to his ear.

"*¿Estamos en el lugar correcto?*" Fancy called out. Are we in the right place? Boot waved at him to shut up, then started a loud conversation with his phone, talking to nobody in loud Spanish—hey, where are you, answer your damn phone, we're here, call me back.

In his ear, Pike said, "In position. Give us cover in three, two, one…"

On one, Boot went back to kicking the front door with his heel, cursing, making a lot of noise. A dozen good kicks, the clanging metal echoing up and down the street. He thought he heard another noise, a faint crunching thud, but it barely registered over the noise he was making.

"*Vamos, esto es una mierda*," Fancy called out to him, still invisible inside the car. Let's go, this is bullshit.

Boot waved at him, and pulled his phone out again. He acted like he was texting someone while listening for noise inside the house. He'd could hear them moving around, then Dog's voice came over the comms. "House is clear."

"*Jodan estos tipos*," Boot called out to Fancy, and stepped off the porch. Fuck these guys. Fancy rolled up the window. Boot walked back across the street, feigning irritation, and climbed into the passenger seat. He landed a little too hard, and winced. "Shit, right in the dick," he said, and as soon as his door was closed he reached down and adjusted the rig stuffed down the front of his pants—a Glock 17 in a Safariland IncogX holster, with a spare magazine caddy right beside it. The spare mag had a TTI extra capacity basepad, and between the two he had forty rounds of 9mm+P onboard to solve any problems. You could hide a big damn gun down the front of your pants with just a loose shirt for cover, but you had to remember to be careful sitting down. He hadn't.

Hand on the grip of the pistol, he looked at Fancy, then out the windshield. He spotted nothing moving on the street. "Anything?"

"No, but..." Fancy shrugged. There could be a lot of eyes out there. He drove away.

"We're clear. Didn't spot anything," Boot said into his mic.

"Roger that," Pike said quietly in their ears. "We're set up. Park it on Playa Lateral and ruck in."

"Copy," Boot said.

They parked the sterile sedan several streets over and threw backpacks over their shoulders before heading out on foot. Across to the highway, then along it for a hundred yards. The sound-blocking wall drew closer. It was broad daylight, with cars passing every few seconds, but there was nothing they could do about that. They just stepped inside the wall like they belonged there, behind two dirty, cluttered yards, literally hopped over the low fence, and jogged up to the back door of the target house. It was mostly closed.

Boot pushed open the door, and they quickly went inside, shutting the door behind them. There was a metal frame, but it had been bent in exactly the right place for the bolt to pop out. Just inside the door Boot saw the long crowbar that had done the deed. He and Fancy knelt down and ripped open their backpacks and began assembling their rifles.

If they had to do anything it was going to be up close

and personal, and noise would probably be an issue, so every man there had a SIG MCX Rattler in his backpack for his main weapon in addition to the pistols they all carried. The rifle had a comically-short 5.5-inch barrel, so with the skeletonized stock folded it was barely over a foot long. They unfolded the stocks, shoved loaded thirty-round magazines into their guns, chambered a round, and then grabbed the sound suppressor and ratcheted it into place using the QD mount. The Surefire SOCOM300 SPS was designed to be the quietest "silencer" on the market for subsonic 300 AAC Blackout ammunition. It wasn't short or light, but it was definitely quiet—even on full auto, the guns were nearly Hollywood quiet, and with the sound of passing traffic in the background it was likely even the neighbors wouldn't notice the sound of shooting.

There was hardly any furniture in the house, as if it was vacant and awaiting sale. The team had their Rattlers up and trained on an open door in the center of the small house. It led to a very small room, a closet or perhaps a pantry, barely four feet wide and six deep, with a few shelves high up on the walls which were bare. When Boot and Fancy had their guns hot Pike raised his hand to get everyone's attention and moved forward.

Pike stood in the open doorway of the pantry, squatted down, and very slowly pulled back the carpet covering the floor inside the small room. He spotted the drilled hole, big enough for a finger, before he spotted the seam in the plywood flooring. Carefully and quietly he laid the carpet back into place, and as he backed away from the room, moving toe-to-heel, he jabbed a knife hand at the open door. He retreated to the furthest corner of the house from the pantry and let the Rattler hang from its single-point sling, one hand loosely on the pistol grip.

"Command, this is Gargoyle," he murmured into his comm. "We are in position. No activity."

"Copy that, Gargoyle. Stand by." There was a very brief pause. "Gargoyle, new orders. You are to capture any wildlife you encounter. Capture, and do not allow any to rabbit back home. Please confirm."

Pike frowned. He didn't need to look around to know identical expressions were on the faces of the rest of his team, who'd heard the conversation. "Command, Gargoyle copies, but...we didn't bring any of the toys we should have for that kind of play date."

"Understood. Make it work."

Pike's frown deepened. "Command, any additional intelligence for us? Numbers, gear...timeline?"

"Negative, Gargoyle. Check back in top of every hour."

"Roger that, command. Gargoyle out." Pike was pleased to see his men weren't looking at him but rather at the pantry, guns held at the low ready, but he could tell they weren't happy. He stared at the closet, and thought. It was nearly in the exact center of the house. To the left was the kitchen in back, and a living room in front. It sat at the end of a short hallway which led to the bedrooms on the other side of the house—three of them, although one was tiny, not much bigger than the pantry/closet in question. If you stood just around the corner, in the kitchen, that was the only spot anywhere close to the pantry where you could position yourself and not be seen by someone in the small room. He switched over to the team channel. "Anyone got any zipties?" he quietly murmured. "I think I've got a couple in my pack."

"I've got two," Dog said. He was talking so quietly that even though he was standing just a dozen feet away Pike could only hear him through the earpiece. "Pretty sure. I'll check. No gags or hoods though, I didn't pack for date night."

"So what's the plan, boss?" Cherry asked.

Pike looked around. Six heavily armed men arranged in a semi-circle, in an enclosed space. They'd needed to blend in, so nobody was wearing armor, but hopefully that wouldn't make a difference. "Stay out of sight, somehow take 'em one at a time as quietly as possible, and when something goes wrong," because it always did, "try not to shoot each other."

"And if they rabbit back the way they came?" Boot asked.

Pike shrugged his big shoulders. "Command said do not allow any to escape."

The first indication they had that their efforts might have some payoff was a soft thump, and a vague noise that might have been someone talking very quietly. Then a faint creak, sharper, louder, and closer.

Cherry and Boot were in the first bedroom, the open doorway just a few feet down the hall from the pantry. The rest of them were stacked up in the kitchen. The creak was followed by a thump. "Okay, good," they heard a man say, with a thick accent. "Let me check out the windows, but we should be okay. You understand? *Coños. Pendejos. ¿No?*" More thumps, then a man stepped into view. He was wearing a dusty navy-blue work shirt over black pants and Nikes. He straightened up with a groan. Putting a hand on his lower back, he glanced at the brightly-lit windows running across the front of the living room, the south Texas glare cut by gauzy curtains and window bars. Then he turned leisurely turned toward the kitchen and took a step before his eyes even registered what he was seeing.

Dog, who was at the front of the stack, took half a step and hit the man with a textbook-perfect jab to his solar plexus. The man's eyes opened wide even as he woofed softly, then Dog had an arm around his neck, dragging him through the doorway into the kitchen.

Dog locked his arm down, tucking his face in tight to take the wild punches to the top of his head as the struggling man's face turned deep red, then purple, then he was out, unconscious. Fancy moved in, and they had his wrists ziptied behind his back barely thirty seconds after Dog had thrown the punch, with only a few vague scuffling noises for their efforts. Everyone in the kitchen froze, listening for more sounds from the pantry. Tommy was now in the lead, at the door. He edged out, leaning, his eye clearing the kitchen doorway, but there was nothing to see.

They waited. Fifteen more seconds passed. There was some very quiet discussion, barely audible, then they heard a man hiss, "Hey. Guy. What do you see?" There was a pause, then a brief, heated argument, the words impossible to make out. There was another pause, then they heard movement. Tommy pulled his head back behind the corner, and they waited.

As soon as he heard the man step out of the pantry Tommy came around the corner, Rattler up. He saw the man was unarmed, and had his back to him, so he reflexively dropped the Rattler on its sling and wrapped a big arm around the man's neck—and all hell broke loose.

The man shouted as he saw the arm, instantly spinning with an elbow up, and kicked backwards and sideways. There was a dull crunch, and Tommy was going down, his mouth opening to scream in pain at his broken knee. Before

Tommy even hit the floor, desperately trying to hold onto the man he'd grabbed, another man was scrambling out of the pantry and he charged at Tommy. Fancy tackled him, but the second man violently twisted in midair and threw Fancy into the front window, the sound of shattering glass loud. Two more men jumped out of the pantry. Boot and Cherry ran out of the adjacent bedroom, guns up and shouting, but the two most recent arrivals didn't back down, instead charging the guns. A wild burst from Cherry's Rattler ran up the wall and the sound of meaty impacts echoed down the hallway. Cherry went down, wrestling with his man. Boot slammed the end of the suppressor into his man's face, stunning him, and another brutal impact of the steel cylinder into the man's forehead sent him down, but as he fell he wrapped his arms around Boot's knees and brought Boot down as well. A fight commenced on the floor of the hallway, four men in nearly one pile, elbows and knees flailing.

Tommy was keening like a dog hit by a car, holding his knee, and Fancy was stunned after his impact with the window, which had sliced up his leg badly. The two men who'd done that damage climbed to their feet as Dog and Pike came out of the kitchen.

Without a sound one of the combatants leapt at them in a flying kick. Pike dodged to the side, and Dog took the foot in his chest with a yelp and went hurtling backward into the kitchen with his attacker. Pike closed with the other man as the fighting raged all around. Pike blocked a flurry of blows to his face and head with his forearm and the Rattler, and lifted his leading leg off the ground as the man tried to kick out his knee but telegraphed the move. The foot bounced off Pike's shin without doing any real damage. Pike blocked a throat punch with the Rattler as his own foot flicked out.

It hit the side of the man's knee hard enough to make him stumble, and one arm dropped. Pike slammed his fist into the side of the man's neck, then punched him in the face with the receiver of the Rattler hard enough to crack bone as he swept the man's legs out from under him. Loud crashes sounded from the kitchen as Dog fought his man. Then a figure was charging Pike from the hallway, both Cherry and Boot on the floor there in a messy tangle, trying to get to their feet.

Pike spun, far too quick and light on his feet than a man his size should have been, and flipped the running man over his hip with far more force than necessary. A surprised look on his face, the attacker flew through the air, rotating, and hit the far wall upside down hard enough to crack the drywall. Pike darted after him, and as the man slid down the wall and hit the floor on head and shoulder Pike kicked him in the face. As the man flopped to the floor Pike planted a knee on the back of his neck. He grabbed his Rattler and aimed it at the room, but the fighting was over. The four combatants were down, semi-conscious, but his team was hardly in better shape. Tommy was rocking, holding his broken knee. Fancy was bleeding heavily from cuts across his back and thighs from window glass. Dizzy, he crawled over to the man whose face Pike had cratered with his Rattler. Fancy flipped him onto his face and pulled out a ziptie. Dog staggered out of the kitchen, a long cut above one eye pouring blood. Cherry was using one arm to hug the other, his face scrunched up in pain from what felt like a hairline fracture. Boot looked dazed from a bad blow to the head. Everyone was panting and sweaty. And, frankly, bewildered at the ferocity of the resistance they'd encountered.

Pike stood, Rattler up, and glided to the pantry. The

carpet was thrown back, and the trapdoor was open, revealing a black rectangle in the floor. Pike aimed his gun down the hole. He saw a short wooden ladder, and dirt walls, but no movement. He jumped through the hole, dropping eight feet and landing in a crouch. His Rattler was up, the red dot of his optic glowing brightly.

He found himself at the end of a tunnel, four feet wide and almost six tall, running straight away from him. It was dimly lit by light bulbs running along one side, spaced every fifty feet along an insulated power cable. The tunnel angled gently downward, but seemed straight as an arrow, pointed perhaps a few degrees off from true west. Pike tried squinting, but that didn't help—the tunnel was so long, and so poorly lit, that he couldn't see to its end. But he estimated he could see at least a hundred yards, and he was alone. No one was close enough to have heard what had happened in the house. He climbed back up the ladder, closed the trap door, and lowered the carpet over the top of it.

"What the actual fuck just happened?" Boot gasped.

Pike walked over to the man he'd flipped into the wall and ziptied him. "These guys were good," he said appreciatively. He could feel he'd have some bruises in a day or so, but at the moment was flying on adrenaline.

"Command gave us charges to blow the tunnel, we still going to do that?" Boot asked, leaning against a wall. He'd noticed Pike had closed the trap door. Upstairs had seemingly known everything about the tunnel—how long it was, how it was constructed, that the other end of it came up in the back room of a gas station on the opposite side of the border, and roughly when this group was going to use it—but they hadn't know the guys coming through it were going to be serious motherfuckers? Talk about an intelligence failure.

"I'll check in," Pike said. "Wouldn't surprise me if they've changed our orders. Again."

"Command could have warned us to look out for ninjas," Dog said, exploring his head wound with tentative fingertips. He'd need stitches.

"No shit," Boot agreed.

"That wasn't karate, that was *wushu*," Pike said. He got a lot of confused looks. "*Gōngfu*. Kung fu," he finally said, giving it an American accent. "Literally translates to bitter work in Cantonese. Karate is Japanese," he said. He dragged the guy he'd just ziptied away from the wall and flipped him onto his back. He was in generic work clothes, a button-down cotton shirt over jeans. All of the men were dressed similarly. Pike pointed at his features. "These guys are Chinese."

"I thought they were Mexican," Boot said. He'd seen the compact builds, and the black hair.

"The guy in the kitchen is," Pike said. "The coyote. The rest of them are military-aged Chinese males. At least one of them has good English. I wouldn't be surprised if they all did."

"And they've had some serious hand-to-hand training," Dog said, pressing a palm to the cut on his head. Head wounds always bled heavily, and half his face was covered with blood. He looked at Pike. "You think command knew? I was thinking they would be cartel guys. Mules, or maybe higher-ups. This is...something else entirely." He looked over his shoulder, toward the freeway, and the wall, and the foreign country just beyond. "What the fuck is going on at the border?"

"Like I said, the rules don't seem to be the rules any more," Pike observed. He didn't look or sound happy about it.

Ghosts and Madmen: Chapter Two

"This is a really bad idea," Dave said, staring out the windshield. "A really, really bad idea." He clenched his hands nervously. They didn't sweat, not any more, not after the third-degree burns and skin grafts, but if they did, they'd be dripping.

"Why?" Lori said, sitting behind the wheel. "You don't think it's a good boost for...public morale, or whatever the Sheriff said?"

"No. I mean, yes. I mean...I don't know." The crowd was big. Bigger than he'd been expecting, but of course it was going to be big. Not only was Sheriff "Shotgun John" Osterman there, and the mayor, but so was the freaking Governor of Arizona.

Lori was parked halfway across the lot, which was packed with cars, but through a freak of luck they could see past all the vehicles and the people to the front of the Cracker Barrel. The Sheriff was standing on the sidewalk there, accompanied by his fireplug of a wife on one side and the governor and mayor on the other. There was also another woman; Dave didn't know who she was, but he guessed either the manager of this restaurant, or perhaps a district manager. Maybe a Cracker Barrel corporate rep. And hundreds of onlookers. News media. Everyone but the local high-school marching band.

They'd been planning to close the restaurant. Demolish it. It has been the site of a horrific terrorist attack, as the news media described it. Technically it had just been a distraction, an assassination attempt by a cartel on a very high-profile Sheriff while another team went after a witness hidden at a nearby motel. Three cartel soldiers had died in the Cracker Barrel, one inside the gift shop. Four citizens had been injured in the gunfire, not including the sheriff, who'd been shot three times in the chest and abdomen with an AK-47. Now, six months later, he was still using a walker or cane to get around, but he'd left all of that in the car for the ceremony today. Which had all been his doing. He'd reached out—to someone at Cracker Barrel, Dave presumed, but he didn't really know—and talked to them. The city had taken a huge psychological hit—the incident at the Cracker Barrel, the bomb and random shootings outside the sheriff's department, another distraction, and the gunfight at the Pima Motel. People didn't feel safe, not nearly to the extent they used to. The bomb crater outside the sheriff's department had been filled, and the damage to the building repaired, but the Cracker Barrel had sat dark and closed, the yellow crime-scene tape fluttering in the wind.

Until the sheriff had talked to someone. Maybe a lot of someones. Probably using motivational phrases like "You can't let them win" and "Fear only works if you give in to it." He could be very persuasive.

They'd turned the grand re-opening into something

more. Dave was glad to see it...but it made him nervous, too. Uneasy. He'd practiced his draw for an hour at his house, trying to burn off some energy, and Lori had just let him be. He rubbed unconsciously at the throbbing spots on his hand—the inside of his middle finger knuckle, which pressed against the underside of the trigger guard, and the web of his hand, which pressed tightly against the rear of his pistol's frame. Which was now on his hip. And there was a spare magazine on the opposite side. It still didn't feel like enough.

Dave saw several vans with brightly-colored logos plastered across their sides, and at least three camera crews. And a shit-ton of deputies. There were a dozen of them, in uniform, helping to keep the crowd back, and also keep an eye on everyone. There was no reason for the cartel to go after the Sheriff again, but that didn't mean anything, and he was there with the mayor and the governor. None of the deputies were carrying rifles, but that was only because the Sheriff thought it would send the wrong message, one of fear. However, Dave did spot a lot of familiar faces in the crowd, cops in plainclothes. And he saw one unmarked Sprinter van parked right beside the building—he assumed it was full of officers in full tac gear, armed to the teeth, just in case.

It looked like the sheriff was speechifying for the cameras, smiling and gesturing while his wife stood by his elbow, looking up at him, smiling. Dave cracked his window. He could hear the talking but couldn't make out the words.

"He looks good," Lori said. Dave thought he looked pale and weak, but compared to how he'd looked in the hospital for weeks, in an induced coma with tubes everywhere, he was vastly improved. But the man looked old. His age had finally overwhelmed his force of personality.

After a short speech the sheriff and mayor and governor moved closer to the building, where a wide yellow ribbon was strung across the front door. Someone produced a giant pair of scissors, and all four of them, awkwardly holding onto the oversize handles, cut the ribbon. The cheer from the crowd was deafening, and rolled across the lot like a wave.

"God, everyone loves him," Lori said, a smile curling the corner of her mouth. The sheriff's wife, taking those short quick steps of hers, moved up to his side and firmly gripped his elbow. They followed the governor and the mayor inside the building, the sheriff walking like he was atop black ice. After a brief delay, the deputies doing their best to organize the crowd, the public followed after. The Cracker Barrel was open for business.

"You either love him or you hate him, there's no middle ground," Dave agreed. "I'm actually surprised there's no protestors."

"Today, here? Everyone knows he killed one of the cartel guys in the gift shop. Even though they never released that video." Unlike the video of the citizen gunfight with the cartel hit squad at the Pima Motel, just a mile down the road, retrieved from the security cameras and sold to the cable news networks. That had been seen. By everyone. Dave front and center, running a liberated AK, covered in blood.

"Yeah, well." He'd never thought the people who protested as especially discerning. More like kids who needed attention. And a spanking.

They sat and watched for a while as the crowd slowly filed into the building. Everyone was smiling and laughing. It was a party. A celebration.

"There's no way everyone's going to fit," Dave said. He

saw the reporters and camera people were not being allowed into the restaurant.

"Then they'll sit on the porch in the rockers and wait their turn," Lori said. "I heard there was memorabilia inside the gift shop."

He frowned. "What, shirts that say 'I survived the cartel attack'? I bet most of them weren't even fucking there."

She punched him in the arm, hard. "Don't be an asshole."

He glanced at her. One of the photos of the incident, taken by a diner with their phone, was of the sheriff on his back on the sidewalk outside the front door. His shirt was dark, so the blood soaking it from collarbones to belt wasn't so obvious, but it was bright red where it covered the hands of the woman putting pressure on his wounds. And was smeared all over the front of her white shirt. It had taken weeks before Lori had been recognized. "Sorry." He rubbed his arm. She knew how to hit.

"So?" she said. She tilted her head toward the restaurant and raised her eyebrows. He made a face.

She frowned at him. "You're a part of this." A big part. He'd killed two men inside the Cracker Barrel, including the one who'd shot the sheriff. Killed at least three more at the Pima Motel, driving there at double the speed limit, two motivated armed citizens in his wake, and they'd prevented the assassination of the young woman in witness protection through a by-God gunfight with the cartel hit squad in the motel parking lot. All caught on camera. "And everyone knows it. Plus, you were invited. So was I. If you're not going in, fine, you can wait in the car. I'll crack a window."

"Fuuuuck." He tilted his head back and closed his eyes.

"Besides, I want to meet the governor."

"I don't know if she wants to meet you. Knowing the

sheriff, how he feels about her, he neglected to mention he invited us. You."

"Me?" she said. "Hey, you're the one under FBI investigation. And he knows. And doesn't care. Well, maybe it's not that he doesn't care, but..."

"Oh God. This is a really bad idea," he said, but he opened his door.

He'd been sitting in the car too long, and his leg had stiffened up. He'd been shot in the hip, and the leg, and had been beaten nearly to death, although he was healing nicely. Could even jog a bit, although he wasn't going fast, or far. The scars across his face were still pink, but thin, and his beard covered most of them up. If you weren't looking, you might not notice them.

There was a party atmosphere outside the restaurant. They were hardly noticed as they walked up, a slender young man in his late twenties hand-in-hand with a pretty but unremarkable blonde. The news vans were parked at the curb nearby, and Dave forced himself to not look in their direction, as they had cameras set up on tripods. Several deputies were standing nearby, positioned to make it look like they were assigned to watchdog the media rather than posted outside the door on guard.

Inside, the gift shop-slash-lobby was packed with people, literally jammed in shoulder to shoulder, talking at the tops of their lungs. Dave traded a look with Lori and then pulled her along. Moving through the crowd was like wading through waist-deep mud. Finally, they reached the hostess stand. Just past it was the wide doorway into the dining room, and there was a deputy posted there, hands on his belt.

"Hi there," Jack said.

The hostess had vaguely been aware of his approach.

"Oh, honey," she said apologetically, shaking her head. "I can put you on the list, but it's going to be two hours at least."

"Supposed to be a couple of seats for us at the sheriff's table," Jack said as quietly as he could.

The hostess, a middle-aged woman, blinked at him and her eyes squinted, then widened. Her mouth worked a couple times, but no sound came out.

"He's in the back, Cujo, he's waiting for you," the deputy said to him. "And you're damn lucky you didn't stand him up. She would have been quite offended."

"She?" Lori said.

"His boss," the deputy said wryly. He didn't mean the mayor, or the governor.

Smiling, Jack nodded at the man, who looked vaguely familiar, and headed into the dining room. After the densely packed gift shop the dining room seemed airy, even though every chair at every table was filled. Dave spotted the Sheriff immediately—the last time they'd been in the Cracker Barrel, he and Lori had been seated with the sheriff just inside the door. This time, he'd taken command of a large round table against the back wall of the restaurant. Like a king occupying his throne. It was meant to send a message, him eating brunch at the same place where he was shot showed that he was unafraid.

Dave and Lori wove between the tables filled with chatting diners, the noise level quite loud. It was mostly families and large groups he saw, some with kids. Quite a few people had their cameras out, discreetly (or not so much) taking photos and videos of the sheriff and mayor and governor.

As he and Lori drew near the sheriff spotted them, and with some difficulty rose to his feet. His wife did the same, and hurried around the table to them, as the mayor and governor turned to see who had arrived. There were two empty chairs at the table. "You look good, it was so nice of you to come," Lillian Osterman said warmly. She was nearly a full head shorter than Lori, who wasn't tall, and Lori bent down so the woman could give her a peck on the cheek. Lillian reached out and warmly squeezed Dave's arm. He was vaguely aware that the noise level inside the restaurant dropped to zero, then resumed in a frenzy of whispering, as everyone there recognized him. Up close, Dave thought Osterman looked like a shrunken, pale, old version of his former robust self...but then again he was in his seventies, and recuperating from being shot three times with an AK-47 at point blank range. Most men who'd suffered that would likely have died.

Osterman nodded his head. "Governor, mayor, this is Jack and Lori. The last time I was here I was dining with them, and this young lady ended up with my blood on her up to her elbows trying to save my life, beside a cardiovascular surgeon recently retired out of Boston. I consider her family, and would be offended if you don't as well." The corner of his mouth twitched as he looked at Dave. "And Jack, well, he was here too."

Both the governor and the mayor shot the sheriff disbelieving looks. Osterman had told them he was expecting two more, but hadn't said who. But everyone in the state knew who Pima Jack was. He'd killed two cartel soldiers at the Cracker Barrel, not twenty feet from where they were sitting. Bitten the nose and lips off a third man who been beating him in the face with an AK-47 inside the gift shop. Raced over to the Pima in the sheriff's car and killed more at the motel in a massive gunfight. And became a huge, unequivocal local hero, for a few months—then men from Detroit, with ties to organized crime, showed up and reportedly tried to abduct him, and he killed them too. And the mobster that they worked for was murdered a day later in Vegas. Now 'Pima Jack' was under investigation by the FBI, although that wasn't common knowledge. The Arizona electorate still considered him a hero, but...

The mayor was blinking erratically, a hesitant smile flashing on and off his face. The governor couldn't decide to smile for the onlookers, or frown. She turned her face toward Osterman, who looked absolutely delighted at her discomfiture. "I've heard of ambush journalism," she said. "Is this an ambush brunch?"

"This is a celebration, of life and its many wonders and endless surprises," Osterman said. He sat down with some difficulty, grabbed a plate, and held it out to her with a look of childlike innocence on his face. "Biscuit?"

Ghosts and Madmen: Chapter Three

Gogolak much preferred physical files. Hard copies in his hand. Pages he could turn. With hardcopies it was so much easier to flip back and forth, find that one quote or interview note or the one specific crime scene photo. Spread them around a large table, or an entire room. But physical files just weren't as convenient, especially when they grew from bulging folders to filling boxes. So, for the trip east, he had everything on his Bureau laptop. Much easier to deal with on the road, especially when flying.

He had a bit of room to spread out, make notes—one seat back table for his laptop, another for a pad of paper—as they'd bumped him into first class. That happened a lot; as a gun-carrying federal agent he was required to carry his gun onboard, to serve as an ersatz air marshal. Not that they really had those anymore. Nobody in the federal government seemed to care about terrorism anymore, unless it was domestic terrorism, and those guys never bombed or hijacked airplanes. They never did much of anything, not that you'd know that from the huge amount of money and manhours the FBI was throwing at them.

For this trip he didn't just have folders or boxes worth of material he could review, there was a literal warehouse worth of stuff, dating back thirty years. More. And he'd read it all, at one time or another. But for this trip he concentrated on the material generated in the last five years and pertinent to his investigation, which was comparatively narrow in focus.

He was only supposed to be in Detroit for twenty-four hours, but he remembered a twelve-hour trip to Cleveland early in his career that had turned into a five-day marathon of surveillance, interviews, and arrests, so he'd checked a bag. He grabbed it off the luggage carousel, after waiting what felt like an hour for them to unload the plane, then jumped into the front passenger seat of the waiting Bureau car. The yawning agent behind the wheel looked like a teenager to Gogolak, but he was getting close to mandatory retirement age.

The young man drove them to the FBI headquarters in downtown Detroit, where Gogolák checked in with the ASAC, then grabbed a bland G-car and drove northwest for his appointment. He arrived in the area almost an hour early, and drove around, checking the place out. Spaced every mile north or south, east or west, was a main road, ruler-straight and usually two lanes in each direction, with a center left turn lane, but between them was nothing but narrow, twisty turny residential streets, green with spacious lawns and looked over by mature trees. There were a number of lakes in the township, and all the streets seemed to curve this way and that, like the lakes were exerting gravitational pull. The houses visible from the street were larger than average, and the ones set further back on big lots, mostly hidden from view, appeared to be bigger still. Most of the neighborhoods didn't have sidewalks—the well-manicured lawns stretched down to the streets, where no one parked. Very few vehicles were visible in the driveways, as every house had an attached two- or three-car garage. While he didn't see as many Mercedes or BMWs or Audis as he was expecting, most of the cars he did see were new.

He had an address memorized, and his phone got him there without incident. It seemed one of the nicer areas, with every house set on a one- or two-acre lot. The house was mostly out of sight behind a hedge. Gogolak turned in his seat and looked around. Most of the neighboring houses were hidden from view but for a sliver of roof or brick or siding visible above or between manicured hedges and mature trees. If anyone came down their driveway he and his G-car would be plainly visible, sitting on the street, but apart from that he was as hidden in plain sight as you could be in upper-middle-class suburbia. The streetlights looked like new LED models, but were spaced quite a distance apart, and he guessed that at night the street would be dark.

He left the scene and arrived at his ultimate destination twenty minutes early, sat in his car for fifteen minutes staring at his laptop, reviewing his notes, then stuffed the laptop and what physical files he had into his leather briefcase and headed in.

There was one uniformed officer at the elevated front desk, sitting relaxed behind armored glass. He took note of Gogolak, but one middle-aged white male in a suit didn't ping anything on his threat radar. He barely paid attention when Gogolak reached inside his suitcoat.

Gogolak stopped before the desk, and flipped open his badge wallet. "FBI Special Agent Gogolak," he announced. He tried a smile. It felt awkward on his face. He'd never been good at smiling. They rarely felt natural, and from people's reactions, they didn't look natural either. "I've got an appointment with Detective Dixon."

The officer nodded, and reached for a phone. "Hold on a minute."

West Bloomfield Township Police Department Detective William "Billy" Dixon commandeered a small conference room for their meeting. While Gogolak pulled out his laptop and folders Dixon brought two cups of coffee, then carried in his own files. There wasn't a box of them, but there were a good eight inches of folders packed with incident reports, surveillance logs, crime scene photos, witness statements....

Dixon saw the FBI agent eyeing the stack. "I'd like to close this case before I retire," he said. "I'm coming up on my twenty." Dixon was short, but looked like he might lift weights. Unlike Gogolak, whose thin hair was balding, and whose pale blue eyes were tucked behind glasses, Dixon had a full head of thick brown hair and Hollywood looks.

Gogolak asked, "And then to greener pastures?"

Dixon shrugged. "I've got an ex-wife, one kid in college, and one about to be. A corporate security gig with that private sector paycheck, on top of my pension, would make me breathe a little easier."

Gogolak nodded. His laced his fingers together on the table in front of him. "Well, I've reviewed everything you've sent us. Read and re-read it. Since I was in the area I did a drive-by of the scene of the original hit-and-run. Do you have anything new that we're not aware of?"

The veteran West Bloomfield Township detective breathed deep, through his nose, and worked his neck. Talking, even thinking about David Anderson made him tense. "Okay, I agreed to this meeting with the understanding that you'd be sharing. Yes, you have every report this department has generated investigating the murder of Paolo Bufonte. I like Anderson for it. He's my only hard suspect. I've turned up circumstantial evidence that shows he might have had Big Paulie under surveillance prior to the man getting run over—twice—in front of his house, but that's it. He's got motive—Paulie killed his parents in a DUI, and then got off on a technicality—and he doesn't have an alibi. He's never cooperated with us and lawyered up immediately, which is somewhat suspicious. Everything about this kid is suspicious. The FBI—supposedly, according to all the news reports—working for the father, Pietro Bufonte, the head of organized crime in Detroit, twice tried to have him killed, the second time using Detroit SWAT cops out on bail, that they'd just arrested—"

"Not the FBI," Gogolak interrupted him, his voice soft. "An errant, compromised special agent."

Dixon had been trying to get confirmation, and jumped on that. "So you're confirming that? Because that's never been officially confirmed. And it never sat right with me."

"Really, why is that?"

Dixon shook his head. He knew all the interrogation techniques, and he wouldn't be manipulated. Distracted. "Are you confirming that? That your special agent was working for Bufonte?"

Gogolak paused, then shook his head. "No. That recording, it's real, we've authenticated it, and it's incontrovertible proof FBI Special Agent Peter Hartman enlisted Paul Wilson of the Detroit Police Department, out on bail for his arrest related to a string of strip club robberies, to murder David Anderson. In exchange for making certain evidence disappear. But there's no proof that it was for Bufonte. For whatever reason. That Detroit organized crime was involved at all. That's just been the assumption. But let's be honest. No other explanation seems plausible, you have to admit. Twenty-five year old kid—who'd applied to the FBI, if you hadn't heard—with no criminal record, no known criminal associates, working for an armored car company, and a private investigator. Why would anyone want him dead? Why would a senior FBI agent risk his entire career to arrange his murder? Mob involvement is the only thing that makes sense, because Bufonte blamed him for his son's death." He peered at Dixon. "Do you know something that I don't?"

Dixon paused and thought. He looked at the wall behind Gogolak, then said, "I know someone. Not quite a confidential informant, but he knows a few things. Told them to me from time to time. And he assured me that Bufonte had nothing to do with those attempts on Anderson's life."

A dubious look settled across Gogolak's face. "Well, then, it seems clear that this source is lying to you. After what happened in Arizona? All four of those men were associates, employees of Pietro Bufonte. And they didn't show up at Anderson's house at dawn, in a car filled with firearms and duct tape, for a book club meeting."

Dixon shook his head almost violently. "At that point Anderson had been in the wind for, what, a year? And that whole time, the entire world thought Bufonte had already tried to have him killed. Twice. And Bufonte was dying of cancer, or so I heard. So what did he have to lose?" Dixon frowned, and leaned back. "So what the fuck happened in Vegas? That's mostly why I agreed to this meeting. Quid pro quo. Four men dead, including Pietro Bufonte, in his mansion in Vegas. Murdered, it was announced shortly thereafter. Normally, something like that, you'd assume it was rivals. An inter-family dispute, or whatever you would call it on the organized crime side. But it happened less than twenty-four hours after his four men show up at Anderson's house. And Anderson burned them down before half of them got out of the car or got a shot off. That fucking kid, every year it seems like he gets into a gunfight and walks away. He's killed I don't know how many people, and he's never even been *charged*. He's been living under a fake name in Arizona since he left Detroit. Isn't that illegal?"

The FBI agent paused, considering. "Not when the new identity was issued to you by law enforcement, as part of an ersatz witness protection program."

That was news to Billy Dixon. He blinked in surprise. "Osterman?" The Arizona sheriff had been all over the news reports from down there. He'd been the one to bring the recording of FBI Detroit office Assistant Special Agent-in-Charge Peter Hartman soliciting murder to the media. How he'd gotten it…no one seemed to know. After being suspended, pending an investigation, Hartman was found in his home at the end of a rope, so no one could ask him any questions. Pretty much everyone involved in these incidents, other than Anderson, was dead, and Anderson wasn't talking. Gogolak nodded. "Well…shit." The news made him think. He peered at the FBI agent. "What does the FBI have to say about that?"

Gogolak shrugged. "Officially we don't have a position on it."

"Okay. And Vegas?"

"Four dead. Two shot, two bludgeoned to death with a hammer, and then the house was torched, using alcohol as an accelerant. Pietro Bufonte was shot in the face, sitting behind his desk. The fire was put out before it completely destroyed the house—turns out marble doesn't burn so well, and he loved his white marble—but no useful physical evidence was recovered. The gun used was found at the scene. Registered to one of the dead men. Not believed to be a perpetrator, he was a known associate of Bufonte. The hammer used was left at the scene as well. In someone's head, actually. No fingerprints on the pistol or hammer."

"A hammer? Like a regular hammer? Is that weird? It seems...weird."

Gogolak shrugged. "Weapon of opportunity, maybe? Nearly as many people killed by blunt force objects every year as gunshots. You grab what's at hand."

"And do you like Anderson for it? I mean, Vegas is only a few hours from where he was in Arizona."

Gogolak made a noncommittal face and shrugged. "He is on the suspect list, but...he's not former military. He's never even been a cop."

"Maybe not, but do you know how many people he's killed? I know you know, if you're looking into him."

Gogolak frowned as he thought, doing the math. "Sixteen. Confirmed." Which didn't include the half-dozen bodies found around Anderson's Arizona cabin. The details of what exactly had happened there were still murky. But most of the men who'd died there had extensive military records, with documented time in combat.

Dixon gave him a pointed look. "I know guys who did tours in Iraq who don't have that many confirmeds. You try to talk to him? Let me guess, he's lawyered up, and isn't talking."

"Correct." In fact, traffic cameras had picked up Anderson's Jeep entering the city earlier that evening, but they had absolutely no direct evidence tying him to the murders. Couldn't place him within miles of the house. They'd attempted to interview him, but he'd refused to cooperate in the investigation, as he assumed—and rightly so—that he was a suspect. His high-profile defense lawyer —on loan from Osterman, it seemed—had stated that Anderson, distraught over the attempt on his life earlier that day, had driven around for hours in an attempt to clear his head, including through the city of Las Vegas, to look at the lights of the Strip, but until the FBI had enough evidence to charge his client, that was all they were going to get out of Anderson. He would not be sitting down for any interviews.

Anderson—clearly—was a person of interest for the murders, but many of the higher-ups in the Bureau simply couldn't believe he had done the deed. One guy, who was still suffering from wounds received in a terrorist attack, had somehow gone all ninja and taken out four guys by himself? Quietly enough that the neighbors hadn't even been sure they'd heard any shots, before the smoke started billowing out the windows of the house, and a passing dogwalker had called 911. The FBI brass thought it was much more likely Bufonte had been taken out by one of his rivals, or by the organization itself because they considered him a liability. Especially since Bufonte had died sitting at his desk, on the second floor of his house, like he was talking to someone he knew. Gogolak had no opinion, and would follow the evidence, wherever it led.

In truth, Bufonte's death cleared up a big mess, a big headache for the FBI. Whether it was true or not, the man was thought to have co-opted a senior FBI agent. Been involved in arranging a murder through the FBI, or so the story went. With both Hartman and Bufonte now dead, that story should now fade away.

"How many times have you met with him?" Gogolak asked the detective.

"Anderson?"

Gogolak shook his head. "Bufonte."

Dixon hadn't been expecting the question. He frowned as he thought, eyes moving back and forth. "Total? I have no idea. His son was killed in the only unsolved homicide we've got in this town. And I mean the *only* one, we're not exactly a hotbed of crime. If you drove around, you saw. Generally, the most serious crime we've got here is stolen cars, and once or twice a year somebody—usually from Pontiac—robbing one of the gas stations on Maple or Middlebelt; we're gated communities and golf courses. My investigation's been open the whole time, and I'd go back to it from time to time, but rarely got anywhere with it. And, you know, Bufonte's not a regular guy. He or his people would check in for updates. I know I met with him personally at least two or three times. Here, I think. I believe I talked to him more on the phone. Him and his people."

Gogolak raised his eyebrows and cocked his head. Dixon nodded. "I know what you're thinking, but I didn't give them any more information than I would give the average person. Not on an active, or at least open, investigation. But, I mean, the last year or so, I didn't need to tell him anything, did I? His face and name were all over the news, how he'd used the FBI to arrange the murder of Anderson. He was tried and convicted in the court of public opinion. Did the FBI ever talk to Bufonte about that?"

Gogolak nodded. "He denied it. He denied everything, including even knowing who Hartman was. But, generally, these guys deny everything as a reflex when talking to us."

"Okay," Dixon said forcefully. "That happened, the FBI as murder-for-hire by the mob was splashed all over the news. I don't need to tell you. So what did you do? The FBI. Don't tell me you didn't do anything. I know you had to have wiretaps all over his phones already, and once all that shit with Hartman happened I imagine you had to be up on all of Bufonte's electronics, his houses, his cars. Well, maybe not everything, if you'd had a bug in his Vegas house you'd have heard everything and would have already made an arrest, but what about that? You ever hear him admit to hiring Hartman?"

"Pietro Bufonte has been in organized crime his entire life, since he was a teenager. He was well aware he was under surveillance, electronic and otherwise, and frequently employed countermeasures."

"That's not an answer."

"I can't comment on an ongoing investigation."

Dixon gave him a dirty look.

"Can I speak with your source?" Gogolak asked.

"My source?"

"The man who told you Bufonte had nothing to do with FBI Assistant Special-Agent-in-Charge Hartman arranging the murder of David Anderson. Your source, who's not a CI, but who knows things."

"No." Dixon shook his head. "Because he was Tony Gianucci."

Gogolak blinked twice, which was all the time it took him to place the name. "Anthony Gianucci. One of the three men found dead in the Las Vegas home of Pietro Bufonte, along with Bufonte himself."

Dixon nodded. "You got it. He and I...well, we didn't become friends, but he was the guy Bufonte had call me for updates on the investigation, and he liked me, so I cultivated him as a source. Occasionally he'd tell me things. Like how Bufonte didn't have fuck-all to do with Hartman."

"Unless he was lying. Everyone lies to cops."

Dixon nodded. "That they do. But good cops learn how to spot liars."

Gogolak stared at him through his glasses, his pale blue eyes steady. He made a noncommittal grunt.

"I'm surprised there's just one of you," Dixon said, after a beat.

Gogolak sighed. "Victims of our own success. I'm probably the lead guy in the Bureau who specializes in American, domestic, organized crime. In the sixties, seventies, and eighties, I'd be a rock star, meeting with the Director, my arrests splashed all over the front of the New York Times. But we're victims of our own success. Between wiretaps and RICO and forcing cooperation using immunity, we crushed the five families. Gotti was the last real big fish, and he died twenty years ago. In custody. You go onto the FBI website, look at the page on our organized crime task force, we don't even talk about the mafia in this country, it's all about transnational organized crime. Smuggling and human trafficking, cybercrime, money laundering for terrorists. The only mention of the mafia is in Italy. I'm not saying organized crime in this country doesn't exist, or isn't still a problem, but after Nine-Eleven the Bureau forgot about it to jump on the anti-terrorism action, and never really came back to it."

"So...with Bufonte dead, and Anderson not cooperating, and it sounds like you've got nothing on him, what are you doing? Trying to clear the FBI's name in all this? Prove you weren't involved?"

Gogolak tried another smile. "Something like that."

Grab your copy...
vinci-books.com/madmen

Author's Note

I firmly believe that the merit of a society, culture, or nation should be based on its relationship with two things: dogs and bacon. Both are man's best friend, but in completely different ways.

Residents of Prescott, Arizona, know two things: 1. It's pronounced *Preskitt*, and 2. The Wagon Wheel Café in this novel across from Prescott's Courthouse Square could very well be The Lone Spur Café.

The breakfast I had a few years ago at The Lone Spur was so legendary, with excellent coffee and eggs and bacon worthy of ballads, that I have been afraid to go back in case subsequent meals didn't measure up. Halfway through this novel I returned to The Lone Spur Café with my fiancée and was delighted to find the bacon was just as good as I remembered.

I have to thank Tesla Missig (my future daughter-in-law) for the "Beefaroni-stained Ninja Turtles t-shirt and Kool-Aid lips" quote, which was such urban poetry I had to write a scene in which to use it. And a special thanks go to my son

Author's Note

Barrett, always my harshest editor, who once again came up with several suggestions which made this a better novel.

I've had hard, horrible jobs. Writing for a living isn't one of them.

Currently my day job consists of writing novels like this and articles for gun magazines, as well as occasionally appearing on outdoorsy/shooting shows on several cable networks. Because of this rather interesting and offbeat occupation, I have been fortunate enough to meet a lot of interesting and offbeat people, many of whom helped provide details for this book. Any errors, of course, are mine.

Both Tim Yan and Howard Toy recommended Summerlin as an upscale Las Vegas neighborhood to me when I was looking for a setting for the climax of this novel. Tim Yan is a friend, fellow gunwriter, and a former U.S. Marine who deployed to Somalia. A few years ago he relocated from a hostile socialist country (California) to Las Vegas, and has never looked back.

Howard Toy is the Senior Vice President of Operations for the Treasure Island Hotel and Casino in Las Vegas and the nicest guy you'd ever want to meet, in suits that would be the envy of Hans Gruber. In spite of being very busy with a real job he answered every stupid question I had about living and working in Vegas, including sharing some nice photos of his rose bushes.

I've been friends with Scott G. since 1984, and for about twenty years we were brothers-in-law...now we're back to just being friends. He's also been with the Drug Enforcement Administration for over 25 years, and he helped correct a few details about Mexican drug cartels and likely clothing choices for a DEA SAC.

I've been a police officer, drove an armored car around

Author's Note

Detroit, and spent 17 years as a private investigator. Yet compared to most of the people whose brains I picked for this book I've led a boring life. One of the quotes I've got at the beginning of a chapter comes from Kyle Lamb. Kyle and I have done a little work together on the Guns & Ammo TV show, and Kyle is one of those very interesting people. Officially he is SGM (Ret.) Kyle Lamb SFOD-D (most commonly known as Delta Force), and the other person I know who spent some time in Somalia. FYI Kyle is a lot more entertaining in person than Eric Bana, who played him in the movie.

Thanks to my day job I've gotten to know/talk to/work with four SFOD-D veterans, a couple Green Berets, two Navy SEALS, two Army Rangers, the former head of FBI HRT, lots of current and former private contractors who did time in Iraq and Afghanistan and Africa, regular Army and USMC combat veterans, street cops, SWAT team members, and four people who have worked for the CIA in various capacities including one gentleman who spent time with the CIA's Ground Branch and another whose story was told in "13 Hours". All of that has helped inform the characters and details in this novel.

Chris Pappas, M.D. graciously acted as my "technical medical advisor" when it came time to accurately depict the injuries done to Dave Anderson and Sheriff Osterman, and the recovery and treatment thereof. Currently Chris is a General Practitioner, and I wonder how many of his patients know that in his youth he travelled around the world doing interesting and offbeat things and was very familiar with the proper spelling of SFOD-D.

It is because of my day job writing non-fiction articles for what could be termed "men's magazines" that I have met a lot of people who have seen serious combat. Far more

Author's Note

than what I've depicted in this book. Such as Dillard Johnson, whose autobiography *Carnivore* I helped write. The official—*official*, mind you—U.S. Army enemy body count for Johnson's Bradley Fighting Vehicle on the first day of combat in Iraq was 488. 488. Look at that number and think about that. Talking to him and a lot of other people helped inform the parts of this book dealing with Dave Anderson's PTSD.

Once again, thanks go to Darrin Anselm, for being such a character. Aaron Abruzzo is merely a faint shadow compared to him.

Professional shooter and Hollywood technical advisor Taran Butler continues to be more colorful in real life than most fictional characters. And a great friend. He is everything in person that he is in these pages. With better hair.

Angus Hobdell is not the only transplanted Brit living in Arizona that I know, he's just the first I met. The very first business trip I ever made as a struggling "media professional" was to CZ Custom in Mesa, Arizona, which Angus runs, and he treated me like a rock star. For that and many other things I'll always be grateful.

Anyone who knows Angus might see some of his colorful personal life reflected in some of the incidents and supporting characters in this book, and on that note I would like to thank Angus and his better half Lauren for having me as a guest in their home.

Trust me, not only is truth stranger than fiction, quite often it is much more unbelievable.

About the Author

James Tarr is a regular contributor to numerous firearms/outdoor publications and has appeared on or hosted numerous shows on The Sportsman Channel cable network including *Handguns and Defensive Weapons* and *Guns & Ammo TV*. He is also the author of fourteen books (and counting), including the critically-acclaimed *Dogsoldiers*, *Whorl*, *Bestiarii*, and *Carnivore* (with Dillard Johnson), which was featured on The O'Reilly Factor. He lives in Michigan with his fiancée, two sons and three dogs.